Praise for Cathy Gohlke

"Cathy Gohlke is a master at mixing intrigue, romance, beauty, history, and faith into her action-packed plots. . . . *Saving Amelie* swept me away. A fascinating, heart-pounding, and heartwarming story."

MELANIE DOBSON, AWARD-WINNING AUTHOR OF
CHÂTEAU OF SECRETS

"Fans of *Promise Me This* will find they will love [*Band of Sisters*] just as much. It still has Cathy's excellent storytelling, historical accuracy, and is a page-turning book you can't put down."

RADIANT LIT

"A wonderful story. . . . The characters are strong . . . charming, witty, and some even have a little bit of devil in them."

ROMANTIC TIMES, 4½-STAR REVIEW OF *BAND OF SISTERS*

"Historical detail is lush and evocative and keeps the reader riveted. High conflict keeps the reader turning page after page, breathless at the ending, and wishing there were more pages to turn."

TITLETRAKK.COM ON *BAND OF SISTERS*

"Compelling . . . well-crafted . . . impressively emotional story-telling. Gohlke has written a page-turning mystery within the pages of a tender story of friendship and the unbreakable bond between sisters."

FRESHFICTION.COM ON *BAND OF SISTERS*

"Captivating."

CHRISTIANBOOKPREVIEWS.COM ON *BAND OF SISTERS*

"[*Band of Sisters* is] a compelling and inspiring novel. . . . Gohlke's fast-paced prose, exceptional pacing, and vibrant characters make for believable historical fiction with a subject matter as resonant today as it was during Maureen and Katie's time."

NOVELCROSSING.COM

"Rich with characters and story lines . . . an extremely intricate and compelling story."

"Gohlke tells a gripping tale of sacrifice, loss, love, and hope against the setting of familiar historical events."

"This dramatic and heart-wrenching interpretation . . . will enthrall fans of character-driven Christian fiction and readers who enjoy Francine Rivers."

"[*Promise Me This*] grabs the reader from the first sentence."

"Gohlke's attention to detail provides believable characters, good dialogue, and historical accuracy."

"Explores the depth of human nature and emotions through its three-dimensional, compelling characters. . . . *Promise Me This* will certainly satisfy romance readers who enjoy historical details and character-driven plots."

"Gohlke does not disappoint with her third novel, a carefully researched story full of likable characters struggling to cope with the difficult realities of grief and wartime. . . . [A] sweet, compelling story."

"[A] riveting story [that] is mesmerizing and compelling as well as historically accurate. This novel of hope, redemption, and promise amidst profound despair is one that will bring the story of the *Titanic* alive during her centennial."

Cathy Gohlke

SAVING *Amelie*

Tyndale House Publishers, Inc., Carol Stream, Illinois

Visit Tyndale online at www.tyndale.com.

Visit Cathy Gohlke's website at www.cathygohlke.com.

TYNDALE and Tyndale's quill logo are registered trademarks of Tyndale House Publishers, Inc.

Saving Amelie

Designed by Stephen Vosloo

Edited by Sarah Mason

Published in association with the literary agency of Natasha Kern Literary Agency, Inc., P.O. Box 1069, White Salmon, WA 98672.

Scripture quotations are taken from the *Holy Bible*, King James Version.

Saving Amelie is a work of fiction. Where real people, events, establishments, organizations, or locales appear, they are used fictitiously. All other elements of the novel are drawn from the author's imagination.

Library of Congress Cataloging-in-Publication Data

Gohlke, Cathy.
  Saving Amelie / Cathy Gohlke.
    pages cm
  ISBN 978-1-4143-8322-4 (sc)
1. World War, 1939-1945—Underground movements—Germany—Fiction. 2. World War, 1939-1945—Children—Germany—Fiction. 3. Medical ethics—Germany—Fiction. 4. Family secrets—Fiction. I. Title.
  PS3607.O3448S38 2014
  813'.6—dc23   2013048548

Printed in the United States of America

21   20   19   18   17   16   15
 9   8   7   6   5   4

For Dan

Celebrating thirty-two years and all our adventures
I love you—forever.

*"Therefore shall a man leave his father and his mother, and
shall cleave unto his wife: and they shall be one flesh."*

GENESIS 2:24

Acknowledgments

In the research and writing of this book I am deeply grateful to . . .

The late Dietrich Bonhoeffer, dissident German pastor, prophet, spy, and martyr, who early recognized the corrupted ideology of the Nazis and the eugenics movement, who challenged the church to protect others, stand against evil, and live for Christ. Before his death at the hands of the Nazis, Bonhoeffer wrote *The Cost of Discipleship*—a book that set my heart on fire.

Natasha Kern, my agent and friend, who believed in this book from its conception and championed its ideals.

Stephanie Broene and Sarah Mason, my wonderfully gifted editors, and Shaina Turner, acquisitions assistant, for patiently working through the complexities of this manuscript and helping me bring to the page the vision God placed in my heart; Julie Dumler, my innovative marketing manager; Christy Stroud, my enthusiastic and dedicated publicist; the wonderfully talented Stephen Vosloo for cover design; the excellent PR and sales teams; and all at Tyndale House Publishers who've worked so diligently to bring this book to life and to readers.

Terri Gillespie, dear friend and writing colleague, for capturing this book's vision, for helping with research and sharing your passion for the unity of God's people in Christ, Jew and Gentile. Thank you especially for your encouragement and prayers when Nazi research became too dark, and for your critique and repeated readings of this manuscript.

Carrie Turansky, dear friend and writing colleague, for your faithful encouragement and prayers, your unflagging support, and for your early critique of this manuscript.

Dan Gohlke, my husband, for generously donning your chauffeur cap and sharing research adventures through England, France, Germany, and Poland, and for your early critique of this manuscript. I could not ask for a better husband or traveling companion.

Elisabeth Gardiner, my daughter, for trekking with me through Berlin in search of the Nazi book-burning site, for climbing through overgrown cemeteries in Poland, for your insights and brainstorming of this story, and for your reading and early critique of this manuscript. I've loved sharing this literary journey with you.

Daniel Gohlke, my son, for combing through museums and research sites in Berlin, Oranienburg, and concentration camps in Germany and France—all difficult research that tried our souls but inspired story and voice, amid so many discussions. I cherish your companionship in this writing journey.

Karen and Paul Gardiner, dear family and friends, and parents of my son-in-law, Tim, for inviting us to join you in your tour of Germany and to see the Passion Play in Oberammergau. That trip cemented our friendship at the time our children wed. Now we are celebrating the birth of our precious granddaughter from that blessed union!

Bob Welch, retired music director at Immanuel Bible Church in Springfield, Virginia, who envisioned taking your choir to Oberammergau to view the Passion Play. When your magnificent choir sang "Silent Night" in the tiny Oberndorf *Stille Nacht Kapelle*, I wept for the beauty of that moment. Little did you know that you fulfilled a treasured dream from childhood.

Brigitta Salyers, for enthusiastically guiding the Immanuel Bible Church tour through southern Germany and Austria, including Oberammergau's Passion Play. You are an amazing woman, a brilliant and patient tour guide, and a dear sister in Christ.

My families of origin and marriage, my church family at Elkton United Methodist, and readers who regularly pray for and encourage me in this writing journey. This is not territory I could traverse alone, and I am so very grateful to you.

Museums and historical sites and their staff in England, France, Germany, and Poland; tour guides in London, Dover, Natzweiler, Berlin, Sachsenhausen, Ravensbrück, Bavaria, and Eagle's Nest; Oberammergau's Passion Play; the many writers of histories, journals, diaries, and interviews from WWII, Berlin, and Oberammergau during the Nazi era; and the Bavarian State Library in Munich.

Four very readable books that helped tremendously are William L. Shirer's *Berlin Diary: The Journal of a Foreign Correspondent, 1934–1941*; Helena Waddy's *Oberammergau in the Nazi Era: The Fate of a Catholic Village in Hitler's Germany*; Eric Metaxas's *Bonhoeffer: Pastor, Martyr, Prophet, Spy*; and Michael Van Dyke's *Radical Integrity: The Story of Dietrich Bonhoeffer*.

Most especially, those who survived or helped others survive the Holocaust and continue to tell your stories in the hope of "never again." There is no way to adequately thank you. But I will never forget. I promise.

And thank you, always, Uncle Wilbur, for reminding me that a sure way to know if I'm working in the will of God is to ask, "Do I have joy? Is this yoke easy? Is this burden light?"

Writing this book taught me that such joy is a matter of spirit and discipleship, especially when the research makes me weep.

Part I

August 1939

1

RACHEL KRAMER dropped her linen napkin across the morning newspaper's inflammatory headline: "Cold Spring Harbor Scientist in League with Hitler." She glanced up, willing herself to smile innocently as her father strode into the formal breakfast room.

"You needn't bother to hide it." His eyes, bloodshot and mildly accusing, met hers as he took his chair at the head of the polished mahogany table. "I've already received a phone call from the Institute."

Rachel glanced at their butler's stoic face as he poured her father's coffee, then carefully framed her statement. "It isn't true, of course."

"In league with the Führer? You believe the ravings of that maniac hack Young?" he scoffed. "Come now, Rachel—" he jerked his napkin from its ring—"you know me better than that."

"Of course, Father. But I need to understand—"

"Which is why this trip is essential. You'll see for yourself that those foreign correspondents exaggerate—to sell American papers, no doubt, but at the expense of international relations and good men doing crucial work."

She might be little more than an inexperienced college graduate, but she wouldn't be shot down. "He also claims that Hitler accuses the Poles of disturbing the peace of Europe—that he's blaming them for impending war, creating a ruse to justify an invasion. If that's true—if he'd truly attack Poland—then you really can't trust him, Father. And if this reporter is right about that, then people will believe—"

"People will believe what they wish to believe—what is expedient

3

and profitable for them to believe." He pushed from the table, toast points in hand. "You mustn't pay attention to the rags. It's all propaganda. I'm sure Herr Hitler knows what he's doing. The car will be here any moment. Are you packed?"

"Father, no sane person is going to Germany now. Americans have evacuated."

"I assure you that I am completely sane." He stopped and, uncharacteristically, stroked her cheek. "And you are destined for greatness." He tugged his starched cuffs into place. "Remember, Rachel, it is 'Herr Hitler.' The Germans do not take kindly to disrespect."

"Yes, Father, but you and I—we must have an understanding—"

But he'd already crossed the room, motioning for his coat. "Jeffries, watch for the driver. We mustn't miss our plane. Where are your bags, Rachel?"

She folded her napkin deliberately, willing her temper into submission—for this trip only . . . *until I make you understand that this is my last trip to Frankfurt—to Germany—and that our relationship must drastically change . . . just as soon as we return to New York.* "My bags are waiting by the door."

❖

Two days later, Rachel tugged summer-white gloves over her wrists, as if that might erect a strategic barrier between her person and the German city once familiar to her. It had been five years since she'd ridden down the wide, pristine avenues of Frankfurt. The medieval spires and colorful geometric brickwork looked just the same. But every towering, spreading linden tree that had graced the main thoroughfare—each a landmark in its own right—had been ripped from its roots, replaced by steel poles slung with twenty-foot scarlet banners sporting black swastikas on white circles. *Ebony spiders soaked in shame.*

"There is no need to fret. It won't be long now. The examination will soon be over. You missed the last one, so you mustn't object if this one takes a bit longer." Her father, his hair thinning by the minute, smiled absently, moistened and flattened his lips. "Our train leaves at seven," he muttered, staring out the window. "We will not be detained."

She forced her fingers to lie still in her lap. His affected reassurance gave little comfort. Why she'd agreed to the hated biennial physical examination by doctors she detested or to coming to Germany at all, she couldn't fathom.

Well, yes . . . she could. Rachel sighed audibly and glanced at the too-thin, self-absorbed man beside her. It was because he'd insisted, because they'd argued as never before, because he'd begged, then badgered, and finally ordered. Because, being adopted, she'd known no other father, and because her mother had loved him—at least the way he used to be, the way he was when she was alive. And, significantly, because Rachel's new employer had agreed to delay her date of hire until September 20.

She leaned back into the comfort of the cool leather seat, forcing herself to breathe. She supposed she could afford him this parting gift of time, this assertion of her belief in him, though she'd come to question—if not doubt—his life's work.

That work had taken a twisted turn from his quest to eradicate tuberculosis, her mother's killer. The publicity against his beloved eugenics research was growing, getting ugly, thanks to the outcries of investigative-journalist crusader types at home and abroad. She would be glad to distance herself when the ordeal was done.

Perhaps this peace offering would soften her announcement that she'd been hired by the Campbell Playhouse—as a gofer and underling to start. But if she proved herself indispensable, they might include her in their November move to Los Angeles—one step closer to radio theatre performance. All of which would send her father into a tizzy. He disdained radio theatre more than he'd detested her modern theatre productions in college, blaming the influence of her professors and "theatrical peers" for her independent thinking. She'd tell him the moment they returned to New York. As far as Rachel was concerned, that could not be soon enough.

But there were the medical examination in Frankfurt and the gala in Berlin to endure first—the gala to honor her father and German scientists for their breakthrough work in eugenics. The gala, which would include Gerhardt and her childhood friend Kristine. She brushed the air as if a fly had landed on her cheek. What had Kristine meant in her letter about "Gerhardt, and things impossible to write," that she was "terrified" for her daughter, Amelie? It was the first letter Rachel had received from her former friend in five years.

She placed one ankle deliberately over the other. *Perhaps Kristine's grown tired of playing the sweet German Hausfrau. It would serve her right for betraying me.* Rachel bit her lip. That sounded harsh, even to her.

The black Mercedes skirted the banks of the free-flowing Main and glided at last into the paved drive of the sprawling Institute for Hereditary Biology and Racial Hygiene. The driver—black-booted, square-jawed, the picture of German efficiency in the uniform of the SS—opened her door.

Rachel drew a deep breath. Taking his hand, she stepped onto the walk.

◆─◆

Lea Hartman gripped her husband's hand as she waited her turn in the long, sterile corridor. What a gift that Friederich had been granted a three-day military pass! She couldn't imagine making the train trip alone, especially with the fearful knot that had grown and tightened in her stomach with every town they'd passed.

She'd been coming to the Institute every two years for as long as she could remember. The money and demand for the examinations had come from the Institute itself, though exactly why, she'd never understood—only that it had something to do with her mother, who'd died giving her birth at the Institute.

As a young child it had afforded the opportunity for a long, exciting train trip with her Oma. Even the doctors' authoritarian stance and scathing disapproval hadn't entirely dimmed the joy of the magical journey far from Oberammergau. But as a teen she'd grown shy of the probing doctors, intimidated by the caustic nurses, yet fearful of refusing their demands. At sixteen she'd written, bravely stating that she no longer wished to come, that her health was quite good, and that she no longer saw the purpose. The next week a car from the Institute had screeched to a stop outside her grandmother's door. Despite Oma's protests, the driver had produced some sort of contract that Oma had signed when Lea was given to her and raced the teen all the way to Frankfurt—alone. She'd been kept in a white enamel room, in a confined portion of the sterile Institute, for a fortnight. The nurses had woken her hourly; the doctors examined her daily—intimately and thoroughly. Lea dared not refuse again.

She shifted in her seat. Friederich smiled at her, squeezing her hand in reassurance. Lea breathed deeply and leaned back against the wall.

Now she was married—almost eighteen months—and though she dreaded the ritual examination, she dared hope they could tell her why she'd been unable to conceive. There was no apparent reason, and she and Friederich wanted a child—several children—desperately. She closed her eyes and once more begged silently for mercy, for the opening of her womb.

Her husband encircled her with his arm, rubbing the tension from her back. His were the strong, roughened hands of a woodcarver—large and sensitive to the nuances of wood, even more sensitive to her needs, her emotions, her every breath. How she loved him! How she missed him when he was stationed with the First Mountain Division—no matter that the barracks flanked their own Oberammergau. How she feared he might be sent on one of the Führer's missions to gain more "living space" for the *Volk*. How she feared he might stop loving her.

The door to the examination room opened.

"Dr. Mengele!" She recognized him from two years before. She would not have chosen this doctor, though she could not say precisely why. The examinations, no matter who performed them, were technically the same. It was only a feeling, and hadn't they told her countless times not to trust her feelings, her instincts? They were not reliable and would mislead her. Neither they nor she could be trusted.

"May I come with my wife, Herr Doctor?" Friederich stood by her side. Lea felt her husband's strength seep into her vertebrae.

"For the examination?" Dr. Mengele raised eyebrows in amusement. *"Nein."* And then more gruffly, "Wait here."

"But we would like to talk with you, Herr Doctor," Friederich persisted, "about a matter of great importance to us."

"Can a grown woman not speak for herself?" Dr. Mengele's amusement turned scornful. He didn't acknowledge Lea, but snorted and walked through the door.

Lea glanced once more into her husband's worried eyes, felt his courage squeezed into her hand, and followed Dr. Josef Mengele into the examination room.

❧

Friederich checked his watch. If the clock in the hallway was to be believed, Lea had been behind the closed door for only forty-seven minutes, but it seemed a lifetime.

He'd not been in favor of her coming to Frankfurt. He'd never understood the hold the Institute maintained over his wife, why she both feared and nearly fawned at the feet of these doctors. But he'd married her—the woman he saw much more in than she saw in herself—for better or for worse, and this, he'd decided, was part of that package. He would not forbid her to come; she feared them too much for that.

And these days, putting your foot down against authority figures carried consequences—consequences Lea could not afford now that Friederich was not regularly at home. The last thing he wanted was men from the Institute on his wife's doorstep when he was not there to protect her. Better for her to remain invisible. From what little he knew of the Führer's "negotiations" with Poland, he and his unit could be shipped east at any moment. He'd been lucky to get leave at all.

Friederich pushed his hands through his hair, sat heavily once again on the backless bench, and knotted his fingers between his knees.

He was a simple man. He loved his wife, his Lord and his church, his country, his woodcarving, Oberammergau with all its quirks and passion for its Passion Play. He was a grateful man, and the only thing missing in his life was children that he and Lea would bear and rear. He didn't think it selfish to ask God for such a thing.

But he wondered if Lea would ask the right questions of the doctor, if she might miss something. She was a smart and insightful woman, but the nearer they'd come to Frankfurt, the more childlike she'd become. And this Dr. Mengele, whoever he was, seemed less than approachable.

Friederich checked his pocket watch, then the clock again. He wanted to take his wife from this place, go home to Oberammergau—home to their cool Alpine valley, to all they knew and loved. He only wished he didn't have to return to his barracks, wished he could take his wife home and make love to her. It wasn't that he didn't want to serve his country or that he loved Germany less than others. At least, he loved the Germany he'd grown up in. But this New Germany—this Germany of the last seven years with its hate-filled Nuremberg Laws that persecuted Jews, its eternal harassment of the church, its constant demand for greater living space and focus on pure Aryan race—was something different, something he could not grasp as a man grasps wood.

Like any German, he'd hoped and cheered when Adolf Hitler had promised to raise his country from the degradation of the Treaty of Versailles. He wanted to be more than a stench in the world's nostrils and to forge a good life for his family. But not at the expense of what was human or decent. Not if it meant dishonoring God in heaven or making an idol of their Führer.

He closed his eyes to suppress his anxiety about Lea, about politics, to clear his head. This was not the time to argue within himself about things he could not control.

He'd focus on the Nativity carving on his workbench at home. Wood was something he could rely upon. Just before being conscripted, he'd finished the last of a flock of sheep. Now he envisioned the delicate swirls of wood wool and the slight stain he would tell Lea to use in their crevices. Yes, something with a tinge of burnt umber would add depth, create dimension. His wife had the perfect touch. Watching her paint the wooden figures he'd carved was a pleasure to him—a creation they shared.

Friederich was counting the cost of the pigment and stain mixtures she would need for the entire set when the sharp click of a woman's heels on the polished tile floor caused him to lose focus. Her perfume preceded her. He opened his eyes, only to feel that he'd fallen into another world. There was something about the woman's face that struck him as frighteningly familiar, but the window dressing was unrecognizable.

Striking. He'd say she was striking. The same medium height. Her eyes were the same clear blue. Her hair the same gold, but not wrapped in braids about her head as they'd been an hour ago. Her locks hung loose, in rolling coils, so fluid they nearly shimmered. Her nails—fiery red—matched her lips. She wore seamed stockings the color of her skin and slim, high-heeled shoes that, when she paused and half turned toward the door, emphasized slender ankles and showed toned calves to good advantage.

All of that he noticed before he took in the belted sapphire suit, trim and fitted in all the right places. He closed his eyes and opened them again. But she was still there, and coming closer.

The thin, middle-aged man beside her stepped in front, blocking his view. "*Entschuldigung*, is this where we wait for Dr. Verschuer?"

But Friederich couldn't speak, couldn't quite think. And he didn't know a Dr. Verschuer—did he?

At that moment a pale and agitated woman in nurse's uniform pushed through the door at the far end of the corridor, hurrying toward them. "Dr. Kramer—please, you have entered the wrong corridor. Dr. Verschuer is this way." Casting a furtive glance toward Friederich, she hurried the man with the thinning gray hair and the beautiful young woman back the way they'd come.

"Lea," Friederich whispered. "Lea," he called louder.

The woman in the belted suit turned. He stepped expectantly toward her, but her eyes held no recognition of him. The nurse grabbed the woman's arm, pulling her down the hallway and through the door.

Friederich stood half a moment, uncertain what he should do, if he should follow her. And then the examination room door beside him opened, and his wife, her face stricken and braids askew, walked into his arms.

2

GERHARDT SCHLICK pulled a cigarette from its silver case and drew the fragrant tobacco beneath his nostrils. He was appreciative of the little things that life in the SS afforded—good food, good wine, beautiful women, and the occasional gift of American tobacco.

He smiled as he lit his cigarette and inhaled—long and slowly. After tonight he expected to replenish his stock of at least two of those items. The rest would come in due course to a man of his station. He checked his reflection. More than satisfied, he squared his shoulders and tugged the coat of his dress uniform into place. Then he checked the clock, and his mouth turned grim.

"Kristine!" he barked. It would not do to be late—not tonight. Every SS officer of note in Berlin would be there, including Himmler, and every Nazi Party man of letters. Only the Führer would be absent, and that, Gerhardt was certain, was by Goebbels's design— some scheme for greater propaganda, no doubt.

It was an evening to honor those entrusted with designs to strengthen Germany's bloodline through eugenics—to create a pure race, free of the weaknesses introduced by inferior breeding with non-Nordic races. It was nothing short of a drive to rapidly increase Germany's Nordic population. A perfect plan to restore Germany to its rightful position in the world—over the world.

Within that grand design Gerhardt saw himself rising through the ranks of the SS. Marrying the highly acceptable adopted daughter of eminent American scientist Dr. Rudolph Kramer would be one more rung in that ladder. A perfect blending of Germanic genes—Nordic features, physical strength and beauty, intellect . . . a perfect family for the Reich.

He smiled again. He wouldn't mind doing his duty for the Fatherland, not with Rachel Kramer.

He could count on Dr. Verschuer and Dr. Mengele. And he suspected, since this afternoon's telephone call from the Institute, that with minimal persuasion he could also count on the cooperation of Dr. Kramer where his daughter was concerned.

One thing stood in his way. Perhaps two.

At that moment Kristine Schlick walked into the room. She twirled self-consciously. The ice-blue satin evening gown brought lights to her eyes as it floated, rippling round her shapely form.

Their four-year-old daughter, Amelie, clapped delightedly as her mother twirled. Kristine lifted the child in her arms and planted a kiss on her cheek. Amelie patted her mother's cheeks and gurgled an inharmonious stream of syllables.

Taken off guard, Gerhardt felt his eyes widen. There was no doubt that his wife was beautiful. Breathtaking—he would give her that. And there were other acceptable features. But she bore genetically deficient children, and in the New Germany that was unforgivable.

"Well?" she asked tentatively. "Do you like it?"

The question of a woman who knows the answer but is afraid to believe. The question of a woman who begs to be told she is beautiful.

But Gerhardt disdained begging as much as he disdained Kristine and his unacceptably deaf daughter. Turning off emotion—any form of weakness—was not difficult once he'd set his mind to it. And he had. He slapped his evening gloves against his thigh, ignoring the sudden terror in the eyes of his child as her mother set her on the floor, shielding her from his approach. "The car is waiting. You've made us late."

⟡

Rachel turned one way before the full-length mirror in her hotel room, tilted her head, then turned the other. She loved green. But wearing it for the gala would've been fodder for yet another argument with her father. He'd insisted she wear royal blue, in a style that would frame her face and set her eyes and hair to best advantage. Because the gala would honor him and his work, celebrating the eugenics research shared between the two countries and the world, he'd asserted that it was essential, especially in these uncertain times, to appear their best and most gracious in every way. Rolling her eyes, she'd acquiesced.

She had to admit that the deep color, draped neckline, and fluid silk did more for her than anything she owned. And because it was the color he'd chosen, her father had not balked at the outrageous price. She supposed it would come in handy for events in New York City—maybe the opera house or a first night at Radio City Music Hall.

Rachel lifted her chin and straightened her spine. She didn't mind turning heads, and she wouldn't mind showing up Kristine and Gerhardt Schlick. She mightn't have cared if Kristine had kept in touch. That's what hurt most—her sudden abandonment.

She'd always known that Kristine wanted a life, a husband and family of her own—those were things girls told one another. And why not? Kristine was a warm, intelligent, and beautiful woman in her own right. Rachel admitted—if only to herself—that she'd relegated her friend to the shadows too often, too long.

Kristine had been so quick to comfort Gerhardt's wounded pride five years ago when he'd stood in the Kramers' New York parlor, furious and unbelieving, his marriage proposal rejected by nineteen-year-old Rachel. He'd married Kristine to spite her; of that she was certain. But Kristine had married him because she'd been swept off her feet, eager for her moment in the sun, her time to shine on distant German shores without Rachel to dim her reflection.

If she regrets her choice now . . . well, what is that to me?

"Rachel?" Her father knocked at her door. "It's time."

"Coming," she called, pulling her light wrap over her shoulders and applying a last deliberate swipe of lipstick. She blotted, picked up the blue-and-silver silk purse dyed to match her shoes, and marched toward the arena.

⸙

Jason Young checked his hat outside the lavish ballroom door, tightened the knot in his tie, and squared his shoulders. He couldn't believe his luck. For two years he'd tracked the elusive Dr. Rudolph Kramer through Cold Spring Harbor's Eugenics Research Association. Not once had the "mad scientist," as Jason had dubbed him, been available for an interview on either side of the Atlantic—and Kramer visited Germany frequently. Not once had he returned the phone calls his secretary promised he would. But that hadn't kept Jason from dishing up the dirt on the man's research and splattering it across news copy—research Jason saw as inhumane and, with Germany's unchecked collusion and Hitler's sterilization campaign, inescapably criminal.

But those obstacles were past. Because tonight he had a press pass to the gala—a legitimate opportunity to watch and record, word for word, everything the man and his cohorts said. If all went well, he'd get directly in Kramer's face before the clock struck midnight. Jason wasn't about to miss this flying saucer to stardom. "Watch out, Pulitzer, here I come!" he whispered.

"Hold on, hotshot." Daren Peterson laid a hand on his colleague's shoulder, gently pushing him toward a linen-covered table with a direct view of Rudolph Kramer and his stunning daughter. "All things in time. Let the man get comfortable. Let him get through his glad-handing. Then I'll shoot the artwork and you can eat him alive."

Jason rubbed his hands together and licked his lips.

❧

Rachel had had more than enough. Nearly three hours of sanctimonious speeches on the growth of Aryan purity and toasts brimming with laudations for the scientific community's systematic plans to rid the world of diseased and inferior stock had passed before the music and dancing, the serious tippling of champagne, and the ultimate loosening of tongues began.

She'd felt undressed by nearly every roving masculine eye and sized up and scathed by every feminine one. Gerhardt Schlick's undisguised stare reminded her of Margaret Mitchell's scene in *Gone with the Wind*—when Rhett Butler's gaze seared Scarlett O'Hara ascending the stairs of Twelve Oaks. Only she doubted that Gerhardt's intentions were as gentlemanly as the ungentlemanly Rhett's.

She actually felt sorry for Kristine. Gerhardt had clearly distanced himself from his wife, paying her mind only to reprimand her with openly superior and snide remarks. Kristine, though tipsy, just as clearly felt his rebukes.

"You must dance," her father whispered, distracting her from watching the couple on the inside of the horseshoe-shaped seating arrangement several feet away.

Rachel bristled. "I don't want to dance."

"Allow me." He stood and, ignoring her response, led her to the dance floor.

At least it was better than dancing with the SS officers or the fawning Dr. Mengele. Rachel was always surprised and pleased when dancing with her father. The moment he stepped onto a dance floor his carriage, his entire demeanor, changed from intent, slump-shouldered scientist to man about town. He bowed, lifted her hand, and they began a Viennese waltz. Perfect frame, perfect timing with the orchestra, and just the right pressure on her back, against her hand. Ballroom dancing was something he and her mother had shared, and though Rachel could not waltz as wonderfully as she remembered her mother waltzing, in his arms she knew she could be made more beautiful still.

They'd taken one sweeping turn round the ballroom floor when her father stopped in response to a tap on his shoulder. He smiled, bowed slightly, and stood aside.

Sturmbannführer Gerhardt Schlick was waiting, smiling in a way that made Rachel shudder, though she refused to show it. She allowed herself to be led round the floor. On the second turn he pulled her closer. "It's been a long time. It's good to see you again, Rachel."

She swallowed, smiling confidently, but her throat was dry. "Has it? And how is Kristine, and your daughter?"

A coldness passed through his eyes. "You must judge that for yourself."

She raised her brows.

He sighed. "Oh, come now. There must have been signs before. You should have told me, warned me. I thought we were friends, at least."

"I've no idea what you're talking about."

"Your friend is not—" he hesitated—"genetically sound. She is not emotionally . . . I would use the English word *stable*."

"Kristine is more stable than any girl I know."

"And so I thought when I agreed to marry her. But as I said, you must judge for yourself."

"What have you done to her?"

He looked the aggrieved, terribly injured party. "You wound me, Fräulein, and do me injustice."

"I doubt that very much."

"Ever the champion of the underdog." He smiled. "And as beautiful as the moment I first saw you." He pulled her closer still.

"And you are married, Herr Schlick." She stepped away from him.

He snorted softly. "Truly, my mistake." Gerhardt bowed, but held her hand and kissed it. "I should have waited for you, no matter how long."

She turned, but he did not let go of her hand. "You'll be in Berlin for several weeks, I understand, Fräulein Kramer."

She didn't respond.

"I look forward to seeing more of you, and often."

"That will not be possible." Rachel pulled away, more disgusted than frightened. She sensed that he followed her toward her seat. Her father was not there, but standing oblivious, deep in conversation within the doctors' circle several feet away. Kristine was gone.

All the you-should-have-known-better cuts she'd loaded in her arsenal, ready to aim at Kristine, evaporated. No matter the headlong foolishness of her rebound marriage, Kristine didn't deserve Gerhardt Schlick.

Rachel retrieved her bag from the table and headed for the ladies' room, trusting that Gerhardt would not follow.

3

DESPITE CLOSE PROXIMITY and creative lurking, Jason Young had not maneuvered one minute alone with Dr. Kramer. "Himmler's got him smothered and Verschuer's got him dwarfed."

"Kramer's a pale fish out of water," Peterson agreed. "Doesn't look like much beside those SS and the charismatic Mengele."

"So, who does? I'm thinking we'd all ought to wear jackboots and carry riding crops."

"Well then, what's next?" Peterson grumbled, licking the base of a new flashbulb.

"They don't want him alone with the press. We've got to get him off to the side." Jason edged toward the tight clique of officers and doctors.

"Muscle through that crowd and you'll find yourself on a swift vacation to hard labor," Peterson whispered. "Perfect opportunity to buddy up with those concentration-camped German priests and pastors you love to champion." He twisted the bulb into his camera, smiling into the face of a particularly nasty-looking SS officer with a monocle.

Jason pushed a hank of sandy hair from his eyes. "We're not supposed to know about that."

"Right," Peterson snorted. "Neither is half of Germany."

"And I don't do prison interviews—nasty smells."

"Wasn't trying to be funny."

Jason skirted the small group, trying to ingratiate himself into the

19

conversation, person by person. But it was no use. It was as though they'd formed a seal around the American scientist.

Except that Jason knew the great doctor was fluent in German, he might have suspected Kramer did not understand the speeches—those from the platform or those given by the men standing next to him. Pretty radical rhetoric, even for the mad scientist. He didn't appear the pompous, driven man Jason had shadowed in New York City. *So what's changed?*

Peterson nudged him. "You're not the only vulture circling." He nodded toward Kramer's daughter, who seemed to be trying to capture her father's attention. "Why not try the circuitous route?"

Rachel Kramer wasn't his first choice. Jason doubted she was privy to her father's research or the alliance between the Eugenics Research Association and the Third Reich. He'd checked her out for just that purpose back in New York but had been convinced she had her head buried in modern theatre. He reconsidered now, giving her the once-over, head to toe—all business. Then he did it again—pure pleasure. She just might be a link to the great doctor off court.

He swallowed. That was an excuse, and he knew it. It wouldn't do to get distracted. Beautiful women had a way of doing that. Still, it was worth a try. He stepped closer and opened his mouth to speak.

"Rachel." A black dress SS uniform muscled between them, pulling her from the group. "I must speak with you."

But she turned on the German. "I don't wish to speak with you. Take your hands off me."

"Please, my dear, let's not make a scene. Consider your father." The SS uniform leaned closer, wrapped his arm around her, but she struggled against him.

"We're on." Jason elbowed Peterson and pocketed his notepad and pencil, picked up a glass of champagne from the nearest place setting, and slammed into the SS officer. "*Entschuldigung*, Herr Sturmbannführer. My fault entirely."

"You imbecile!" the officer exploded, releasing Rachel.

"You're absolutely right; I'm a clumsy oaf. Here—" Jason grabbed a linen napkin, dramatically sopping the man's arm—"let's clean you up."

"Get away from me, you *Dummkopf*!"

"Now, now." Peterson stepped between the two, steering the officer away. "There's no need to get riled. International relations and such. Simple mistake. How about I get your photograph for the newspaper? What was your name again?"

Jason just as smoothly cupped Rachel's elbow. "Would you care to dance, Miss Kramer? Give this homesick American a Berlin memory?"

Clearly relieved, Rachel stepped onto the dance floor. "Thank you. That was—"

"Uncomfortable," Jason finished. He took her hand, twirled her twice, then pulled her closer than necessary into a fox-trot. "Damsel in distress from the nasty Nazis and all that."

Rachel laughed, pulling back slightly. "Precisely. And who is this chivalrous Yank I must thank?"

"Sir Jason, at your service." He mocked a bow.

She mocked a curtsy, smiling warmly. Jason felt his blood race.

"Well, Sir Jason, what brings you to Berlin? It's not exactly tourist season in the nation's capital, is it?"

"Hardly." Jason took a half box turn to keep Peterson and the uniform in his peripheral vision. "First big gala assignment in the new regime."

"You're a foreign correspondent?"

He felt her tense. Jason laughed. "From your mouth to my editor's ears! Confidentially—" he twirled her again—"I'm guessing he's laying ten to one that I'll fall flat on my face before the New Year, get kicked out of the country by the Gestapo, and be back on NY's city beat before you can catch a cat's meow."

"You're that bad?"

He grimaced. "Do you always say exactly what you mean?"

Now she laughed. "I hope so. I don't have a journalist's gift for flattery."

"You give me too much credit." He dipped her once.

"And you're a flamboyant dancer!"

"Not so staid and serious as your German uniform?" He grinned, though he caught the uniform's glare from across the room.

She shuddered—enough that he felt it through her evening gown.

"So, who is the creep?"

"The husband of an old friend—who's acting like neither."

"Check. Do you want me to walk you out?"

"No, no, of course not—thank you. I'm here with my father." She nodded toward the clique against the far wall.

"Not one of the military types, I take it."

"No. The American scientist—Dr. Kramer." She lifted her chin slightly but diverted her eyes. Jason caught her mixed glimmer of pride and uncertainty.

"Ah—part of the cooperative eugenics program Himmler was going on about."

"I'm fairly certain Herr Himmler overemphasized America's contribution."

"No need to be modest. It's all the rage here in Germany—master Nordic race breeding. Sterilization of questionable bloodlines. Elimination of undesirable elements." He twirled her again. "So, what do you make of it?"

She looked taken aback, and Jason knew he was losing her. "What does your father think? Will the US be accelerating their program—keep pace with the Führer?"

Her smile gone, she pulled away. "I don't discuss politics, Mr.—Mr. Jason."

He raised his hands in surrender. "My apologies, Miss Kramer. No offense intended. It's just that this is a gala to celebrate the research shared between countries. I figured you'd be all for it, or at least your father would." He stepped closer, staged his best repentant-little-boy look, and held out his hand. "I'll behave. Promise."

She placed her hand in his.

Jason couldn't believe his luck. "Here's something neutral. What will you do while in Germany? Need a tour guide?"

"I've been coming to Germany ever since I was a child. What could you show me?"

"Anything you want. Say the word." He grinned. "I'll become the best tour guide Germany has to offer, if I have to bribe every cabbie in Berlin!"

At last she smiled, and he twirled her, glad to be in her favor once again.

"As a matter of fact, Sir Jason, I probably know Berlin better than you. Perhaps I should give you the tour."

"Now you're talking!"

"But only if you stop twirling me—I'll be too dizzy to walk!"

They both laughed as the music faded.

"Thirsty?"

"I thought you'd never ask."

Before they lifted champagne flutes from the waiter's tray, Peterson cut in. "Young, I'm out of here. I need to get these photos developed. See you tomorrow." He nodded appreciatively toward Rachel. "Miss Kramer."

But when Jason turned back to Rachel, her jaw had gone rigid and her eyes cold. "Young? Your name is Young? Jason Young?"

Jason swallowed, fairly certain what was coming.

"The bounty hunter masquerading as a crusader out to ruin my father?"

"Hey, that's not my intention."

"You knew my name. You knew who I was. That's why you danced with me—you wanted a story."

"I don't rescue women in distress to get a story. I didn't set up the uniform. You looked like you could use some help." But he couldn't hold her piercing gaze.

"Your incessant hounding is driving my father into an early grave."

"My hounding?" He couldn't let that pass. "Do you know what they're doing as a result of his research and the research of his counterparts here in Germany? Did you hear what they said tonight?"

Rachel turned to walk away, but Jason kept pace. "If he's innocent, if there's a good side to this, then help me get the story. Convince him to talk to me. I'll be fair—honest."

"Honest?" She nearly snorted, reducing him to dung with her glare. "You've shown just how honest you are, Mr. Young. I don't think either Germany or America can stand much more of your brand of honesty."

Jason stopped short, the wind knocked from his sails. "Hey, I don't make the news," he called after her. "It's people like your father who do that! I just write it."

❧❧

The piercing headache between Rachel's eyes would not relent. Even the headlights of oncoming cars made her wince. But her father was in high spirits.

"Quite the affair, if I do say so." He spoke as if expecting an answer, but Rachel knew better. She closed her eyes and leaned back against the seat of the Mercedes.

"I daresay Herr Himmler came across rather stronger than I would have, but Germany's on the right track. They've moved ahead of us in America. We'll benefit greatly from their studies."

She turned away, uncertain which was the culprit that made her feel sick—her headache or her father's skewed reality.

"We'll be leaving for the conference on Tuesday. I'm driving to Hamburg with Major Schlick and Dr. Verschuer, then taking the ship to Scotland. There will be meetings after the conference. Two weeks is a long time on your own."

"I prefer it. I'd like to do some shopping while we're in the city, and I'm eager to see what the local theatres are producing." She tried to push back the throbbing. "I didn't know Gerhardt was part of the eugenics conference."

"He's taken an interest. He's quite the favorite with Dr. Verschuer. Someone worth knowing . . . a rising star in the SS."

She felt her father's eyes upon her, even in the darkness. The thought of Gerhardt Schlick numbered among Germany's finest made her queasy.

"The trip would give you opportunity to get to know him better."

"I have no desire to know him better. He was beastly tonight—to his wife and to me."

"I don't imagine their marriage will last."

"Why do you say that?"

Now he turned his head away, toward the opposite window. "You saw how things are between them." He hesitated, but only a moment. "Did you speak with Kristine?"

"No." Rachel felt her exasperation rising. "I'd intended to, but we were not sitting near enough during the speeches, and by the end of dinner she was completely cowed by Gerhardt."

"She was drunk."

"I can see why. He's horrid to her."

"You don't know what he contends with. You mustn't judge harshly."

"Harshly?"

"It was a poor match from the start. You could have handled him so much better. You were . . . hasty."

Rachel could not believe her ears. Surely her father must have had too much to drink. "What about their daughter? Amelie must be—what—four, by now?"

But her father dismissed her and the notion of Amelie with a flick of the wrist. Rachel was just as glad to drop the conversation. Perhaps by morning he'd regain his senses.

※

Rachel woke to find a note pushed beneath her door. Her father had gone out to an early breakfast meeting with colleagues. He'd apologized that she must eat alone and promised to see her that evening for dinner. They were invited to join the American ambassador and his wife. Rachel knew it was an order.

She opened the balcony door of her hotel room, glad for the morning sun, glad she would not need to spend the day with her father and his cronies. Rather than call for room service, she decided to go exploring—find an outdoor café specializing in strong ersatz German coffee and good rolls.

She was nearly out the door when she remembered her room key. Rummaging through her evening bag, she pulled out her comb and lipstick, her compact and passport—but no room key. She turned the bag upside down. Still no key. She massaged the purse all round, could feel the key in the bottom, but couldn't see it. Taking her bag to the window, she opened it. When it was held up to the light, she saw that a hole had been torn in the lining—a hole she knew was not there before. Rachel wriggled her finger through, felt the errant key . . . and something else.

She tried to grab hold of the paper, but both slipped away. Retrieving her nail scissors, she snipped the hole a little larger. Out came the key and a slim, rolled paper. Rachel recognized the hastily scrawled handwriting as Kristine's.

4

FRIEDERICH TURNED the small block of limewood over, and over again—first this way, and then that. It was the finest piece he owned, with the finest grain. He'd saved it until last. There was something about carving all the other figures of the Nativity first—the magi and shepherds, the sheep and donkeys, and even the archangel—that brought him with great satisfaction to the holy family, and finally to the *Christkind*. By saving its carving until last, he knew intimately the nature of the wood and the deeper personality of the family. For surely each was unique.

Ever since he'd married Lea he'd been carving her loving, concerned, and doting smile into Mary's face. He'd carved his own protective nature into Joseph's stance. And the babe—the babe was the child they hoped for, prayed for. The perfect child they imagined suckling and gurgling by day, the child Lea would sing to sleep at night. He'd carved a dozen in the last year—each one a work of which he was proud.

Friederich dropped the wood onto his worktable and stood. He walked to the window of his small woodshop and stared at the sun-drenched mountain. Mockery. There would be no babe to imagine. No babe for them—ever. What hope, what contentment could he carve into the holy family's faces now?

Lea's stricken eyes and grim mouth had not changed in the week since he'd brought her home, and there was no prospect in sight.

Why, Lord? Why Lea? The doctor, that coarse Dr. Mengele, had told her she'd never conceive, that she'd been sterilized the summer she turned sixteen—the summer she'd evidenced an obstinate nature.

"Like your mother," the doctor had told her. "Such flagrant refusal to acknowledge authority is the evil strain that has run rampant through Germany, the very nature that puts our Fatherland at risk. We must weed out those strains."

Lea had not understood, had dared to beg the doctor to reverse the process, citing her marriage to the older, stable Friederich, his longtime employment as a fine craftsman, how they'd faithfully supported the winter fund, his service to the Fatherland, how very much they wanted to raise children for God and Germany. Dr. Mengele had laughed at her stupidity, her naiveté, and said such simplemindedness was better erased from the New Germany. They'd clearly made no mistake, and there was no reversal possible. He was surprised that a man of Friederich's caliber had married her.

Friederich pounded his fist into his palm, so angry was he at the cruel and senseless doctor. Lea had not been able to speak at the Institute. She'd fled the building and he behind her, not knowing what had happened. He'd been frantic with worry but determined to get her home. And once he did, she broke down. Such gut-wrenching sobs.

Even now, he wondered if she'd told him all.

A week later, his afternoon pass had not moved her. She sat, staring from the window. He'd waved his hand in front of her face, and she'd not noticed. If she would cry again, he thought that might help. But no more tears came—at least not when he was with her. With Oma, he prayed it was different. Lea would surely let her defenses down with her Oma. She must.

And now he was being deployed. He'd told his commander that his wife was ill and begged that he be allowed to see her one last time. He was not above begging where his wife was concerned. But she'd barely blinked. When he kissed her good-bye she'd leaned into his chest, then pulled back, resignation in the slump of her shoulders.

Friederich sighed, placed the wood on a high shelf, and straightened his workbench. He'd leave everything in order. There was still small satisfaction in that.

He'd pulled the workshop door closed when he noticed the Christkind missing from the large Nativity, the one on display in his shop window.

Heinrich Helphman—certainly. The six-year-old had stolen it twice in the last month. Friederich frowned. The door was always locked. How did he get in? He checked the door. There was no sign of forced entry. *Whatever possesses the child? He must know his parents and the priest will punish him for stealing, even if I do nothing.*

If Friederich had all the time in the world, he'd carve a Christkind for the boy to keep, but this one was too valuable to let go, and part of a set—a set that had represented his hopes with Lea more than any other.

Even so, Friederich hadn't the heart to go after the boy. He'd write Lea and ask her to deal with him or his parents in time. Perhaps it would give her purpose. And if not, it was only wood, after all.

❧—❧

Hilde Breisner, Lea's Oma, who'd kissed away each hurt since Lea was born, could not mend this one. Lea did not tell her until Friederich had been deployed.

"Did you tell this doctor that your mother was raped? That the pregnancy was not her fault?"

"He knows this!" Lea sobbed in her arms. "He said she must have had 'that look' that drives men wild. That she must have wanted it."

"This is not true!" Oma trembled in anger. But her fury did Lea no good, and her daughter was long dead and could not stand up for herself.

"He said the sterilization process cannot be reversed. That he wouldn't, even if he could. He said that with such a lineage we would never be allowed to adopt, no child will be placed in our care. He said I am no more trustworthy than my mother."

Lea sobbed with such a vengeance that Oma feared for her sanity. Oma rocked with her granddaughter's head across her breast, back and forth, back and forth, until Lea pulled away and ran from her cottage door, leaving Oma to weep alone.

❦

But Lea didn't go home. When she found her Lutheran church door locked, she'd crept to the Church of Saints Peter and Paul. Now that she'd cracked open the dam to her heart, there was no stopping the outpouring. She desperately needed comfort. Comfort and mercy—no matter that she could not tell a soul.

She slid through the back door of the ornate sanctuary. Not knowing if she'd be welcomed, uncertain about the procedures of genuflecting and crossing herself, and intimidated by the gold and the carvings, she stole up the aisle—nearly halfway. Slipping into a pew, she sank to her knees, to weep, to pray, to beg forgiveness for she didn't know what. There had always been some secret shame, something dirty and vile within her that others saw—at least that the doctors in Frankfurt had seen and condemned in her since birth. Something that kept her from deserving, from living, a normal life. She'd never told Oma, had never hinted at the horrible things they'd said to her each visit—not until today. If Oma knew what they knew, saw what they saw, might she not stop loving her too? Lea couldn't bear it.

Lea didn't hear the curate enter the pew beside her. She simply realized that the light in the church had changed.

The horror of finding herself alone in the darkening building with this man of the Catholic church, and in the state she was, undid her. Shamefaced and broken, she tried to stand. But her feet and knees had gone numb, and she sat back upon the bench.

"Frau Hartman." The curate spoke softly. "Take your time, *bitte*. You have been drinking?"

"*Nein,* Curate Bauer!" she nearly cried. "I am so very sorry. Excuse me. Please excuse me. My feet went numb while I prayed; that is all."

"There is nothing to excuse, my child. You are welcome to pray here—always."

His kindness broke her defenses, and her lip trembled. She tried to hold it in, but her grief and shame erupted, and she wept again.

He handed her his handkerchief. "How can I help you?"

"You must think me mad." She wiped her eyes, trying to regain her breath.

"You are not the first woman to seek comfort in the church—thank God. Especially in these times."

Lea breathed deeply, doing her best to compose herself.

"Herr Hartman is serving his military time," the curate observed. "That must be very difficult."

Lea shook her head. "I would not have my husband see me like this for all the world."

"How can I help you, Frau Hartman?" he repeated.

"There is nothing to be done."

"There is always something."

Lea laughed, choking on her laughter. "No, not this time."

"You must have faith, Frau Hart—"

"Faith," she snorted, "will not help us."

"Frau Hartman," he admonished.

"We can have no children!" she blurted. Then, horrified by her outburst, by the humiliation of her confession, she slapped her hand to her mouth and stood to leave.

"But you can't know that. You've been married but a year." He shrugged. "Perhaps it's not God's time."

"Eighteen months!"

"Even so, God can work miracles. Think of Sarah—in her nineties! And the womb God opened for Hannah!"

In her heartbreak, in her brokenness and anger, Lea told him exactly why miracles were not meant for her. She told him all that Dr. Mengele had told her in Frankfurt, taking a perverse pleasure in the shock that widened his eyes. She told him that the sterilization had been done as a pronouncement on her wickedness—wickedness so vile that even she couldn't see it, inscribed as it was in her soul. And when she'd spewed her worst venom—for herself and for the doctors who'd played and continued to play God—she dared him to report her ravings to the Gestapo. She gasped and heaved. The church grew dark before she breathed normally, before there was silence. And still Curate Bauer did not speak.

Lea stood at last, relieved, ashamed only that she'd told a man not her husband. She knew he must be embarrassed, too horrified by her outburst and so conscious of her indecency that he could not speak. She didn't care. Something had snapped, and she would not be cowed.

When the curate reached, trembling, to lay his hand on her head, she fled the pew and stormed up the aisle. She pushed wide the outer door, letting the Alpine wind suck her breath and lead her home.

5

RACHEL WAS RELIEVED—glad for the reprieve and freedom—when, midmorning, three days after the gala, Drs. Verschuer and Mengele joined her father and Gerhardt Schlick en route to the seventh International Congress of Genetics in Edinburgh, Scotland. They'd be gone two weeks—a week in Scotland and another in meetings with the doctors in Frankfurt.

Two days later, Rachel, against her better judgment but consumed by curiosity, followed Kristine's directions, minutely penned onto the paper hidden in the lining of her purse. It was not far to the small café, a quaint but secluded open-air affair edging the Tiergarten.

The woman she found waiting at the two-seat table along the walkway was not the schoolgirl she'd grown up with, nor was she the intoxicated, intimidated woman in blue satin from the gala. She was—Rachel frowned—something she could not quite pin down.

Kristine looked up. Rachel would have appreciated more time to study her longtime, if former, friend.

But Kristine smiled as if no time had passed since their sleepovers in high school. "You came—I knew you'd come!" And she nearly squeezed the life out of Rachel, just as she'd done in those long-ago school days.

Rachel was more than a little confused. "Kristine." She hugged her back, but limply.

Kristine pulled her to the chair opposite her. "It's been so long."

"Five years," Rachel accused.

Kristine blinked, her cheeks brightening in color, but quickly added, "I'm sorry. I'm sorry I hurt you."

Much against her will, Rachel's eyes welled. *But you did hurt me. You hurt me badly. And now* . . . "What do you want, Kristine? And why the cloak-and-dagger routine?"

Kristine sat back, pulled off her gloves, moistened her lips. "I want you to take Amelie. I want you to take her to America."

Whatever Rachel expected—and she'd not known what to expect—it was not this.

"Amelie? Don't you think she's a little young for the grand tour in reverse?"

"Take her, and raise her as if she is yours." Now Kristine's eyes welled, and she did not blink the tears away.

Rachel's mind ran through Kristine's cryptic letter, through her scribbled hidden note, through Gerhardt's accusations. She tallied them, inserted her father's criticism of their marriage and child, but still they didn't add up. "Are you leaving Gerhardt?" It was all she could think—the only thing that made even a little sense.

But Kristine laughed hoarsely. "I would go in a heartbeat!" She sobered. "Amelie is deaf."

"What?"

"Do you know what it means to be deaf in Germany now?"

Rachel shook her head, as much to shake off the fog settling there as to say that she did not—did not know that Amelie was deaf, did not know what it meant to be deaf in Germany, could not comprehend what Kristine was asking her.

"Did you hear the speeches at the gala? Did you listen?" Kristine leaned toward her, lowering her voice. "They are going to rid Germany of every genetically imperfect man, woman, and child. Handicapped physically, mentally, emotionally—it doesn't matter. They will all be gone for the greater good of the Fatherland. That means Amelie."

"What do you mean 'rid'?"

Kristine grasped Rachel's fingers, her grip stronger than Rachel would have expected. "They're going to kill them—murder them."

Gerhardt's words came back to Rachel. *"She is not emotionally . . . I would use the English word stable."* Rachel tried to focus, tried to understand what Kristine was saying—what she could possibly mean. Simply because she detested Gerhardt, she wanted to give Kristine the benefit of the doubt. But she shook her head. "That can't be what they meant, Kristine. That's absurd."

Kristine's blue-gray eyes flashed, and she gripped Rachel's fingers more tightly. "That's what they'd have the world think."

The waiter came then, and Kristine pulled back, sat straighter. Rachel rubbed life back into her fingers beneath the table.

"Shall I order for you?" Kristine offered brightly, her demeanor changing in an instant before the waiter. "Two coffees and a sweet?"

"Nein." Rachel rattled off her own order in the native tongue, determined to remain independent, separate from Kristine.

When the waiter had gone, Kristine apologized in English. "I'd forgotten your excellent German."

"You've learned well," Rachel acknowledged.

"It was the first of many things Gerhardt insisted upon—perfect German, Berlin accent." Kristine pulled a cigarette from her purse and lit it. "Little good that's done me." She puffed, inhaled. "I know this must sound insane to you."

"Impossible. It sounds impossible and improbable. I'm sorry Amelie is deaf. That's surely hard—and a disappointment for both of you. But Gerhardt wouldn't allow his own child to be killed. And when did you start smoking?"

Kristine inhaled long. She did it again. It seemed to steady her nerves as she stared out over the Tiergarten. "I've seen the plans. In Gerhardt's briefcase, though he doesn't know. T4."

She gave a short, rueful laugh. "Do you know why they call it T4? Because they were having lunch one day, just across the way—"

she pointed behind Rachel, a general direction—"and conceived the plan. This plan to eliminate thousands upon thousands was conceived between courses. What do you think? Between consommé and beef tongue? Or over dessert? The address of their luncheon was Tiergarten 4." She dropped her barely smoked cigarette onto the flagstone and ground it with her shoe.

"You must have misunderstood."

"Misunderstood?" Kristine's voice rose. Heads turned their way, and she reined in her posture, the decibels of her voice. She waited until their neighbors had returned to their coffees, their newspapers, and whispered, "Have you read *Mein Kampf*? The Führer calls these 'unfit' and 'life unworthy of life.' Those who will be a drain on German society and resources when the nation goes to war—when the German army fulfills its 'destiny' to gain more living space for the *Volk*."

"He can't be serious about going to war. There will be a last-minute armistice or something like they did in Austria."

"Do you think Poland will allow an *Anschluss*? Open the border and happily allow Hitler to march through their breadbasket?" She leaned forward again. "Rachel, this is not like you. Open your eyes!"

But it wasn't like mild-mannered, go-along-to-get-along Kristine, either. Rachel couldn't get her bearings.

"Every doctor and midwife is ordered to report children with genetic defects on their records, retroactive to 1936. I've seen the order. I don't know if the mandate's gone out, but it will."

"That's not unlike the eugenics work being done in America or England or Scotland. They keep all kinds of lists and details about families—for generations. Sometimes they recommend sterilization in severe cases. But for the most part, they're just observing."

Kristine kept on. "They'll encourage at first. Invite parents to bring their children to centers for special training and treatment—training and medical attention they can't receive at home."

"Well, perhaps that's true. Caring for a handicapped child must be—"

"And then when a little time has passed—very little—they'll kill them."

"Kristine!"

"They'll put them in vans and drive them round, gassing them as they go. Or they'll use injections. For the infants, they'll starve them—it's cheaper and they can starve whole rooms at a time. They've thought of everything, and in typical Germanic precision and orderliness, they've written up every contingency."

Rachel pushed away from the table and grabbed her purse. "I won't listen to any more, Kristine. You're married to a man you don't love—who apparently doesn't love you. And I'm sorry for you. Gerhardt is a cad and doesn't deserve you. But you've got it wrong. He's not a monster."

Kristine pulled Rachel back to her seat as the waiter, eyebrows raised, delivered their order. *"Danke."* Kristine slipped him two Reichsmarks.

The waiter nodded, his eyes lighting appreciatively, and backed away. Both women sipped their ersatz coffee—black and strong.

Rachel winced. "I don't know how you drink this stuff."

Kristine ignored the gibe. "Once Amelie is gone, Gerhardt will find a way to eliminate me."

"Oh, Kristine . . ." Rachel could take no more, though her heart broke for her friend. Truly, she was unbalanced.

"Gerhardt is rising within the ranks of the SS. It is incumbent upon every SS officer to bear children for the Reich—genetically perfect Aryan children. And to do that they must have genetically perfect Aryan wives."

"But there's no absolute proof that deafness is hereditary. There's no reason to think—"

"They are not certain of that. They believe that such things would not occur if there was not a weakness in the bloodline, or a predisposition to that weakness. And those weaknesses must be eliminated."

Rachel paused. That was true. She knew from her father that was precisely the rhetoric common among eugenicists. And she'd heard as much touted at the gala. "They recommend sterilization—not elimination! And even then, it's not a law to sterilize parents of handicapped children."

"Not in America. Not yet."

"But here? You're saying that it's a law here?"

"Hitler changes the laws to suit his grand design." She leaned close, looked down to whisper, as if studying Rachel's pastry. "And if he doesn't order it directly, he has it done through his emissaries—all made to appear as if it's done for the greater good of the Fatherland."

Rachel sat back. *What if the rhetoric about creating a master Nordic race is not just talk, not just the hope and fantasy of dreamers? What might they do to increase the segment of the population with those features and characteristics and decrease the population without? What if . . . ?*

"Once he's rid of me, Gerhardt will be legally free to remarry—" Kristine's eye twitched—"someone more suitable. In the meantime he's free to propagate his bloodline, to do his duty for the Fatherland with prostitutes the Reich deems fit."

"I'm sure you're mistaken. There must be another explanation." Rachel couldn't take it in, couldn't grasp that she was defending Gerhardt.

Kristine pulled the gray silk scarf from her neck to reveal a perfect circle of purple bruises round her throat and beneath her collarbone, thumbprints obvious. "This is not a string of pearls." No tears welled this time. "Is this the necklace of a woman valued?" She rewound the scarf.

Rachel could not breathe, and Kristine gripped her fingers once more. "Take Amelie, I beg you. Take her with you to America."

6

RACHEL TURNED OVER IN BED. She'd not slept well since her meeting with Kristine. She closed her eyes and repeated to herself for the twentieth time that she did not want a child. What did she know about raising or even communicating with a deaf child? She didn't even know if she wanted marriage—ever. Never mind the unlikelihood that she'd be allowed to leave Germany with someone else's offspring. Especially when that someone was SS Sturmbannführer Gerhardt Schlick.

Rachel sat up, slipping her feet into her sandals. What she did want was to return to New York, take up her first real job, begin her career with the Campbell Playhouse, and not look back. She'd studied four years for just this kind of breakthrough. Small—she knew it was small—but any kind of breakthrough in NYC's theatre community was amazing, nearly impossible to snag.

She wanted to forget about Kristine and her ravings, forget the smug, licentious Gerhardt, the wild accusations of Jason Young. And she desperately hoped that her father had not stepped onto a moral and ethical slope so slippery that he could not regain his footing or his soul.

But she'd promised Kristine she would think about taking Amelie to New York. And she had—for nearly a week.

Rachel rang for room service and coffee, glad for once that the Germans loved their coffee—or whatever was substituting for coffee these days—strong.

It was a good thing her father was away. Had he been there, she might have gone to him, confided in him, and sought his advice, even against her better judgment. Rachel had sensed an uncomfortable bias on her father's part toward Gerhardt, a cold dismissal of Kristine—one that made her skeptical of his fair counsel, even made her question his motives. But in whom else could she confide?

Perhaps he was right. Perhaps Kristine had let her imagination run wild. At any rate, her father would return in another week. She could do nothing about any of it now.

The thing Rachel could control was her shopping and theatregoing, and she'd taken good advantage of these days on her own to frequent Berlin's best department stores, and the less traditional, more experimental modern theatre venues—places her father would not appreciate, places the Reich had formally disapproved of but that still thrived. She planned a night of Wagner's *Meistersinger*, staged at the Volksoper, for his return. That, she was certain, would meet his approval.

Unhappily, her favorite stores had been closed—Jewish stores now sporting six-pointed yellow stars with a woeful string of empty windows and signs forbidding Germans from shopping—never mind that there was nothing to sell. Equally, Jews were forbidden to shop in Gentile department stores, eat at Gentile cafés, buy food from Gentile cart vendors—*Juden Verboten* signs were plastered everywhere.

Rachel pulled a blue serge suit from her wardrobe and wondered where Jews were allowed to shop, where they ate, if there was enough of anything available to them. Her father had told her to mind her business, not to question or speak her opinions aloud. "You're not in America," he'd said, "and things are tense, uncertain here just now. You don't want to leave a mistaken impression or—" he'd half smiled—"create an international incident."

As nearly as Rachel could tell, she wasn't in Germany either—not the Germany she remembered from her childhood visits. This one was covered with black-jackbooted SS and grim-faced Gestapo, awash with brown-shirted Hitler Youth goose-steppers—hard-faced, energetic, and intimidating. She knew her father wasn't teasing; he was warning, ordering. Rachel appreciated neither. She wanted to go home.

⭑⭑

Friday morning, September 1, dawned gray and cloudy. Rachel's sleepy late-summer morning was sharply interrupted by Reich Chancellor Adolf Hitler's radio broadcast at seven, proclaiming that German troops had crossed the Polish frontier at four that morning, advancing in a "counterattack."

She scanned the morning paper slipped beneath her door, but there was nothing about the invasion, making the radical reports seem surreal, more like radio theatre than reality.

Not a face in the hotel dining room an hour later registered surprise. Guests breakfasted on dark rye bread covered in sliced meat and cheese just as they did each morning, as if invading a bordering country happened every day. Waiters with steady hands poured hot drinks from steaming silver pots.

Rachel hovered round the hotel, almost afraid to venture through its front door. Luncheon was soup, salad, meat, and vegetables as usual, waiters still steady, though more reserved. By three in the afternoon Rachel felt as though she'd slipped through a rabbit hole where nothing was as it appeared. She remembered Kristine's words about the execution of T4. *"When the nation goes to war . . ."*

Her father wasn't back yet. There was no one to talk with—no one she dared talk with. But if she sat another minute, she'd crawl out of her skin. "Shopping," she said aloud, dabbing the corners of her mouth and throwing her napkin to the table. That was something she could understand, something she could do besides eat apple strudel and dunk coffee cake and pace her hotel room floor.

She stepped into the late-afternoon throng of shoppers and workers, most walking Berlin-briskly about their business, but with faintly dazed expressions, a hint of uncertainty shading their brows. And then there was the underlying apathy . . . which she understood least of all.

Hawkers of newspapers cried out their specials with the only true emotion she witnessed: "Counterattack on Poland! Army advancing! War is on!"

Rachel could not believe such madness. Even she knew that Poland's army was no match for Germany's. To imagine that they had sprung first . . . she simply couldn't buy it.

She headed for the main shopping district and the stores she knew. Surely her father would see they needed to leave immediately, to return to the US earlier than planned. Anything she wanted to take home, she must purchase today.

She wasn't prepared for the army of curb painters. "Blackout preparations, Fräulein," she was told. "Tonight'll be the first. Just a precaution, these lines, to help us find our way in the dark. Our Führer will never let the enemy through." He stood, arching his back. "But you might want to keep your gas mask handy, if you're out tonight."

Poland bomb Berlin? It was hard to imagine. But if Hitler didn't withdraw his troops, Britain and France would surely join the fray by sundown. They were bound to Poland by treaty. Rachel walked faster, determined to be back before dark. She didn't have a gas mask.

It was nearly seven when she stepped from her last store, pleased with the new season's rich-brown and belted cardigan she'd bought at a fairly reasonable price, only slightly embarrassed that she could think of fashion when war was declared and there was already talk of greater rationing in Berlin. But the war wasn't here—not yet. And she'd bought something for her father, after all—his favorite writing paper, available only from Berlin stationers. She was contemplating buying a box of chocolates for their return trip when sirens blared so loudly from every direction that she dropped her packages and shopping bags to cover her ears.

Faces in the waning light paled; steps around her quickened, some heading for the nearest newly appointed air-raid shelter. But once the noise subsided, most pedestrians and the few shopkeepers who'd run into the streets to look up into the sky for Polish bombers masked the tension in their faces, picked up, and moved on as though nothing out of the ordinary had just occurred. Shaken, Rachel pulled her hands from her ears and breathed. That was when she spotted Jason Young across the street.

Knowing she blushed, she refused to acknowledge his wave, but stooped to retrieve her jumble of packages. The heaviest slipped from her grasp. Vainly she swiped the air in an attempt to recapture the ream of linen stationery that burst open. Jason was suddenly beside her, piling brown paper parcels into her arms, chasing stationery as it turned head over heels in the late-day breeze, rushing up the pavement.

When he chased the last sheet into traffic, to the tune of impatient taxi drivers laying on their horns, she screamed, "Let it go! Let it go!"

But he gallantly trotted back, errant sheets in hand. Ordering the linen jumble just so, he handed the ream to her as if on a silver platter. "Lady Kramer—" mouth serious, eyes smiling—"we meet again."

She didn't want to return his smile. She just wanted this miserable, frightening day to be over, and she didn't want to think about social graces or crude reporters. But she forced a smile, embarrassed though she was to be in his debt again. "Sir Jason to the rescue. You make a habit of saving damsels in distress."

He grinned from ear to ear. She hated that her breath nearly caught at his shining brown eyes. *Devilishly handsome—there ought to be a law. Does he know? Brash? Boyish?* She couldn't tell, but wouldn't mind getting to the bottom of it. The thought startled her. *He's Father's enemy!* And then she wondered if perhaps her father needed an enemy . . . or at least a conscience. As horrendous and browbeating as Jason Young's investigative pieces had been, they'd also proven thought-provoking—for her.

Perhaps there were things Jason Young knew about Germany that she didn't—things he could explain. She could ask. But how? "That infernal siren!"

"Meant to keep us on our toes and off our guard. I'm sure they'd claim they're running essential tests to see that they work properly in the event of air raids—for the safety of the *Volk*, of course." He almost looked serious as he scanned the sky.

Rachel felt the blood drain from her face. "Poland. You don't think they'd really—?"

"You expect something different?" He eyed her cryptically and swept his arm across the expanse. "Preparation—for weeks now. They'll massacre the Poles, and if the Poles don't blast them back, shame on them. Already, Hitler's—" He stopped short. "My apologies, Fräulein Kramer. You don't want to know." He tipped his hat as if to move on.

She felt the rush of heat to her cheeks. "That's not true." But his accusation echoed Kristine's: *"Rachel, open your eyes!"*

"No?" He turned back. "What's changed?"

A million things—Kristine, Amelie, talk of killing centers and of gassing children. This insane invasion of Poland—and what will that unleash? Surely the Allies won't abandon Poland as they did Austria. Czechoslovakia. And if Hitler would do this, what else might he do? Is anything too far-fetched?

Jason waved his hand in front of her face. "Earth to Fräulein Kramer."

She blinked.

"Where's your father? Back from Scotland yet?"

Red flags went up in Rachel's mind. Her face must have registered the same.

"I'm asking because they're likely closing borders. You might have a tough time getting through. Time to go home to the good old US of A."

"Father's well connected—the German scientists, the SS," she defended.

Jason nodded, though she saw he disapproved. "That might be his ticket. They're giving travel priority to military."

"There's something I must ask you, Mr. Young."

But he was no longer with her. His eyes narrowed, following a black van down the street, its driver apparently searching for an address. He watched it slow, then turn the corner.

"Go home, Miss Kramer. My best advice to you and your father is to go home and stay there. Get out of Germany before things get any worse—and they will get worse."

"That's just it. I . . . Perhaps over dinner we could—"

But he cut her off, never meeting her eyes. "Sorry, ma'am. Don't mean to be rude. Gotta go."

It felt like a slap. "Another rescue mission?" She couldn't keep the sarcasm from her voice. Now that she was willing to give him her attention, he refused her!

He simply tipped his hat—more to the air than to her—and took off at a clip.

Rachel watched, stunned, curiosity battling indignation, as he neared the intersection where the van had turned. He hustled across the street, disappearing beyond the corner building. She'd never been left standing in the street by a man who clearly wanted her number, never been refused the time of day by any man. "Forget you, Jason Young!" she spat in frustration.

Shouldering her purse and hefting bags, Rachel set her jaw and a steady pace in the opposite direction. She'd missed the afternoon coffee hour, but if she caught the streetcar, she might just make it back to the hotel in time to ask for a light supper. *Maybe I can convince them to make a good cup of tea—a strong cup of tea.* The headache building behind her eyes seemed intent on lodging.

She rounded the corner just as the trolley pulled to a stop at the end of the block. Walking quickly, she raised her arm to signal she was coming, but the conductor ignored her. Two people stepped up into the car. The trolley bell dinged. She jogged faster, calling out. Still ten steps behind, the car pulled away from the curb.

A stitch in her side and a stone in her shoe, she dropped her packages to the corner bench and swore. There was nothing to do but wait for the next car. *Unchivalrous—that's what they are!*

She retrieved the pebble from her shoe and straightened the seam in her stocking. When she stood, she saw the black van parked halfway down the block—the vehicle Jason had been so taken with, or one very much like it.

But Jason Young was nowhere in sight. Curious, she strolled across the side street to get a better view.

A line of children, perhaps ages three through ten or eleven, filed down the sidewalk, the last one exiting the doorway of a two-story brick building. A man in a white coat led them behind the van, and a woman in a black dress herded the children forward. But there was something about the children. . . . Some were stiff and stilted in their gait. Their arms didn't swing in rhythm with their stride, or if they did, it was exaggerated. One tall girl, clutching the shoulder of the child before her, was obviously blind.

A very small boy with a moon-round face, flattened in the front, stumbled and fell. Rachel was too far away to hear what he said as he cried out, but the woman at the end of the line hurried forward and jerked the boy to his feet, shook him soundly, and pushed him back into line. The boy stumbled forward, catching his scraped arm to his chest. The woman happened to glance Rachel's way. Their eyes connected. Grim, she turned quickly away.

Rachel knew she shouldn't intervene in Berlin's affairs, but the woman was rougher than was called for, surely. It must be some kind of institution.

Kristine's words came back to her: *"They are going to rid Germany of every genetically imperfect man, woman, and child."*

"That's ridiculous," Rachel whispered. But the memory of

Kristine's urgency remained. Rachel returned to her packages across the street, still watching, anticipating that the line of children would emerge on that side of the van. But they didn't. They'd disappeared. Shortly, the white-coated man rounded the vehicle and climbed in the front passenger seat. As soon as he did, the driver pulled away, toward Rachel's end of the street. She stepped back onto the curb.

The children must have climbed into the back of the van. There was nowhere else for them to have gone.

The van pulled to the intersection, passing Rachel, pausing for traffic, and turned left.

Windows painted black—the children can't see out, and I can't see them.

Rachel's heart began to pound. *"They'll put them in vans and drive them round, gassing them as they go."*

"There's some other explanation," she said aloud.

The woman in the black dress was already stepping through the doorway of the brick building. A trolley pulled to a stop near the curb. Rachel looked up into the face of the conductor. He waited for her to enter, to hand him her coins. But she stepped back, shaking her head.

Rachel harnessed her shoulder bag and, leaving her parcels on the bench, headed quickly for the brick building—before she could think it through, before she could change her mind.

The sign, small and white with gold letters, read, *Schmidt-Veiling Institut*. She thumped the brass door knocker beneath it. No one came, so she thumped it again, louder this time. She waited, but still no one came. Not accustomed to being ignored, frightened now by her imaginings, she banged it loudly, continually. At last the door flew open and the woman in the dark dress emerged, her face flush with . . . with . . . with what? Anger? Fear? Suspicion? Rachel couldn't tell.

"The children," Rachel stammered in English. She saw the woman's fear change to contempt and switched to German. *"Die Kinder—* where have they gone? What's happened to them?"

The woman tried to shut the door, but Rachel pushed her foot through it and forced her way into the dark foyer. "Tell me."

"And who are you? What is your business here?"

Rachel's theatre training kicked in, as though she'd deliberately summoned it. "My cousin brought her daughter here. I demand to know what you've done with the children."

The woman paled as Rachel spoke. "They are sleeping. It is afternoon nap time. That is all. Tell your cousin to call before she comes to visit."

"The ones I saw getting into the van—the black van, just now."

The woman's eyes grew unnaturally bright. She looked over her shoulder, then back again. "They—they are being . . ." She hesitated barely a moment. "Taken for treatment."

"What kind of treatment?"

"That is up to the doctor, what they need. What each one needs." She stepped forward, urging Rachel backward, toward the door. "You will excuse us, Fräulein. We have work to do."

Rachel nearly gave way, uncertain, knowing she couldn't truly be sure, couldn't prove anything. But a mournful wail filtered through the hallway, reaching her ears as she stepped away. "Who is crying? Who is that?"

"Children cry often, Fräulein. In a house as large as this it is only common. You must go now."

"That was not a child!"

The woman's frustration erupted. "It is Frau Heppfner. If you must know, her only son has been sent to the front. She is a good German, but she is frightened for him." She pushed Rachel through the open doorway. "Now you must go."

❦

From behind the shrubbery covering the corner of the street, Jason watched Rachel step from the orphanage. He had a good idea about what had happened to the children; he'd been tipped off to expect as much. But he'd no idea what role Rachel Kramer played. He'd expected her to be coldhearted and pretty much an ostrich, hiding her head in the sand about things that impacted anyone other than herself. He hadn't expected that she might be in some way linked to Hitler's nightmare.

He shoved his camera deep into his coat pocket and followed, several steps behind, to the corner.

She walked slowly. When she turned, looking lost and troubled, he knew for certain she wasn't part of the horror he'd just witnessed, and his heart pricked for her.

"Miss Kramer?" He reached for her arm. She pulled away, staring at his hands, then up into his face, as if she didn't know him. He stepped closer. "Rachel? Are you all right?"

Jason pulled her to the bench amid her jumble of packages and bags, some of which had been rifled and emptied. She lifted a torn brown wrapper.

"You can't trust anybody." He tried to make light.

But she looked up with tears in her eyes. "No. No, you can't."

"Do you want to tell me what happened back there?"

She slumped against the bench back.

"What did that woman say to you?"

Rachel stared straight ahead. It was getting to be a habit with her. Jason thought that if he waved his hand in front of her face now, she might not notice.

"She said that the children have gone for treatment—what each one needs, what the doctor thinks each one needs."

"Did she say when they're coming back?"

Tears welled in her eyes and fell down her cheeks, making her look vulnerable, almost childlike. She shook her head slowly, finally whispering, "I don't think they're coming back."

She knows—but how? "Is this part of your father's research?"

She looked at him, her eyes regaining focus. "What?"

"You know what they're doing in the van, don't you? Did your father tell you?"

She cringed. "He's got nothing to do with that! He works to make the world a better place, not—not that!"

He leaned closer, wishing he could shield her, knowing he mustn't. "This is where eugenics leads, Miss Kramer. This has been the end goal all along—to rid the world of the disabled, the elderly, the politically expendable, and any race or group of people Hitler deems unacceptable."

"No," she nearly whimpered. "It's not the same."

Jason sat back, and though he wanted to shake her into reality, he also pitied her. "If you believe that, you've bought into the lie. There's nothing I can do to help you if you won't open your eyes." He pulled a card from his coat pocket. "Here's my number. Call me anytime, day or night, if you want to talk. They'll know where to find me." He hesitated. "Let me walk you back to your hotel. Tonight's the first blackout. You don't want to be out alone."

"No, thank you. It's not far. I can manage very well."

"That's not a good idea, Miss Kra—"

"I can manage!"

He stood, rebuked but undecided. He hated leaving her there distraught, especially with the gathering dusk and impending blackout. But she was arrogant, even in her misery. He'd have to wait around the corner, follow her, make sure she made it safely back.

He knew she was thoroughly frightened. Yet he also knew that she and the whole world needed to be terrified. There was no other way to wake them up, to force their hands.

7

SUNDAY DAWNED CLEAR AND SUNNY, a perfect late-summer morning caressed in breezes—the kind of day meant for boating on the Spree or picnics and ambling along the Tiergarten's shaded pathways.

But Rachel had not left the hotel since she'd returned from her ordeal Friday night with the van and Jason Young. Traipsing back to her hotel in the darkness, hearing footsteps echo off the pavement around her but unable to see anyone in the blackout, hearing hushed whispers—every whispered voice equally afraid—had been more than enough of Berlin for her.

Besides, she was intent on staying by the phone in case her father called. She gathered all the frightening news she could stomach through Reich-approved radio stations and through her chambermaid.

"I heard Herr Hitler with my own ears, over the loudspeaker in Wilhelmplatz this noon!" the girl had insisted. "At eleven o'clock Britain declared war against us! But our Führer let them have it—lambasted those warmongering British and those capitalist Jews!"

Rachel's stomach churned.

"There's a new decree. Listening to foreign broadcasts is *verboten*. The Führer doesn't want us discouraged by foreign propaganda, like in the last war. Too many women wrote their husbands at the front about what they'd heard of the war, and about the harsh rationing and such—*meine Mutter* told me how it was. It brought our soldiers low, and they gave up the fight too soon. It was all Bolshevik Jew lies behind it, you know, meant to destroy morale." The girl spoke knowingly while she snapped pillow slips and shook the eiderdown. "*Meine Mutter* says it's why we suffered the humiliation of Versailles. The Führer says we needn't have lost at all. But thanks to him, we're stronger now. We'll not listen to the lies this time, and we're to report those that do."

"You've no idea what war will mean," Rachel tried to persuade her.

"We don't want war, but we'll not lose to those that force it upon us!"

Berlin women sewed cloth bags. Men and boys packed them with sand, slamming them by the hundreds against the bases of houses, intent on breaking the impact of explosions. Government stations distributed gas masks—to Aryan residents—but did not evacuate women and children.

Rachel dared hope Hitler's boast that the British and French planes would never breach the city's lines was true. And then she wondered if she should regret that, if she should hope instead for the crazies to be blasted from the Reichstag.

Lists of blackout regulations were posted in the newspapers. Only the whitewashed curbs helped navigate the darkened streets.

But Rachel was done going out after dark. Even the theatres, which still opened their doors, could not compel her. She was packed, ready to leave for the US the moment her father returned from Frankfurt. The only person she'd telephoned since she'd witnessed the van of children being driven away was Kristine. She'd phoned her on Saturday, intending to say she would do whatever she could for Amelie, but hung up without speaking when Gerhardt answered the phone.

If Gerhardt is back early, why isn't Father?

Rachel paced the carpeted floor of the sitting room between her father's bedchamber and her own Sunday morning and afternoon. Rehearsing her lines over and over—what she would ask him, what she could say while shielding Kristine and Amelie. He couldn't possibly be part of this madness. He would know what to do. And they must leave right away—before they couldn't.

When her father finally returned, it was nearly the dinner hour and she was spent with worry. Neither had dressed for dinner, and going to the theatre was out of the question. He complained that he was tired from the journey and asked if she'd mind if they had something served in their sitting room.

"Not at all. I'd prefer it." Rachel kept a grip on her emotions but knew she spoke too brightly. "And we must talk of going home—as soon as possible!"

After placing their order for room service, he sank into the sofa. "You've no idea the stress of this trip, my dear. The war—not unexpected, but still . . . I'm glad you were here in Berlin, waiting for me. It makes . . ." He swallowed. "At least, something . . ."

"Are you ill?"

He waved his hand as if to dismiss the idea. "It's just . . . so many decisions, all the preparation for the conference in Edinburgh. And such a disappointment. So little cooperation between nations and ideologies. The tension between monarchs . . ." He closed his eyes. "They all want the same thing eugenically—ultimately—but refuse to align themselves with Germany for fear of what the world thinks. They don't understand. We're standing on the precipice!"

"We're in the middle of a war!"

He brushed the air again. "It will blow over. France, Britain— they're no match for Germany. They'll soon see and come to their senses. As will Poland."

She couldn't believe what she was hearing. "I'm afraid I'm like those nations you met with, Father. I don't understand either."

He was massaging the bridge between his eyes. "What is it? What do you not understand?"

Taking the deep chair opposite him, she leaned forward. "On Friday—the day the Führer declared war on Poland—"

"A counterattack, he said."

She ignored him. "I saw something that disturbed me greatly—something I hope is not what it seemed."

He opened his eyes. "And what is that?"

"I was shopping in the city. As I was waiting for a trolley I saw a van—its windows painted black—stop before an asylum for handicapped children."

"Perhaps the children were going on a trip."

"I didn't say they'd gone anywhere. What makes you think they went somewhere?"

He waved his hand in dismissal once more, but she saw his shoulders tighten. "A supposition—you said there was a van."

"Actually—"

But a knock at the door startled Rachel.

"Come in!" Dr. Kramer called, seemingly relieved, rejuvenated by the sight of the waiter wheeling the cart with their dinner.

They'd barely begun their meal when Rachel tried again. "You're right, Father. The children were loaded into the van, but I don't think they were going on a pleasure trip. The woman in charge said they were going for treatment. What sort of treatment would an entire vanload of handicapped children be going for—children with different handicaps?"

"How can I know that? Only their doctor would know."

But she persisted. "At the gala I heard Herr Himmler talk about those who would become a drain on German society in the event of war—those whom the Reich could barely sustain in peacetime could not be supported during war. What did he mean?"

Her father was clearly annoyed by the turn in conversation. "How can I know what he was thinking? Rachel, you take these things too much to heart."

"But that's the nature of eugenics, isn't it—to weed the weak from the strong?"

"Yes, of course. But you needn't worry. You're a perfect specimen." He winked, as though he'd made a joke.

"How? How will they do it?"

"What Germany does is Germany's affair. Just as what America does is America's affair. We share our research, we benefit mutually from the findings of that research, but we do not dictate medical policy from one country to another."

"But I've heard—"

"Rumors? Never give credence to rumors. You know better than that. What is important is that Germany is at war, and all her resources are needed for her soldiers. We'll be fortunate indeed if Herr Hitler continues to channel funding to Dr. Verschuer's work."

Rachel tried again, but her father cut her off. "We owe Germany and Dr. Verschuer a great debt. Do you understand what it will mean to eradicate diseases such as tuberculosis, polio?"

"But not at the cost of other lives. You can't justify—"

"Unusual sacrifices are sometimes called for in order to achieve a greater good. We must all make sacrifices. And contributions."

Rachel's frustration built so that she barely knew how to respond. "Father," she pleaded.

"You're in a position to make a valuable contribution. Your bloodline is pure; you are healthy and intelligent."

"What are you talking about?"

He reached for her hand. "You carry the Aryan bloodline that all Germany, all the world, craves. By choosing someone of a similar, suitable line and continuing your bloodline, you contribute to strengthening the human race—the ultimate purpose of all our work."

"I'm not a project, Father. Besides, I don't have this 'suitable someone' tucked in my back pocket—I'm not interested in marriage now! Please stop changing the subject."

Weariness replaced his affected charm. "Choosing someone you know is preferable to having the choice made for you." He stared at her until she, confused, looked away. "I'm tired, Rachel. I must say good night. But you must think about all I've said." At the door to his room he paused, not looking back. "We will meet Gerhardt and his wife for dinner tomorrow evening. You will see her condition for yourself."

"Kristine—her name is Kristine," Rachel insisted. *The girl I grew up with—the girl who spent nearly every weekend at our house!*

He did not answer but closed the door, the latch clicking into place.

Rachel wrapped her hands round her head. *What is the matter with him? What was he talking about? And what about those children? What about Amelie?*

An hour later, in the middle of a radio broadcast concert, the program was interrupted by another speech from the Führer, once again thundering about Poland and the importance of needed living space for the German Volk.

Rachel shook her head and snapped the dial, silencing the urgency. *He sounds as theatrical as* The War of the Worlds! *No wonder everyone back home was terrified by that radio broadcast. Invading Martians were like Hitler turned loose. If only Herr Hitler were a figment of the imagination too.*

8

HELPLESSLY, CURATE BAUER trailed Frau Fenstermacher round the schoolroom. She wouldn't sit, wouldn't stand still, and couldn't seem to pack her bags fast enough.

"Demons! They're demons, Curate, I tell you, and I'm finished—*kaputt!*" She slammed sheet music into folders. "You must find someone else!"

"Now, now, Frau Fenstermacher, they're children—a little high-strung, perhaps, with so many of their fathers being called into service, but good children in need of stability." He pulled her bag gently from her arm.

"In need of stability? That's the understatement of our decade!" she snapped. "Our own village children are handfuls quite enough. At least I can threaten that if they don't behave, they'll never be allowed to perform in the Passion! But these refugee children—there's no such hope for them, and I've no leverage!"

"Perhaps in these unusual times we should make an exception. They're truly good children."

She jerked the bag away. "Ha! You'll never get Father Oberlanger, nor the mayor, nor the town itself to allow a child not born in the village to perform in the Passion Play—that's sacrilege. It's a right of birth and a privilege to perform, not something passed round the table!" She sighed heavily, purposefully. "Not to speak contrary, Curate, but I don't see good children when I look at those runny-nosed hooligans! Your rose-colored spectacles need polishing, and my nerves need a good shot of schnapps!"

"I'll buy you a bottle myself, if you will only stay through Advent, Frau Fenstermacher," he pleaded. "I'll buy you the best and biggest bottle in Oberammergau—in all of Bavaria!"

She stopped suddenly and stared at him, pity in her eyes. Her shoulders slumped and she laid a hand on his arm. "That's good of you, Curate, what with your vow of poverty and all. But you can't afford the schnapps that would make me stay another week with these wild things, let alone through Advent. And you may as well face facts. If the Führer doesn't settle this thing and pull our troops back, well . . ."

"What will we do?" The young priest plopped on the desktop behind him. "The choir director has been sent for training. A third of the Passion cast is on military duty and more on alert. They'll be called any day now. The schoolmaster is gone. We need someone who can control these children, someone who can direct and sing—not to mention direct their after-school auxiliary practices."

"A tall order, all of that, requiring at least three stalwart souls." She paused and looked away, speaking softly. "It might be time to think of calling off the Passion, though I don't envy you the job. The entire village—we live for it every ten years."

"They'd hang me, and I wouldn't blame them. Call off the play?" He moaned. "Never. Oberammergau *is* the Passion."

"Well, I'm not so sure we'll get many patrons if Jesus and the disciples are off to war, and if Britain and France are shooting at us, never mind the tighter rations on *Benzin*. Folks are getting mighty nervous. It's stirring too many memories of the last war, no matter that we've barely started in Poland. If we go on like this, it won't matter that the Führer thinks our Passion is 'the best example of anti-Jewry in Germany and should go on forever.'"

Curate Bauer moaned again. He loved the true Passion of Christ and supported the town's mission to present the play every ten years, but he hated the anti-Semitic slant the script conveyed, the way it demonized

Jews—the very thing that had, for centuries, roused Christians to perpetrate pogroms, intent on killing off the "Christ killers." The very apple of God's eye, brothers and sisters Jesus had died for.

Frau Fenstermacher shoved the music folders into the bookcase opposite the door and hefted her shopping bag. "Well, you know a thing or two about the miracle business, Curate. I'd say you'd best get to it."

"You border on sacrilege, Frau Fenstermacher," he chided, but without heart.

"Not at all, Father." Though she crossed herself. "You yourself said that the Lord turned water into wine."

"Wine I can get; a children's choir director I cannot." He sighed. "Please, Frau Fenstermacher, just until I can find a replace—"

"All I'm saying is that under the present circumstances you might not be able to find a good Catholic choir director to get these refugee children ready for Advent. What you need is a Gestapo agent! In lieu of that, you might try the evangelicals. Wouldn't they just love to slip in the back door and insinuate themselves into our play! Maybe it's time we trained them."

A yowl shot up from the courtyard. Curate Bauer knew he should investigate, but it would have to wait. "See here—"

She cut him off with a wave of her hand. "All you need at this late date is someone who can read music and keep them in line—that's all you can expect with everything gone helter-skelter, thanks to—oh, never mind. The scallywags born and bred here know their parts, if they'd just settle down. But those refugee children won't settle for me, and my old heart won't take another rehearsal."

"But—" He could barely hear himself for the howling in the corridor beyond the door.

"My best advice, Curate, and I thank you for asking, is to take the first person through that door who knows anything about drilling children. Give them the job before they can say no. Don't even ask if they can sing."

The distinct knock at the door and the sobbing beyond cut the wind from Curate Bauer's sails. "What is it?" he shouted, defeated.

The door flew open and a furious Lea Hartman stood with six-year-old Heinrich Helphman's ear in a death grip. "I'm sorry to disturb you, Curate Bauer, but Heinrich has been snitching the baby Jesus from Friederich's Nativity scenes again. I really must ask you to do something about . . ."

Curate Bauer did not hear the rest of Frau Hartman's tirade. He was too impressed with Frau Fenstermacher's raised eyebrows and the significance of miracles.

9

A SINGULARLY UNCOMFORTABLE AFFAIR, Rachel decided of their meal with Gerhardt and Kristine. Gerhardt, the picture of Germanic efficiency gilded in arrogance; and Kristine, the intimidated and nervous mat on which he wiped his boots. His affected chivalry in holding chairs for the ladies and in ordering for his wife served more to underline his control over her than his gentlemanly attention.

Each time Rachel tried to draw Kristine into the conversation Gerhardt answered for her or swiftly corrected and ridiculed her responses. *She's absolutely cowed, just as she was at the gala.*

"Tell me about your daughter," Rachel pushed. Gerhardt's smile remained, though his eyes turned cold. Kristine looked suddenly paralyzed. "She must be four by now."

"Amelie is something of a throwback." Gerhardt glanced at his wife, accusingly. "How do you say in English—feebleminded, slow?"

Kristine leaned forward, a lioness shielding her cub. "Amelie has a hearing difficulty; that's all. She's bright—truly bright—and says the funniest things." Her eyes begged for Rachel's understanding, her belief.

"She speaks?" Dr. Kramer questioned.

"She signs—quite well for a small child," Kristine enthused.

"She grunts like an ape." Gerhardt shuddered. "Kristine has convinced herself that the child is nearly human."

"She is hum—"

"Enough!" Gerhardt stopped Kristine cold. "She will be sent for treatment." He spoke as though the matter had long been settled. "As you know, Dr. Kramer, there has been much research done of late on such cases. She will be well cared for in ways that will no longer drain Kristine's energies."

"She doesn't drain my energies." Kristine rose to the occasion, though the dark circles under her eyes belied her statement. "I love our daughter. She wants only to be loved by us." She seemed to gain courage from Rachel's presence. "I can't imagine life without her. I don't want her sent away."

But Gerhardt silenced his wife by placing a firm hand on hers. "You are so exhausted you don't know what is necessary. You will see; it is all for the best." He smiled, but Rachel saw his grip tighten on Kristine's fingers until the tears glistened in her eyes.

Dr. Kramer offered little throughout the meal, Rachel thought, as though the entire affair were a script in which he had no part. *So why are we meeting?*

"I would be delighted to show you the improvements our Führer has brought to our fair city, Fräulein Kramer. Perhaps we could begin with a stroll through the Tiergarten tomorrow afternoon, when the day has cooled."

"I'd be afraid of being caught in the blackout," Rachel quipped. "I'm surprised you're not in Poland, Sturmbannführer Schlick. It seems most of Berlin has been deployed."

"Our Führer requires various means of support, and as you may have heard, we are doing quite well in Poland. We'll take Kraków soon, and should be in Warsaw before the week is out. My role is here, for the time being." He raised his glass to her.

By the time coffee came, Rachel had grown weary of Gerhardt's repeated attempts to draw her into his company.

"It would do you good to get out, Rachel," her father encouraged.

At last Rachel could take no more. "Father, you must realize that it is highly inappropriate for me to accompany Sturmbannführer

Schlick without his wife." She reached across the table to Kristine. "I will only go if you and Amelie join us, Kristine. It's been so long since we've seen each other. I want to catch up on all your news, and I want to meet Amelie. She sounds delightful."

Gerhardt laughed. "You Americans surprise me with your conventions." But he acquiesced. "Certainly Kristine and Amelie must come, if it makes you more comfortable. I tend to forget the two of you were children together." He eyed Rachel appreciatively. "You are so very different from one another."

Rachel smiled politely but couldn't miss the pain, the fear in Kristine's eyes. She had no doubt that Kristine and Amelie would not make that date in the park, that she would have no further opportunity to speak with her friend—alone or in company. And so she knocked her glass of red wine from the table, targeting her own skirt.

"Rachel!" Her father groped for the glass as the dark wine spread across the pristine tablecloth, and Gerhardt called for a white-coated waiter.

"My best poplin!" Rachel gasped, standing in horror, knocking her table setting to the floor.

"Rachel, calm yourself!" her father ordered to no avail.

Kristine pressed her linen napkin to Rachel's skirt while Dr. Kramer, never good with messes, pushed back from the table.

Gerhardt shouted, ordering the waitstaff as if they'd been the culprits.

"Kristine, come—help me rinse the stain from my skirt." Rachel pulled her friend toward the stairs leading to the lobby.

"I'll send a waitress," Gerhardt intervened.

"I don't want some stranger seeing me undress, Gerhardt! Kristine can help me." Rachel's indignation silenced him, and she pulled Kristine behind her.

Once in the powder room Kristine headed for the washstand, but Rachel drew her to the sofa. "We don't have much time and will probably not have another opportunity to talk alone. I'm sorry I didn't believe you, Kristine. I'm so sorry—I didn't know about the order or the children being—" Rachel couldn't say the words. "I want to help you, to help Amelie, but I don't see how I can—how I can get her out of the country."

Kristine shook her head. "Gerhardt has given me an ultimatum. I must take Amelie to the center in Bradensburg before Saturday, before he returns from another trip to Frankfurt, or he will do it. I don't know what to do, how to stop him." Her eyes filled. "He'd never let her go to another family—never let her leave the country. He says Amelie must be sent away—no 'loose ends' that might call his bloodline into question."

"Isn't there someone you know who would take her? Hide her?"

Tears of frustration spilled from Kristine's eyes. "No one. And I know he does not mean to let her live. I couldn't hide her long. Everyone is afraid. Neighbors report neighbors. Children in the Hitler Youth report their siblings, their parents, their teachers." She covered her face. "My poor Amelie!"

Germans can't be so heartless—they can't possibly know and allow this! But they weren't the only ones to turn blind eyes, and Rachel knew it. Never had Rachel felt so helpless, so tied and without options. She raked her fingers through her hair in desperation.

What was it Jason Young had said? *"There's nothing I can do to help you if you won't open your eyes. . . ."*

Well, my eyes are open now, Mr. Young. Show me what you can do to help—I'm ready to listen.

"You mustn't give up, Kristine. Tell Gerhardt not to worry, that you'll take Amelie to the center before the end of the week—that you just want these last days with her."

"Are you crazy? I can't do that!"

"No, but I know someone who might be—maybe—just crazy enough to help us. Give me the address of the center."

❧❧

Her father was in no mood to talk when they returned to the hotel. "You embarrassed us both. I've never known you to be so clumsy. It's as though you tried to humiliate me."

"Because I dropped a glass? Father, it's my dress that's ruined, not your reputation. It was only Gerhardt and Kristine. What does it matter?"

"It matters," he snapped, pounding a cigarette onto its silver case, tamping the tobacco hard enough to smash its end.

In that moment Rachel pitied him, but she couldn't hold back. Amelie's life depended on it. "Father, I'd like to take Amelie home with us."

"What?"

"Amelie," she insisted softly. "You heard the way Gerhardt talked. Germany is no place for a deaf child now. We can make sure she receives the help she needs in New York. There are schools for the deaf."

"Stay out of it, Rachel. It's not our affair."

"I'm not asking you to do anything, except perhaps to help persuade Gerhardt. He respects you, and—"

"Leave it!" He'd hardly ever raised his voice to her, and the novelty took her aback. "I don't wish to argue with you. I've argued with half of Germany's eugenicists to no avail." The lines in his haggard face underlined his words.

"Then you know what they're doing—and you know we must save Amelie. Father, she's Kristine's daughter!"

"Before we came you wanted nothing more to do with her."

"I was hurt that she ran off with Gerhardt, that she never even wrote. That doesn't mean I want to see her child murdered!"

He collapsed to the sofa, pushing his head into his hands, leaning forward over his knees. "There's nothing we can do. You don't know what is at stake. Gerhardt said she is going for treatment—"

"We can take her home! Kristine is like a sister to me!"

"She is not your sister! She is not your equal!" he exploded.

Rachel knelt before him. "I didn't say she is. Father, I don't know what to think about all this; I don't know what to believe. I only know that killing children is wrong."

He paled. "Great causes call for extraordinary sacrifices."

"You can't believe that means killing children!"

He slumped against the sofa back, closing his eyes. "It's a fine line. The work I've done my entire life—it was to eradicate tuberculosis, to strengthen the human race. It was for good. I meant it for good, and the sacrifice—the sterilization—was only for those who carried disease, so they wouldn't pass it on again and again." His voice quavered.

"Then—"

But he cut her off. "No more. Say no more." He opened his eyes and gripped her fingers. "What they do here is beyond my control. There are other things we must think about, talk about."

"What could be more important than—?"

"You must intimate—no, you must make it clear when in the presence of my colleagues that you are interested in marriage, that you intend to marry soon."

"What?"

"Lest they think . . . lest they think you are not normal. It is most important to be—and to seem to be—healthy, robust, and normal in Germany today."

"Father, this is not about me!"

He leaned forward, weary but urgent. "You are wrong. You are so wrong, Rachel. It *is* about you—it is all about and has always been about you. Never forget that!"

Rachel knew that was precisely what she'd thought too, what she'd always thought—been raised to think: Me first. But after seeing Kristine so distraught over the intended euthanization of her deaf daughter, she wondered.

"There were stipulations, you know. Things that involve you and your adoption."

"What things? I'm an American citizen. What has—?"

"You are also a German citizen by birth—you know that. I will do my best for you. But you must be prepared . . ."

"Prepared for what?" Rachel felt her anxiety rising.

"I'm tired now, Rachel. I will know more after my meetings in Frankfurt." He stood. "We'll talk more when I return."

"You just got back!"

He placed a hand on her shoulder, giving it an uncharacteristic, affectionate squeeze. "Our plans have changed. I leave early. I will not wake you. We'll be back by the night train at the end of the week."

"Is Gerhardt going with you?"

"Yes." He sounded as though he carried the weight of the world, then closed his door.

She needed to know what he meant, what she had to do with his meetings—why he was returning to Frankfurt so soon, and what this growing link with Gerhardt Schlick meant. Why would an SS officer spend so much time with a eugenics scientist?

Her only connection to Frankfurt had been her many medical examinations at the hands of Dr. Verschuer. She'd always assumed that was simply because her father knew and trusted Dr. Verschuer, because he and her mother so highly prized their adopted daughter, and because they thought German doctors were better than American doctors. But that didn't sound logical to her anymore. What was their real purpose? *What is his purpose now?*

❦

Lea stepped from the curate's office as dusk fell, determined to take the longest road home. She needed time to think.

He'd called her a miracle. Lea had never been called a miracle, she was quite sure.

That morning, Curate Bauer had questioned her carefully; she'd answered truthfully.

"Do you read music?" he'd asked.

"Yes."

"Do you sing?"

"I love to sing."

"You can control a classroom of unruly children?"

"Oh—possibly." She could make time for the rehearsals each day—absolutely.

But he hadn't asked the important questions—about the day she'd screamed in his sanctuary of the evil burned so deeply into her soul that she could not see it, name it. He'd just kept explaining her duties, as though he was offering her the job. She'd heard him, and yet she hadn't absorbed it all, so loudly had hope beat in her chest.

Curate Bauer—good, kind Curate Bauer of the Roman Catholic Church of Saints Peter and Paul—had offered the despised, barren Protestant Lea Hartman the opportunity to conduct his youngest after-school children's choir—seventeen unruly, rambunctious, obstreperous hooligans below the age of eight, if Frau Fenstermacher was to be believed. It was not for Passion rehearsals, simply to keep them singing and out of trouble. There was nothing Lea wanted more. If only the Institute did not learn of it.

She'd accepted. But later, the fear grew inside her—a living, coiling, recoiling thing. Late that afternoon, she'd stopped at the curate's office door. Knowing she could not endure another disappointment, could not help but believe this joy, too, would be ripped from her the moment she set her heart to it, she spoke again to the curate of the day he'd found her in the church.

She could barely believe that she'd dared such a thing in a practical, matter-of-fact voice. Curate Bauer wasn't married, had no children of his own—by choice and vow. How could he understand the anguish of sterilization? The scorn of being barren and despised, demeaned by doctors who professed to know her heart and nature when she barely knew them herself? The terrible fear that her husband would stop loving her? And she'd told the curate all of this—twice.

Confessing again—reminding him of her sinfulness—might make him reconsider his offer. But it would be better never to meet with the children than to have them ripped away. She knew this. Still, the curate did not despise her. This time, Curate Bauer wept with her and prayed with her. He said something so strange—that he couldn't pity her for the journey that was her own, for in it was her Father's good pleasure to give her the Kingdom.

She wasn't entirely sure what he'd meant. She could hardly believe that God would despise her and then bless her with the care of these precious children. Perhaps He would yet see He'd made a mistake and take them away. But until He did, Lea resolved to be the best choir director Oberammergau's youngest after-school choir had ever known—not for the sake of the coming Advent celebration, but for the children.

She would pour every ounce of love she had into them.

She'd squander her rations and buy or beg whatever was needed to bake strudel and kuchen and turnovers and bring fresh milk from her cow to each rehearsal, no matter if she had less to sell in the market. No, perhaps not milk before they sang; that tended to muddy the vocal cords. Water—that should do. But she would give them milk after they sang, so they would walk home on full bellies.

She would sew new robes for the celebration—for each child. Friederich would never begrudge her the cost or trade of the fabric, she was certain. And if it was too dear or new could not be had, well, she had old fabric from curtains no longer needed. That might be even better—might fit the tenor of the celebration even better.

Lea laughed—a soft and gentle laugh known only to her and God. She couldn't wait to write Friederich. He would understand what this meant to her. But she would not tell him what she'd told Curate

Bauer. She'd not told even Friedrich so much about the Institute and the doctors' branding of her. She pushed those memories away—at least for now.

As she walked clear around the village, she began to sing, softly. Night fell. By the time she reached her gate the sky was inky black and the stars stood as white flames against it—burning brighter than they had perhaps ever. Lea felt cleaner, clearer inside, than she could remember. She wondered if this sensation would last or if it was only a momentary lifting of the cloud that was her life. She wouldn't ask. For this moment, she would sing praise.

She smiled and, laughing, crying, hugged herself. This night, though he'd not returned the baby Jesus and had stubbornly vowed to Curate Bauer that he never would, even Heinrich Helphman wore a halo.

<hr />

Jason Young yawned and stretched. He'd been on the trail of a story for seventeen hours—the last three of which he'd spent pounding the keyboard. He'd just phoned his story to New York and was about to call it a night—a very long night—when his desk phone rang. He checked his watch. One thirty. He'd be spending the night on a cot in the downstairs newsroom. The phone rang again. He wanted to ignore it, but that went against his newsman's grain.

"Can you talk?" The breathless female American voice at the other end of the line bore the trademark tensions of nearly every one of his sources in Germany.

"To my femme fatale? Sure!" Jason smirked, suddenly wide awake.

"You're very funny, aren't you?"

"A regular riot—that's me. What can I do you for?" He was careful not to use her name, certain as he was that every phone in the newsroom was tapped.

"Coffee. Do you like coffee?"

"Real coffee—by the boatload."

"So do I. Eleven o'clock tomorrow morning? Our corner?"

"See you then." Jason thumped the phone to its cradle. *She's scared. Something's happened.*

He rolled down his sleeves, swung his jacket over his shoulder, and headed for the door, wondering what was up, more than glad she'd called, and dubious he'd get a wink of sleep.

10

JASON WAITED at the corner where he'd found Rachel after the murder of the innocents. He tipped his hat as she approached and fell into step beside him. The Tiergarten café wasn't far, and it felt good to walk in her company.

Half an hour later the waiter delivered their order and she'd finished her story.

"Let me get this straight." Jason leaned across the café table toward Rachel, distracted as much by the scent of her perfume as he was by the silver flecks in her blue eyes. "You want me to hide a deaf kid who can't understand anything I say until Hitler and his cronies go belly-up and disappear, then restore her, unscathed and smiling, to her doting mother, the wife of an SS officer—which officer, by the way, wants to slit both their throats?"

Rachel sat back, blinking in the morning sun as it streamed through the linden trees. She sipped her coffee slowly, then set it down. "I realize it sounds difficult—"

"Difficult? It sounds impossible, dangerous . . . a suicide mission."

"I didn't know where else to turn, whom to trust." She looked desperate.

"I'll do it."

"If we don't do something, her father will take her to the center at the end of this week—" Rachel stopped short. "You'll do it?"

"I'll do it." He sat back, concentrating. "I don't know how— exactly. But I know some people who might have connections to others who will. I'll need a little time. The first thing is to find some-place to hide her—somebody who'll take her in. And then some way to make it seem like she's gone for good."

"I want to take her to America with me, without Gerhardt knowing."

"You'll never get a deaf kid out of Germany. In case you hadn't noticed, you didn't come in with one. They're sure not gonna let you leave with a German kid on the lam, Miss Kramer."

"I wish you'd stop talking like a Chicago gangster, Mr. Young." Rachel frowned.

"You heard that the US declared neutrality today? I'm not sure we can count on them to help—not now, maybe not ever."

"Then what do you propose?"

"Give me forty-eight hours. Let me see who can help, what I can arrange."

"You know people that influential?"

He shrugged and looked away. He couldn't share the little he knew. "We'll see."

"Why? Why are you willing to help me?"

Jason didn't know what to say. He wasn't sure he knew the answer. He only knew he couldn't stop Hitler or the eugenicists or the crazy things he'd seen perpetrated in the name of building a strong Germany. He was sick of seeing the world go askew and doing noth-ing. Maybe if he saved this life . . . maybe that meant something.

He looked at Rachel—beautiful and bewildered and vulnerable and proud at once. Her helplessness reminded him of the impotence he'd felt in Germany for months, and of a recent conversation.

"I interviewed a Jewish professor last week—a guy who'd been at the top of his game at the University of Berlin for years. Over the last three years he's been ousted from the faculty and stripped of his citizenship, his property has been confiscated—Aryanized—and he's been reduced to half rations. He's cleaning streets now—on good days. Those are the days he eats a little, as opposed to nothing. Even that he shares with his wife and their Jewish neighbor. After the interview, I gave him my lunch. You'd have thought I'd given him the world on a platter. He gave me a saying, a proverb, in return: 'He who saves one life saves the world.'"

Rachel blinked. He recognized the ungainly wheels spinning in her brain, the wrestling and slow dawning of an idea.

"I don't know how that rates with thousands of people being cut out of society, so many being imprisoned and some even worked to death. But I want to find out, and this is as good a time as any. Besides, maybe we can save more than one."

Jason stood, pocketing the address of the medical center. "Lunch at the Ummerplatz on Thursday—noon. No more telephone calls. The newsroom is tapped. Goebbels keeps an eye and ear on everything that comes in and goes out with the press. He doesn't want Germany's reputation 'tarnished' before his world audience, and killing kids might have a way of doing that, no matter the propaganda."

Rachel nodded, her eyes wide.

Jason knew this was a new world to her. He was glad she was seeing it as it was. Somebody needed to. He wasn't making much headway through the press.

"You can't print this in the newspaper," she whispered. "Not here and not in America. It would be too dangerous for Amelie, for Kristine."

"Not to mention you." Jason tossed coins to the table. "I won't print it now, and not with those names. But there'll be a story in it sometime, somehow—and it's my scoop. Don't forget that."

❦

Two days later, Rachel received general instructions from Jason and passed them to Kristine, whom Jason promised to contact directly with details. The day after that—the day before Gerhardt and her father were to return from Frankfurt—the rescue would be carried out. Rachel didn't know what that meant, only that Jason's broad plan sounded just wild enough to work—as long as none of them got caught or killed in the process.

Rachel had come to understand through Jason that getting caught could mean arrest and a prison camp—what he called a "concentration camp"—for Kristine, grilling and certain deportation for Jason, and possibly one or the other—thanks to her dual citizenship—for Rachel herself. She couldn't think of the consequences for Amelie.

She was to stay at the hotel—to be visible to the hotel staff, creating her own alibi. But that meant she would know nothing of the outcome until word came from Jason, verifying Amelie's safety. Rachel would pass that word to Kristine. Jason believed knowing little beforehand would enable the women to act naturally in response to whatever he had planned. But Rachel knew that merely waiting patiently was outside her capability. Acting innocent and alarmed was something she'd learned to do in theatre class.

⊹⊱⊰⊹

Kristine's last days with her affectionate Amelie were too precious to share. She memorized every smile, every sleeping moment, every blink of her daughter's eyes and blush of her cheek. She signed constantly, reminding her daughter that she loved her, telling her she was the joy and light of her life. Telling her, as best she could, all the things she would never be able to tell her again.

Kristine rose early Friday morning and took great care in bathing and dressing her little girl and curling her hair. She pinned a pink satin bow to Amelie's golden ringlets, one that perfectly matched her smocked cream-and-pink frock—Kristine's favorite, one she'd stitched by hand.

She packed her daughter's case with only her best summer clothing, a few dresses, and a bright-red jacket for fall—as though she believed her daughter would need it. She signed that Amelie, now a big girl, was going on a journey without her mother. And then Kristine held her close, before Amelie could sign her lack of understanding.

Several times Amelie reached up to trace her mother's silent tears and taste the salt, then creased her small brow in worry lines. She poked her tiny finger between Kristine's lips until she saw her mother smile. Then Amelie would smile as if all were right with the world and sign, "I love you, Mutti." It broke Kristine's heart.

Twice Kristine sat down in defeat, knowing she couldn't go through with it, knowing she must. There was no other way, no better plan. But it was so dangerous—dangerous for Amelie. If Jason Young and those he trusted made one mistake, if they were even a moment too late . . . But she couldn't think of that. She must trust that they would do only and all that was necessary—that God would fight with them and allow the ruse to be accomplished.

At nine o'clock, Kristine hefted the small suitcase by its handle, ushered her little girl along the hallway, and closed the door of their home behind her. She tucked Amelie's small, pink hand in her own and walked toward the train station, desperately trying to stay in the moment, memorizing each breath her daughter drew.

By the time they reached the medical center, Kristine trembled. Amelie, usually delighted by outings with her mother, crowded into her skirt, pensive and fractious. Kristine knew Amelie was only responding to her mother's tension, but she couldn't force herself to act more normally. She knew that whatever happened, she would never see her daughter again once she walked out the center's door.

"Do not frown so, Frau Schlick," the admitting nurse chided. "You have made the right decision for your daughter. The girl will thrive under our discipline and receive the most advanced treatment."

Kristine's eyes filled and she nearly sobbed as she signed the papers.

"This is only your duty as a good German mother," the nurse admonished, clearly put off by the young woman's display of emotion.

It was more than Kristine could take. "I am not a 'good German mother,' Frau Braun." She threw the pen to the desk. "But I assure you that I am the very best of mothers, and I love my daughter more than I love my life. Now give me the papers."

Frau Braun colored, then made a show of concentrating, of signing and separating duplicate copies of the forms. Standing, she thrust one set toward Kristine. "You don't want to miss your train, Frau Schlick."

Kristine folded the papers deliberately, placed them in her purse, and closed it with a snap. But her anger evaporated when she turned back to her daughter. Kneeling, she scooped Amelie into her arms, smothering her with kisses. Amelie, blue eyes wide, clung to her.

Kristine squeezed her eyes shut, memorizing the feel of the muscles in her daughter's arms as they wound round her neck, of the warm and tiny body, heart beating wildly, pressed against her own.

"You must go, Frau Schlick. You're upsetting the child," Nurse Braun insisted. She pulled Amelie's arms from Kristine's neck.

For one wild moment Kristine thought to grab Amelie and tear from the center, running, running with her forever.

"This is the best plan, I assure you. Shall I call for help?" the nurse threatened.

The plan—yes, the plan. I must stick to the plan—for Amelie. Kristine whispered into her daughter's hair, "I will love you forever— as long as I have breath, and beyond." Kristine knew Amelie could not hear her, but she knew with all certainty that the girl understood her heart.

Kristine stood, pushing Amelie away, and signed that she must go with the woman. But Amelie didn't want to go. She struggled, her eyes large in alarm, reaching for her mother. "You must go, my darling." Kristine straightened her arms, increasing the distance between herself and her daughter.

Frau Braun pulled Amelie by the waist. The child cried out in panicked, guttural yelps. The nurse called for assistance. An orderly appeared and swept up the kicking Amelie, hoisting her none too gently beyond a door that closed with a resounding click as the latch fell into place.

Kristine could see nothing for her tears but Frau Braun's grim-set mouth. She could not hear or comprehend what the woman was saying to her. All she could think was, *Amelie! My Amelie!*

Love for her Amelie drove her from the office, down the hallway, and into the street. Distraught, but desperate to know the plan would be carried out and her precious daughter safe, she slowed her steps. She'd not walked a full minute when the explosion came from behind her.

※─※

Jason had watched Kristine kneel before Amelie at the door of the clinic, tuck something inside the neck of the little girl's dress, and press her forehead against her daughter's. They communicated something between them through their fingers, a sign Jason could not understand. A perfect picture—mother and child.

Jason turned away, feeling an intruder into such intimacy. He'd waited for Kristine to exit the building before signaling the all clear to his coconspirator. The resistance group was so secret, so tightly woven, that he didn't even know who'd set the bomb, who proclaimed loudly that they'd called the fire department, who blocked the roadway with delivery carts and a faked bicycle accident, further delaying the firemen who'd been sent to the wrong address.

He didn't know the name of the woman who argued vehemently with Frau Braun and the medical staff in the courtyard, or from where the sudden influx of pedestrians came to rescue the remaining children from the burning building. He didn't know who stole away in the smoke and confusion, a child-sized bag bundled beneath his arm.

Jason held no part in the resistance, and his peripheral contacts were there one day and gone the next. But he'd dug up and shared enough Nazi dirt to make friends with those who knew people who knew people who made things happen. He trusted his "friends of friends" to do their job, and concentrated on badgering the medical staff for a story—how could such a thing happen and why weren't they more responsible with their equipment and didn't they realize the children could have all been killed and the detailed spelling of names. Confusion reigned as he ordered photographers to capture the burning building and the frightened but safe children from every angle.

Before the fire brigade finally arrived in force, a crowd of genuine locals had gathered, further blocking access. By the time hoses were pulled from the truck and turned on the blaze, the building had been gutted, the heat so intense there was no hope of entering.

Kristine Schlick, eyes wide and hair wild, ran from child to child, from nurse to orderly to nurse again, searching for Amelie—crying and screaming for the daughter she'd only just left behind. She played her part well, but Jason knew it was more than acting.

It was all Jason could do not to grab her, comfort her, tell her that Amelie and the other children with secret places to go had been safely spirited away. But he could not, dared not even speak to her for fear of giving everything away. Instead he sent photographers to capture on film the nearly hysterical, grief-stricken mother. And all the while he invented good copy for the news story that he prayed would rock Berlin and New York.

11

RACHEL WAS HORRIFIED when she read the heartbreaking story buried on page five of the morning paper. The story outlined the bungling phone call that first sent firefighters first to the wrong address, and lauded heroic locals who'd appeared from the streets to rescue most of the children when the medical center's ancient boilers exploded. No bodies had been recovered. The intense heat had prevented firemen from entering the building until everything inside was in ashes. Four-year-old Amelie Schlick and two others from the greater Berlin area were presumed dead. Case closed. A memorial service for the three children would be held Sunday morning after services.

Rachel would never have agreed to the explosion, never have risked such danger. Her stomach churned for Kristine's sake. If only she could place Amelie in her friend's arms once more, or at least assure her that her child was safe. But she could do neither, and there was no proof that all was well. She dared not contact Jason for fear she was watched or that her phone—or his—was tapped. She, and therefore Kristine, could only wait.

Amelie remembered the strong hands that had wrenched her from her mother's neck, her mother's arms. She knew that the man in the white coat had shut her in a room with other children. She was intrigued by the children—most bigger than she. But she wanted her mother. None of the other children had mothers. Where were all the mothers?

When the pungent smell and vapory cloud began to fill the air, grown-ups had thrown open the door, picking up children and pulling them from the room into the burning hallway. Amelie had been frightened by the chaos and the eyes of grown-ups filled with terror. She'd cowered back, behind a crib, into the corner.

The man in the white coat returned. Through the rungs of the crib she could see his mouth making shapes, could see his features distort, see him cough in the growing smoke and heat. But he looked so mean, so angry—like her father when he was frustrated with her. She didn't want the man to see her, to touch her again. Amelie shut her eyes tight and made herself as small as she possibly could, curling into a ball beneath the crib.

She didn't see when the strong hands jerked her out, banging her head sharply on the bottom of the crib. She yelped in pain. And then the hands dropped her to the floor. Their owner stumbled backward. Different hands grabbed her up, tucked her beneath a blanket so tight she could barely breathe.

The hands carried her, bumping her up and down as they ran. Her head throbbed. She tasted the sticky blood oozing from the gash on her forehead. And then everything went dark.

❦

Rachel received a note, scribbled across a napkin, with the Sunday morning coffee delivered to her room. Three words had never meant so much.

Safe and well.

She accompanied her father to the Sunday-morning memorial service held in the largest Lutheran church in Berlin. Two dozen people gathered to mourn and pay their respects in the dark church—mostly curiosity seekers from the neighborhood of the fire.

Gerhardt portrayed the stoic German officer, proudly humbled in his grief. Kristine hunched, tearful and pale beneath her black veil.

Nothing the Lutheran pastor said could comfort the young mother, and though Rachel sensed Gerhardt's kindness toward his wife at the front of the church was show, she was glad he had the decency to make a display for the public. She hoped that was in some way a help to Kristine.

But as the few mourners began to leave, while Kristine knelt at the altar and the pastor spoke with her, Gerhardt stepped back, joining Rachel and her father, as though they were his family, more his concern than Kristine.

"My condolences for your loss, Gerhardt," her father said, extending his hand.

Gerhardt nodded. "An unfortunate end."

Rachel seethed inside. "Unfortunate, Herr Schlick?"

"You can see what her death has done to Kristine. I've seen daily what the child's life did to her." He straightened. "Kristine will grieve. We shall see if she is able to overcome her grief."

"She needs to get away." It was a sudden inspiration on Rachel's part. "Father—" she laid her hand on his arm—"I want to take Kristine home with us. Let her get away for a time." She turned to Gerhardt. "It will do her a world of good."

Gerhardt's eyes registered surprise, then a hint of frost. "Out of the question."

"Why?" Rachel demanded. "Look at her, Gerhardt—she's desperate. She needs help."

"Precisely why I cannot allow her to leave my side. The best doctors are here, in Germany. I will see that she gets the help and care she needs." He leaned closer. "You forget, Fräulein Kramer, that Kristine is my wife, that we have lost this unfortunate child together, and that we must certainly grieve together. It is only seemly."

"You don't strike me as the horribly grieving father."

"Rachel!" her father admonished. "Lower your voice."

She did, but she couldn't stop herself. "Her absence will give you freedom to throw yourself into your all-important work. And I dare-say you know how to find comfort elsewhere."

Half a smile pasted Gerhardt's lips. He leaned closer, whispered in her ear. "If that is an invitation . . ."

Rachel felt the rush of fury up her neck and face extend down her arms and to the tips of her fingers. She would have slapped him had Kristine not begun walking toward them.

Rachel stepped to meet her friend, enfolding the broken woman in her arms. "I want you to know that I love you, Kristine, and I want you to come home—to New York—with Father and me. The rest will do you good." She turned her head and, clasping Kristine's arms, whispered into her friend's ear, "She's safe and well."

Kristine gripped her hands in return, squeezing them for dear life.

"Rachel," her father counseled, "you must not interfere. A wife's place is by her husband's side."

"I could not have said it better myself, Doctor." Gerhardt pulled Kristine from Rachel's arms. "Come, Kristine, hold your head up. You are an officer's wife. There will soon be family deaths for some of those attending today, a natural by-product of war. You must set an example."

12

IN LESS THAN A WEEK Kristine's body was dragged from the River Spree.

Rachel and her father stood again behind Gerhardt in the dark and flowerless Lutheran church, one week after Amelie's service, and listened as the same pastor, this time looking ten years older, read the funeral liturgy through.

Fewer mourners attended this time—the neighbors living on either side of the Schlicks, two SS officers and their smartly dressed wives, an elderly black-veiled woman who said she'd sold Kristine flowers on occasion, and Drs. Verschuer and Mengele, up from Frankfurt on business, wearing pristine summer suits. Kristine had made few friends during her time in Germany. Gerhardt had seen to that.

Rachel glanced at the back of Gerhardt's neck, her heart railing against her chest. She knew he'd murdered his wife, as surely as she knew Kristine had seen it coming. But Rachel had not expected it so soon. She'd been certain there would be time to help Kristine escape, to organize a plan with Jason Young's help to eventually reunite mother and child.

Only now did Rachel realize how naive she'd been, how right Kristine was, how much she wished she could go back and change . . . everything. But what could she have done differently? Whom could she have turned to for greater help? Rachel twisted her handkerchief in gloved fingers and dabbed at the bitter tears beneath her veil.

"She fell mad in her grief," Gerhardt, the stalwart grieving widower, commented to the pastor as the coffin was carried out. "She had no strength, no stamina."

"Sturmbannführer Schlick." Dr. Verschuer extended his hand. "Unfortunate." Rachel saw him search Gerhardt's eyes.

But Gerhardt did not flinch. He simply agreed, "A weakened strain." He lifted his shoulders. "The river called her name, and she, apparently, could not resist."

Rachel wanted to slap them, to shout at them for their melodrama—melodrama they did not even mean. But her father pulled her toward the door. "I am meeting with Dr. Verschuer and Dr. Mengele this afternoon and evening, while they are in Berlin. I may be late. Shall I call you a taxi?"

Rachel shook her head. *What is the matter? Doesn't he see?* "Father, you know this was no suicide. You know Gerhardt—"

Her father elbowed her sharply, glancing over his shoulder. She saw Dr. Mengele watching them. Her father acknowledged the doctor with a nervous nod. Rachel allowed herself to be pulled from the church, walking quickly, in a viselike grip arm in arm with her father, down the outside steps. He whispered urgently, "Say nothing, Rachel."

"But—"

"Nothing! Whatever happened is none of our affair. There is nothing to be done."

"It's murder, Father!"

"Stop it." Still walking, he shook her. "I warn you! You're hysterical. Go back to the hotel and stay there. I'll return as soon as I'm able."

But she'd taken all she could stand and wrenched away. "Father, I want to go home! I want to go back to New York now!"

"That is not possible."

"What do you mean? You said we'd go home after . . . Our plane leaves tomorrow!"

"Fräulein Kramer!" Gerhardt's call came from behind them as he hurried down the church steps, flanked by Verschuer and Mengele.

Her father shot her a warning glance.

"Will you be joining us for luncheon?" Gerhardt asked—too bright and eager for a man who'd just closed his wife's coffin.

Unnerved by her father's behavior, she played the game. "No, no—I'm going back to the hotel. I have a sick headache, and I'm not hungry."

"Regrettable, Fräulein. I was hoping for your company."

She felt she might vomit at his audacity. *What's the matter with him—with Father and all of them that they don't see Gerhardt's behavior for what it is?*

He took her hand. "You were a great favorite of Kristine's, you know."

She tried to pull away, but he maintained his grip. "She was my friend."

"Yes. I understand. There is just one thing. I am certain Kristine would have wanted you to have something—something special to remember her by."

Rachel nearly choked. Tears of grief and frustration, of heartbreak, threatened to spill.

"I would like for you to come to my home, to go through her things with me. Take anything you wish."

She couldn't speak—her mixture of disgust, regret, and the terrible longing for Kristine's life threatened to drown her.

"As you will understand, it is a task I find most difficult. It would be a gift to me—and to Kristine—for you to do this." He squeezed her hand again. "Say you will come."

Rachel fought her instincts. But her longing to be near some semblance of Kristine, her futile wish to let her friend know how desperately sorry she was that she had not believed and acted upon those beliefs from the start—and her fear of Gerhardt's unnatural grip of her fingers—held sway. She nodded miserably. "I'll come. But it must be tomorrow, before our evening plane." She said it in challenge to her father, but he looked away.

"Excellent!" Gerhardt barely restrained his jubilance. "I shall call for you tomorrow at noon."

The tears welled in earnest, and she could not stop them. But she would not cry in front of Gerhardt Schlick or the doctors. Rachel turned away, ready to bolt. In five long strides her high heel caught on a seam in the walkway, the black leather pump slipping from her foot.

It was in retrieving her shoe that she heard Dr. Mengele's words, carried softly on the breeze.

"Things are falling into place." And then, decidedly, firmly, "No more loose ends."

"She will comply," her father answered. "I'm ready to seal the file."

Rachel glanced up in the shade of her veiled hat brim. Each man's eyes swallowed her whole.

<hr />

Jason had been waiting, watching the front of the church from behind a newspaper a block away. He registered the interchange between Gerhardt and Rachel on the church steps as he scribbled beneath the front-page headline. When the group of four men entered a black Mercedes and drove past, he folded the paper and walked in the opposite direction.

He waited until Rachel reached an intersection, stepped beside her, and casually let the paper fall between them. He retrieved the paper and, handing it to her, spoke clearly enough for bystanders to hear. "Excuse me, Fräulein, you've dropped your paper."

Before she could acknowledge him or speak, he lifted his hat and swung up onto the trolley just rolling away. He'd ride for half an hour and backtrack to the café address he'd written beneath the headline. He'd wait an extra hour to give her enough time to return to the hotel and make a second trip out the back door in case she was being followed.

Jason knew he was acting as though he were in the midst of a spy novel. He wished he didn't feel the need.

※—※

At half past one, Rachel followed the waiter to an outside table of the Zillheln Street Café. Urns filled with trailing, blooming flowers—in shades of red and white—bordered the cast-iron tables. Rachel ordered ersatz coffee and a plate of warm apple strudel ladled with custard sauce—comfort food her mother had made for her when she was a little girl in need. If only her mother were here now. She would know how to reach her husband, shake him back into his moral fiber, bring to life the good man that he once was—at least that she'd believed him to be.

The crusted shell of a man that had shaken Rachel on the church steps, that had leveled the bomb that they may not be returning to America tomorrow, that allowed children to be euthanized and her childhood friend to be murdered—this was not someone Rachel recognized or knew how to confront. He was not the father who'd raised her.

"Penny for your thoughts." Jason was suddenly opposite her.

"They're not that valuable. They're certainly not pretty." She bit her lip and looked away, determined not to cry in front of him.

He reached for her hand. "Your little package is safe—as are the others who disappeared."

Rachel closed her eyes, a tear of gratitude slipping down her cheek. "Thank God, and thank you for getting me word."

"God, and some very good, very brave Germans."

"And you." She swallowed, meaning it.

He squeezed her fingers and sat back. "She won't be able to stay there much longer . . . too risky."

Her heart tripped. "Then—"

"Then we'll have to keep moving her."

"Does she look like Kristine?" Rachel almost didn't want to know.

Jason smirked, taking her fork and biting into her strudel. "Not now."

Rachel waited.

He leaned forward, whispering, "They cut her hair short and dyed it—still blonde, but darker. Dressed her like a boy. Not sure that will take. She's the prettiest boy I've ever seen." He sat back, sipping his own coffee. "It's the deafness that's hardest to conceal. From a distance she's fine—like any other kid. But up close, if someone speaks to her, she doesn't answer, doesn't respond to sudden noise. And she communicates through sign language—or tries to. But nobody can understand her, and they just try to keep her still so she doesn't draw attention. It's risky, for everyone. So—" he shrugged—"there's the rub."

Rachel pressed her palms into her eyes, her temples. She couldn't help Amelie. She couldn't even help herself. No longer hungry, she pushed the strudel toward Jason, who gladly dug in. It wasn't long before he set the empty plate aside.

"I'm sorry about your friend. I never thought she'd—"

"She didn't!" Rachel snapped. "Gerhardt murdered her."

"That's a tall accusation. You have proof?"

Rachel stared at him, trying to decide what to tell him. But there was no one else to confide in. Her father was no help, whether from fear or because he'd sold the last remnant of his soul to Gerhardt and the doctors of the eugenics movement—perhaps to the Reich's Führer himself; she didn't know. She only knew that she had no one, and that Jason had saved Amelie.

"Kristine told me that Gerhardt wanted to get rid of her, that he wants to produce perfect Aryan children for the Reich—that it is required of those rising in the ranks of the SS."

Jason nodded. "That's true. Hitler's even created homes filled with 'genetically pure' unmarried women to help increase the birthrate—all at the disposal of those great German specimens of manhood, Hitler's supermen."

"The SS." Rachel felt the bile rise in her throat. "Kristine said that Gerhardt wanted to be free to marry someone who was genetically—eugenically—strong and pure. Someone who would not produce a deaf child."

"Did deafness run in her family?"

"No!"

"Then how does he know he's not the problem? I didn't know deafness was even hereditary."

"It's not—at least they have no definitive proof that it is. But the eugenics movement believes that handicaps and deformities are caused by weakened strains in the bloodline, and that those blood-lines should be eliminated."

"That's what I was trying to get your father to say—to publicly admit!"

"So you can sell more papers? So you can secure your byline?" She couldn't stop the sarcastic rise in her voice.

He leaned across the table. "So it wouldn't come to this."

She stared him down until he sat back.

"But if I get the byline, I'm not opposed," he admitted.

"In the US they advocate sterilization—so certain bloodlines won't continue."

"Germany sterilizes too, if they can wait out the generation. If not, they just do away with them. Quick cure." His sarcasm matched her own.

"That's what Kristine said Hitler is mandating for those who are considered a drain on German society—'life unworthy of life.' But I don't think even those laws would have allowed Kristine's murder."

"Which is why he did it so soon after the explosion—to make it look like the grief-stricken mother took her own life."

"But she didn't—I know it! I told her Amelie was safe once you got me word—the very day of Amelie's funeral. She would have lived for that, and for the hope of one day seeing her." Rachel closed her eyes, shutting out images of a struggle on a bridge, a pier, the shore—wherever it was. The terror of Kristine's last moments. She felt Jason push a handkerchief into her hand. Without opening her eyes she took it, grateful for his silence.

At length, he said, "I guess when this is all over, assuming we can keep Amelie safe, you'll still want to take her back to America?"

Rachel opened her eyes. She would have laughed if it hadn't all seemed so impossible, so preposterous, so absolutely frightening. "That was my hope—when this stupid war is finished. But there's more. It looks like I may not be returning to New York after all."

"What?"

She told him what her father had said on the church steps about not leaving tomorrow, about Gerhardt's invitation to his house, Dr. Mengele's words carried on the morning breeze. She told him the mysterious things her father had said about her adoption, told him about Frankfurt, about the files she knew those doctors had kept on her from childhood, the frequent medical examinations requiring trips to Germany. She remembered more as she spoke, including her father's insistence that her German be fluent, with a Bavarian accent. And finally, his words about closing the file.

For the first time since she'd met him, Jason Young looked truly worried.

13

THE AFTERNOON WAS GONE when Rachel locked her hotel suite door, barricading it with a wooden tea trolley. If her father returned, she hoped his struggles with key and trolley would give her sufficient time and warning.

She'd never played private investigator, let alone international spy, but there would not be a better time. Her father had said he'd be late, and because of the funeral she knew he hadn't taken his briefcase and files to his meeting with the doctors and Gerhardt.

Everything Jason had said, had urged her to do, made sense. If there was a link between the doctors and Gerhardt Schlick that concerned her, it would likely be detailed among her father's papers. If they were lucky, there might even be something there—or as a last resort, something she would find in Gerhardt's home—to link him to Kristine's death.

She'd expected her father's bedroom and study doors to be locked. But picking locks with a hairpin was something she and Kristine had perfected during their adolescent sleepovers. It took less than a minute.

She drew the drapes and found his briefcase beneath his bed. Picking that lock was out of the question. It was a combination lock, the numbers of which she spent nearly an hour trying to guess. She tried birthdays, telephone numbers, ages, days of the week, their address—everything she could think of—to no avail.

Oh, Mother! Mother! If only you were here. What would you do? I don't know what to do! I don't know what to do, and time is running out!

Love him. The image of her mother's smile, her embrace, her solution to all of life's ills was so strong, Rachel gasped.

You don't know how he's changed, Mother. He's changed so even you wouldn't recognize him!

But the image persisted, the impression in her brain waxing strong.

I can't! I'm so angry—so hurt. I don't know what he's thinking. I know you loved him, but he was a different man when you married him . . . when you married him . . .

Not daring to breathe, Rachel keyed in the date of her parents' wedding anniversary. The tumblers clicked into place. She pushed the latch, and it snapped open.

The first set of files detailed peculiar symptoms of tuberculosis patients, everything from skin lesions to diminished lung capacity. There were photographs, charts of patients, descriptions of treatments and the efficacy of drugs used experimentally.

The second set of files dealt with sets of twins, separated at the beginning of the experiment. One of the twins in each case was injected with a tubercular serum, or in some cases fed milk from tubercular cows. The other twin was raised on wholesome foods in a wholesome environment. The files charted the devastating development of the disease in the exposed twin. Once the untreated disease was full-blown, the healthy twin was reunited with and kept in close proximity to the tubercular twin. Reports indicated that some patients appeared to develop immunity to the disease, while in the majority of cases, the disease became full-blown and eventually fatal to both twins.

In conclusion, she read, *this is the desired strain . . .* She could read no more.

Experiments on human beings. I knew you were researching tuberculosis. I had no idea you murdered in the process.

She pulled Jason's small camera from her purse and photographed the last few pages of the file, hoping it was only her tears that made the words appear blurry through the tiny viewer.

The clock struck eight, and she pressed forward. The next several files dealt with more sets of twins but seemed to be largely clinical observations—no treatments. *What is it about twins?*

At last she came to a file on Gerhardt Schlick. There was mention of a failed experiment—something about subject B-47. There was an after note about his marriage to Kristine, and more detailed notes on the birth of Amelie. A midwife's notation that the child appeared to be healthy, and two years later a doctor's diagnosis of deafness. There was nothing incriminating—nothing about Kristine but a recent notation on her death and something about an aborted experiment. It was primarily a detailed record of Gerhardt's lineage, his physical and mental development based on clinical examinations made at the Frankfurt Institute over the last several years, each detail compared to an ideal Aryan model.

Hitler's supermen. Rachel cringed. She'd reached the last page of Gerhardt's file when she saw a scribbled note—her father's handwriting—at the bottom of the page. *Insert subject B-47.*

Insert subject B-47? What does that mean? She had no idea, and no time. Her father would surely return any moment.

She replaced the files and was about to close and lock the case when she realized that there was something of bulk in a separately latched compartment in the lining of the lid. She pulled the smaller group of files from their hiding place.

Each of the files was lettered and numbered. She flipped open the first one and saw the photograph of a young boy, not more than three or four years of age. There were subsequent pictures of the boy, at different ages and only in his undergarments. Each photograph was accompanied by a chart detailing the subject's physical and mental development. There was something familiar about the background in each picture. What was it?

By the time she'd flipped through the second file, Rachel recognized the sterile walls of the clinic in Frankfurt. She remembered being told to stand against that wall, to turn, to bend this way and that and hold the position. As a child it had been a game with the doctor present. As a young woman she'd been perturbed but obedient to the longtime regimen and the nurse who'd replaced the doctor due to her state of undress. She'd had no idea there was a hidden camera taking photographs.

Though she felt the heat of shame, she flipped through the remaining files, certain now that she'd find her own set of humiliating, revealing photographs, her own file with details of her growth and development.

The numbered and lettered files apparently designated individual subjects. A-25, A-36, A-37, A-42, A-47, A-51 for male subjects. B-29, B-34, B-47, B-56, B-71 for female subjects. Beyond the photographs taken during clinical examinations, there were numerous family photographs of each subject, details of family life, of the parents' background, of athletic abilities, education and intellectual achievements, religious, political, and community affiliations.

She snapped random photographs of the files, uncertain of their usefulness, changed the film, and snapped dozens more. Nothing she saw could hold any of the doctors or her father accountable in a court of law—not even an American court—unless she could prove the files were kept for some lurid purpose.

Public opinion could be swayed by reports of injecting innocents with tubercular serum, not by files and growth charts of children, no matter how demeaning.

She'd been searching for, expecting, her own file, but was not prepared when she opened the folder. That her father would have sanctioned such an invasion to her privacy cut her; that he would have detailed her life in such a clinical fashion debased her. But that he saw her as a specimen, part of his eugenics research, entirely unnerved her. Clipped synopses of her studies and relationships, of every facet of her life, filled the folder labeled *B-47*.

The clock struck nine. She couldn't read more, couldn't stomach more, but knew that she would want to know all he'd said—later, when she'd had some sleep and could digest what she'd seen. She spread the pages across her father's bed and photographed them, one after another. She'd just returned the last of the files to its hiding place when the image of her father's scribbling on Gerhardt's file flashed to the forefront of her mind—*Insert subject B-47. I am subject B-47!*

She pulled out her file, flipped to the back, and read. She was not only part of his research. She was an "experiment and an element in experiments." Rachel felt the room tilt, the light fade. She shook her head, forced herself to concentrate. Notes near the end of her file were in handwriting other than her father's: *It is imperative that this subject reproduce in order to achieve its purpose. Noncompliance will result in an aborted experiment.—Dr. J. Mengele.*

Dr. Josef Mengele, who doesn't like loose ends. My father, who antici-pated closing the file. They mean for me to marry Gerhardt. I was raised to marry Gerhardt Schlick—or someone like him! That's what Father meant about demonstrating interest in marriage, about choosing some-one, about not returning to New York.

Rachel closed her eyes, sick to her stomach, trying to get her bearings. *Kristine was murdered because she didn't produce a "perfect" child. Gerhardt was ordered to marry me—all part of this sick breeding program. And now that they've eliminated Kristine, they intend to get their experiment back on track. But what happens if I don't comply?*

She reassembled the file, placed it in the case, and reset the lock. She slid the briefcase beneath the bed, making certain to angle it just as it had been. She switched off the light, opened the drapes, and stared into the dark, trying to absorb what she'd read.

Rachel did not believe in God—had been raised to view such belief as a crutch for the weak. And she, a member of the elite, was not weak. But for the first time in her life she wished she did believe. She knew she was weak, and she needed help.

14

My dearest Friederich,

You will never believe what has happened. . . .

The young refugee and village children are precious beyond measure, trusting and starving for attention—and for apple strudel! Their sweet voices carry the timbre of cherubs, barely in need of tuning.

Curate Bauer has asked me to oversee some minor tweaking of crooked halos here and there, admonitions for improved behavior. To my great surprise, that is more easily accomplished than I'd have imagined. They're so eager to please, to be part of something wholesome and cheerful. What could be more cheerful than a choir of young children? Even Heinrich Helphman is a pleasure, a treasure, a joy—though he adamantly refuses to return your Christkind. I don't know what possesses him, but I haven't the heart to press him.

I cannot tell you, my husband, how they fill my heart, how their questions spark my mind and their small hands tucked into mine as we walk from school lift my life.

I love you, my darling. Hurry home to me and you will see. You will love them too.

Friederich lay back on his pallet and folded the letter. He closed his eyes as he held it, envisioning the smile of his angel wife.

He'd worried when he first read of Curate Bauer's request. He'd heard from Frau Fenstermacher of her nightmares with the children's choir—the entire village had heard for weeks. He couldn't understand how the priest had come to ask his wife such a favor—how it would ever be approved by the board or the Catholic parents, even though Lea wrote that she'd accepted minimal pay, so anxious was she to do the job.

Friederich shook his head as he tucked the letter inside his shirt, next to his heart. Lea not only looked the part; she sang like an angel. And Oma had seen to it that she'd learned to read music and play the piano from childhood. That was normal in Oberammergau, for Catholics, Protestants, or Jews. Music was mandatory in every child's education—always the singing, and often an instrument. Catholic children, especially, were watched and early on encouraged in music, acting, and singing. All were watched for woodcarving or hospitality skills. How else could the village be prepared to launch and host a Passion Play every ten years, with all the attending theatricals and musical programs year round?

But Lea had no special training with children. None of it made sense, and Friederich feared for his wife's mental state if the priest should decide to withdraw the opportunity or offer it to another—someone better trained, someone a member of the Catholic church. He wished he could caution Lea, perhaps even talk her out of it.

But it was as though a fire had been lit in his wife's heart. He saw it in the rush of her handwriting across the page. She was radiant—he knew it by her words, by the bright lifting of her *i*'s and the happy tails on her *k*'s. And it turned out that she was a natural teacher, a disciplinarian when needed, but even more a mentor and guide to the children. She said so herself in so many words. It was the first time she'd recognized her own strength in all the months they'd been married.

How could he deny her or advise against it? If things did not change in some way he could not imagine, she would need all the validation and joy this life could afford her. She might even need the income.

Friederich pulled from his pocket the small babe he'd carved from pine in his rare free time and ran his thumb over the face, the limbs of the child.

Since coming to Poland his unit had done nothing but obliterate Poles. He'd not been assigned to the burning of the synagogue last week, but his friend Gunther Friedman had returned from the mission as white as a sheet. He'd whispered that they'd herded the men, women, and even the children from the village into the synagogue. Just before slamming the door, he'd locked eyes with a little girl, the age and size of his own Gretel back home. Gunther said she seemed to understand better than he did what was coming. He'd slid the outside bolt on command, and his unit burned the synagogue to the ground. The screams—before the helpless were overcome by smoke—had haunted Gunther's dreams for days. The sickly sweet smell of burning hair and flesh clung to his jacket for less than a night. But Friederich thought he, too, would vomit.

There was no way he could continue this killing, be part of the murder of villagers whose only crime was to live in the path of the German army. But he knew there were few alternatives. None of them boded well for him, or for the possibility he would see his Lea again.

He'd nearly stained the small Christkind through rubbing it with his muddied thumb. He thought of little Heinrich and his fascination with the Christkind—the babe Lea wrote she'd not been able to retrieve from her most difficult but nevertheless endearing pupil.

Heinrich Helphman? Endearing? Friederich shook his head. Lea was besotted. *Are all children so fascinated by other children, by babies, as is Heinrich?*

He smiled for the first time since coming to Poland, and it warmed him through. *Who would not love a child? And what could be better for my Lea? I could not give her a child, but sharing in the lives of these children gives her a family. It gives her life again.*

❧❧

Jason waited for Rachel two hours past their appointed meeting time at the Tiergarten café. He'd read through two morning newspapers and finished two plum turnovers and three cups of black coffee—or something like coffee—thanking his lucky stars that foreign correspondents received special ration cards. Still, she hadn't shown.

He raked tense fingers through his hair, massaged the back of his neck. *Stupid, Young—stupid! No story is worth this. What kind of risk did I put you through, Rachel? If they killed Kristine . . . if your father was in on it . . . if he found you going through his files . . .* He couldn't complete the thought.

He'd determined, for both their sakes, not to telephone her at her hotel, not to have her telephone him at the news office. He'd bet a week's wages that the Reich had every phone in both places tapped. But two hours was too long. *Something's happened.*

Jason threw coins to the table and set pace for the hotel. He couldn't leave her in the lurch, no matter what that meant.

He'd nearly reached Wilhelmstrasse when he saw Rachel's slim figure, curves wrapped in a navy traveling suit, emerge from the stream of morning shoppers. He didn't try to disguise his relief, but the tension in her face drew him.

He met her as she crossed the street. "You sure know how to leave a guy hanging, Miss Kramer." He hefted the case she carried. "Going on a trip?"

She pushed past him, never slowing, not looking him in the eye. "Help me get a plane, a ship—whatever will get me out of Germany and to New York the fastest. I need it now." She glanced over her shoulder. "And not from Berlin."

He matched her pace, confused, needing to understand what that meant, what had happened, what it meant for Amelie, knowing she wouldn't ask such a thing without reason. "Can we change your ticket?"

She missed a beat, and he thought her voice cracked. "Father's holding our tickets—at least he said he was." She walked half a block, heels clicking the pavement in sharp rhythm. "I've no idea what's safe. But I have money. I emptied his cache."

What happened? "Does Dr. Kramer know you're leaving?"

"Not yet. I waited until he'd gone." She walked faster, her voice coming thick. "You were right about him. And his research." She passed the camera and a small bag of film canisters to him. "You'll find everything you need there. Use it as you wish, except—" She stopped abruptly, and the pedestrians behind them nearly collided.

Jason pulled her aside, saw her bite her lip.

"There are files about me—about others like me. Promise you won't—you won't use those pictures."

Jason frowned, not knowing what she was talking about.

"Promise me!" she insisted.

"I promise; I promise," he said.

"Be careful." Rachel locked eyes with him. "Be so very careful."

Jason had been in plenty of tight spots. It came with the territory. This should be no different. He took her hand, leading her through the busy street, down a back alley, and to the only place he knew to borrow a nondescript car on short notice. Whether they could make it through the border checkpoint into Austria was another matter.

After spending the equivalent of three hundred dollars and an hour on the road, Rachel had quietly filled Jason in on the files, what she understood of the work done at Cold Spring Harbor, her father's focus on tuberculosis, greater detail of the medical examinations she'd been part of in Frankfurt, and her discovery of research done on twins—both for tuberculosis studies and for other programs she'd not had time to identify.

"They're playing Cupid, as near as I can tell, though love has nothing to do with the matching. Apparently it's all about pairing bloodlines—eugenically ideal Aryan bloodlines." She glanced at Jason, embarrassed to have been an unwitting part of such a program. But the greater pain was the betrayal of her father.

"And Gerhardt Schlick is your match."

"Evidently designed that way for years."

"So when you turned him down and he married Kristine, they weren't happy to begin with. It had nothing to do with Amelie's deafness after all."

Rachel sighed. "I wouldn't say that. If Amelie had been 'acceptable,' they may have left everything alone—at least as far as their marriage was concerned."

"But now, according to the good doctors, you're slated to marry Gerhardt and produce lots of little Aryan thoroughbreds."

Rachel winced. "I'll not do it. I've seen the posters promoting fertility and the 'obligation of every strong German woman' to bear multiple children."

"Maybe that's the twins connection. Maybe it has to do with increasing the Aryan population."

"I don't know. But there's more to it than that. The experiments for tuberculosis infected one twin who was given no treatment. Only when the disease was full-blown was the other twin exposed."

"Medical experiments for eradicating diseases?"

"And for detecting and eliminating 'weakened strains,' and I don't know what all." Rachel had been nauseous ever since she'd begun reading the files. Racing down the autobahn did not help. "But they let the twins—one or both—die, and they do nothing to help them, unless one is declared immune to the strain."

"You don't suppose you have an infected twin running around somewhere, do you?"

Jason's sarcasm grated. It was no joke. *Father's betrayal! How could he?* Rachel straightened. *Did Mother know?* She could not entertain such a possibility. "He didn't start out like this—he didn't," she insisted. "Father was so different before Mother died. . . . At least I want to believe he was." She swallowed, but it felt like lead in her throat. "I didn't get to finish reading the file. I—I was afraid Father would return, and—and I just couldn't take any more in."

"So you don't know anything about—?"

"After I'd gone to my room, I wished I'd looked back in my file—made myself read it. There may have been something about my birth mother and father. I know my mother was German and died in child-birth, that I was born in Frankfurt and adopted by my American parents almost right away. They said I was her only child. That's all I know." She turned to Jason, glad that he had to keep his eyes on the road. "I nearly went back to read more, but Father's key turned in the lock of the suite. I couldn't face him without showing how I feel toward him. I'm sure he wouldn't invite me to have a peek, even if I confronted him."

"And this morning?"

"I left a note last night saying that I wasn't feeling well and would be sleeping in. I'd see him for dinner tonight. By the time I came out of my room he'd gone for the day. I think he's meeting with the doctors at the Kaiser Wilhelm Institute. He left a note saying he'd be late. He probably imagines I'll spend the day going through Kristine's things with Gerhardt."

"By the time he gets back, you'll be gone. He won't know where." Jason drummed the steering wheel with the tips of his fingers. "It might have been better to wait until they'd be gone longer—would have given you a head start."

She shook her head, miserable. "I couldn't stay there another day—I couldn't. I left him a letter."

"A letter?" The incredulity in Jason's voice brought her up short.

"I told him I'm ashamed of him, that he sickens me, that Mother would be disgusted, and that he's dishonored her memory by selling me out. Whatever good he's done in his quest to rid the world of tuberculosis is undone and spat upon by his murder of innocents."

Jason whistled low.

"I'll never see him again. I told him I'm returning to New York and that he's not to try to contact me. I want nothing to do with him." Her voice broke.

"He'll come after you, Rachel. They'll come after you," Jason insisted. "They've spent twenty-odd years raising you as a broodmare; they're not going to let you off the hook because you say you don't want to play their nasty game."

"When I get to New York, I'll move; I'll change my name."

"You underestimate them."

Rachel couldn't be defeated before she'd begun to fight. There would be battles enough ahead, and she wouldn't use her energy to fight with Jason. "Just get me out of Germany."

❦

Five hours later, as dusk settled in, Jason pulled to the curb of the train station nearest the Austrian border. "I just hope this is still an option. If you get through Austria, next stop is Switzerland." He took the hand Rachel held out to him, awkward though it seemed.

"Thank you. Thank you for everything," Rachel stammered. "Especially all you've done for Amelie—all you will do."

"Don't thank me yet."

"You'll let me know that she's safe."

He nodded.

"When you . . . If you find a way to get her to America, I'll take her." Rachel looked up helplessly and said, "I don't know anything about children—or deaf children. But I'll find her a place."

"I'll let you know. Through my US editor—using our code words."

"I'll contact him when I get settled—wherever that is." She turned, but Jason wouldn't let go.

"Be careful. Be safe."

She smiled, a tight and worried smile. "And you." She pulled away, was already out the door, reaching for her bag in the back. He jumped out and took it from her.

"I'm not leaving until I see you safely over that border."

She breathed, touching his arm. "Chivalry is not dead, then?"

"Not yet," he grinned, feeling a little stupid, not one bit sorry.

15

Jason hung back, as they'd agreed, pretending to read a newspaper as he stood against the newsstand pillar inside the station. Rachel's American passport might get her through the border, but he'd spent too much time in the New Germany to leave anything to chance.

They waited until the lines were long and the room busy. Rachel placed her German marks on the counter beside her passport.

The official barely looked up. He counted the money, issued and stamped the ticket, and returned her change. He took a cursory glance at the passport, hesitated a moment, searched her face, and handed it back. He asked her something in German—something Jason couldn't hear. She nodded, replied, and was smiling when she stooped to pick up her overnight bag.

Jason breathed.

But the official called her back, apparently asked her to wait. She complied, demurred, asked a question. The man hesitated, frowned, pointed across the room toward two hallways. She smiled and held up her hand, as though promising something.

The man was still frowning as she walked away.

The next customer placed marks on the counter, momentarily blocking the official. Jason saw the official step aside, sweep the room with his eyes, and motion to an armed uniform. His eyes and a nod followed Rachel, who was just stepping into the ladies' room.

The uniform pulled a paper from his inside coat pocket, flashed it to the official, who nodded in return. They motioned for another—a bookend of the first uniform—to come.

The hair on the back of Jason's neck prickled. The nerves in the backs of his hands tingled. He folded his newspaper.

The armed uniforms strolled past. Jason lowered his eyes to the newspaper, forced himself to count to five, breathe, and look up. They'd taken the short hallway leading to the stairs beneath the train platforms and stationed themselves on either side.

I don't like it.

The man at the counter watched the door to the ladies' room.

A boarding announcement came over the loudspeaker. Passengers hefted bags, hugged loved ones good-bye, poured toward the stairs to the platform. Late customers lined the ticket windows, holding passports and marks high to urge officials at the windows to hurry. Rachel opened the door.

Jason blocked her, grabbed her bag and cupped her elbow, turning her toward the arched door to the street. "Just walk."

"But—"

"Trust me."

Sharp whistle blasts came from behind as they reached the door to the outside. But the press of passengers intent on catching the late-afternoon train surged forward, creating a blockade in front of the armed uniforms.

Jason pushed through. Once they hit the fresh air, he grabbed Rachel's hand and raced for the car.

"Jason! What—?"

"They're looking for you—get in!"

They peeled from the curb and made for the autobahn. Sirens erupted behind as train whistles blared from the station.

❦

"What choice is there?" Jason was tired of arguing. "Either you get out with your father or you go into hiding until we can find a way to get you out."

"I told you—I don't think my father means for me to leave Germany! I don't even know if *he's* going to leave!"

"Or if he can."

"What does that mean?"

"What if he's just as much a prisoner in all this as you are?"

"That's ridiculous. I saw his files." She hesitated. "I just don't know where the line is concerning me, or if there is one."

"He may not either."

"Why are you defending him?"

"I'm not defending him, but think about it. They already have your photograph—I'm sure that's what those guards were looking at. There's no way your father would have been able to get that out to the border patrols today, even if he'd read your letter by noon."

"Unless he suspected earlier that I'd run." She looked at him. "Or unless they suspected that he and I might both run and had sent them ahead—even days ago?"

"Exactly. They have no intention that you leave the country—never had." Jason slowed, pulling off onto a side road, cutting his lights.

"What are you doing?"

"We can't get back into the city unseen tonight—especially with the blackout and checkpoints. And where would we go?" He turned to her in the dark. "You can't go back to the hotel, and I can't exactly take you to my hotel room or hide you in the newsroom. We'll have to find someplace tomorrow."

Rachel pushed the heels of her hands into her eyes. "I just can't believe this is happening."

"Believe it."

"Maybe I should go back to Father. I could plead with him, try to reason. If we could both just go home!" She groaned.

"The Krauts won't let you do that." Jason slumped behind the wheel, creating a headrest of the bench back, and closed his eyes. "Major mess!"

"I'm sorry." Rachel's voice came thick, sounding like a little girl about to cry. "I've roped you into hiding a deaf child, drawn you into a murder conspiracy, and now you're stuck with me. Your picture will be plastered on wanted posters across Germany. You'll probably lose your job—at least."

He grunted. "They certainly have your picture. Not mine—not yet—at least not beyond what they have on all foreign correspondents. I can blend into the crowd—like the Shadow." He grinned, tapping his nose. "The worst that can happen with my job is that I'd be sent back to the US for creating an international incident."

"The worst? Right, Mr. Shadow." She leaned her head on his shoulder. "Now who's living in a fantasy world?"

❧❦

Morning came softly. Jason pulled onto the main road, thick and dreary fog shrouding the headlights for their return to Berlin. "Maybe we can get through with nobody stopping us."

"I've been thinking about it all night," Rachel said. He didn't like the sound of that. "I think you should take me back to the hotel."

He was glad there was no oncoming traffic; he'd probably have run off the road.

"I'm going to try to reason with my father, to get him to go home with me. They won't stop me going with him."

"But you said—"

"I know what I said. Only now I'm thinking—I'm wondering if I've overreacted."

"Are you kidding? I guess you didn't see those guys back there—the ones with guns. They're not toys. They were already looking for you—waiting for you. Now they know you're trying to leave the country. Your father's probably blown the whistle on you. You left him a letter, Rachel! He won't pretend he didn't read it. They're not gonna let you breeze out."

"But . . . I can't get out on my own."

Jason gripped the steering wheel. "Let me talk to some friends. This new church—the Confessing Church—helped a Jewish journalist I know get out of the country with his family. They just might—"

"No, I won't let you risk any more. I never should've pulled you into it. And nobody in some radical church bent on helping Jews is likely to help the daughter of a eugenics scientist eager to eliminate them! Let me off a block before the hotel." She sat back, folding her hands in her lap. Jason recognized the female "this is settled—this is the way things are" posture. His mom and sister did it all the time.

Only you're not my mom or sister, Rachel Kramer. He narrowed his eyes, determined to focus on the road.

The kilometers passed. They were less than a half hour from Berlin when he spoke again. "Amelie. You could hide with Amelie."

Rachel snorted.

"Ladylike response."

She blushed. "I'm sure your miracle goodwill family is ready to take in a twenty-four-year-old 'child' as well as a deaf four-year-old. That would be easy to sweep under the rug."

"Don't be sarcastic."

"Don't be ridiculous. We've no idea how long this insanity will go on."

"As long as Hitler's in power. And I can't see how that can go on much longer. There's resistance forming within, and Britain's in on it now."

"They've not even sent planes to Berlin! Hitler's gaining momentum every day."

She was right. It was exactly what he'd told the mole who fed him resistance information. "They say Britain's waiting for the right moment."

"The right moment?" Rachel snorted again. "When will that be—when he takes Paris? Or London?"

Jason frowned at her.

She didn't blush this time. "They're all afraid of him. Terrified—just like we are. I'd rather take my chances with my father. He must feel something for me."

Jason swallowed. *What kind of father would do what he's done to you?* "I have an idea."

She rolled her eyes, shaking her head.

"There's this reporter, ready to go stateside. She's already got her passport, ticket—everything."

"Will they let her through?"

"Sure, she's press."

"Will they let her through with a sister?" She looked hopeful.

"Not a chance, but you could send your passport with her."

"Stay in Germany with no passport, no papers?" Rachel turned away. "You're mad."

"Hear me out. Sheila's going by passenger ship. She walks on board as herself—nothing unusual. But just before leaving the ship in New York, she drops your passport in a broom closet or somewhere—somewhere not connected with her—to make it look like you'd been on board the whole time, hiding, stowing away."

"All the while I'm still in Germany with no passport."

"We could drum up papers—a fake identity. I know people who know people. The point is that they'd stop looking for you here. They'd think that somehow you got ashore—back to the US. And we could hide you here until we figure a way to get you out."

"You 'know people' willing to blow up buildings, hide children from the Reich, and do passports? Are you even a reporter?"

He raised his eyebrows in a Groucho Marx imitation.

"Don't tell me. And what if they catch her with my passport? What if she forgets to drop it? What if she can't find a place to drop it?"

"You sound like my grandmother!"

"It's insane, and it puts too many people at risk—including me. I don't want to stay in Germany; I want to go home."

As they turned onto the street housing the hotel, the morning traffic ground to a standstill. Black cars with official insignia lined both curbs and blocked the street. Armed SS in black jackboots flanked the hotel's entrance.

"What's going on?" Rachel craned her neck.

"I can't see. Wait, they're hauling someone out."

Rachel leaned across him to get a view from his side.

Jason didn't know whether to shield her from seeing or to make sure she did. A pale-faced Dr. Kramer, rumpled, holding his left arm and bearing the shadow of a stubbled beard, was escorted, none too gently, by two SS guards and a familiar figure in uniform.

"Get down!"

"Father! Why are they taking him—?" Rachel began. "It's Gerhardt! He's got Father's briefcase!"

Jason pushed her back and hissed, "Get down! Don't let him see you!" The traffic inched forward. "I can't get out of this blasted line! Hit the floor."

"But where are they taking him?" She slid from the seat.

Jason kept his eyes facing forward, draping a nonchalant arm across the wheel to shield his face. "I don't think we'll be getting an answer to that question—at least not today."

"What's happening now?" Rachel peered up from the floor.

"They're shoving him into a car. Schlick's getting in the other side. I don't recognize the others." Jason inched the car forward, his fedora tipped toward the steering wheel. "There're still a couple of guards stationed outside the hotel."

As soon as the black cars pulled from the curb, traffic began to flow. Rachel pushed herself back into her seat.

Jason rounded the block and drove the length of the boulevard, heading for the Brandenburg Gate. "We need a plan."

"They're looking for me. It looked like they'd beaten him."

Jason cradled the hand she nestled in his.

"I should turn myself in."

"Did you forget that he was planning on turning you in, closing the file, subject B-47?"

She closed her eyes. "I keep thinking, maybe I was wrong. Maybe he didn't mean it as it looked in the files. He's my father. He couldn't . . ."

"Sell you out?"

The sob she'd held so tightly broke through.

16

"YOU'LL BE SAFE HERE." The thickset Frau pushed open the wooden trapdoor in her narrow hallway ceiling with the handle of a broom. "But you must keep very quiet and absolutely still during the day. My neighbor, Frau Weisman, is the courtyard monitor. She will report anything she thinks suspicious." She eyed Rachel sharply, waiting, Rachel thought, for some reassurance.

"I'll be very still."

The woman nodded. "You can come down to use the toilet and to wash when my husband has gone to work and the children are at school. If that is not possible, there is a bucket in the corner. But you must not use it until they have gone. They might hear you. I will pass food to you once in the morning and once before my family returns for the evening."

She pulled a chair from the kitchen, motioning for Rachel to step up. Rachel bit her lip, tentatively smiling her thanks, and climbed. She braced her elbows on the attic floor and attempted to hoist herself through the opening. The Hausfrau pushed from behind—to Rachel's chagrin. But she made it.

"When I play the piano, that is my signal that you may move and stretch. The piano will cover your movement. I will always play Wagner last, so you will know you must be quiet. When I stop, you too must stop."

Rachel nodded, now peeking down through the attic's square opening. "Thank you, Frau Himmerschmidt—thank you for helping me."

"*Ja*, well, we all need to help one another now." The woman motioned for Rachel to set the wooden door in place.

Rachel remained where she was, sitting cross-legged on the dirty floor by the little door, around which showed the faintest rim of daylight. The attic peaked in the center, but even there she couldn't stand. Corners of the attic room revealed shadows, faint outlines of trunks and boxes, broken furniture—a chair turned upside down and the railings of what might have been a bedstead. The air hung heavy, dusty, musty. Rachel wasn't about to go exploring—not yet. She just hoped she was the only thing that lived and breathed in the attic.

Late that night, while she listened to the soft snores of the family below her, Rachel stretched, fully dressed, on the lumpy, sour-smelling pallet she'd found stashed in a corner of the attic. Running through the events of the last three days, she remembered the itinerary she'd believed to be real, at least what she'd believed from her father when they first set foot in Germany. They should have landed in New York this very evening. She should be lying in her luxurious bed, dreaming of tomorrow—her first day working in Manhattan as the newest gofer for the Campbell Playhouse.

Rachel bit her lip to keep from crying, silently rolled over, and stared into the darkness.

❦

Jason rubbed the stubble on his face. When he'd returned the car and seen Rachel to safety, he'd stopped by his room in the hotel only long enough to rumple his bed, make it look as though he'd crept in late. *As if the nosy maid service will buy that!* If necessary, he'd come up with a story—drop a couple lines that he'd bunked in the makeshift newsroom, been working late and caught unaware by the time, the blackout—something.

He squinted. Things were getting complicated. The family hiding Amelie had refused to take Rachel—too risky. But their contact said

115

he knew someone who might. Jason had dropped Rachel off, praying the woman was a safe bet. But how could he know?

He cupped the rolls of Rachel's film in his pocket several times throughout the day, waiting, wondering how he could get Peterson out of the darkroom long enough to develop them alone. The last thing he wanted to do was share this scoop. He had no doubt it was a doozy.

The afternoon wore long. Jason found himself nodding off, elbows on his desk, more than once.

"Long night, Romeo?" Eldridge, his colleague and archrival for the next best news story, dumped a file at his elbow, jarring Jason awake at half past five.

Jason sat back, yawning, and rubbed his eyes. "Me and Mrs. Hitler—a hot time on the ole town last night."

"Show me Mrs. Hitler and I'll take her out myself. That's one story I'd like to scoop."

"You, me, the rest of the world."

"New York wants an editorial by midnight. Something on the way things are going here in Berlin since the war started—rationing, blackouts." He thumped the file. "Everything's here. Be a pal and whip something up—something the censors will allow through. I've gotta cover some hobnob dinner conference over at the US ambassador's."

"Plum piece. Kudos to you. Save me a slice of cake and you're on."

"Done. I'm taking Peterson along to see what we can get on film."

"Feed the waif while you schmooze—he's looking peaked on the new rations." Suddenly Jason was wide awake. A dignitary dinner guaranteed an empty darkroom for at least a couple of hours—probably until morning unless something big broke. Plenty of time to develop Rachel's film. He opened the file, pretending to read, and tried not to look too eager.

Less than an hour later he pulled the first set of prints from the chemical bath and clipped them to the line to dry. As near as he could tell, Rachel had done a good job with the camera—no shakes or shadows. He should be able to read the documents once he got the prints into the light.

The first images of people she'd snapped looked like head shots for passport photos. But as prints developed, more revealing images began to line up—shots taken during medical examinations, but ones he felt fairly certain were taken without the patients' knowledge. He whistled low. *No wonder she made me promise.*

While waiting for the images to dry, he perched at a desk outside the darkroom, sitting guard—even though the floor was empty—and pecked out the bargained editorial. It wasn't hard, but still he made several false starts, doing his best not to snark about the Nazis but to reveal the state of Berlin, hoping Americans could read between the lines. He wasn't optimistic. They hadn't raised their voice against Hitler's Nuremberg Laws that dispossessed Jews of their citizenship, nor shed many tears over Jason's reports on *Kristallnacht* when synagogues were torched and Jews were thrown out of their homes, imprisoned, and their stores and businesses ransacked.

Not even when he'd done the feature on Jacob Goldman, the seventy-six-year-old owner of a little family bookstore—a Berlin landmark as old as time. Storm troopers had pulled the old man and his wife from their beds above the store and thrown them both into the street. After clubbing the terrified couple into silence, they'd smashed the windows of their store and set it—and two stories' worth of inventory—ablaze.

Jason shook his head. Even with the Nazis' heavy censoring, enough came through to New York that it should have infuriated the country. Where was his "Christian nation," anyway? Weren't they supposed to help the oppressed and needy?

Two hours later, the editorial done, the darkroom so squeaky clean that Peterson would never know he'd been there, Jason sat alone in the newsroom with the prints.

He'd read everything, and it was hard to swallow. He was sure Rachel didn't know much about her father, about her adoptive mother's role in her upbringing, let alone anything about her family of origin.

What a story! Not just about Rachel, but all the victims. The very kind of personal profiles that would paint these monsters of manipulation for what they are. But can I print it? What will it mean to them if I do? He breathed deeply, squeezing the bridge of his nose. *In any other time and place it would be an exposé—bring the bad guys to their knees. But publicizing this here, now . . . it's more like signing the victims' death warrants—and mine. More than a few have blown the whistle and disappeared. An idea—I'd settle for an idea!*

Jason stacked the photos and slid them into an envelope. Then he slipped the negatives into a separate, smaller envelope and taped it to the bottom of his top right desk drawer. He switched off the light, welcoming the dark to better think.

It's time you stop worrying about your doctor father, Miss Kramer— he's not worth it. It's a sure thing you've been little more than a guinea pig to him. Trouble is, with or without him, the good doctors of Germany are just getting started.

But if I tell you the truth, if I show you these files, will you stay where you are? And if you don't, if you race down to Oberammergau to meet your long-lost family, it puts them at risk—and ultimately Amelie, and me, and all those who've helped save your hide.

Jason closed his eyes. He'd just stepped onto his own slippery slope.

17

Nearing the end of a long day, Curate Bauer stopped by the after-school program, pausing just outside the classroom door to listen to the children singing. Frau Hartman had a way about her—a way of leading the voices of the children into such harmony that they sounded like one angelic host.

The curate didn't even bother to pull a chair from one of the other rooms. He simply slid down the wall, resting his back and head against the cool plaster. He closed his eyes and allowed the blending of voices to raise him above the earth, away from the worries of the parish.

"Curate," a voice whispered, so near that it tickled the hairs in his ears, making him start. But he didn't open his eyes. He recognized the voice.

"Why aren't you in choir practice, Heinrich? Frau Hartman has already begun."

"I know," Heinrich whispered. Still Curate Bauer did not open his eyes. But he felt the little boy, all arms and legs, slide down the wall and plop beside him. "I have a confession to make." The voice was lower still, but determined.

Curate Bauer opened his eyes. "A confession? But you've not made your first confession yet. And you won't until you've completed catechism next year."

"But, Father, I've sinned."

"No doubt." For the first time that day Curate Bauer smiled.

"But I won't take it back," Heinrich insisted.

"The sin?"

"No, the baby."

"The what?" Curate Bauer was awake, fully alert.

"The baby Jesus—I won't take him back."

"You mean Herr Hartman's Nativity carving?" Curate Bauer had recovered more holy infants from Heinrich Helphman in the last six months than he'd done from all other parishioners combined in all the years of his life.

"Yes, Curate—stealing was the sin. And I know stealing's not right."

"No, it's not right. There seems something especially blighted about stealing the Christkind, Heinrich. Frau Hartman's been so good to you. Why would you steal from the Hartmans?"

"It's because Herr Hartman is the best carver. And because of his smile—he's got such a lovely mouth."

"Herr Hartman?" Curate Bauer agreed that Friederich Hartman had a ready laugh and a warm smile, but what had that to do with stealing his carvings?

"No, the baby Jesus." Heinrich spread his hands as though patiently explaining to a toddler.

"I don't think you can convince yourself that stealing makes the Lord Jesus smile, Heinrich." Curate Bauer was getting a headache. To deal with near-starving families bound for who knows where and who knows what in the morning and a belligerent little thief in the afternoon was more than should be required of a saint, let alone a penitent sinner like himself. He'd like to take a strap to the boy. "Give me the carving and I'll return it for you—only because you've confessed, and only this once. It must not happen again."

"I can't. I won't." Heinrich scooted away from the priest. "I'm just confessing; that's all."

"Heinrich." The priest's patience was wearing thin. "You must—"

But before he could repeat what Heinrich must do, the boy was up and off, fleeing down the hall and out the door.

Wearily, Curate Bauer found his feet. He liked to think of himself as fairly fit, but he was no match for the pumping legs of a mountain child. He stopped at the school door and watched the youngster sprint through the hedges and down the cobbled hill. The curate threw his hands up. He wasn't old or decrepit, but he refused to chase the fleet feet of Heinrich Helphman through the village. He and Frau Hartman could deal with Heinrich another day.

※

Lea had just locked her classroom door when two black Mercedes, swastika flags flying, barreled through the quiet village streets. It was a rare-enough occurrence that shopkeepers quickly closed their doors and mothers bade their children inside, shuttering windows. As if anything could keep the Gestapo or SS out!

Unsettling though it was, such things had happened before—usually preceding raids. In fact, the same cars had roamed the streets of Oberammergau the week before, parking first in one place and then another for hours, as if watching. Then they'd disappeared. Why were they back now? Lea pitied the object of their attention. Perhaps someone had been reported for hiding political enemies.

She took her time. No one would be visiting or looking for her. She'd nothing to hide, and she'd promised to walk five-year-old Gretchen Zuckerman home that day, as her mother helped to midwife a laboring neighbor. By the time they arrived, Gretchen's older siblings would be home from their Hitler Youth meetings and could watch her.

Such extra moments with the children were like icing on cakes for Lea. She loved it when Gretchen tucked her small hand into Lea's larger one, happy to walk with her teacher, dimples punctuating her smile. Lea's heart swelled to feel the child's sturdy body move in rhythm with hers, arms swinging. It was a happy trust, and Lea was thankful.

She forced herself not to linger at the Zuckerman gate despite the temptation to stay until the children's mother returned. It wasn't necessary, might even be thought presumptuous. She squeezed Gretchen's hand good-bye and smiled as the child waved her up the street.

Lea had nearly reached home when the red-and-black swastika flags appeared round the bend, pulling to a sudden stop in front of Oma's gate. Lea's heart skipped. *They must have the wrong address!*

But two black-clad warriors piled from the official car, thrust open the gate, and strode to her grandmother's front door while two more pulled revolvers and crept round the side. Lea's heart pounded as she hurried up the hill. Mistake or not, Oma's poor heart couldn't take such shock.

Lea heard them barking orders and shouting before she ever reached the neighboring garden. She walked faster, fear holding her back, fear propelling her forward. In slow motion, Lea saw Oma open the door, saw one of the guards shove the older woman aside and push into the small house. Lea raced uphill.

"Oma! Oma!" She slammed open the gate and sprang through the door but was jerked off her feet by one of the SS guards, her arm wrenched behind her.

Amid stars she saw Oma grasp her heart as the guard closed the door.

18

Jason loosened the knot of his tie, then pulled shirt and tie over his head in one fell swoop. *Good enough for tomorrow.* He tossed shirt and pants to his bedside chair and collapsed into bed, too weary to worry about food or drink. He'd spent the last forty-eight hours interviewing every foreign ambassador left in Germany, getting their take—their country's official take and digging for their unofficial take—on Hitler's bulldozing.

The war on Poland had not lasted long. The Poles did not have the military might or air power to fend off Germany's war machine. When Russia entered eastern Poland, the job was all but done. Warsaw fell in twenty days. The foreign press hunkered down in Berlin, taking unholy bets on how long their British friends across the North Sea would take to enter the war they'd declared on Germany.

September was nearly over. Just that morning Jason had learned that Dr. Rudolph Kramer was reported to the world press as being in critical condition. He cringed to imagine what kind of interrogation the doctor had received at the hands of his tormentors. He'd no doubt that Dr. Kramer had been condemned as an accomplice in Rachel's escape from the moment she showed up at the border. What father would not have helped his daughter escape a life of misery with the likes of Schlick?

Only Rudolph Kramer had done nothing of the sort, intended nothing of the sort. Jason shook his head, remembering the files. *It stinks. It all stinks. And where does that leave Rachel?* He was glad she was in hiding. *At least I don't have to tell her—yet.*

———❦———

Frau Weisman, the nosy neighbor and courtyard monitor, had stopped to visit Frau Himmerschmidt during Rachel's second week in the attic—just before lunch, ostensibly to borrow a knob of lard.

She'd wondered about the extra portion in Frau Himmerschmidt's pot, how it was she even had a knob of lard to share considering the new rationing restrictions, and where she got it.

Rachel listened, her chest tight, her ear pressed to the attic floor above the kitchen, as the women talked of this and that, as Frau Himmerschmidt, perhaps too cheerfully, advised her neighbor on the best ways to stretch potatoes, which supplements could be mixed with flour for bread.

Without seeing, Rachel could tell that Frau Weisman did not buy her neighbor's frugality. More was more, and rationed meats did not lie.

By the time Frau Weisman and her many pointed questions had gone, Frau Himmerschmidt, frazzled to the bone, had decided it was simply too risky for her family to hide Rachel in the attic any longer. Just before her children bounded in from school, she whispered to the attic door that Rachel must find another place, and right away, so certain was she that Frau Weisman suspected her secret and would find them out.

By midafternoon, Frau Himmerschmidt's children had finished their luncheon and returned to school. Rachel heard her call good-bye to her courtyard monitor as the curious woman, martyr that she was, plowed through rain puddles toward her local hospital to fulfill volunteer obligations. Less than two minutes passed before Frau Himmerschmidt pushed the attic door open and helped Rachel down.

Rachel layered her clothing and stuffed her pockets beneath the Frau's raincoat to make herself look heavier. She powdered her hair and made up her face to look older, using whatever Frau

Himmerschmidt could provide and all the theatrical tricks she'd learned in the makeup department at NYU. *This isn't how I'd planned to use that knowledge.*

Rachel knew she should be frightened. But she was sick of the attic, and the anticipation of walking out of doors revived her.

Frau Himmerschmidt telephoned the foreign correspondents' office and asked for Jason Young. "Your laundry is finished and ready to be picked up. I'm sorry, but I've decided that I will no longer take in laundry. I have enough to do with my own family. You must find someone else." Not waiting for a response, she hung up, turning to Rachel. "I'm sorry—" she spread her hands—"but I have children. I don't know why they are after you—you seem like a nice young woman." She helped Rachel into her raincoat. "You're not Jewish, are you?"

"No." Rachel blushed, then felt ashamed that she'd blushed. "Would that matter?"

The woman sighed. "I don't want it to matter."

Rachel nodded. She understood, at least as best she could. Everyone was afraid to hide Jews—afraid of the Nazis, of the Gestapo, of the SS, of the brownshirts, of the Hitler Youth, of the monitors in their apartment blocks and courtyards, of nosy neighbors quick to report longtime friends and quicker yet their enemies. Fear reeked. She'd just been too self-absorbed and blind to see it before. She'd not needed to see it—it hadn't threatened her until now. "Thank you for hiding me these days. I know it was a risk."

Frau Himmerschmidt blinked, then pulled the curtain from the corner of the window, whispering, "Through the courtyard and turn left. The trolley stop is up one block and over one."

Rachel hesitated, terribly aware that she had no place to go, no one to trust. But the woman stepped back and lowered her eyes. She'd been dismissed. Frau Himmerschmidt pulled open the door, and Rachel slipped through. Imitating her benefactor's heavy walk through the courtyard, she made her way toward the next block.

Riding the trolley was a risk, but so was walking the streets.

She prayed Jason had understood the message, prayed he would once again come to her rescue and find her a place to stay—all before she remembered she didn't believe in praying. She walked slowly, not increasing her pace to catch the trolley just in view.

She was halfway through the second block when a taupe BMW pulled beside her. "A lift, *meine Frau?*" It was an attractive young woman.

"Nein, danke." Rachel pointed toward the trolley stop.

"Friend of Jason's," the woman whispered, leaning across to open the door.

Rachel hesitated.

"Come, Frau Wagner." The woman spoke well and brightly, but with a distinct American accent. "I'll give you a lift. It's no trouble at all. I'm eager to pick up my laundry."

Rachel drew a deep breath and slipped into the car.

"Sheila Graham." The woman extended her hand.

Gratefully, Rachel clasped it.

"Don't say anything. Jason's told me not to ask."

"Then how—?"

"It's better I don't know. We all operate on that basis from time to time." She grinned, pulling back into the line of traffic. "Jason will meet us at my apartment later. You can get a bath—relax, maybe get some sleep before he comes over. I'm guessing those lines aren't all about great stage makeup."

"I'm afraid they're not," Rachel breathed. "Thank you."

Sheila nodded, shifting gears. "I have a date tonight. You and Jason'll have plenty of time to talk. I don't know what's going on, but I'll help any way I can. You can stay with me—for now."

Rachel shuddered, nodded her thanks, and determined to keep tears of relief from spilling down her made-up cheeks.

⸙

Never had a bath and hair wash felt so good. Rachel thought she could stay in the small tub forever, and she might have fallen asleep there had Sheila not called her from the other side of the hanging comforter. "Jason will be here soon. You might want to get decent."

Rachel dressed quickly, glad for Sheila's loan of a skirt and blouse. She pulled back her hair in a taut ponytail, hoping it would dry without springing tiny ringlets all over her head.

She was tucking the blouse into the band of her skirt when Sheila opened the door. Jason slipped through, bearing dinner.

"Takeout Chinese—Berlin style!" He grinned, mouth triumphant, eyes relieved and alight at the sight of Rachel.

"My favorite!" She couldn't stop the grin spreading between her ears.

Sheila glanced between the two of them and laughed. "I'm outta here. Keep it down and keep the door locked. Keep those lights low. I'll jingle the key in the lock before I come in."

Rachel felt herself blush.

Jason, too, turned crimson, but was quick on the draw. "I'll be gone before you get back."

"If you do, make sure you're not seen. You know about my courtyard monitor."

He nodded, and Rachel was surprised how easily, how smoothly they communicated. She must not be the first secret they'd shared.

When the door closed behind Sheila, Rachel felt suddenly shy. "Sheila made some coffee. Would you like some?"

"Real coffee? Sure. That's a rarity outside the best restaurants these days. Sheila must be using up her stash. I'll dish up the grub."

"Sounds good."

But as they ate, Rachel couldn't think of a thing to say. She kept lifting her napkin to make sure she'd not left a smidgen of rice or a dab of soy sauce on her lips.

"Pretty good, but not like American Chinese food."

"No," she agreed, "but it sure beats potatoes every meal."

"Ah—" he smiled halfheartedly—"the plight of refugees."

"Refugees," she repeated, disheartened, and sat back, pushing her plate away.

"Rough in the attic?"

"It's not like home." She winced, not meaning to sound ungrateful. "I'm not sure where home is now."

That killed the conversation.

Jason pulled a large envelope from his jacket.

"New passport?" She lifted her brows hopefully.

"Pictures." He licked his lips, as if deciding how to proceed. "I developed your film."

Rachel felt her heartbeat quicken, her chest tighten. She'd been wondering what else was in her file—what she hadn't seen.

He pushed the envelope across the table. Holding her breath to steady her fingers, Rachel pulled out the sheaf of prints. Five minutes passed as she read, peeling away the years of her life. "He changed after Mother died," she confided. "Even his notes show that he took a different path."

"Maybe she held him back."

"Or kept him sane," Rachel insisted, then continued to read. "A sister? I have a sister?"

"An identical twin. Which explains the trips to the clinic—the examinations—every two years. Both of you."

Rachel had realized she was an experiment as soon as she'd seen the file in her father's hotel room, but she still couldn't grasp that reality—that he'd used her. Now, to learn that she had a twin was more than her mind could absorb. "I—we—were part of a long-term research project."

"*Are*—you *are* a long-term project. That's why they're determined to keep you here. And read this." Jason took back the file, separating portions, and pushed another photograph toward her. "This shows that your father never had any intention of allowing you to leave Germany. It's his handwriting, isn't it?"

Rachel nodded.

"He forged your signature, attempting to withdraw your US citizenship, effective the Friday you arrived in Berlin." Jason sat back while she absorbed that idea. "There's no confirmation that it worked, but I think you can safely stop worrying about him."

Which is harder to believe? That he's betrayed me, sold me, raised me for science and his own egotistical research? Or that I have a sister? "How long have you known this?"

"Since I developed the film—two nights after you gave it to me."

"But you didn't tell me—get word to me?"

He reddened. "I was afraid you'd want to find her, that you'd run off like a crazy person. It's the first place they'll look—maybe already have, if they suspected you'd seen your father's files, if they thought he'd told you."

"He never told me any of this."

"Schlick and his goons wouldn't know that. They must have figured you knew something, learned something, to make you run off. Your letter would've made them think so. Trust me, the SS covers their bases."

"But you knew, and—"

"And you were safe where you were," he shot back. "Now you're not, so we've got to figure out something else."

"Who is she? Where's my sister?" She must focus on that.

He flipped through the pile and pulled a photograph. "Her name is Lea Hartman. Looks like she's been married something over a year.

No children. The last record shows she lives in Oberammergau—I think always has."

"She looks exactly like me," Rachel gasped, "only—old fashioned. . . . Oberammergau . . . the town of the Passion Play."

"You know it?"

"I was there once—in 1934. Right after Hitler came to power. It was a special year—the three-hundred-year anniversary of the play. Father—" Rachel stopped. Her heart ached. She blinked and pressed on. "Father and I attended in August—the same day the Führer attended. Father pointed him out to me." She sank back against the chair. "But he never said I had a sister living there." She looked at Jason, wishing for a lifeline. "Perhaps he didn't know."

"He knew, and his wife knew . . . from the beginning." Jason looked her squarely in the eye. "He and your adoptive mother were researchers, Rachel. You were their project, raised as an experiment—as was your sister, though it doesn't look like any of your biological family knows that."

She turned away, feeling suddenly gritty, dirty. *To be so devalued, so debased by my own father! But Mother . . . I truly thought she loved me. I don't know what to believe.* She swallowed. "Does it say who my real parents are?"

"Your mother's listed, but it looks like information on your father is missing."

"Missing?"

"I mean there's nothing about him—as if they didn't know who he was."

Rachel sighed, feeling another door to her life close. She leaned toward him. "Tell me about my birth mother. What is her name? Is she alive, after all?" Her heart beat with hope.

"No, I'm sorry."

She bit her lip.

"But there's a grandmother. I think she's still living."

"I have a grandmother?"

He sat back and pushed the remainder of the file across the table. "Look, you might want to read all this for yourself."

"And my sister?"

"She's alive—like I said, she's living in Oberammergau. Not always had an easy time of it, apparently, but she's there."

"My sister." Rachel said the words aloud. Two words that tasted as new as Creation. "I want to see her, to meet her." She wanted it more than anything she could imagine.

"There's something else."

"More?"

"My sources tell me Schlick has made a quick trip south—to Oberammergau. He returned less than happy."

Rachel felt her eyes go wide.

"I don't know what that means, but I'm guessing it can't be good for your sister or grandmother. I can't ask without tipping too many people off, and you never know who to trust for sure, who will hold out if they're picked up." He sat back, his eyes registering all the worry she felt.

Schlick had not hesitated to have his daughter killed, nor his wife. Rachel could only imagine what that might mean for the women in her family.

19

By THE TIME the SS roared away, Oma's house had been upended, closets torn to pieces and holes gouged in woodwork thought too hollow—possible hiding places for whom, neither Oma nor Lea comprehended. The attic had been ripped apart and the storm cellar's shelves emptied—canning jars of fruits and vegetables crashed to the floor and dried herbs and flowers batted back and forth in fury.

They'd twisted Lea's arm, and the taller man in charge had ripped her shirtwaist, running his hands where he pleased, demanding she tell him where *she* was hidden. Lea could only weep. Another had threatened Oma and slapped the old woman, forcing her to the floor, bruising her cheek. But neither understood whom they meant, what they wanted.

It was twenty minutes before the nightmare thundered back the way it had come, angry but apparently satisfied that *she* was not there. Still, the one in charge, the one with the driven eyes, threatened that it was no use to hide her, to hide anyone, and if she appeared, they were not to give her refuge but to turn her in right away. He tucked his calling card, with the name Sturmbannführer Gerhardt Schlick and a telephone number, into Lea's skirt, assuring the women that he had methods of finding her. When he did, if they'd done anything to help her, each of them would pay. He would be back.

Once they'd left, both women stayed where they were for some time, crumpled on the floor, barely daring to breathe, summoning their courage and bearings.

It was too frightening, too bizarre to comprehend.

Lea helped her grandmother to bed, bathed her cheek, and brought her hot tea. They didn't speak of the invasion, the violation. There were no words.

Once the old woman was settled, Lea returned to the kitchen sink, drew the curtains, and scrubbed her arms, her chest, her torso, with a vengeance. She did her best to straighten her torn clothing and hold her tears at bay. *Friederich! Friederich, I need you!*

She wrapped her grandmother's shawl around her, tying it tightly across her chest. She would return the next morning to help clean and straighten the house, but for now she must go home—home to Friederich's carvings and the quilt that had covered them both before he'd been called into service.

Lea walked quickly through the dark, glancing over her shoulder at every sound. When she finally reached her threshold, her heart stopped. The door stood wide. The same vandalism had stormed her home. The haven she and Friederich had built and shared and treasured had been trashed, his rows of carvings thrown against the wall, her porcelain figurines and the teacups she'd been given by Oma smashed.

It was too much. Lea shoved her nightdress into a bag, pushed Mildred, her calico cat, through the door, closed it, and retraced her steps, trudging up the hill. She would deal with it all tomorrow. But tonight she would sleep in the bed she'd grown up in. She would listen to Oma breathing in and out, and she would pray that Friederich would come home soon.

⊰•⊱

Rachel refused to change her mind though Jason had tried to reason with her for nearly an hour, to talk her out of racing to Oberammergau, saying he was certain that was the first place the Nazis would search for her, positive they'd lie in wait when they didn't find her the first time. Finally he'd given up, begged her to sleep on it, promised they'd talk the next day.

As soon as she locked the door behind him, Rachel drew the lamp close on the kitchen table. She pored over the photographed file, squinting to make out some of the wording. Pushing away conflicting memories of the only parents she'd known, Rachel concentrated on family she'd never met, never imagined existed.

"Lea. Her name is Lea." Rachel traced the facial features that could have been her own. But the hairstyle was different, the woman wore no makeup, and something about her eyes and mouth didn't match Rachel's own. Not in their shape, but in what they conveyed. Rachel couldn't quite put her finger on it, but it was something—some spark not there, a confidence lacking.

She shook her head. It could just be a trick of the photograph. She'd know when she met her.

"When I meet her," she whispered, closing her eyes, letting the words seep through her brain and into her bones. "My sister."

Rachel owed Jason everything; she knew that. She'd trusted him with her film, her story, her life—and Amelie's. He'd put his job and reputation at risk to help her—even his freedom, his life. And now she was asking him to help her again, to get her to a little Bavarian town far away, where they might already be looking for her. No wonder he didn't think it was safe. He probably believed it wouldn't take much to get her to spill everything she knew, incriminating him.

But he doesn't understand what it's meant to be alone—at least inside—all my life. To have always felt that some part of me was missing, and now, to suddenly learn that I have a sister—a sister and a twin—and a grandmother . . .

It was late when Rachel closed the file and turned down the light. She slipped beneath the blankets Sheila had left for her on the sofa, glad the generous young woman was not back yet. She wanted to be alone with her thoughts, her imaginings, for a little while longer. But her eyelids were heavy. It had been a long, emotional, frightening, thrilling, and exhausting day.

She closed her eyes—just to rest them a minute—and fell into a deep sleep, rich in magnificent snowcapped Alps, Bavarian window boxes spilling over with bright-red geraniums, and variegated ivy attached to cream-colored stucco houses painted in gigantic scenes from the Passion Play she'd seen years ago or domestic scenes from the village's country life. In her dream she walked the village, from end to end. At the very last house in the very last lane sat a quaint and cheerful cottage, a white-haired grandmotherly figure in Bavarian dress standing atop the stoop by the open door, arms spread wide, smiles wreathing her weathered face, welcoming her home.

When Rachel woke she closed her eyes again and bit her bottom lip, desperate to retrieve details, any tiny remnant of the dream. Because she knew it was just that. Life was beginning to show her that dreams were not always fulfilled. At least this way, she'd have something.

❦

By midday Lea had returned order to Oma's small kitchen and parlor. Together they mended the torn eiderdown, shaking their heads.

"As if someone could hide in an eiderdown!" Oma clucked her tongue.

"They meant to terrify us—to bully us."

Oma sighed. "They certainly did that. But why? What did they want? *Whom* did they want?"

Lea had no answer. Both women decided it best that Lea move back indefinitely—until Friederich returned. "Safety in numbers," Lea decided.

"At least comfort in numbers." Oma smiled, reaching for her granddaughter's hand.

Lea stayed all day until she walked into the village to teach choir practice. She slept at Oma's again that night and tackled her own home next morning.

Most of Friederich's carvings could be salvaged. Chips here and there—a nose or finger or staff gone that might or might not be found. But she would preserve them. She wasn't sure Friederich would want to keep them, but she could not bear to throw them into the fire. Her porcelain was not so fortunate. Painstakingly, she glued the larger pieces together—like a puzzle. When they were dry, she packed everything away. She would not invite destruction. It seemed it needed no invitation, and the hateful SS officer in charge had sworn he would return. She shuddered.

While packing Friederich's carvings, she made the decision not to write to him of the raid. *It will only worry him—drive him nearly mad that he can't be here to protect us. No, I won't have it on his mind as he faces all he must. It is enough. And if God should bring us together again, as He must—oh, He must!—then we will share what we've been through.* Lea brushed away a tear as she locked the door. In June, they'd been so hopeful for their future. But as the summer wore on and Friederich was conscripted, as she'd learned that she would never conceive, as Friederich had been deployed . . . all their hopes had fallen apart. And now this.

She lifted her head. *But it's not the end. No, I have the children's choir and I have Oma, and I will hold this day.*

Because nothing escaped the villagers of Oberammergau, everyone knew Lea and Frau Breisner had been visited by the SS. And everyone was curious why. What had two simple women done to bring the scrutiny of the SS to their village and terror upon their heads? But Lea couldn't tell what she did not know.

A month ago she would have felt their stares and suspicion intimidating, judgmental, perhaps even calculating. But in many eyes she now saw fear, pity, concern, a "there but for the grace of God go I" camaraderie. And she was grateful. She would take that, embrace that.

The children, with their high, lilting voices, so lifted her spirits that by the time choir practice was over, Lea had determined to lift Oma's.

When she opened Oma's back kitchen door late that Friday afternoon, the magnificent aroma of apple strudel baking welcomed her home. Lea smiled as she unwound her muffler and hung it by the door, glad that she was cut from the same frugal but celebratory cloth as her grandmother. They would be vigilant and better prepared if they should be visited again. Together, they would survive.

An hour later, aged and wrinkled hands that had trembled in fear in the presence of the SS days before trembled in mirth. Oma spooned a second helping of steaming cabbage soup and weak coffee—the last of their real coffee—while Lea regaled her with tales from the children's choir.

Oma finally begged Lea to stop the hilarity, but to no avail. Helpless, she snorted coffee and doubled over at Lea's impersonation of the irrepressible six-year-old Heinrich.

"One stunt after another—and another—and another!" Lea spouted. "He tied ribbons together from the girls' plaits in front of him, and when they were to separate in staid formation both girls fell to the floor, skirts flying above their knees and scrambling like sea crabs—their heads bound together!" She threw up her hands. "How the room howled! And such a straight face! I never saw such a devil with an archangel smile!"

"Oh, Lea—you mustn't say such things!" Oma admonished, eyes twinkling.

"It's true!" And both women erupted again.

Oma wiped her tears with her napkin, then reached across the table to wipe the liquid laughter from Lea's cheeks. "You are happy, aren't you, my child?"

Lea grasped her grandmother's hand. "Yes. They're not my own children, I know, but most like my own that I'll ever experience. I want to give them everything I have to give—every ounce of love and help and devotion, while I can. I want them to feel the joy they give me! I won't waste these precious days being afraid."

"I'm so proud of you, my Lea!"

Lea hesitated, then whispered, as though someone might over-hear, "Sometimes I fear that this—working with the children—is a dream that will be suddenly swept away. The way those men came so suddenly. Everything is . . . is temporary, isn't it?" She breathed, then caught her breath. "I'm almost afraid to be happy, especially in the midst of such madness and uncertainty—as though it might be wrong. As though *I'm* wrong."

"No, oh no, my Lea. Joy is the gift of God, and you are His child. He loves you so. He rejoices over you with singing!"

Lea lifted her head and smiled. She wanted to believe that. But shades of doubt crept through her heart.

20

RACHEL FELT LIKE a ping-pong ball bounced between Jason and Sheila as they sat round the table in Sheila's apartment just before curfew.

"You can't carry any portion of that file with you," Jason insisted. "If it's found on you, every person listed is in deep trouble."

"But I want my sister to see it—she'll need proof that I'm who I say I am," Rachel argued.

"If you're stopped," Sheila said quietly, "they'll want to know where you got it."

"I took the photographs myself—from my father's files. I'm not afraid to implicate him. They already have him in custody, for pete's sake!"

"But you'll drag Jason down with you. They'll want to know who developed the film—when and where. You need to memorize your family details, as well as names, addresses, train schedules—as though you've known them all your life. You absolutely have to remain in disguise at all times." Sheila sat back. "Your twin's identical; you shouldn't have trouble convincing her or your grandmother that you're Ibine Breisner's daughter."

"The tougher job will be convincing her to take you in—and maybe Amelie—for the duration, or at least until I can arrange safe passage for both of you to Switzerland. Or better yet, the States. If I can find Amelie." Jason drummed his fingers across the table.

"What does that mean?"

"My contact was arrested two weeks after the explosion. The

Gestapo doesn't look kindly on supplying Jews with forged ration books. I can't get in to see him. The brass isn't in the mood for prison visitors from the foreign press."

"Jason." Rachel didn't know what to say.

Jason shook his head. "I'd agreed to one connection for safety's sake. Big mistake. Now some guy's demanding more money—he claims it's too risky, and the woman hiding Amelie needs more incentive to keep her. I've got to get her to you and both of you to safety."

Rachel hesitated. It was one thing getting Jason to save her friend's child, to see that she was settled in a German home with a German woman who probably knew something about raising children. It was another to care for her personally. If she'd been able to take Amelie to New York, there were homes, schools for deaf children. She hadn't imagined raising her herself.

But she didn't like the way Jason was looking at her. He seemed to see her hesitation in a new light, as if he'd tasted something sour. Rachel pulled her best acting face, assuring him that she could hardly wait. If it came to pass that she actually needed to take care of Amelie, she'd pull that off too . . . somehow. It promised to be the most convincing performance she'd ever give. As long as she could imagine acting the leading role in a challenging drama, she just might be able to hold fear at bay.

The threesome spent the next two evenings inventing a character for Rachel and perfecting her disguise. The third night Jason arrived with her new passport concealed in the lining of his jacket: Elsa Breisner, age fifty-seven, from Stelle.

Sheila offered to dye her hair several shades darker and streak it heavily with gray. "It will grow out. But at least guards at the station won't see a honey blonde when they're looking."

"But if I've the same color hair as Lea, that will help convince my family." Rachel loved the words *my family* and used them at every conceivable opportunity, savoring their taste on her tongue. She didn't want to admit vanity—that she loved the color of her hair, that it was a significant part of who she believed herself to be. "A wig and a kerchief will work. Can you get them?"

Sheila lifted her brows, clearly not fooled. They'd settle for powdering her hair gray.

During the next week they perfected her papers, her story, her disguise, and did the best they could with her accent. Rachel alternately panicked and champed at the bit to go.

Ready or not, the time of departure finally came. The night before, Rachel hugged Jason in an awkward good-bye. Sheila packed her bags to leave for the States, where she would drop Rachel's passport aboard ship as it neared New York. Jason's plan just might work, since the Germans already knew of Rachel's attempt to leave the country.

They all hoped that Germany's fixation remained on London's response to Hitler's peace proposal and the end of recognized Polish resistance, that the circulation of Rachel's photograph through checkpoints was no longer news.

"I can't thank you enough—for everything." Rachel allowed Sheila to fold her in her arms before they left separately for the train station.

"I sure hope you'll thank me later, kid." Sheila's eyes clouded. "Be careful. Be safe. Don't write!" She grinned. "But when this is all over—and someday it will be—you owe me a meal, a bed, and a drink in New York."

"Done." Rachel shook her hand, clinching the deal. "A night on the town and a place to crash—for as long as you want—in New York." Those words sounded so good, so impossibly far away.

And then Sheila was gone. They'd agreed that Rachel should wait until the courtyard monitor left for his daily marketing, then slip down the apartment stairs and out through the back gate.

Rachel washed the breakfast dishes and stacked them in the cupboard. She wiped the hot plate and table, folded up her flannel sheets and returned them to the top shelf of the closet. Domestic duties were new to her, but for now it all seemed like part of the script.

She set her bag behind the door, then perched on the edge of a kitchen chair to wait another hour. Never had the minutes passed so slowly, or the clock on the wall ticked so loudly.

21

BERLIN TO MUNICH, the train stopped several times, both to take on and discharge passengers at appointed stations and to heed military checkpoints. At each checkpoint, armed guards roamed the aisles, checking papers at will.

"They're looking for Jews, you know," the woman beside Rachel whispered. "As if they don't know enough now to ride in the baggage car." The woman clucked her tongue.

Rachel swallowed. She'd barely paid attention to the talk at her father's table in New York of reducing immigration quotas of undesirable Eastern Europeans. She simply took it for granted that he knew best, that they would indeed weaken American bloodlines. But here she saw the prejudice, the hate, living and breathing before her.

Even if the Jews are not the same as us, the harassment is inhuman. Why don't the German people stand up, do something—revolt? As the officer neared, she sat back, knowing why.

Just before they reached Munich, the papers of a woman two seats in front of her were checked, and those of her son beside her. Rachel could barely see the boy's profile. He was young, too short for his head to reach the top of the bench back. "Your name is Cohen? Jewish?"

"No—I mean, that was my husband's name. He's . . . he's no longer living." The woman spoke out, her voice shaking only a little at the official's intimidation.

"So, a Jew whore. This is your son?"

"Erich, my son." She didn't acknowledge his slur.

"This boy's name is Cohen?"

"Yes, of course."

"And he's half-Jewish, *ja*?"

"*Ja*, but he's only a child, and he is with me."

"A Jew is a Jew—he sits in the baggage car or goes off the train."

"Please, *mein Herr*, I—I'll hold him on my lap, if that is more acceptable."

But the official was not about to lose face in front of the other passengers. He'd make an example of the woman and her son. Rachel saw it in his expression. She drew in a breath and held it.

"Up!" The official jerked the boy from his seat, shoving him along the aisle. The mother grabbed her bag and the parcels they'd stowed, stumbling after him.

"Not you!" the guard shouted, forcing her back toward her seat.

"But he's my child!"

"A child by the road if you don't sit down. This is what comes from sleeping with *der Juden*!"

The boy, eyes wild in terror, said nothing.

The horrified woman looked from one passenger to another, a desperate plea for help. But Rachel saw them look away, bury their heads in newspapers and books, look out the window, even feign sleep—as if anyone could sleep through that.

Rachel wanted to stand, to stomp after the repugnant official and give him a sharp piece of her mind, put him in his place for the outrageous bully he was. When the young mother glanced toward her, Rachel felt as if she must see into her soul, must know what she was thinking, imagining, refusing to do.

Rachel looked away. She could not help the woman or the boy, dared bring no attention to herself lest she be discovered. *But what if I wasn't running, wasn't hiding myself? Would I help him then? And even if I am . . .* She closed her eyes, leaned back against the bench, and feigned sleep. She only knew she was very much afraid.

22

HILDE BREISNER laid her heavy, braided carpets saddle-style over wooden benches set squarely in her garden and beat them with a vengeance. There was nothing she liked better than beating the swirling dust from her rugs when she had something on her mind. She found it satisfying in the extreme—no matter the doctor's warning about overtaxing her heart. *Whack!*

She'd tried for days to push the SS raid from her mind. But something they'd said—before Lea arrived—kept running through her brain.

Whack!

They'd demanded to know if her granddaughter had come. She couldn't imagine why they wanted Lea, but she didn't want to tell them where she was.

Whack!

And yet when Lea suddenly appeared, they didn't seem to want her after all. They said they wanted "the other one." It was so puzzling. Surely they had the wrong Breisners.

Whack!

"Frau Breisner?" A halting, middle-aged voice with a slightly strained accent spoke from the back garden gate.

"Ja?" Hilde jumped. "I'm Frau Breisner." She hated when visitors came to call in the midst of her housework. Everyone in the village knew you didn't make calls until after midday meal and the washing up! It was an unwritten rule that only outsiders would not observe.

"May I speak with you, Frau Breisner?" The woman with gray-streaked hair stood patiently on the garden walk. "Alone?"

Hilde spread her hands wide, open to the great out-of-doors. "We're quite alone here." She wiped them on her apron, eyeing the woman's carpetbag. "But if you're peddling wares, *meine Frau*, you'd best go along. I've no money to buy." She turned back to her rug beating.

"*Nein, meine Frau!* I'm not peddling anything at all, but—" the woman lowered her voice and spoke with some urgency—"I must speak with you—privately."

The voice rang stronger than the woman's appearance warranted, and that gave Hilde pause. There was also something familiar about her. Her face? Her eyes? Hilde shook her head. She'd never seen this woman before; she was sure of it. "What is it you want?"

The woman glanced from side to side—nervously, Hilde thought. "Please, Frau Breisner, allow me to come inside—to sit and talk with you. It's . . . it's important to us both . . . and very personal."

Hilde frowned, discomfort rumbling in the lower regions of her stomach. She'd heard about foreigners slipping into Oberammergau, begging to be taken into homes as parts of Germany emptied of its Jews and Poles.

She felt sorry for them, of course. Hitler had created havoc and there were rumors of random cruelty. But those things were far from Oberammergau. The people of the Passion Play would not behave so—it violated everything the Passion stood for, at least ideally. Of course she knew the play, as it stood, was anti-Semitic. That didn't mean the villagers were. At least she hoped not. At least not all of them.

But we're not likely to bite the hand that pays our bills, are we? Still, she doesn't look Jewish, or even Polish. But who can tell these days? "How did you get here?"

"Excuse me?" The woman leaned closer, anxiety apparent in her eyes.

Hilde sighed. She was never good at refusing to help beggars, no matter that she could not afford another mouth to feed. "You couldn't have walked far with that bag, *meine Frau*. Where did you come from? Who's with you?" Hilde wasn't about to be reported for harboring fugitives—Jews or others—or at least she wouldn't be tricked. If she harbored anyone, it would be with full information and because she chose to help.

"No one—I walked from the train station in the village."

Hilde walked to the street and looked up and down. Not a soul in sight.

"Please," the woman begged, "please don't do that. Let me talk with you in private."

"Whatever you want to say to me can be said out here—in the bright light of day."

The woman's eyes widened, looking even more agitated. Hilde thought again that there was something familiar in the woman's expression, but she determined to hold her ground.

"Oma," the woman whispered.

Hilde felt a catch in her heart. "What did you say?"

The woman, still stooped, stepped closer. But her voice lost its crackling as she whispered, "I've news of your daughter."

Breath sucked from Hilde's lungs. She recognized the eyes—her daughter's eyes. Lea's eyes. But she insisted, "My daughter is dead."

"Yes, yes, she is. But I'm her daughter—your granddaughter, Rachel."

The garden spun in all its lovely colors. As Hilde tottered, the woman dropped her carpetbag and caught her, but with the surprising strength of youth. Confused, desperate for her rocker in the kitchen, Hilde motioned toward the house.

<hr>

Tenderly, Rachel settled her grandmother in the rocker just inside the kitchen door, then filled a stein from the spigotted barrel on the counter. While her grandmother drank, catching her breath, Rachel retrieved her bag from the garden, careful to take up her slow gait while outdoors.

Once inside, she locked the door and drew the nearest curtain across its rod. She pulled a low stool near the rocker and waited. But she could not take her eyes from those that mirrored her own.

She searched the lines of Hilde Breisner's face, the cheekbones, the length of her knotted fingers—more similarities than she could count. It was as if she gazed upon herself fifty years into the future. And it was all she could do not to laugh, to cry over the old woman before her.

When the woman seemed to calm, Rachel reached for her hand. "I'm Ibine's daughter."

Hilde pulled back, her eyes wide and brow furrowed. She shook her head. "You're from the Institute. The SS sent you, didn't they? Please, please leave us alone!"

Rachel's heart sank. Jason was right. Gerhardt had already been here, had probably tormented her grandmother, perhaps Lea as well. She brushed the powder from her hair to show its mask.

Hilde gasped, sputtered, but no words came.

"I know this sounds fantastic—impossible." Rachel leaned forward. "I have so much to tell you, to ask you, but I must warn you that there are people looking for me. If I'm found here, it will be dangerous for me and certainly for you and Lea."

"Why are you doing this?" The old woman's eyes filled with tears, fury and fear and wonder so clearly mingled. "What do you want?"

"Oh no—please—I don't want to hurt anyone. I wanted only to meet you, to ask you—"

The door latch rattled, and a knock came at the door. "Oma?" a lilting voice, tinged with worry, called. "Are you in there? What's going on? Why is your door locked?"

But the older woman didn't answer, didn't seem able to answer. She couldn't catch her breath, and then a wheezing started. Panic sprang to her eyes, and she motioned toward the far wall. Rachel dropped her hand, not knowing where to turn, what to do.

The knocking became a pounding. "Oma—open the door! Are you all right? Who is with you? Will you not open the door?"

The old woman grasped her throat, her chest. Rachel threw open the door to the young woman with the pounding fist—a young woman who looked for all the world like a provincial mirror image of herself. "She's having a seizure—a heart attack—I don't know! Help her! Oh, please help her!"

Rachel hadn't finished her plea before the young woman pushed her aside and ran to the gasping Oma.

Oma threw her hand toward the far wall.

"Your tablets? In the cupboard?" Jerking open a cupboard door and rummaging through a host of small pottery and jars, the young woman grabbed a brown bottle and pulled the cork. "Hold on, Oma, I'm coming."

But Oma seemed to be losing focus.

"Open your mouth." She forced two tablets between Oma's teeth, beneath her tongue, then sat back on her heels, gently rubbing her arm, her back. "Rest there. Just rest a bit." She waited until Oma calmed, began breathing easier.

Never had Rachel witnessed such a tender and proficient bedside manner, not in all the doctors she'd encountered through her father's work.

But when the young woman turned toward her, her back to Oma, her face clouded and her eyes threatened. She pulled Rachel into the next room. "What happened?"

Frightened as much by the younger woman's anger as by Oma's attack, Rachel sputtered, "I don't know. She just . . . What's wrong with her?"

"Her heart is weak. She can't—" But the young woman hesitated, staring, as if she'd just seen Rachel.

"Lea. You're Lea." The wonder Rachel felt at seeing her twin nearly stopped her own heart.

"Who are you?" Lea looked as if she gazed upon a ghost.

"I'm Rachel. I'm your sister."

"My—sis—?"

"Your twin," Rachel pressed. "Ibine Breisner was my mother—and yours."

But the woman named Lea paled, shaking her head. "That's not possible. My mother died in childbirth. I was her only child."

The old woman gasped again. Rachel and Lea both turned. "Oma!" they said, almost in unison.

Lea's brows rose and she stepped between her grandmother and Rachel. "Did Dr. Mengele send you to torment us?"

"No!"

"Dr. Verschuer, then," Lea accused. "We've had enough—*enough*. Get out!"

"I'm not from the Institute!" Now Rachel was very near tears. "I'm trying to escape them!"

"It was you they were after. The SS came looking for you. They terrified Oma and nearly destroyed her house—and mine. They said there is a woman who looks like me. They said if she came, not to believe anything she said. They vowed they'd be back, and if we took her in, we'd pay."

"I'm sorry they hurt you, but that should say something for me—that I'm not part of them." Rachel leaned forward. "Our mother birthed twins. We were separated when she died." She lowered her voice. "I think they let her die, may have even helped her die. They sent me to America, to be raised there, but sent you to be raised by our grandmother."

Lea shook her head. "You're making this up."

Rachel hardly knew how to respond. Her script had fallen apart.

Oma groaned again, trying to regain her breath.

Lea fetched and rolled a towel, tucking it beneath Oma's head at the back of the wooden rocker. "Just rest, Oma," she crooned.

Rachel knelt before her. "I'm sorry I upset you. I just wanted to meet you—to meet you both."

Oma reached her hand out to Rachel. Rachel grasped it like a lifeline.

"Well, you've met us," Lea said coldly.

"Lea, Lea," Oma scolded gently. Her eyes turned again to Rachel, back and forth between the two young women. "Can it be—?"

"No, Oma. Don't let her fool you. *Meine Mutter* had only one child."

"That's what I thought too," Rachel asserted, the words thick in her throat. "That I was an only child. That's what I was always told at the Institute and by my adoptive parents."

"My Ibine—twins," Oma said in wonder.

Rachel bit her lip. "I would not hurt you for the world, but I must talk with you. I must know about my mother, my father—so many things." She hesitated. "And I must ask you to hide me."

❧❦

It was a full hour before Oma had sufficiently recovered, before Lea felt she could take her eyes from her grandmother. In that time, Rachel told them enough that Lea came to believe her—though Rachel's story was fantastic, something she might read in a suspenseful thriller novel brought from England by one of Friederich's customers.

It was the details of the link through the abominable Institute in Frankfurt that convinced Lea—that and the fact that when Rachel had washed her face and combed the powder from her hair, she looked like Lea's own reflection, only more modern. She could only shake her head at the impossibility of it all and do her best to push the besetting weight from her heart.

Lea couldn't think only of herself or her fear that the SS might appear on their doorstep again in search of Rachel. She saw in Oma's eyes the horrific realization that the Institute had allowed her precious Ibine, her only child, to die in order to conduct experiments on her identical twin daughters. *Help us, Holy Father; help us.*

But what could they do with Rachel? How could they help her leave Germany with border patrols searching for her?

"You'll stay here with us, of course!" Oma proclaimed. "Lea's here while her Friederich is away."

"They'll come back looking for her. We've no place to hide her!"

"Then we'll make a place." Oma reached for her granddaughters' hands.

"There's more," Rachel confessed.

"More?" Lea wasn't certain they could take more.

"A child," Rachel began.

"You've a child?" Oma gasped. "My great-grandchild!"

Lea's heart tripped.

"Not mine; she's the child of a friend. But I'm . . . responsible for her. I'll take her to the United States, just as soon as we can find a way out of Germany." She told them about Gerhardt Schlick and the T4 program, about the ruse to make him believe his child had been killed and about Kristine's murder. It was evil beyond Lea's imagination or Oma's ability to speak.

"So now this madman is looking not only for you but for his child! Here, in Oberammergau!" Lea nearly cried.

"He doesn't know that Amelie is alive! He's certain she's dead, and he doesn't know I've come."

"We can't hide you—and can't hide a child." Lea couldn't believe she was saying it. "The neighbors see everything—know everything!"

"She's here?" Oma's eyes clouded.

"No, but a friend will bring her here—if you'll allow it. I'm to send a note through the mail in a kind of code. She's very small—only four years old." Rachel's eyes pleaded.

"Bring her!"

But Lea squeezed Oma's hand, urging her to slow down, to think.

Inspiration sprang to Oma's eyes. "Lea teaches children from the orphanage, from town, and from the refugees trickling into the village. We can say we've taken in refugees. She can blend right into the village." She half smiled in wonder. "But you must remain in disguise. If anyone saw the two of you as you are—even separately—they would know immediately that you were sisters."

"Amelie's deaf—she can't blend in." Rachel looked the most uncomfortable Lea had seen her. "She wouldn't be able to sing, and she can't be seen. She truly can't be seen by anyone."

❧ Part II ❧
October 1939

23

AMELIE HADN'T sucked her thumb in a long time. But in the dark of night, tucked into a makeshift pallet beneath the eaves of the farmhouse attic, she slipped it into her mouth. It comforted her a little, though it was no substitute for her mother.

She couldn't understand what had happened, what she'd done to deserve being pulled from her mother's fragrant arms weeks and weeks ago, or shoved into the smoky, smelly woolen blanket, or jostled over bumping roads and finally thrust into the arms of a woman she'd never met—a woman who immediately cut the curls from Amelie's head and shaped her hair like a boy's.

Amelie didn't like the scratchy shirt or the lederhosen or the dirty woolen cap she'd been dressed in. She missed her pretty dresses and her mother fussing over her hair. She missed the soft ringlets that her mother sometimes twitched to tickle her cheeks, and she even missed bath time.

She dreamed of her mother, but when she woke the image of her smile faded as quickly as the morning dew outside the kitchen window. Amelie feared that if she forgot her mother, her mother would forget her.

The woman with the greasy apron fed her, smiled sometimes, and moved her mouth in kind ways—much as her mother had done. But she couldn't speak in signs at all, no matter how desperately or often Amelie signed her questions. "Where is Mutti? Where is Mutti?" brought no response. Amelie placed her hand on the woman's chest, her throat, her face, and felt the same sort of soft rumbles that she'd felt when leaning against her mother.

But the woman didn't smell the same, and her skin was not soft and silky as her mother's had been. The woman carried the lingering fragrance of the animals in the barn and farmyard just outside the kitchen door—the big-eyed cow, the strutting goose, the wallowing pig, even a tinge of the humble brown donkey with the rough and scruffy coat. All of that was enveloped with the yeasty smell of baking bread.

Never had Amelie tasted such delicious freshly baked bread or such creamy yellow butter, spread thinly though it was. The woman even spread her buttered bread with sweet black-currant jam—a rare thing. Her mother had tended to withhold the dark-purple sweet, smiling but shaking a gentle finger when Amelie reached for the crockery pot.

Still, Amelie cried herself to sleep at night. Sometimes the lady would climb the attic stairs and scoop her up and rock her gently. Amelie never knew when or if this would happen, or why she chose to do it. In those tender moments Amelie tried signing again, but it seemed to frustrate the lady, and she pushed Amelie's hands away.

People came and went all times of the day and night, and sometimes Amelie was quickly shown to sit beneath the kitchen sink, behind a curtain that draped to the floor. The woman motioned for Amelie to keep very still, and Amelie tried her best to obey. She usually fell asleep obeying.

❦

That first night, Lea's pen dripped a blot of ink on the kitchen table as she hesitated over her letter to Friederich. *Another secret—a litany of secrets. Another "something" I will not tell my husband . . . for fear he'd worry about things he can't help or prevent? For fear he would have me turn Rachel out for the danger in which she and this hunted deaf child will place us? No. For fear he would have me embrace them beyond my ability. For fear she is so like me—but more of everything than I can ever be—and comes with a child in need of love! How she would appeal to Friederich—to his manliness and protective nature.* Lea bit her lip. *She's said nothing of whether the Institute—* She choked back a sob.

Lea did not finish the letter, but folded and placed it in its envelope. She'd work on it again tomorrow. She turned out the light, checked on Oma, who breathed softly and rhythmically in her sleep, and walked to the little room she'd grown up in. She slipped her shoes beneath the bed, turned down the coverlet, and slid in next to her sister.

Lea turned to her side, facing away from her roommate. Rachel might indeed be her twin, her decidedly more beautiful twin, but Lea was the one married to Friederich, and she was the one Oma had raised as her own daughter. She must make certain this interloper did not forget she was exactly that. And she'd remind her, at every opportunity, of the danger in which she'd placed them.

24

THE CLOCK in the newsroom ticked off the half hours: four, four thirty, five, five thirty, six in the morning. Jason stretched, pushing the heels of his hands into his eyes, trying to rub some life into his spent brain. He'd met his deadline an hour before but couldn't bring himself to dodge the overzealous early-morning patrols back to his hotel. He'd wait an hour longer, then try to find someplace that served breakfast on a Sunday morning.

There might be just enough time to get to his hotel, shave, and grab a fresh shirt before the underground church service. He stood, stretching again, reaching for the ceiling and plunging his hands toward the floor, arching the ache in his back like a cat.

He wasn't a churchgoing man—no time or inclination, and nobody made him go growing up. But this was for the sake of a story about some rebel pacifist preacher who'd helped found that new church he'd covered before—the Confessing Church—and who'd dared to thumb his nose at Hitler's policies. He'd declared, when Hitler had barely settled into office, that no one but Jesus Christ is the true leader, the true teacher. For that first tirade, his radio program had been cut midstream. More recently, Bonhoeffer'd been banned from preaching in Berlin.

The thing that puzzled Jason and interested his editor was why Dietrich Bonhoeffer had returned to Berlin at all. Granted, his family was here. But Bonhoeffer had been safely stowed away in America, according to Jason's sources. He'd returned to Germany because he said he couldn't allow his church to go through these days alone, that he'd have no right to take part in the restoration of Christian life in Germany after the war unless he shared the trials of this time with his people. That sort of rebellion and heroism—misguided or not—was right up Jason's alley, and fodder for a great story.

And he needed a story. The whole thing with Rachel Kramer had blown up in his face. When a rival American news reporter had scooped him on the detention of Dr. Rudolph Kramer and the mysterious disappearance of his daughter, Chief had raked him over the coals, threatening to ship him to China—especially since Jason had pegged Kramer's daughter at the gala in August.

If the chief only knew! The real story was a dynamite tale—one worthy of a novel, if not a Pulitzer. But Jason dared not print it—not here, and not in America. He couldn't be linked to any of the players.

Jason knew Rachel's picture had been circulated to newspapers, Gestapo, checkpoints, and border patrols. She was as good as labeled an enemy of the Reich, was to be arrested on sight and brought to Berlin for questioning. Jason closed his eyes, sighed, and wished for the hundredth time that he knew she was safe. That's all he wanted—all he asked. But he knew that safe now was not safe later. Rachel, her grandmother, and her sister were all targets for the SS.

If all had gone well, Sheila should have dropped Rachel's passport aboard the ocean liner by now. Once the authorities found it, they'd presume she'd somehow slipped into the States without being documented. The fat should hit the fire when she didn't turn up in Manhattan. There'd be accusations flying back and forth between the US and Germany—unless, like all the other stories Jason felt mattered, it was buried in the back pages and no one cared after all. No one but Gerhardt Schlick and the Institute's pack of pseudoscience doctors.

If I want to stay in Germany, I'd better make good and dredge up something that shows just what rot the Reich is up to, without rubbing their noses so deeply in the stench they kick me out of the country. He sat up. *Okay, so that's my specialty—skate the thin edge, trip the light fantastic.*

Jason wound his watch, setting it against the wall clock. He straightened his tie, slung his jacket over his shoulder, and stuffed a small notepad and pen in his shirt pocket. He hoped Bonhoeffer could keep him awake.

Two hours later, with a hot breakfast in his stomach and a fresh shirt on his back, Jason slipped through the side door of the address he'd been given. A woman welcomed him to her home. He scanned the faces of the balding and middle-aged men congregating near the front of the large parlor. Surely one of those was his man.

Jason had heard of the Bonhoeffer family plenty of times—everybody knew the preacher's father, Dr. Bonhoeffer, eminent psychologist. But he hadn't run into the preacher. The overflowing home church shifted to life and order. Two hymns were sung a cappella, infused with more feeling than Jason had expected. Midway through the second hymn, a man in a tweed suit walked from the back of the room, stepping up to the makeshift pulpit. He was a tall, blond fellow, not much older than Jason. Athletic, broad-shouldered, square-jawed. He looked more like a German soccer player than a preacher.

He sang with gusto—a far-reaching baritone. But when the room fell silent and he adjusted his wire-rimmed glasses, preparing to speak, the action lent him a studious, professorial bent.

Jason leaned forward, determined to catch every word, to find a story his editor would buy. But three minutes in, he knew he'd never get the fiery oratory of a rebel—certainly none of the pulpit-pounding passion he would've expected to hear from a man of such reputation in the US. Short on sleep, Jason pinched his arm to concentrate, translating the German in his head.

The man spoke quietly, earnestly, peering into their eyes, as if they'd just sat down for a cup of coffee but he had something urgent to share. His sentences tended to be lengthy, his thoughts complex, as though through reason alone he could implant his message, ensure stability.

The preacher's physical presence dominated and his sermon challenged, though it was not overtly political. What Jason knew at the end of the hour was that Dietrich Bonhoeffer had foreseen the stripping of Christ from the altars of Germany. He'd seen the Nazification of the German church as they'd accepted their Führer as its head and sovereign, replacing Christ. He'd read the truth in Hitler's *Mein Kampf* about the intended murder of innocents—long before anyone on either side of the Atlantic had believed the madman could be serious about eliminating Jews or Poles or handicapped children or infirm elderly. Hadn't it all been there in black and white? Wasn't Hitler doing just what he'd written?

"Germany is at stake—heart and soul!"

Jason nearly whistled and stomped. *He gets it!*

Bonhoeffer declared, "When the church stops standing for Jews—for anyone—then we stop being the church. Grace is costly—it took the death of our Lord Jesus Christ, our Savior, to achieve that grace. It requires just as much from each of us.

"But we've come to practice cheap grace—grace that appears as a godly form but costs us nothing—and that is an abomination, a stench in the nostrils of God!"

Jason had not heard anyone so openly address the responsibility of the German church to stand against Nazi cruelty to Jews, against Hitler's manipulation of the National Reich Church—not even behind closed doors. It was a death sentence. And yet the young preacher didn't seem afraid for himself—only for the fate of Germany, and for the soul of the collective church.

Glancing around the room, Jason wondered if the others got it too. The woman who'd welcomed him smiled in return and nodded, a fire of purpose in her eyes.

He couldn't sing the last hymn for the preacher's words ringing in his ears. All he could think was, *What now? What can we do?*

❦

Late in the afternoon, as the three women drank roasted chicory and shared slivers of sugarless seedcake, Lea explained to Rachel that she never knew who their father was.

"My poor Ibine was raped while visiting friends in Munich," Oma insisted. "She never told me the man's name. I don't even know if she knew him. There was a party, and she was found unconscious in the bushes the next morning." Tears streaked Oma's cheeks, and she drew a deep breath. "She was never the same. So we sent her to stay with relatives near Frankfurt until she had the baby, hoping it would help her. Such a mistake! They took her to the Institute to deliver her child. It was the closest medical facility to their home. They never imagined—*I* never imagined my daughter would not return . . . or that she'd borne twins."

Lea didn't wait for Rachel to absorb that information but grilled her about her adoptive parents, her life in America, her father's research, details about the files she'd seen, and about Amelie. She'd barely finished when Oma, somewhat recovered, made the observation about their names.

"Rachel and Lea . . . names from the Bible. They were sisters—daughters of Laban." She puzzled, "If my Ibine did not live to . . . to see you, I wonder who chose your names? The doctor or midwife who delivered you? They aren't typical German names."

Rachel shrugged helplessly.

"From the Bible—both good wives of Jacob." Oma nodded approvingly, then blinked, as though she'd just thought of something.

"Do you think that's why we were named so—some literary allusion? Does that mean something?" Rachel looked from one to the other. "I don't know the story. Can you tell me?"

164

Lea knew that Oma would not say. So she did what she must, what would come out sooner or later anyway.

"A man named Jacob—heir to the covenant God made with Abraham—loved Rachel and wanted to marry her. Her father, Laban, promised his daughter to Jacob on the condition that he work for seven years. But on the wedding night Laban tricked Jacob and sent the older daughter, Leah, to his tent." Lea moistened her lips and glanced at Oma, who stared into the coffee cup cradled in her hands. "When Jacob discovered he'd been fooled, he was furious and demanded Rachel as well. Laban gave her to Jacob soon after, but forced him to serve another seven years for her."

Rachel's eyes widened in disbelief. "That's horrible! What a long time to work for, to wait for someone."

Lea did her best to control her voice. "Laban said it was their custom that the older daughter marry before the younger. But perhaps it didn't seem so long—because Jacob loved her. Rachel was the more beautiful of the two, the woman he desired." Lea forced herself to look Rachel in the eye, challenging her reaction. She glanced again at Oma and knew her grandmother understood her heart.

"At least he ended up with two wives." Rachel laughed—self-consciously.

"And many children," Oma observed, as if trying to match Rachel's optimism and engage Lea. "Just like your children's choir."

"Yes, she gave him many children. Leah was not barren." Lea glimpsed the flush across Oma's cheek. "But he only truly loved one." The perpetual knot in Lea's stomach tightened.

Oma shifted in her seat, as if that would change the subject. "We must decide on a hiding place for you—and the child." Determination strengthened her voice. "I won't—I can't—let you go so soon." She looked from Rachel to Lea. Lea had rarely seen her grandmother so happy. "And when they come looking again, they will find no one."

Rachel responded in kind, radiating gratitude, happiness, no matter that they could all be signing a death warrant, no matter that they'd thought of no way to hide her or the child. Lea watched the familial bond spring between the two—withered flowers soaking in spring rain. Brightening, straightening, strengthening before her eyes. And that, too, was dangerous.

She stood. It was nearly time for the children's choir practice. "Do you have everything you need before I go, Oma?"

"I do!" Oma reached for Lea's hand, beaming, still clasping Rachel's with her other. "I do!"

"If it's settled then, I'll write the note to bring Amelie." Rachel beamed in return. "Can you post it for me tomorrow? It would be safer not to post it here in the village."

Lea nodded, though her heart was not in it. The coded letter would bring the child—now Rachel's child. Leah fingered her letter to Friederich, tucked into her pocket. She'd post that today—general as it was and omitting so many important events.

Keeping her emotions in check, she pushed her arms through her coat sleeves and wound her muffler round her neck. Rachel strode from the room to prepare her note, purpose in every step. It was the first moment since Rachel had arrived that Lea and Oma were alone.

"It will be all right," Oma whispered. "Everything will be all right; you'll see."

"Rachel and Lea. It's almost laughable, were it not so pitiable—so true a picture."

"But it's Lea your Friederich loves—has always loved. You're the one with the home, the husband, the lifetime we've shared, the Passion Play, the children's choir. Rachel is running, hiding. She's been betrayed—no home or family but us, no understanding of life beyond herself, no faith as near as I can tell. You are the one with abundance, my dear. It's possible to be generous, isn't it?"

"They probably said that to Leah when Jacob spurned her."

"He did not spurn her for long," Oma teased. "They had seven children!"

Lea pulled away from her grandmother. "Because she'd not been sterilized. And, I'd wager, neither has Rachel."

❦

For two days Bonhoeffer's words haunted Jason, the challenge they issued in his brain growing ever louder.

"It's not even my country," he argued with the mirror as he shaved in miserably cold water. "And even if it was, who can stop Hitler?" He scrutinized the question one way after another as he ate, as he tossed and turned before sleep, as he stepped from the trolley, then found himself in the newspaper office—never realizing he'd walked the distance between the two.

He couldn't get the preacher or the image he'd created of Jesus' costly grace out of his head. *What is this costly grace that compels Bonhoeffer? What compelled Jesus?*

It wasn't until the third morning that Jason summoned enough courage to face his own shortcomings. He'd track Bonhoeffer down and talk with him. But it was too late. Frau Bergstrom, the woman who'd hosted the preacher's service in her house, told him that Bonhoeffer had left for Pomerania. She gave Jason his book, *Nachfolge*, saying that would better explain the preacher's position.

Jason read, mentally translating *Nachfolge*, or *Discipleship*, into English over the next three days, though he had to reread portions five and six times before he understood them. The German was difficult enough, but Bonhoeffer's ideas were astounding.

Is it possible to live like that? Like Jesus did? And if it isn't, what was the point of Him teaching us? Showing us? That's what Bonhoeffer was saying. And much as it went against the grain of "get all you can as long as you can" and "scoop the next story before some other guy scoops you," Jason knew he was right. It was the missing link—in Germany, in everything.

Bonhoeffer's book had forced him to look inward. He wasn't too happy with what he saw. Life wasn't about him. It wasn't even just about Rachel and Amelie, though helping them was part of it.

One thing was certain: from the time he closed the book, all Jason's reference bars changed. They shot higher, out of his line of vision, too high to reach. But he knew, for the first time, that he couldn't and wouldn't have to reach those bars alone.

When Jason finally turned in his Bonhoeffer story, his editor nearly choked. "You can't say that! You want to get the guy arrested? Sent away for good? Rewrite!"

Jason leaned back in his desk chair. He pushed strong fingertips into his temples, willing the pain to go away as he reworded the article in his brain.

Everything he'd written was true but sensational, intended to incite, to make readers think. Yet Nazi censorship had grown so severe, he bore no hope of seeing it in German print. The truth might get him a quick trip home, or maybe a long vacation in a concentration camp. And New York editors tended to bury Germany's stories in back pages, certain nobody wanted to read or could believe the atrocities—the mowing down of Jews in Poland; throwing political activists and pastors and priests into concentration camps; using girls too young to be mothers to breed SS babies; killing children deemed expendable because they weren't picture perfect.

Did readers think it was all propaganda? Jason shook his head. He'd been told a dozen times that America had its own worries, and he knew that was true—the miserable stock market, lousy crops and poor harvests, lynchings throughout the South that looked more like Germany's treatment of Jews than they'd want to admit. The Yanks couldn't be bothered with Europe's mess.

"Face it, Young," his coworker Eldridge had laughed, "you've gotta play to win. Give 'em enough to sell a story, but get off your high crusader horse. Martyrs don't win, and in this climate, that'll only get you busted by the censors—or crucified—and your heroes killed. Schmooze a little with the Krauts; a little groveling won't kill you." He laughed at his own joke and thumped Jason's chest with his forefinger. "It'll get you some juicy tidbits and keep you in the game."

Jason walked the long way back to his hotel room that night. All he could think about his work, his very life, was *cheap grace*.

25

JASON HAD WORRIED about Amelie ever since his first contact was arrested. The little girl could have no idea what had happened to her mother, why she'd been made to look like a boy, why she was suddenly swept from the city life and home she'd known and plopped with strangers in the country. He guessed she must be frightened, confused—no matter how good the woman who kept her might be. And somehow he doubted the woman's maternal nature based on the continual increase of money she'd demanded.

But not in a million years would Jason have anticipated that Mark Eldridge, ready to scoop him at every turn, would be his link to helping Amelie. Jason, Eldridge, and their editor in chief were just closing the stale and smoky newsroom for the night when Eldridge complained, "It stinks. Hitler's silent crusade to rid the world of anybody different from him."

"Jews, you mean." The chief pushed his pencil behind his ear and ground his cigarette into a tray.

"Yeah, Jews—but not just," Eldridge countered. "Anybody."

"Those with divergent political views. Communists," Chief agreed.

"Poles, Czechs, Gypsies, homosexuals, Jehovah's Witnesses, priests," Jason jumped in. "Confessing Church members who don't want the Führer for their god. Christians in general who aren't happy replacing pictures of Jesus with Uncle Adolf—you name it."

"Them too." Eldridge shrugged.

"You're right—it stinks." A desk phone rang and the chief turned to pick it up.

"And?" Jason continued, sensing Eldridge wasn't done.

Eldridge glanced up, then away. "I heard he's having kids and sick elderly gassed behind closed doors—ever since he invaded Poland."

Jason's heart flagged an alert. He wondered about Eldridge's sources, but agreed. "At least the handicapped, the mentally ill. Calls them 'life unworthy of life.'"

"There's no such thing."

"There is. He calls it his T4 program—euthanasia. My source says the Führer no doubt believes that a few hundred missing handicapped kids won't be noticed in the glorious rush of war, that their elimination will elevate the Reich to even greater heights by freeing up beds for wounded soldiers."

"I mean there's no such thing as life unworthy of life."

Jason stared at the man who'd raced him for nearly every story, every deadline, for the last twelve months. He'd thought his rival driven, merciless. But he agreed again. "Every life has value."

"Every life." Eldridge rubbed the three-day stubble of his beard.

"We'll never convince US papers to print that story on the front page."

"Miffing the great Adolf's not worth the risk of losing Germany's goodwill—or more to the point, their war reparations," Eldridge sneered.

Jason grunted. "Like we'll get them now."

"Not a chance."

Jason turned to pack up his desk for the night.

"I have a kid brother back home."

Jason hadn't imagined Eldridge with any family. He was too competitive, too isolationist, not the family-man type. "Lucky you." The thought of his kid sister so far away made Jason shove his rough draft into a folder so hard that it missed and slid off the desk. Embarrassed, expecting a gibe, he stooped, picking up pages.

"He can't hear—can't even see so hot."

Jason stopped.

"But every thought in his head is worth three times that stupid Kraut brandishing his riding crop and raving about increased living space." Eldridge's jaw worked back and forth, his lips tight over his teeth.

"How do you know?" Jason realized how that sounded, felt the heat creep up his neck. "I mean, how do you know what your brother thinks?"

"We talk." Eldridge looked at him like he was stupid.

"You said he's deaf."

"Sign language, facial expressions, lip reading, touch—even some finger spelling into his palm."

"You know how to do all that?" Jason couldn't form that picture of Eldridge in his mind.

"Our mom made us learn—the whole family. Not hard—just takes practice."

"So, you could show me?"

Eldridge looked ready to rip Jason's face off, as though Jason were messing with him.

"I mean it. I have a friend. But I can't talk with her."

"You have a deaf girlfriend?"

"I didn't say she's my girlfriend—just a friend. She signs, but I don't know what she's saying or how to communicate with her."

Eldridge pulled his jacket over his shoulder, ready to push off for the night. "Why not? But if I were you, the first thing I'd tell her is to stay out of the Fatherland."

He was out the newsroom door before Jason could reply.

Stay out of the Fatherland—right. What are the chances of hiding long-term a child the Reich wants to kill? Jason knew the answer, and he knew Amelie must be moved.

❦

Rachel turned to the right and then to the left before Oma's bedroom mirror.

"Lea's dress fits you perfectly! You are two peas in a pod." Delighted, Oma clapped her hands.

But for each praise Oma lifted, Lea bristled.

"You really think this will work?" Rachel wasn't so sure that even her best acting skills could turn her into a provincial mountain woman.

"Why not?" Oma cooed. "By the time we finish with your hair and wardrobe, no one could tell the difference between you."

"That's not true, Oma." Lea spoke softly. "She needs to stand, to sit, to walk and talk like me if we're to fool anyone enough to get her through the train station."

"You're right." Rachel eyed her sister critically. "I must practice your accent. It's close, I think, but not quite true."

"Nothing about this is true," Lea countered.

Oma pinched her lips. "You girls will get it right. You must, for all our sakes."

"Yes, Oma," Lea acquiesced.

Her very demeanor annoyed Rachel. *Why does she have to be so two-faced and mousy? She's obviously jealous. She despises me but won't say it—would never say it to Oma.* Rachel cast her twin a glance meant to put her in her place, but when Lea's flaming face and iceberg eyes made clear she'd understood, Rachel felt an unfamiliar twinge of regret. She turned away to tie her stout German shoes—Lea's shoes, which Rachel thought ugly—pretending she hadn't seen.

But Rachel knew neither of them had fooled Oma. Their grandmother was observant, quick, and still the most patient, grace-filled woman Rachel had ever met. *She's not taken in by either of us. And still she seems to like us—to love us!*

Oma was Rachel's picture of a Bavarian grandmother living in her quaint gingerbread cottage. But there was something different—something not so "Oberammergauish" in her home and garden, in her very nature, that Rachel couldn't articulate. She wanted time to unravel that mystery—time she wouldn't have.

Many houses and cottages in Oberammergau were painted with scenes, either from Bavarian community and life, German fairy tales, or the Passion Play. Oma's cottage bore no scene but was painted a plain cream-colored stucco with black shutters—not so different than the basis of the others. Traditional black window boxes lined the base of each window, brimming over with scarlet geraniums, trailing ivy, and another green filler plant Rachel didn't know—all quite Bavarian. But her narrow, hedged back garden ran deep with winding fall flower and hedgerow trails, little benches tucked here and there beneath flowering or weeping shrubbery—more like an English fairy garden than a Hansel and Gretel sort.

Lea boasted that before blackout regulations had plunged the community—the entire country—into darkness, their grandmother had lit a dozen small lanterns at night tucked here and there along her garden paths. Her neighbor had fussed at Oma's extravagance, but Oma loved them and claimed their flames made the night come alive, like fireflies.

"Are there fireflies in Germany?" Rachel couldn't imagine it.

"Not many," Oma had admitted. "But you'd be surprised the places I've lived and traveled, my dear. The things I've done . . . England, Ireland, the Netherlands. I wasn't always an old German *Hausfrau*." She'd winked and said no more, but it was one more enticement for Rachel, and one more reminder that Lea had lived an entire lifetime knowing and being known and loved by their grandmother.

Oma and her home were ideally placed, Rachel decided, against the backdrop of the snowcapped Alps. Early snowfall had painted the mountains white against the brilliant-blue October sky—the thing of storybooks.

But as Lea quickly reminded them, those beautiful snowcapped mountains portended an early winter, more difficult travel, and uncertain rations. The sooner they could get Rachel and Amelie out of Germany, the safer it would be for everyone.

Oma had chafed, clearly not wanting Rachel to go so soon. But Rachel knew Lea was right. She must leave with Amelie as soon as Jason found a way to get the child to Oma's. Impersonating her petulant sister was part of a potential exit plan, and Rachel determined to focus on those preparations.

"Sit here, my dear," Oma ordered, "and let me braid your hair."

Rachel straightened her dress—Lea's dress—and sat, returning her grandmother's smile in the mirror.

"I'll do that, Oma." Lea took the brush and comb from her grandmother. "You see about the coffee."

Oma released the tools reluctantly. Rachel, too, was sorry. She would have liked to have her grandmother brush her hair—once, before she left. That thought was cut short by Lea's sudden twist of her long hank of hair and the coarse digging of the comb through her roots.

Rachel bit her lip, determined not to let her sister see her wince. Lea jerked the comb, not bothering to untangle the knot that always formed at Rachel's neck. She carved a deep part straight down the middle of her scalp—forehead to base of neck. Dividing the hair on either side of the central part, Lea wove tight braids, yanking each time she overlapped, and tied off the ends. She wound them round Rachel's head and pinned, pushing the pins into her sister's scalp.

Rachel said not a word, no matter that she'd had to grit her teeth to keep from crying out.

Both sets of eyes met in the mirror. "Do you feel better now?" Rachel asked.

Lea's face flamed, but she wore the mask of triumph.

"I look nothing like you. Your braids are loose and full," Rachel accused. "Do it again."

The red in Lea's cheeks rushed to her ears. She glanced at Rachel's hair in the mirror, a foot below her own. Rachel saw that she'd hit her mark and waited to be obeyed.

Lea threw the comb to the vanity and turned. "Do it yourself."

Rachel grabbed her sister by the wrist and spun her back. "What is your problem?"

"Your coming brings nothing but trouble, and when you leave I'll be picking up the pieces of Oma's heart. You've put her—all of us—at terrible risk."

"I wanted to find you, to meet you. We're sisters—twins! I wanted to know about our parents, and I want to know Oma. I need to know her!"

Lea jerked her wrist free, but stepped nearer, closing the space between them. "Well, that's just it, isn't it—it's what *you* want. I imagine you've always gotten what you want, haven't you?" She walked out.

Rachel felt as if she'd been slapped. This was certainly not what she'd wanted—not like this. She sank to the vanity's bench. *She has no idea what it is to grow up believing you're loved, believing you're special, then have it torn away, to learn it was all a lie without love—worse than without love.*

Slowly, as the tears she'd held back trickled down her scrubbed cheeks, she pulled the pins from her hair. She brushed it out, gently, and massaged life back into her burning scalp. She braided her hair in loose coils, then wound them round her head, pinning the braids gently into place, a nearly perfect copy of Lea's. Her dress and shoes were Lea's. Her hair matched. But the soul that stared back from the mirror was someone different—neither Rachel nor Lea. Someone Rachel no longer knew.

—❦—

Jason figured it was a game for Eldridge to pass the time during the long hours of waiting at the news office for a phone call from New York, an assignment, the whiff of a scoop. At least Jason hoped his colleague saw it as a game, hoped he believed that Jason's fascination with learning sign language was because of his crush on some girl back home.

He picked up the finger spelling quickly. It took longer to grasp common hand signs. Some made sense, were sort of intuitive, but there were so many.

"Not bad," Eldridge conceded. "Guess pounding the keys keeps those fingers limber after all."

Jason grunted. He'd kowtow to Eldridge long enough to learn for Amelie's sake—whenever, *if* ever he had the chance to communicate with her. He hoped the hand signs were universal. He imagined she was too little for finger spelling. Learning to sign was his only means of helping her now, or of easing his own desperation to do something—anything.

But Jason's lessons were cut short. The message from the farmer's wife came sooner than even he had expected. Jason translated the crude note folded into the sandwich thrust into his hands by some youngster in the street pretending to hawk lunches: *Storage costs doubled—pay immediately. Surplus not wanted. Remove or destroy.* It couldn't be plainer than that.

26

Jason had one connection—one hope he'd met through the Confessing Church—and he tried it before sundown.

It was nearly blackout when he rang the back doorbell on Potsdamer Strasse. A stocky kitchen maid came to the door and cracked it open. "What do you want?"

"I need to speak with Frau Bergstrom."

"You are American." It was an accusation.

"I can't help that. I still need to speak with her."

"Come back tomorrow. It is time to black the windows." The maid pushed the door, but Jason was quicker, planting his foot over the threshold. She grabbed his coat collar and sleeve, almost bodily lifting him from the floor and out the door.

"Tomorrow might be too late," he pleaded. "Frau Bergstrom knows me. I'm a friend of Pastor Bonhoeffer—a friend of Dietrich." It was a stretch, but he was desperate.

"You do not need to roughhouse my poor maid, young man." He heard a smile in the cultured voice coming from the darkened room to their left. "Let him in, Greta. Let us hear what he has to say."

Jason gasped as the short but burly maid he now respected more than the Tiergarten police thumped him to the kitchen floor.

"You were saying?"

"Frau Bergstrom—we met when Dietrich spoke here. You gave me his book."

"I remember you, Herr Newspaperman. But I do not remember

that you knew Dietrich personally." She drew him into the next room and closed the door. "Could you not come in daylight?"

"I'm in a bind, and I'm hoping you can help."

She waited. He couldn't read her face.

"There's a kid—a little girl—who needs a place to stay."

"Ah." Frau Bergstrom hesitated. "She is Jewish?"

"No, she's deaf." He knew he must be up-front. "And she's the daughter of an SS officer."

She blanched. "Surely this officer can find a place to . . . to care for his own daughter."

"He believes she's dead. He wants her dead."

"But how did you—no—no." Frau Bergstrom stopped. "What is it you want of me?"

"I want you to hide her, to save her, and if you can, help me get her out of the country—to the US, if that's possible. I don't know if this is something you can do or help with, but after hearing Dietrich preach, after reading *Nachfolge*, I . . . I just want to save her. I only have a room at the Adlon—no place to hide a kid. But she's a good kid—a great kid."

She shook her head. "And how do you know this child—this wonderful German child for whom you feel such compassion? This child of an SS officer for whom you risk, and ask me to risk, everything?"

"That's a long story, ma'am." Jason felt the weariness descend as the craziness, the audacity of what he was asking caught up with him.

"It is a story you must tell me if you want me to help you, to risk my family." She opened her hand, indicating Jason should take a seat at the dining room table. She nodded to the maid, who slipped coffee between them as Jason talked.

Jason told her—all he knew. He never doubted he could trust this woman who'd opened her home to a dissident preacher watched by the police, the Gestapo, the SS—a preacher who risked his life helping, teaching, warning Germans and foreigners alike, encouraging all in need of backbone. That kind of guts in the midst of Nazi brutality was contagious, and he'd seen the fire in her eyes.

Frau Bergstrom placed her cup in its saucer when Jason finished his story. "Perhaps the safest place for the child would be with her mother's American friend. She is a link to the mother—someone who evidently cared enough for both of them to try to save the child."

"I haven't heard from her yet. She might have found a way to leave the country," Jason hedged. "We didn't realize the Nazis would move so soon."

She folded her hands. "Few did. Dietrich saw so much of their evil in its infancy—before Herr Hitler came to power. And he saw the weakness, the crack, within the church—the church's refusal to stand up, to shout back, to protect before the evil spread so far, so wide." She sat back and observed him. Jason felt he was weighed in the balance. "You said you read his book?"

"I did. That's why I hoped you'd help me—help Amelie."

"Bring the child here by night and I will help you get her to her mother's friend, because I believe that is what my Lord would have me do. But I think, Herr Young, before you ask others to risk their lives and the lives of those dear to them, you must answer this question: Why am I doing this?"

Jason swallowed. "It's the right thing. It's wrong to kill little kids."

"Why? You must ask yourself why it is wrong to kill this child if by doing so you can make room for others who are strong in mind and body."

Jason couldn't believe she'd said that.

"That is what our Führer maintains—that some are more worthy of life than others. Indeed, he asserts that an elite few in the world are worthy of life and procreation." She paused. "Ask yourself, if you do not believe that to be true, why is it not?" She waited again. "If this child is not able to contribute to society in the same way you and I are able, does it make her less valuable? How do you know?"

Jason knew Hitler had it wrong, but Frau Bergstrom's run around the issue and his lack of sleep made his head hurt.

"Are you doing this for a newspaper story?"

"No. I can't print this—not now."

"But later? Are you hoping, laying the groundwork for a sensational story? Or are you willing to lay your life down for the sake of this child?" She waited. Jason squirmed. "Will you abandon her if things do not go smoothly? If no one else can take her?"

"I thought . . . I just thought someone could—someone would."

"Who, if not you? When, if not now?"

Jason felt his chest tighten. They were the questions that confronted him each time he turned out the light at night, each time he tried to sleep. Bonhoeffer's challenge rose before him, shadowed him, haunted him. He wanted to do the right thing but was in over his head.

"This is the cost of discipleship."

"Costly grace," Jason remembered, knowing he understood so little.

She nodded and stood, taking his hand. "Bring the child here. I promise to help you find out about your friend—if she is still in Oberammergau. If so, I have friends able to transport the child there. In return, you must promise me to read the passages I will mark for you in my Bible. And then you must tell me what you think, whom you do this for, and why. And then you must tell me if you are willing to do it for others."

Jason nodded, returning the pressure of her hand in agreement.

He was halfway back to his apartment, Frau Bergstrom's Bible hidden inside his jacket, before he realized he'd just agreed to a long-term relationship with Frau Bergstrom and her friends—friends whose convictions might draw his neck in a noose alongside theirs. Oddly enough, he felt a weight lifted and wasn't one bit sorry.

27

STURMBANNFÜHRER GERHARDT SCHLICK read the dispatch from Frankfurt a second time, then threw it to his desk. Rachel Kramer could not have disappeared without a trace—not in Germany, and not in New York.

Her passport had been found aboard a liner in New York Harbor, but Rachel had not appeared—not at her home, not at the Long Island Institute, not at her New York University, and not at the Campbell Playhouse, where a job was reportedly being held for the young woman. She was presumed dead, having stowed away aboard ship and disappeared en route to New York.

Rachel's disappearance, accompanied by her scientist father's sudden death in Berlin, had created quite a stir in the international press and recriminations on both sides of the Atlantic.

But Gerhardt refused to believe that anyone in Germany's ranks had eliminated the young woman. Drs. Verschuer and Mengele still wanted her; they'd questioned—such a mild word—Dr. Kramer until he was not fit to answer questions. They were furious, as was Gerhardt, that the experiment they'd invested over two decades in had been thwarted. He and SS troops had been sent to Oberammergau on the chance that Rachel had learned of her twin. The interrogation had been thorough, but to no avail.

More than angry, Gerhardt was humiliated when Dr. Kramer confessed that he was unable to control his daughter's willful streak, that she was determined to have nothing to do with Schlick. It was for that remark that Gerhardt had struck him, perhaps too hard. The idea that Rachel would spurn him a second time was not to be borne.

No, he didn't believe she was dead, nor that she had disappeared. Every border patrol had her photograph in hand—well before the doctor was interrogated, before she could have possibly reached Germany's borders. They'd reported her at a border train station, but she'd run away. How? Where could she have gone? Who would have helped her? Whom in Germany did she even know once Kristine was eliminated?

He had the staff at the Institute interrogated, along with the hotel staff in Frankfurt, the driver of the car that took them to Berlin, the maids of their rooms there, the waitstaff, the doorman, the bellhop. Nothing.

Gerhardt racked his brain.

Then he remembered the gala. And a particularly obnoxious American who'd spilled champagne on his chest, his sleeve.

The second American—the one with spectacles—had pulled Gerhardt aside, taken his photograph, made quite a pretense of getting the exact spelling of his name, his address. He'd promised his photograph would appear in the foreign press, right beside Himmler's—a tribute to the gala and the men leading the eugenics movement. A moment in the sun Gerhardt could not afford to miss.

Gerhardt had checked. He'd had his staff check every paper in Berlin. Their contacts had checked papers in New York and London—nothing.

The Americans had formed a team—a ruse to sweep Rachel from his arms. And while he was being photographed and questioned, where was Rachel? He closed his eyes, recapturing the vision—a swirl of blue, laughing, talking . . . with the champagne-spilling American. *A reporter. Foreign press. Did she know him from New York? Who was he?*

Gerhardt lifted the telephone receiver from his desk. It should not be hard to find out.

28

RACHEL'S ANONYMOUS, coded note finally reached Jason, looking as though it had traveled halfway round the world and been opened and resealed half a dozen times.

He telephoned Frau Bergstrom from a public box, saying that he'd heard the symphony and, knowing how she loved music, highly recommended it—the score was excellent and the evening worth sharing with friends. It was playing tonight. He'd have the tickets sent round.

Thirty minutes later Jason had borrowed a car and made his way to the country and the farmhouse where he believed Amelie was hidden.

The woman who answered the door denied that she housed a child, but when he produced thirty marks, her eyes widened and she showed him into the kitchen.

He'd seen Amelie from a distance the day Kristine had taken her to the clinic. He'd seen her just after they'd dyed and cut her hair and changed her clothes. Even so, the timid, sad child pulled from beneath the kitchen sink was barely recognizable.

"We call her—call *him* Herbert," the Frau said.

Jason swallowed. He'd thought he was prepared. The disguise was for the little girl's safety, after all. But he couldn't have guessed this was the pink-and-cream beribboned cherub who had walked into the clinic with her mother—her mother who was dead. "She doesn't look like herself."

"But that is the point, *mein Herr*." The woman huffed, motioning

Amelie to the table. "Your coming here is dangerous—for her and for me. As you can see, she is well. In these times that is all you can hope for." She lifted her chin, defensive.

Jason winced. "I appreciate that."

The woman softened, sighing. "Come, sit with her at the table while I tend to my dishes. Eat something. That is the only thing you can share with her."

Jason didn't openly disagree but was relieved he'd thought of something to bring the child. When the woman stepped from the room he pulled a small picture book, one with the brightest colors he could find, from inside his jacket pocket.

Amelie's eyes widened and the first spark of life filled them. Jason felt a spark to match. He signed, *My name is Jason,* then made a *J* beside his ear, a whimsical sign he'd chosen for his name. Nothing in Germany could rival the tentative smile the little girl gave him as she made her name sign, an *A* beside one dimple in her cheek, in response.

Jason laughed, and Amelie pushed her hand to his chest.

"You feel that?" He laughed again.

Amelie smiled shyly up at him, but he could barely see her for the sudden dam behind his eyes. He coughed, pointed to the book on the table before them, and made a sign Eldridge had taught him, pressing his palms and fingers flat together, then opening them in an offering, like the cover of a book. He signed that it was a gift for her.

Amelie tilted her head and made the sign for *thank you* but looked puzzled. He made the sign for *book* again and waited.

She blinked, waiting too.

Jason smiled, then opened his arms.

Amelie climbed into his lap, all the while searching his eyes. Apparently satisfied, she settled in and opened the book. She began to mouth shapes, and Jason knew she was mimicking reading—surely memories of her mother's reading aloud to her. She turned, clasping his face between her small palms, circled his mouth with her finger, then pointed to the book.

"You want me to read to you?" He stroked her hair. "But you can't hear those words, can you, kiddo? You don't know what they mean."

But Amelie shook her finger at the book and leaned against him. Jason wrapped his arm around her and opened his palms again. Amelie opened hers.

The squat woman shook her head, wiping her hands on her apron. "She's like a monkey—imitating everything she sees." She set a cup of hot but watered-down chicory before Jason and a tumbler of milk before Amelie. "A pity—she'll never be more than that." The woman went back to her washing at the sink.

A monkey? Jason gritted his teeth to keep his opinion to himself. *She's bright. She's quick. She can sign rings around both of us!*

Amelie tugged his sleeve and pointed again to the book. Then she nestled her head once more against his chest.

"You feel the vibrations when I talk—that's it." He smiled. "I guess I can read anything, say anything, and that will be all right, as long as we point to the pictures."

Amelie wriggled against him, and he knew she was content.

The book seemed to open a world of memory for her. As soon as he'd finished, she held up four fingers and proudly pointed to herself.

Jason held up all his fingers, peeled shoes and socks from his feet, and pointed to his toes, then his ears, eyes, nose, mouth, and one elbow. He pointed to himself, then mimicked astonishment. The Hausfrau laughed in spite of herself, and Amelie giggled in delight. She had a beautiful giggle, just a little off-key.

Barely an hour had passed when Jason stood and stretched. Amelie looked up at him, and he saw in her face a tentative fear that he was preparing to leave.

"Not on your life, kiddo," he whispered, smiling. "I just needed you to know you can trust me."

The Hausfrau walked in with a filled wash basket, linen fresh from the line. "Good. You're leaving. My neighbors will return from the town soon. They must not see your automobile. Too many questions it would raise."

"I'm taking her with me. Thank you for keeping her this while. I know it was dangerous for you and your family. If you'll just pack her things—"

"Taking her? Where are you going? The man who brought her said nothing about her leaving. He has not yet paid me for this week. He promised to pay me in two weeks."

"There's been a change in plans." *I should have known the urgent note was a middleman ruse for more money.*

"You must not take her—not until I talk with him. Not until I have my money."

Jason scanned the room as she spoke. He'd seen no telephone or telephone wires leading into the farmhouse, but he wasn't about to get waylaid, to allow the woman to call for reinforcements. "Get her things. I'll pay you."

"I don't know. . . ." She hesitated.

Jason shrugged. "Suit yourself. We're leaving." And he picked up Amelie as she was.

"Wait! Wait! I'll search for what she came with—though it was very little."

"Be quick." Jason pulled out his wallet. He couldn't risk leaving a trail of Amelie's things for a blackmailer.

The woman's eyes widened and she nodded, disappearing quickly up the stairs.

She returned in less than a minute with Amelie's dress and shoes, her hair ribbons and underthings.

"Where's her mother's jewelry?"

"Jewelry? For a child? There was nothing."

Jason knew she was lying. He'd seen Kristine finger something at Amelie's neck before walking her into the clinic. He also knew it was likely that Kristine had given her daughter something of her own. Jewelry would have been the ticket—a locket, a ring on a chain, something small and wearable. Jason pocketed his wallet. "You've taken your pay. Try to sell that on the black market and I'll have your name and picture in every newspaper in Germany for kidnapping."

"*Nein!* Wait! Wait!" she cried.

"You're trying my patience, Frau."

"Let me look again. There may be something. One moment!" And the woman ran back up the stairs.

Jason heard a drawer pulled open, a bit of rummaging.

The woman returned to the kitchen, a little more slowly, a little less certain. "Let me see the money," she insisted, her palm clenched.

Jason pulled out his wallet again. "Let me see the jewelry."

The woman opened her hand. A small silver locket nestled there—a filigreed heart.

"Open it."

Inside was a photograph of Kristine.

❦

Jason wished he could drive Amelie to Oberammergau himself. He wanted to, felt the need to protect her. Nobody had ever looked at him with such trust, such hope.

He confessed to himself that he also wanted to see Rachel, to know she was safe, to see if her blue eyes held any response to his concern for her. But a member of the foreign press, an American, traveling with a young German child—male or female—would only arouse suspicion. He'd be headlights beaming a trail to their hiding place.

He knew that Amelie was in good hands with Frau Bergstrom, that her connections in Germany and her ability to see the little girl safely to Oberammergau or out of the country far surpassed his own.

Still, he hated leaving Amelie with more strangers, especially the maid at the Bergstroms' kitchen door.

But this time the sturdy woman placed a comforting hand on his arm. "We'll take good care of her. You can trust Frau Bergstrom. Take the dress and hair ribbons and shoes with you and burn them. They must not be found—they're too easy to identify. We'll save the locket for her." She began to pull the door closed. "Ach! I almost forgot. Frau Bergstrom said to give you this." She shoved a scrap of paper in his hand and pushed him away. "Now go."

Jason nodded miserably and pulled the door behind him. Amelie's guttural sobs broke his heart.

That night, in the privacy of his room, he read the scrap of paper. An address, with the initials *D. B.* "Dietrich Bonhoeffer," he whispered. "Somebody I need to know."

Jason finished reading the Scripture passages Frau Bergstrom had marked for him, and he pored again over passages he'd marked in Bonhoeffer's book. He closed both and turned off the light. It was easier to admit things in the dark—like the fact that he'd hoped to play the hero to Rachel and Amelie and still wasn't entirely sure where his motives divided. He'd fallen hard for the little girl—a kid who'd started life with all strikes against her. He knew about that, had lived that in his own way when his dad, the town drunk, had beaten his mother silly before finally bailing on the family. Jason was six years old at the time, and all he could do was shove his kid sister under the bed, away from their dad's boots. Jason had started out with high hopes to impress Rachel through helping Amelie—first for a story, but it was no time before he fell even harder for one older, shapely blonde.

Sacrificial? Hardly. "Cheap grace." He winced. *There're no words more fitting.*

Frau Bergstrom had him pegged. He'd even imagined the headline: "American Journalist Saves Deaf Child from Ruthless SS Father"—no matter how long he must wait to print the story. And he would have waited—for Rachel's sake, and Amelie's. But the risks he took weren't selfless.

What was it Granddad used to say? "You can fool some of the people some of the time—but you'd best not be fooling yourself, the biggest fool of all."

Jason punched his pillow and rolled over. It was well past midnight. Truth had a way of shining a light too bright, too penetrating, for sleep.

29

LEA HADN'T WORRIED about Friederich's missing letters for the first few days. After all, he'd told her that there might not be reliable post in war zones. So much depended on supply and the time and opportunity to write, the means to send or receive mail. He'd urged her not to worry.

But when October turned to November, and Germany had formally annexed western Poland, Danzig, and the Polish Corridor, she wondered. If things were going so well for the German military, why was there no mail?

Frau Rheinhardt, one of the village shopkeepers, received word that her husband, who'd been deployed at the same time as Friederich, had been wounded outside Warsaw and was recovering in a hospital near there. Widow Helmes received a formal letter stating that her son had been killed in the Polish campaign, that he had died bravely for the Führer. Still, Lea heard nothing.

When other women in the village received letters from their husbands and sweethearts detailing military victories, Lea's heart constricted. It was all she could do to smile at her neighbors and wish them *guten Morgen*.

By the time a brisk knock came at Oma's door late one Sunday evening, Lea's heart had nearly failed her.

But it was simply a delivery. At first Lea argued with the man hefting the large wooden box. They'd ordered nothing, and if it was forgotten wood for Friederich's carving shop, it should be delivered there. She had no way to carry such a load. The driver ignored her and pushed past her into the house, talking loudly. He glanced anxiously into the gathering dark, shook his head, and urged her to sign. She refused without knowing what was being delivered.

"You are Frau Lea Hartman?"

"*Ja, ja,* certainly."

"Then the package is for you." He urged in a whisper, "Close the shutters before you open it, but open it quickly. This goes with the package." He pulled a small envelope from his chest pocket and shoved it into her hand.

Lea blinked, and the man was gone. She closed the door.

"What is it?" Oma asked.

"I've no idea. Friederich said all his orders were in before he left— that I should not be bothered. Who delivers on Sunday night?" She circled the box, clutching the envelope. "The man said to close the shutters and open it quickly." She tore open the small envelope and tipped it toward her palm. Out fell a small heart-shaped necklace. "A locket."

"What does that mean?"

Lea shrugged just as the box gurgled. Both women stepped back.

"What is it?" Rachel whispered from the bedroom.

"We—we don't know," Oma answered. "It—it—"

"Get your hammer, Oma. We must pry off the lid. Rachel, close the shutters and black the windows."

"Isn't it early?"

"Do it," Lea ordered.

Oma handed her the hammer, and Lea expertly pulled long nails from the perimeter of the lid. She pushed the top aside. A tiny whimper came from the box, and Oma's mouth fell open.

"Rachel, I think you'd best come here." Lea spoke in wonder at the child curled in blankets, hair matted into spikes, tearstained eyes wide and blinking in the sudden light.

Rachel stepped beside her sister. She gasped, speechless.

"Is this your Amelie?"

"No—I—I don't know," Rachel stammered. "This is a boy. I mean, I've never seen her—except her picture. But this . . . Jason said they cut her hair to make her look like a boy. So—"

Lea opened the locket in her palm. A woman's smiling face looked up at her—a beautiful, fair-haired woman. She held the locket up for Rachel to see. "Do you know her?"

"Kristine!"

Lea waited only a moment longer for Rachel to reach for the child. When she didn't, Lea lifted the little one from her nest of blankets. "I've surely never seen a boy this pretty!"

The child looked from one woman to the other, fear written in every feature.

"What an ordeal you've had, Amelie," Lea crooned. "To think you've ridden all this long way in a box! You must be famished and thirsty."

"She can't hear." Rachel sniffed and stepped back. "She's soiled the blankets."

"So would you, if you'd been locked in a box for who knows how many hours," Lea retorted.

"Help me pull them up, Rachel," Oma ordered. "We'll set them to soak—see if there's a note in the bottom."

But there was nothing, and no return address.

"Your friend is certainly creative in his modes of transportation," Lea observed.

"You don't think he was here, do you? The deliveryman?" The lift in Rachel's voice raised eyebrows from Lea and Oma.

"He wasn't American," Lea said. But seeing Rachel's disappointment, she softened. "At least he sent the child."

Rachel didn't smile.

Oma filled a basin with water and pulled it by the stove. "A wash is in order, I think. Thank heaven we have enough fuel to keep the stove going. We can heat it at least a little."

"But a drink first, and maybe something to eat," Lea said. "She must be hungry."

Amelie's eyes, round in wonder, searched the faces before her and landed on Lea's.

Lea smiled gently, pressing a cup into the little girl's hands. When Amelie had her fill, Lea pulled the child's lederhosen off and pitied the rash between her legs and up their backs.

"She's been in these boy's clothes too long," Oma clucked.

"Only to disguise her," Rachel defended.

"*Ja*, well . . . Rachel, bring the chamber pot from the bedroom. We'll see if she can go before her bath."

Rachel's shoulders squared, but she did as she was told.

Oma placed her hand on Lea's arm and whispered, "Perhaps you should ask Rachel if she wants to bathe and feed the child."

Lea stiffened. She didn't want to ask Rachel, didn't want to give the little one up. She saw no maternal inclination in her sister. But Oma was right. Amelie was Rachel's responsibility, her child for all intents and purposes.

When Rachel returned with the pot, Lea set Amelie upon it.

"She's a girl, all right," Rachel observed.

"Do you want to bathe her," Lea asked, "or shall I?"

Rachel's eyes opened wide. "I've never done that."

"Then it's time to learn," Oma encouraged. "We'll help you."

It was all Lea could do not to jump in. But she pulled an apple from the bin and began cutting it into slices. While Oma coached Rachel in pouring water into the basin and testing the heat, Lea fed Amelie thin slices and bigger smiles.

Rachel's awkwardness in lifting Amelie set off a chorus of unholy howls from the child, until Lea could take no more and scooped Amelie from her, forming a crooked seat with her elbow for the little girl, who nestled against her chest, tucking her head beneath Lea's chin. "You must let her know that you won't drop her."

"She can't hear me!" Rachel argued. "I can't tell her anything."

"She can feel your confidence in holding her, the security of your arms, your embrace."

Rachel looked at her sister as if she were talking a foreign language.

Lea glanced at Oma for approval, and Oma shrugged. Lea stood Amelie in the tub of warm water, playfully splashing her legs, talking softly, singing sweetly, coaxing her to a sitting position. She drew the flannel over her small body and hair, soaped the cloth, then scrubbed until she was clean. Oma handed her a pitcher of warm water and Lea poured the water gently over Amelie's tilted head, shielding her eyes and crooning.

In time, the little girl relaxed beneath Lea's touch. When she opened her eyes, she rubbed the soap away and smiled.

Lea's heart quickened. "The towel," she ordered, and Oma placed one freshly warmed in Rachel's hands and pushed her gently forward. Lea lifted Amelie to a standing position, and the sisters rubbed her dry together.

"What can she wear?" Rachel looked out of her depth but curiously glad to be working with Lea.

"Just something to sleep in tonight. Her clothes will be dry by morning." Oma was already scrubbing the little pants and shirt in another basin.

"She can have my camisole with the long sleeves," Lea offered. "It will be big, but we can tie it round her and it will keep her warm— like a little nightdress."

"That's good of you," Rachel said.

Lea returned a genuine smile. "She's a precious child."

"Where will she sleep?"

"She could sleep with me," Oma suggested.

"But she'll toss and turn and keep you awake," Lea said. "Perhaps Rachel can sleep with you, and Amelie with me."

"You don't mind?" Rachel asked, clearly relieved.

"Not at all." Lea could scarcely keep the happiness from her voice.

But Oma stepped in. "Amelie is your child now, Rachel. You should keep her with you. She must grow accustomed to you, and you to her."

"But I don't know anything about children."

"You will learn." Oma spoke sweetly but firmly. "You must learn. You've taken on this responsibility."

Lea felt her heart wrench. "Truly, I don't mind. I'd—"

But Oma cut her off with a warning glance and slipped the silver locket over Amelie's head. "So you'll always remember your mother, child," she whispered.

Later that night, after everything had been cleared away and Amelie had fallen fast asleep beside Rachel, Lea lay with her back to her grandmother.

"You are awake?" Oma whispered.

Lea did not answer.

"I know that it hurt you to give the child over to Rachel. But Amelie is not yours, my darling girl. When Rachel goes, the child goes with her. If you let yourself become too attached, it will break your heart all the more."

Still Lea did not answer. She couldn't speak without crying. She knew her grandmother was right. Friederich would say the same, would caution her in a minute, if not forbid her outright to give her heart to a child who would break it simply because she must.

But to hold and feed and wash and cuddle Amelie—to feel the little girl's arms around her neck and the weight of her body against her chest—was heaven. In the space of an hour Lea had conjured a lifetime of feeding and caring for the child, of washing and curling her hair that would later grow long and silken, wound into plaits.

She would sew fitting and pretty frocks for Amelie. To have all of that ordered away by the one woman who knew more than any other what having a child might mean to her . . . it was a hurt too cruel to bear, impossible to speak.

Everything for Rachel, and none for Lea. Lea knew the lament was not true, that it reeked of the self-pity that the Institute had burned into her very thought process from childhood, but she had no strength to hold it back. *Rachel doesn't even want her—doesn't know what to do with her! I could love her, give her a home with Friederich. Oh, how we would love her!*

What she couldn't say, couldn't acknowledge even in the darkness, was that Amelie's arms in some strange way helped heal the loss of Friederich's. No, she wouldn't acknowledge anything more. Lea closed her eyes and lay awake till morning.

30

THE AROMA of Oma's freshly baked breakfast rolls drew Rachel to the kitchen, where she found Lea swirling and zooming spoons of porridge airplane-fashion into Amelie's mouth.

"Those smell heavenly, Oma! How did you ever glean enough ration books?" Rachel inhaled deeply, dramatically. Her grandmother smiled, distracted, as she tore a sweet roll into little pieces for Amelie.

Rachel poured herself a cup of roasted chicory, bit into the fragrant delicacy, and perched across the table from Lea. "Don't you think she should be feeding herself?"

Lea didn't answer, but tweaked the little girl's cheek affectionately. Amelie smiled shyly, offering an inharmonious giggle.

Oma lifted the kettle from the stove. "Draw the washbasin near the stove for me, Rachel. I'll pour this in for her bath."

"She just had a bath last night!" Rachel had wanted water heated for a hair wash for three days, but Oma had insisted that soap and fuel for hot water were rationed, and that she'd have to wait.

"Just enough for an oatmeal bath for her rash. It will be soothing."

Rachel pulled the basin near the stove as ordered but stepped away, sipping her lukewarm drink.

Once Lea settled the child in the basin, she scrubbed gently behind Amelie's ears and scraped dirt from beneath her nails, clucking all the while like an old mother hen. Then she rinsed her all over and began the oatmeal process again.

Rachel rolled her eyes and shook her head. "She's four years old,

Lea. She should surely be able to bathe herself." She reached for another roll. "Just because she's deaf doesn't mean she's stupid."

No one answered. Lea continued with Amelie's oatmeal bath. Oma continued stirring the pot on the stove. At length, she set down her spoon and stood before Rachel. "Amelie has been through things none of us can imagine. Count your blessings. She deserves all the attention and affection we can give her."

Rachel felt heat creep up her neck and into her cheeks. She was not used to being reprimanded by anyone other than her father. "But she must learn to do for herself, to not be seen as handicapped if she's to get on in this world."

"And she will do for herself, as we all do," Oma affirmed. "But today—this day—we will help her, just as we helped you when you first came. All of us."

Lea did not turn from her task, but she smiled a half smile of victory—a half smile Rachel resented.

"Munich? You want to transfer to Munich?" The chief's cigar nearly fell from his mouth. But he caught it. Tobacco was rationed.

"Sure—for now." Jason shrugged. "We're short on press there. I could catch the train out tonight, cover Hitler's anniversary speech on Wednesday, check out a few of the Bavarian villages. See how the war's affecting them as opposed to urban areas like Berlin, talk to the border patrols. Lots of good old Nazi training camps in that loop."

"Ha! As if they'd let you in!"

Jason ignored him. "Maybe check out that Passion Play the Krauts are all so gaga about in Oberammergau. I heard they're gearing up for a production next year—or that's the tradition. Might be interesting to see if Uncle Adolf's activities have skewered that." He shifted his feet. "You've got Eldridge here in Berlin. We're always trying to scoop each other. This way you cover twice as much territory on the same dime."

"You'd report in three times a week by phone to me and twice to New York, and you'd follow up with print. Anything extra you'd send me right away, right?"

"Regular as the glockenspiel."

Chief sat back, like he was hedging bets. "You'd need a photographer."

"I could handle that too. Just send my film back to Peterson."

Chief raised his brows and turned down his mouth, as if considering. "I'll think about it."

Jason nodded, shoved a pencil behind his ear—as if he didn't really care, as if the idea had just occurred to him—and sauntered back to his desk.

But Eldridge had overheard. "Brownnosing the chief? Didn't think you had it in you."

Jason tossed his pencil to his desk and flopped into his chair. "Just tired of racing you for the prize, ole buddy."

Eldridge smirked but caught himself. He squinted, as if trying to get his colleague in focus, to read his mind.

Too smart for his own good, or mine. Which is another reason I need to get out of here. Jason had no doubt that Eldridge would print every lead he was sitting on. And if Eldridge knew why he really wanted to go to Munich—why Frau Bergstrom had suggested it—they'd all be running for their lives.

❦

While Amelie slept through the afternoon, Lea urged her sister, "We've been lucky so far, hiding you in the attic or the closet, when anyone's stopped. But with Amelie here, we must form a better plan."

"She made funny noises all night in her sleep. Imagine if she cried out at the wrong time. There's just no way to make her understand that she has to keep quiet, to realize the danger."

"There may be, but we don't know her well enough yet to

understand how to tell her. Oma's kept her neighbors at bay so far, but I'm worried." Lea bit her lip. "We can't expect Amelie to hide for hours in a cupboard by herself. If those brutes return . . ."

"Gerhardt Schlick doesn't forget. More than wanting me, he hates being outwitted, beaten at his game." Rachel returned her cup to its saucer. "He'll be back."

Oma walked in, eyes weary.

"You didn't get a nap either, did you, Oma?" Lea asked.

Oma shook her head, pulling a chair from the table. "We must think this through. Those SS will be back. They said it, and I feel it."

Lea pushed a cup of strong and steaming chicory toward her grandmother. "We were just saying the same."

"You're squandering our ration," Oma reproved but then sighed, gratefully sipping the bitter brew. "Just this once."

"I know we should leave. I can wear my disguise. I have the papers I came with, and I still have most of the money I took from my father. But traveling with a child is a different thing—especially when I hardly know which end is up."

"Which end is up?" Oma frowned at Rachel's odd expression, creasing her brow in concentration. Both sisters laughed at their grandmother's confusion until Lea brushed the air.

"We can't get you out—not yet, not now." Lea leaned forward. "There's a cupboard beneath the stairs that Friederich built before he left. We didn't mention it before because it's rough—unfinished— and they'd surely look there. But I was thinking that if we build a second wall—a false wall that sits flush against the sides—we can create a separate compartment in the back. A hiding place. We could line it with blankets—hide you both there in case they return. It's not too far from the stovepipe that goes through to the attic, so that should take the chill off."

"*When* they return," Rachel corrected. "And that's only temporary—we couldn't live there."

"You may need to sleep there sometimes, and be ready to go in at a moment's notice during the day. We could open the ceiling and create a trapdoor in the floor of the attic. I can attach rungs to the wall, like a ladder."

"You're a carpenter to boot?" Incredulous, Rachel shook her head. "I appreciate all that you've both done, but we must find a way to get us out. I might still get through Austria all right—might even get Amelie through if the border patrols can be bribed or if we come up with some kind of story and Jason can get us papers. If we don't get out of Europe soon, I'm afraid that the border into Switzerland will be closed—and then what?"

⁂

Jason's train pulled into Munich late Monday night. He stretched, slapped his fedora atop his head, and hefted his bag. He'd find a room for the night if there was one to be had, track down a meal, then hunt for an appropriate boardinghouse in a few days, once the hoopla from Hitler's anniversary speech had passed.

He could take the train to Oberammergau tomorrow. It made sense to see how the Passion Play was shaping up for the coming season. He mentally ticked off his list of leads: Despite Hitler's invasion of Poland, and despite France and England's declarations of war on Germany, will Oberammergau's Passion Play, produced every ten years, open on schedule? Considering the toll of war, will the village still run the play the entire season? Will anybody come?

Jason couldn't imagine enough able-bodied young men left to fill the dozens of prime roles, much less man the hotels and shops, by the time Hitler got done conscripting the village's populace. He couldn't imagine how the town could feed stadiums of playgoers on the current rationing. And what about blackouts?

But he had other reasons for visiting Oberammergau and making the acquaintance of its citizenry. He hoped his long list of ideas for feature stories would afford him repeated trips to the village and interviews with locals for weeks to come. If it didn't or if his editor didn't buy it, he'd think of something else.

Working for the foreign press could keep him in the area, but he must be careful. Gestapo in Berlin trailed him and his colleagues like bloodhounds. Munich would be no different.

31

IT WAS HALF PAST SIX and barely light when Curate Bauer hurried along the cobbled street toward the church. He'd spent a long and sleepless night negotiating the private sale of valuables too heavy to travel, converting them to cash and jewels—portable wealth—for a Hebrew Christian family determined to flee from Oberammergau before they were forced out. Now he must return to the church before Maximillion Grieser, one of the Hitler Youth, made his morning patrol. The teen, eager to rise in the estimation of the Nazi Party, took his duties far too seriously. Such eyes and ears, such inflated ego, could be most dangerous.

The curate had thought, upon taking vows for the priesthood, that he'd be leaving backbiting, selfishness, and politics permanently behind—entering a quiet and disciplined life. But those very issues dogged his every step. They plagued his parishioners and those they persecuted through their fear and through apathy. No one was exempt. He tried not to judge his flock, but the conflict knifed his heart day and night, wearing him thin.

At least, as a member of the clergy, he'd not been forced to join the Nazi Party. He pitied the men of Oberammergau who wanted only to ply their trade, to raise their families, and to keep alive the traditions of the Passion Play. It was no longer enough. If they did not join the Party, if they did not march and carouse and goose-step and "Heil Hitler" on command, they were ridiculed, harassed . . . and sometimes worse.

And now the oppressors were driving longtime neighbors from their land—because of ancient blood that flowed or was suspected of flowing in their veins. As if being Jewish prohibited you from being Christian or German or human. As if Christ Himself had not been Jewish.

Curate Bauer cursed, then prayed for forgiveness. He felt helpless in the face of this hypocrisy, this injustice, this madness. Good men and women driven from their homes, sent to concentration camps or relocated to lands Germany occupied, all so Germany could be "Aryanized." And the rumors were growing that not all camps were for detention or work, no matter that their iron gates bore the assertion *Work Makes Free*. He shuddered at his imaginations.

No moral conscience and no fear of the Almighty! And what do we do—what do I do—but sit back and watch? Curate Bauer trembled in his anger against the impotency of the nation, of the church, of himself.

By the time he'd climbed the steps to the church, he was winded, the fight still churning inside him. He leaned against the door to catch his breath, to forcibly calm his breathing and spirit before entering. He'd beat his head against the door if it would help.

"Curate?" A small voice came from the darkened alcove behind the steps.

Curate Bauer started, descended the steps, and peered into the corner to better see the child—slight; he couldn't have been more than six or seven. "You're one of the Levys." He hadn't meant it to sound like an accusation.

"Y-yes, Curate," the boy stuttered, pulling back.

"Come. I won't bite you. What are you doing here at this hour?"

"Waiting for you, Curate." The youngster crept out, looking both ways, fear of discovery written in his features. "We're leaving today—and we won't be back," he whispered.

Curate Bauer's heart sank. Another family.

"*Mein Vater* said to give you this." The child pulled a package from beneath the steps—a large rectangular box wrapped in a woolen scarf. "He said you'd know what to do with it. He said to tell you it's special—made from olive wood from the hills outside Jerusalem. Grandfather sent it to him last year, a Hanukkah gift."

Curate Bauer remembered the day Jacob Levy had received the paint box, and word of his father's cruel death—an announcement not shared with his children. Carefully, he unwrapped the package. The box, smooth and beautifully marked in runs of dark and light and golden brown, was more than a box to hold a fabulous array of paints and thinners and brushes and rags. It was a painting in itself.

"But there's no time left to use it, and Father said he's just learning to paint. He said you'd know who needs it most—that it should be used for a sacred purpose." The child waited, but Curate Bauer only ran his hands over the beautiful surface. "We'll be in Jerusalem next year, and Father says we can find another." The little boy's eyes lit, hopeful.

Curate Bauer nodded slowly, unable to speak for the knot growing in his throat.

"Father says we don't need our house anymore, either; that someone else is needing it more and will be moving in soon. We're going to Grandfather by and by, and he'll have all the room we need, Father says. We'll just have to wait nearer the border for a bit—until there's a ship we can all fit on."

Still, Curate Bauer could not trust his voice.

The child shifted uncomfortably and the priest knew he must pull himself together.

"Good-bye, Curate. It's been nice knowing you." The child held up his hand, and the priest took it in a firm grip.

As best he could, Curate Bauer made the sign of the cross on the little boy's forehead, then whispered, "The Lord bless thee and keep thee. The Lord shew his face to thee, and have mercy on thee. The Lord turn his countenance to thee and give thee peace."

The child was halfway down the street when Curate Bauer called out, "Tell your father—"

The child stopped and turned, waiting. Curate Bauer tried again. "Tell him thank you—that I will keep this safe until he returns!"

The boy lifted his hand jubilantly. "I'll tell him! But he said to do with it as you wish; we'll not be back!" And he turned and ran home.

Curate Bauer wrapped the wooden box as carefully as if it were spun glass. "No," he whispered, "you will not be back." He pushed open the church door and stepped inside. When he'd closed the door, he walked to the right-side altar, knelt before the intricately carved crucifix, and wept.

⊰✦⊱

Jason packed for one night. He dared spend no more time in Oberammergau and needed to get back to Munich for Hitler's speech, lest the chief fire him before he got started. He didn't know if Rachel and Amelie were still in the village. But if they were, there'd be no better time to get them out with all the focus on Hitler and his safety. A ruse might just be possible.

A story. I'll treat it like any other story. What are the villagers doing about the Passion Play? What about the major roles? Has Jesus been called into the military? The twelve apostles? He pictured thirteen men in beards and long robes—Jesus and the twelve apostles—toting German Lugers. The image made him wince.

He hopped the morning train, stowed his bag, and pulled a notepad from his chest pocket.

"Keep your head down and your nose clean"—that had been the chief's advice as he slapped Jason on the back and showed him the newsroom door. That and "Don't be late with those stories. Make 'em good or you're off the payroll."

Jason sighed and loosened his tie for the train ride. He sure wouldn't last long without a paycheck. He pulled his fedora down over his eyes—all the better to formulate his interviews.

But his mind returned to the conundrum that haunted him. Every passage he'd read in the Bible Frau Bergstrom had marked for him countered the things he'd assumed in life. He couldn't say he'd been taught his values—more absorbed them over time.

The Confessing Church service he'd attended in Berlin had challenged those values—not so strongly as Bonhoeffer had written about them in *Nachfolge*, but his challenge had run counter to Jason's personal belief system just the same.

Personal belief system? Is that the problem? That we've all just assumed truth is what we individually believe? Or is it a collective assumption? That the truth for Germany—and the truth for Britain and Poland and the US—is their own, regardless of how it affects others? Is there no truth—no universal truth—that applies to everyone? He couldn't buy that.

He'd tried to ask a pastor he'd sat next to on the train from Berlin. But he'd sensed that the pastor feared Jason was trying to trick him into saying something inflammatory, so Jason had backed off. He got that a lot—part and parcel of being in the newspaper trade. Sources either wanted to be quoted verbatim, ad nauseam, or remain anonymous.

He couldn't blame them. It was dangerous to be an individual in the Reich today—dangerous to be committed to or allied with anyone but Hitler and the Nazi Party. And that made aligning yourself with the radical Jesus dangerous.

Jason must have dozed because he hadn't heard the conductor call for tickets. The first he knew was a thumping on the crown of his hat. Jason pulled it from his face, blinked, and fished his ticket out of his pocket. The conductor punched it and moved on.

The Nazi behind him wasn't so quick. "Papers."

Jason handed them over.

"American. And where are you going?"

"Oberammergau—just overnight."

"What brings you to Oberammergau at this time?"

"Checking out the Passion Play." Jason hated that every encounter with these guys made his mouth go dry.

"You're early, Herr Young."

The passengers around them smirked, nodded approvingly, egging the Nazi on, eager to be seen in agreement with him.

"Right—well, that's what the world wants to know. Is the show still going on? Is anybody coming? Are tickets available?"

The Nazi's face froze. Jason knew the guy could take everything he'd said as sarcasm and make a scene, an example of him, or he could let it go. But Jason had learned that acting afraid was as much a "come and get me" signal as standing up and brandishing a pistol.

The Nazi chose to play the magnanimous host. "We will eagerly await your story, Herr Young." He thrust the papers into Jason's chest. "One day."

Jason didn't look up but pocketed his papers and pulled the fedora back over his eyes.

⁂

"I can't stay in this stupid cupboard another minute!" Rachel fumed, exasperated. "This is ridiculous and completely unwarranted. It's not as if the SS is standing outside the door."

"Don't take that tone of voice with Oma," Lea retorted. "She doesn't deserve it."

"Girls!" Oma clapped her hands as if addressing a troop of unruly children.

Amelie laughed and clapped in response, as if Oma had started a game.

Rachel threw her hands up. "She's driving me crazy! I can't stay cooped inside that cupboard all day with her."

"You've only been inside an hour! One hour!" Lea accused. "You must practice. You said you spent days and weeks in an attic!"

"That was alone—with room at least to stretch out!"

Oma grabbed their arms and shook them both. "Stop it! All our nerves are frayed, and neither of you are helping."

"Frau Gerda was here early this morning asking if Oma would take in a boarder—a niece of one of her boarders from Hamburg," Lea said. "Do you understand what that will mean?"

"That's impossible!" Rachel felt the nerves tingling on the backs of her hands. "Why doesn't she keep the woman herself?"

"She's already got two boarders," Oma said wearily. "We all take in boarders during the Passion Play year—and the year before, as we prepare for the season."

"Why? The play doesn't start until next spring."

"For the transients," Lea explained, patiently drawing out each word. "There are hundreds of transients in a Passion season year—hotel and hospitality workers, cooks, carpenters, itinerant musicians, tailors and seamstresses—all looking for work, needing food, needing rooms. Even our barns and stables fill up."

"And there are so many more now." Oma shook her head. "The cities are emptying of women without husbands, families who've been evicted because their fathers have gone to the army, or those who fear the bombing and rationing."

"And some looking for a change, who just want to get out of the city, who take advantage of the fact that Oberammergau is known to house transients during play season!" Lea huffed.

"We musn't judge them harshly. We don't know their circumstan—"

"That's it, then! We'll be boarders!" Rachel shouted.

Lea shushed her.

Rachel shook Oma's arm. "Don't you see? You don't have to hide us at all! I can take a position as a skilled laborer—hotel management or something."

"My dear, you can't walk outside that door without the whole of Oberammergau turning its head and seeing that you are the mirror image of Lea. We could never hide you in plain view. The cupboard is the only way."

"They won't let you off the hook for boarders long," Lea warned. "Frau Gerda won't be the only one badgering you."

Oma agreed. "There's simply not enough room in the village to refuse."

"There's not enough room in the cupboard to accept!" Rachel retorted.

❦

Lunch was a quiet affair. Amelie had eaten early and was tucked into bed for a nap, sleeping with her thumb squeezed into her mouth, looking every bit a cherub.

Lea had walked home to scrub and order her house before choir practice. She and Oma had agreed that letting it out to boarders was the only way. If it became clear to everyone that she'd moved in with Oma until Friederich returned, Oma may not be so pestered about boarders.

Oma and Rachel sat across the table from one another. Rachel set her spoon beside her bowl and tore the last of her roll. She watched Oma pass her hand over her brow and sigh.

"I'm sorry for all the worry, Oma. My friend never should have sent Amelie here."

Oma smiled sadly. "I'm only sorry that Germany has come to this. To think that I am hiding my granddaughter and a little child in a secret cupboard in my house—it is unbelievable."

"I don't know how long I can do this—this hiding in the cupboard. I feel as if I'll go mad—I'll scream and give us all away."

Oma reached for her hand. "No, my dear. You won't scream. You won't give us away."

"I'm just not sure I can—"

"You must look beyond yourself, Rachel. You must think of others before yourself."

Rachel tried to rephrase Oma's words in her mind. "I look after Amelie hour after hour."

"Yes?" Oma asked. "She is your responsibility now—your child. Is that such a sacrifice?"

"Well . . . yes, it is. I wasn't raised for such things. It requires so much patience, so much tolerance on my part."

Oma's brows rose in mock amusement.

"I mean I've never looked after children. I certainly never had anything to do with a deaf child."

"Is it so hard?"

Rachel pulled her hand away. "I'm not even twenty-five years old. I don't want—"

"We are all doing things we don't want to do, my dear."

"You don't want me here?" Rachel could not stop the indignation rising in her chest, the familiar bite of betrayal.

"Don't put words in my mouth. Of course I want you here. And I want Amelie." Oma sighed. "I simply wish it were under different circumstances." She folded her hands. "But we must accept things as they are—be glad we're together and make the best of these times. And we must all make sacrifices—willingly." Oma smiled softly but gave no quarter. "It is called grace, my dear."

32

Lea unpacked sheet music in anticipation of her students' arrival. She set a plate of apple strudel cut into small squares and a jar of milk on the teacher's desk, in full view of the class. They tended to perform even better with the promise of treats before their eyes. Several of the mothers had combined their rations to allow Lea the freedom to bake for their children, and for those children who had no families.

Lea loved pampering her students, and she loved teaching them— more than any work she'd ever done. But today she didn't smile. Today she thought about her sister and Oma, about Amelie and Friederich.

Oma was right. With so many restrictions, Rachel could not maintain her composure much longer. Lea knew her sister had tried, but Rachel spun a whirlwind, a bright butterfly ready to burst its cocoon. And now that Amelie was here, she was no longer the center of attention—something her twin didn't handle easily or gracefully. She'd not the temperament for self-control or self-sacrifice or for sharing the limelight.

Lea sighed, throwing her score to the piano's rack. The problem was, she could understand Rachel—to a point. She, too, would have hated being cooped up in a tiny cupboard with someone who couldn't understand her. But a child! How could she not love Amelie? Still, Lea would have done it without complaint because she would have been grateful to Oma for taking her in, for hiding her.

Lea knew she deserved nothing—expected to receive nothing. But Rachel seemed to expect that everyone would bend to her needs, even her wants. Rachel would not have said so, but Lea was certain her sister thought herself superior to all of them—even to Oma.

She'd as much as said their dress was provincial and their ways backward. She'd gasped at Lea's lack of experience with makeup and fashion. She'd cringed at Lea's stout shoes—shoes all German women wore to walk the cobbled streets and climb steep and rolling hills.

Lea sank to the piano stool. She may as well admit it—at least to herself: she did not much like her sister.

Oh, Friederich! Where are you? I need to talk all these things over with you. I need for you to see Amelie—what she could mean to us. I need you to be here, to be strong where I am not, to just be here. . . . Where are you, my love?

"Frau Hartman, are you all right?" Maximillion Grieser, dressed smartly in his Hitler Youth uniform, stood suddenly in the doorway. He was by Lea's side in a moment. "Can I help you in some way?"

Lea roused herself, embarrassed and strangely uncomfortable in the young man's presence. "It's nothing, Maximillion. I'm just a little tired; that's all." She stood, straightening the sheets of music. "I'm afraid you caught me at a poor moment. Is there something you wanted? The children will be here any minute."

"Only to be of service." He stepped closer—too close. "With Herr Hartman gone, you may be in need of help from time to time."

Lea walked round the piano and toward the desk. "I'm quite all right, Maximillion. Thank you for asking."

He followed her. "There is nothing I would not do for you, Frau Hartman. I hope you know that. I'm entirely at your disposal."

Father Oberlanger, the parish priest, stepped silently into the classroom.

"Thank you, Maximillion, but I need nothing. Now, I am about to begin my class. You must have other duties."

He looked crestfallen, thoughtful, but nodded. "You need only send for me."

She turned away, cringing under his stare and Father Oberlanger's open curiosity.

When Grieser had gone, Father Oberlanger, keeping his distance, offered, "I hope young Grieser is not a nuisance. The Party has stationed several of their local Hitler Youth here to be of service. It might not do to shun him."

Lea knew that meant they were stationed to keep an eye on the comings and goings of the church and clergy. Father Oberlanger walked a fine line, fearing the Party's interference and reports, and needing to cooperate in order to maintain as many of the church's freedoms as possible. "He makes me uncomfortable, Father. I'm not sure his behavior is entirely appropriate."

The priest sighed. "What is appropriate these days is up to the Gestapo, as nearly as I can tell, Frau Hartman." He turned to walk out but paused at the door. "Try not to ruffle his feathers. It could make things . . . more difficult. These Hitler Youth are quite full of themselves, but essentially harmless."

⟡

Curate Bauer knocked at the music room door a few minutes later, uncertain if he should disturb Frau Hartman, who looked to be praying before the arrival of her class. Father Oberlanger had told him of the unwanted attention from Maximillion Grieser. She surely didn't need that. He sucked in his breath, hoping, praying the children had not worn her out or turned into the little he-devils and she-devils Frau Fenstermacher vowed they were.

"Frau Hartman? May I come in?"

She lifted her head, and he saw the shine of tears in her eyes, the streaks of those already shed on her cheeks. Embarrassed, she swiped them away. "Forgive me, Curate Bauer. I'll be myself in a moment."

"Tears are nothing to be ashamed of, Frau Hartman. I shed my own."

"You?"

"A priest is not immune to sadness."

"No—no, of course not." Lea cleared her throat. "There are many sad things these days."

"Yes." He nodded. "Yes, there are." He pulled a woolen scarf from a large wooden rectangle, the olive-wood paint box given him by the Levy child.

Lea's eyes lit in eager appreciation.

"You are your husband's wife." Curate Bauer smiled. "You know beauty when you see it."

"It's stunning—the grain and coloring." She ran her hand over the smooth surface. "Olive wood?"

"From the hills of Jerusalem. Excellent craftsmanship with no knots; a more perfect piece I have never seen."

"It is magnificent. Friederich would love to see this."

"A gift for him, and for you."

"Father, that's too much!"

"It was given to me as a sacred trust, to see that its contents are used to paint something precious—something most sacred. I can think of no one better able to bring that trust to life than you and your husband." He smiled. "You paint Herr Hartman's carvings, and as Heinrich Helphman says, Herr Hartman is the finest carver in all of Oberammergau."

"Heinrich Helphman says that, does he?" Lea smiled sadly.

"Yes, and I've meant to tell you that he came to me to confess stealing the Christkind from Friederich's Nativity, though he refuses to give it back."

"Why does he—?"

But Curate Bauer did not know. He simply shrugged. "Each time we retrieve one, he steals it again—or steals another one. He seems to prefer the one in your husband's shop window. We shall talk to him together, and I will try to get him to return it—again."

"Not today, Father. I'm not up to confronting Heinrich about anything but his solo today."

Curate Bauer nodded, remembering her tearstained face, which had dried beautifully. "Is there something I can do for you, Frau Hartman?" He spread his hands wide. "You've done so much for me, for the children. I would be honored."

She nearly spoke but stopped, as if reconsidering. She started again. "I've had no letters from Friederich in . . . in far too long, and I'm afraid—"

The three o'clock bell in the tower rang, and the chimes welcomed the rush of students into the classroom.

Lea swiped her cheeks again and straightened her back, breathing deeply.

Curate Bauer squeezed her shoulder. Hers was a familiar pain for which he had no answer. He bowed and stepped back toward the door, allowing the smallest children to smother Frau Hartman with hugs—hugs he knew would be the best medicine for her soul.

33

Shadows stretched across the backs of the pews when Curate Bauer, deep in conversation with the visiting American newspaperman, looked up to find the mayor and Maximillion Grieser striding purposefully down the center aisle of the church.

Curate Bauer had not been expecting the mayor today. In fact, because of ideological differences neither could breach, the two rarely spoke. So it was with some awkwardness that the priest introduced the men, overlooking Grieser.

"Mayor Schulz, I would like to present Jason Young, who has come to write a news story on our preparations for the coming season of the Passion Play. Herr Young, our mayor."

"Hope I can bring a little publicity your way," Young offered.

"The play, yes." The mayor straightened. "That is most kind of you, Herr Young. But if you will excuse me . . . Curate Bauer, I must speak with you—about our play."

But Curate Bauer didn't like having his interview interrupted and couldn't help but wonder at the mayor's lack of manners. "I'll be with you directly, Mayor, as soon as I show Herr Young our children's choir. Frau Hartman will be finishing up with them any moment." He cupped the reporter's elbow. "This is the choir of our youngest children, and their voices are extraordinary."

The mayor interrupted again. "Please, Curate, before you continue with Herr Young. It will only take a moment. Perhaps Maximillion could conduct our guest."

Jason's eyes widened, but he touched two fingers to his forehead in mock salute. "I'll catch up with you later, Curate." He stuck out his hand. "Good to meet you, Mayor. I look forward to doing so again at a more opportune time."

❦

Jason could not have been more pleased, as long as Junior Hitler excused himself at the door. To think that he'd get a gander at Lea Hartman without the priest along to observe was too good to be true.

"So, you patrol the halls of the church?" Jason asked, thinking the boy marched like he owned the place.

"I serve where I'm needed." Grieser spoke as if on parade. "You will treat Frau Hartman with all due respect, Herr Young."

Jason nearly smirked at the kid's overbearing tone. But he had nothing but respect for Lea Hartman and every hope to be in her debt. "Check," he agreed without attitude.

They'd just stepped into the school section of the building when a piano's melody guided them, and high, sweet voices reached Jason's ears. *Curate Bauer was right—they sound like angels.*

Eager as he was to see Rachel's sister—to know how much she looked like her twin in real life—Jason dared block Grieser's reach for the classroom doorknob. He knew his entrance would distract the students and their teacher. "Let me listen, just for a minute or two."

Grieser frowned, bloated his chest to expound, but Jason closed his eyes and leaned against the outside wall, ignoring the boy's huff. A minute passed. He heard the Hitler Youth stomp off, but Jason didn't open his eyes. The music on the opposite side of the door drifted out on angel's wings. *Can anything so pure, so sweet and true, come from Germany today?*

"It's a mystery, isn't it?" Curate Bauer whispered very near Jason's ear, as though he could read his mind.

"I didn't hear you coming, Curate." Jason was annoyed with

himself for missing the opportunity to catch Rachel's sister alone, and unsettled that the curate had caught him unaware.

"I have some experience in traversing halls silently." The curate leaned closer and spoke earnestly. "I do not wish to intrude. When the children sing, I am transported away from . . . from . . ." Curate Bauer smiled sadly and stepped back. "I forget myself."

"Not something you can afford to do these days, is it, Curate?" Jason suggested.

"No, it is not. So many things we can no longer afford." The priest looked troubled, as though some weight had descended since Jason had left him. The mayor had looked like he was on a mission. Passion Play troubles? In the current political climate Jason would not be surprised if the play was postponed . . . or canceled.

The music stopped. Jason heard the teacher address the class, heard a collective cheer and a slight stampeding beyond the door, then silence.

"That will be strudel and milk time, Herr Young. It is our cue." Curate Bauer half smiled and opened the door.

⁂

Lea loved the half hour after choir practice. Her small charges shone with innocence despite untucked blouses and scabbed knees. They sounded like the well-tuned strings of a harp while singing and yet swooped like carrion crows to a platter of sweets after the last amen.

Children leaned elbows on the desk as they ate and drank. It had quickly become their special time to share with her funny stories, confidences, and sometimes the troubles that beset their day. This, for Lea, was the greatest music of all.

Heinrich Helphman had just begun a gruesome, if exaggerated— Lea prayed—tale of his bloody exploits against the army of rats in his uncle's barn. Little girls squealed and boys clapped Heinrich on the back, giving him a "well done" for the creativity and extreme grossness of the tale.

Lea glanced up, uncertain how long Curate Bauer and his visitor had been standing in the doorway. Merriment ceased. Instinctively, Lea laid a restraining arm on Heinrich's shoulder while sending up a silent plea that the curate had not overheard Heinrich's efforts to rid his world of the vermin.

"Frau Hartman, allow me to introduce our guest. Herr Young is here to do a story for the American newspapers on the preparations for our Passion Play—and how the play shapes our lives." Curate Bauer stood aside. "He's just heard the wondrous fruit of your labors."

Lea stood and smiled tentatively, discomfited by the attention and intrusion, flustered by the familiarity of the stranger's name. "Herr Young."

Jason paled. He began to speak and stuttered. Finally, "I'm sorry— Frau Hartman?" It was a question.

Lea caught Curate Bauer's piqued curiosity at the man's odd behavior. She felt her own face flame. *This is the man who sent Amelie here? The one who helped Rachel find us? Please, Lord, don't let him give us all away!* "This is our youngest choir in Oberammergau." She smiled broadly at her pupils, hoping to divert the man's attention. But he couldn't seem to take his eyes from her face.

Curate Bauer stepped between them. "Frau Hartman took over our choir of unruly youngsters on short notice. We are most grateful to her."

It seemed to give Jason Young the time needed to compose himself. "Right." He pulled his reporter's notebook from his pocket. "The curate here says you've done a great job."

"Good hearts and excellent voices make my work a pleasure," Lea agreed, "even if at times they are a bit undisciplined." She raised her brows at Heinrich, whose cheeks brightened.

Children began to squirm, and Lea added, "If you have questions for the children, Herr Young, you will please ask them now. Their mothers will be expecting them home soon."

"Right." He shook his head again, as if trying to shake away a fog, and focused at last on the children. "How about we start with you?" He pointed to Heinrich. The others giggled and nudged one another.

Lea smiled indulgently. The moment Heinrich spoke, the others were eager to add their version of everything he'd said.

While Jason questioned Heinrich, Curate Bauer pulled Lea aside. "I'd thought to ask you something, Frau Hartman, but after seeing this young man's behavior, I'm afraid it might be indelicate."

Lea blushed warmly. "After all I've told you, Curate," she whispered, "I don't think there is anything you need hesitate to ask me."

Curate Bauer frowned. "I hope that is true. Then I must trust you to tell me if this is not . . . expedient for you." He turned his back to the reporter, blocking the line of vision between Jason Young and Lea. "Herr Young wishes to stay in Oberammergau tonight, and occasionally in the future, I believe, to complete his interviews. He thinks to return now and then to report on our progress. I'm surprised the Gestapo allows it, but perhaps they are eager to paint a more amenable portrait of the Fatherland these days." He shrugged. "At any rate, I'm not certain whom to ask to take him in. He's not a regular boarder, you see, and won't pay unless here. The cast members have already taken in boarders and require consistency in payment. There are so many this year, and with the extra women and children from the cities . . ."

"And you would like me to take him in?"

"I'd heard you were thinking of renting your home, that you are staying with Frau Breisner." Curate Bauer stole a glance at Jason Young. "But if this is too awkward . . ."

"No—no. I'm glad to have him. Oma speaks English, of course, so that is useful, and might be helpful to him. Renting our home from time to time would help me with the finances but wouldn't force me to give up my home altogether. If Friederich—when Friederich comes back, we will return to our home. It will be easier, then, to take an occasional boarder rather than to have our house rented out to a family."

Curate Bauer smiled and pressed her hand between his palms. "Bless you, my child. I am certain your Friederich will return soon. He must." He looked back at the journalist. "His accent is rather pitiable, isn't it?"

Lea smiled. If this was the man she believed, he might have a plan to get Rachel out of Oberammergau—or out of Germany. Why else would he risk coming?

She was packing the empty platter—all but licked clean of strudel—into her market basket when she realized that Jason Young was probably there to help Amelie leave Germany too. Lea's mouth and throat went dry. She swallowed at the thought, then swallowed again. *Help me, Lord.*

34

Jason found his walk through the village in the company of the beautiful Lea Hartman unnerving.

She's the image of Rachel. She could be Rachel in costume, in disguise. Side by side, I couldn't tell them apart.

And yet, as they left the church and walked through the town, Lea Hartman changed. Her posture slackened—just a little. Her shoulders rounded and the light that had shone from her eyes minutes ago was replaced by a clouded anxiety.

Jason didn't usually have that effect on women, and she was married, after all. Maybe she was uncertain that her husband would welcome him staying in their house while he was away. Maybe she'd rather have refused the priest's request and had only agreed in deference to the curate.

He glanced at her from the corner of his eye as they walked. *Does she know who I am?*

Jason picked up his pace and forced himself to smile, be friendly. The sooner he gained Lea Hartman's trust, the sooner he'd find Rachel and Amelie, and the sooner he'd know if Lea and her grandmother might be willing to do more.

❧

Oma had milked the cow and just separated the cream. She'd reached the garden, drawing her muffler around her throat, when she saw Lea in the dimming light. She was not entirely surprised when her granddaughter walked through their garden gate with the handsome American beside her. She'd half expected Jason Young before now, simply hadn't imagined how he'd finagle a trip to Oberammergau without arousing suspicion. An introduction and plea for hospitality from a local priest was ingenious—no matter how he'd done it.

"Of course you'll stay for coffee and supper. We'd have it no other way."

From the little Rachel had told them, the man had risked much in helping her and Amelie. Oma had never imagined that was entirely magnanimous on Young's part. Any man would find her grand-daughter attractive. And how could anyone with half a heart resist helping little Amelie?

"Bring this load of kindling, Herr Young—" she pointed toward the woodpile outside the door—"and I'll pour the coffee."

"It's very kind of you to offer this hospitality, Frau Breisner."

"You'll find Oberammergau quite the gathering place these days."

"Because of the play, you mean."

"The play, and the war." Oma took the man's measure. "Our number of transients has grown beyond skilled laborers for the production and hospitality venues."

"Oma means the women and children coming from the cities," Lea volunteered. "We have more food here in the countryside. Most villagers are taking in boarders these days—into their houses, even their shops and barns. You are most welcome to stay in our home when you come to Oberammergau for your interviews."

"*Danke schön.*" The American dipped his head in a bow.

"*Bitte schön.*" Lea smiled. "Your German is good."

Jason laughed. "But my accent is terrible! Please—I know. You don't have to pretend."

Oma smiled. *A man impossible not to like.* "We're glad you have come, Herr Young. Only remember, we are people of the Passion.

We offer hospitality and shelter—mercy—to those in need, and we expect the same of others."

"'People of the Passion'—that's not a phrase I've heard."

"You will hear it often as you come to know us better. For all of us in Oberammergau, the play is our trade, our commerce. For some of us it is our life and the fulfillment of our ancestors' vow to the Lord. And for some—for us—it is the way we live our own vow to Him. Our discipleship."

"'I was a stranger and you took me in'?" Jason quoted, tipping his head to the side.

Oma nodded, smiling. "*Ja*. So, we understand each other." She pointed toward the kitchen door. "Let's go inside. We've more to discuss, do we not?"

<hr />

It was hard for Rachel to tell who was more delighted, Amelie or Jason, the moment they caught sight of one another. Jason knelt to the floor and Amelie raced into his arms, her eyes lit like candles on a Christmas tree, gurgling in sounds and almost words that ran together so quickly that even Oma gasped.

"How's my best girl?" Jason picked Amelie up and danced her around the kitchen, hugging her tight. "Are they treating you right?"

Rachel knew Amelie couldn't hear a word, but she seemed to understand him perfectly. The two exchanged a string of simple signs that passed like a secret code between them. Amelie laughed, delighted, as if they'd shared the most brilliant joke on Broadway.

When Amelie was at last content to nestle in Jason's arms, he sat at the kitchen table and poured out the news. "Hitler's speaking in Munich tomorrow night. The city's crawling with Nazis. Getting you out is definitely a risk, but the focus is on his security. They won't be looking for middle-aged ladies traveling by train—or children."

Lea pleaded, "But Amelie can't be invisible. Her lack of hearing becomes obvious quickly."

"Right—they can't travel together."

"And you daren't travel with her—an American man with a German child," Oma said.

"They'd stop me in a heartbeat." He looked from one woman in the group to the next and stroked Amelie's hair. "The box worked before. We could—"

"We can't put her back in that box!" Oma insisted. "You didn't see what it did to her. She was terrified!"

Jason sat back, holding Amelie, but raised one hand in surrender, waiting for a better suggestion.

"She was alive, Oma," Lea whispered.

Oma looked up. "I wouldn't have thought you would agree to . . ."

Lea swallowed, her eyes fastened on Amelie's back. "I don't want her to go. But we don't know how long we can safely hide her; and if, as Herr Young says, there's talk in Berlin of invading Switzerland . . . I want her alive more than I want her with me."

Jason looked up at Rachel, still standing in the doorway to the kitchen. "You've not said anything. What do you think?"

"It's so sudden." Rachel felt the rush of adrenaline and the crashing of her confidence at once, mixed in with her growing attraction to Jason. She wanted the others to clear the room, to leave them alone, to let them talk. And she wanted to push back the hank of sandy hair that kept falling across his forehead.

Jason brought her focus to bear. "What do you think about Amelie traveling in the box? Or is there some way to have her travel in disguise with you—or in the same train car as you?"

"No." Rachel knew she said it too quickly. But she didn't want to be responsible for Amelie. "I don't think I could keep her quiet. And I'm not . . . not natural with her."

"I agree," Lea said. "It would be too dangerous for them both."

"Laudanum," Oma said quietly. "That's what we gave babies in the hospital during the last war to make them sleep."

Lea blinked. "But—"

"Give her just enough to make her sleep most of the time—not enough to do any permanent damage. It will not only keep her quiet for a few hours; it will keep her from being so terrified of the box."

"Whom do we send the box to?" Lea asked.

"It could be mine—part of my luggage. A trunk perhaps, rather than a box." This sounded more like a play Rachel could comprehend.

But Oma disagreed. "If anyone is suspicious of you or your papers, they will search your luggage. It could be the undoing of you both."

"Friederich's work," Lea said.

"What?"

"When the box first came, I thought it was wood for Friederich— a mistaken delivery." Lea leaned forward. "Rachel could travel as herself—at least, as the middle-aged woman she has papers for. And I could travel with the box. We'd make a separate compartment for Amelie, just as we've done with the cupboard, and place the carvings in the top. I'd travel as though I'm going to sell my husband's wood-carvings, to find new business clients. I could, perhaps, take them all the way to Austria, or even Switzerland." She turned to Rachel. "We could meet there—or you could buy some and I could have the box relabeled to go with you."

Rachel could hardly believe Lea would put herself at such risk. "If they discover you, they'll—"

"They'll do no more to me than they will do to you—or to Amelie. And I could care for her along the way."

Oma held her hands to her cheeks, her eyes shining with unshed tears. "It's so dangerous—for all of you. Can't we just keep on as we are?"

Jason shifted Amelie to his other knee. "There's more news from Berlin." He looked up at Rachel.

Her mouth went dry. "Father?"

He nodded, searching her eyes.

"Tell me." Rachel stood bravely. "Tell us all."

Jason shared what he'd heard—that Dr. Rudolph Kramer had died of heart failure in prison after thorough interrogation.

Rachel could only imagine what horrors an interrogation from Gerhardt and his cohorts meant. But her father could not tell what he didn't know. Had she betrayed him, left him to suffer at Gerhardt's hands? *But how do I live with my father's betrayal? With my stupidity— my inability to see that he and even Mother used me? How do I live with knowing that he didn't love me—that I was nothing but a laboratory rat for him?*

She turned away, refusing to cry, to shed tears for the man, and yet she couldn't push the crushing weight from her chest, the hope that he'd not suffered long, and the regretful wish that all she'd believed three months ago about her adoptive parents was true.

She heard the scrape of a chair and Amelie's small feet settle on the floor. Jason's hands found her shoulders. She turned into his chest, grateful for the arms that enveloped her.

<hr />

Gerhardt Schlick's driver pulled to a stop before the newly painted barracks on the outskirts of Oberammergau just after midnight. His chauffeur opened the door and stepped smartly aside.

Gerhardt checked his watch by his cigarette lighter. The streets of the Passion Village, shrouded in darkness, lay sleepy and quiet. He smiled as he stepped from the car.

The more Gerhardt thought about it, the more convinced he'd become that Jason Young was connected in some way to Rachel and her family in Oberammergau. A little intimidation was all that had been required to obtain the information he wanted from the reporter Eldridge. Gerhardt shook his head at the naiveté of the American press. Hitler should keep them in Germany for his own amusement if nothing more.

Another telephone call might have given Gerhardt all he needed. But that was too simple, and if Young was more intricately, intimately connected to Rachel than it appeared, such a call could tip the scales unfavorably.

It was significant that Young had been reassigned to Munich in time for the Führer's speech to commemorate his 1923 beer hall putsch. Reporters from every paper would surely need stories marking the anniversary of Hitler's early attempt to rouse the populace and seize power. And Gerhardt himself had been ordered to cover the speech in an official capacity.

He holstered his revolver. With all of Germany focused on Munich, no one would suspect a raid in the little village amid the celebrations.

He'd dispatched SS troops and attack dogs to Oberammergau, where they would be barracked and standing by. In the early-morning hours, they'd greet Oberammergau in a manner the locals would not soon forget. Midnight raids increased terror but too often allowed escapes into the darkness.

Gerhardt moistened his lips in anticipation. When the village was just rising, he'd blare the sirens and release the dogs. Every house and barn would be searched, every shop, the church, the school, every square centimeter of every building and haystack. If Rachel Kramer was hiding in Oberammergau, he would certainly find her.

Before leaving Berlin, he'd placed a final call to Frankfurt. The doctors agreed that it was too early to close the case. Identical twins were not so plentiful that the experiment, particularly one of such long duration, should be abandoned prematurely—particularly in the light of Gerhardt's new leads.

But he didn't have long. Dr. Mengele had expressed novel ideas for obtaining new sets of twins for his experiments through concentration camps—experiments unsuitable for Aryan bloodlines. They'd conceded that Gerhardt's bloodline was still of interest . . . as long as time didn't overrun his prime. Dr. Mengele had laughed at his own joke. Gerhardt had not.

He had no intention of allowing Rachel Kramer to slip through his fingers again. It was not that he cared to please the good doctors beyond what notice the experiment might bring him within the ranks of the SS, or that he could not find a more desirable woman. Stunning women were plentiful and certainly eager to fill any need he required. But finding and mastering Rachel Kramer had become a matter of the hunt, of personal pride—a matter of honor. He'd gladly crucify all those who'd helped her.

Gerhardt tugged the fingers of his gloves into place and smiled. *That should provide a fitting new scene for their Passion Play.*

35

JASON HAD STAYED past curfew, helping Lea prepare the crate. She said the compartment was smaller than the one Amelie had arrived in. But Lea had lined it in soft blankets, even a new pink crocheted piece that he suspected she'd made for the child of her hopes. Only he knew from Rachel's file that there would be no child for Lea.

Lea was clever with wood—things her husband had taught her— and knew how to make the lid secure for travel but easy to remove.

It made Jason sick to think he was sending the two girls he cared most about into such danger—one so beautiful he could barely breathe when he'd held her, and one so small and vulnerable he wanted to stop time to preserve her innocence.

For the first time he felt he better understood "costly grace"— sacrificial living and dying. He only prayed that he wasn't being stupid and that God would watch over them, care for them. He'd whispered a prayer over Rachel before leaving for his room at the Hartmans' house and had taken a couple of pictures on a fresh roll of film—one of Rachel holding Amelie, the two of them smiling at each other, and one of Amelie's hands lifted to Rachel's face as Rachel faced him. If he was not mistaken, Rachel's eyes held all he hoped.

❧❧

By the time the sisters said their good-byes and Oma tearfully released Rachel with vows to find her after the madness of Hitler had passed, gray dawn crept over the mountain—first in lavender hues, then in shades of rose, amber, and melon. Lowing cattle, their bells jingling, heralded their morning milking from the outskirts of town.

Rachel closed her eyes as, bundled against the cold, she walked down the hill and through the village, toward the train station, her frame slightly bent and her gait uneven—a middle-aged woman with a touch of rheumatism. But she was glad to walk slowly. She wanted to ingrain every sound, savor every smell, every nuance of Oberammergau and this window into her mother's—her real mother's—and her grandmother's and sister's world.

Getting out of the village was the important thing. If anyone stopped her, it would likely be here, where everyone knew their neighbors' business.

Lea had wagered that fewer villagers would be Munich-bound on the earliest train. Once they reached the big city, she'd said, they could more easily blend in. No one would likely know or recognize them. They must still pretend not to know each other, and Rachel must maintain her disguise and be on her guard, but they could breathe a little easier until they reached the Swiss border as long as they submitted their papers as required and did or portrayed nothing suspicious to alert Nazi patrols.

Lea would leave half an hour later. It would be best for the villagers to see her leave, to know her business. It might rouse gossip for a woman to try to sell her absent husband's carvings, but stranger things had been done in this new wartime.

The borders were what worried Rachel most. They surely still had her photograph, were surely still on the watch for her. But if they thought Rachel might attempt to reach Oberammergau, wouldn't they also be keeping track of Lea's whereabouts?

Jason had thought so—wasn't sure Lea's participation was a good idea, except that she could be seen as truly innocent. There was nothing to link her to anyone on the train, and that might save Amelie.

Rachel had purchased her ticket and was about to enter the railcar when she heard someone calling.

"Frau Hartman!"

Rachel tried not to stare as the ruddy-cheeked priest thrust his hand toward Lea. Rachel took a seat in the railcar and lowered the window less than an inch, enough to hear.

"Curate Bauer—*guten Morgen!*" Lea returned the greeting.

"You're out early this morning." The priest nodded toward her luggage. "Off on a trip?"

"*Ja, ja.* I'm going to see what I can sell of Friederich's Nativities, a little bit to tide us over until he returns."

Concern—or disbelief, Rachel thought—sprang to the priest's eyes. He eyed Lea as though he were a doctor, checking for symptoms of flu. "A good—a very good plan." *Pity—he looks at her with pity!* "I, too, am going to Munich—just for the day." He hesitated. "You mustn't worry about the children. I'll take the rehearsal tomorrow myself. It won't matter if they miss today."

"*Ja*—of course! *Danke,* Curate Bauer. I should have spoken with you first. I'm so very sorry."

"It is no matter. I'm sure we can manage. I'll get Frau Fenstermacher to help me for the remainder of the week, or the next. You won't be gone longer than that, will you?"

"*Nein, nein.* Only a few days. Just to sell what I can for the Christmas season—the Advent markets should help."

The priest searched her eyes, pity and questions in their blue orbs. He hefted Lea's bag and they disappeared into the car ahead.

Rachel let out the breath she hadn't realized she'd been holding and moved to a seat nearer the rear of the car. She pushed her traveling case onto the shelf above, then took a window seat and closed her eyes, feigning sleepiness, hoping no one would engage her in conversation.

Minutes passed, and though she was conscious of the time, it seemed that the train delayed. She felt more than saw that the car filled and the fresh air diminished. The blast of the conductor's whistle and his last call to board helped loosen the vise grip in her lungs. Still, the car did not move.

She peeked through her lashes. Lea was sitting six or so rows ahead. She couldn't mistake the honey-colored braids wound just above the nape of her neck and beneath her hat brim.

At the front of the car stood two SS officers. All heads lifted toward them. Hands reached automatically into purses and coat pockets for papers. Everyone needed papers, must show papers on request, must have papers on their person at all times.

Rachel knew, before they'd ever reached her, that Lea was their target. She was their reason for harassing the locals and holding up the train. They were just making a scene, a show. It was every bit a play upon the stage as they made their way down the aisle toward her sister.

Rachel opened her leather purse. As she pulled out papers, a man—the priest who'd spoken to Lea—stood, blocking the path of the SS officer. Every eye widened at the man's daring. "Is this delay necessary, Rottenführer Vondgaurdt? You know us. You can see we are all locals here. You've checked our papers a dozen times."

"Sit down, priest." The officer clapped his hand on the man's shoulder and pushed the priest to his seat, continuing his slow descent of the aisle.

Rachel forced herself to breathe deeply, evenly, to keep her heart from jumping through her chest, to ignore the menace in the officer's face.

"Frau Hartman." The officer stopped. "I haven't seen you on the train for some time. May I ask where you are going this fine morning?"

Even Rachel knew he was playing with her. But Lea rose to the occasion.

"I am taking our Führer's advice at last and taking myself to see our Fatherland."

"You are making the joy of journey? Alone?" He did not look amused.

But Lea cast embarrassed glances from side to side, taking in her neighbors. Rachel's pulse quickened to realize that her sister had more of the actress about her than she'd imagined. "If you must know, Herr Rottenführer, I am going to sell some of my husband's carvings." She looked up bravely. "I haven't heard from him in weeks, and I must sell them to care for my grandmother and myself."

"So," the Nazi grunted, ignoring her confession, "our busy little choir director—a bee too busy to join the Nazi Women's Party—has decided to tour the Reich? Before winter sets in with a vengeance? You are not too busy, Frau Hartman, with the training of the children's choir—the Reich's future Passion Players—to be away at this time? Just before Christmas?"

Rachel felt her heart rise in her throat, until all went as dry as cardboard. That was the mistake she'd seen in the curate's eyes. Lea would never leave her children's choir at such a time!

She nearly stood, determined to save her sister. But before she could speak the priest jumped up again. "We've arranged everything, Herr Rottenführer. Why do you bother us? Frau Fenstermacher and I will take over the children's rehearsals until Frau Hartman returns." The priest feigned impatience, but Rachel knew he did so at his own peril.

"Sit down, priest." The order came sharper, the officer's patience gone. "I am afraid that your presence is required in Oberammergau, Frau Hartman. You realize, of course, that the children cannot be without you at this time." He smiled with his mouth, but his eyes sent shivers down Rachel's spine. "Children are important to you, are they not?"

Rachel heard Lea's involuntary gasp. She knew there was more than she grasped in Lea's change in posture.

"It is only for a few days, Herr Rottenführer, and all has been arranged. This is my first excursion in months."

"Since Frankfurt—if I am not mistaken." He tipped his jaw. "I thought not. You see, we place great value on the Reich's citizens." He shook his head and sighed audibly. "It is a great pity, of course. But Oberammergau cannot do without its Frau Hartman—not today, and not in the near future. Do I make myself clear?"

"Herr Rottenführer, I ask you to please reconsider. This once."

"We prefer to keep all our pawns on the chessboard, where we can clearly see them." He stood at attention. "You will leave the train, Frau Hartman. Or do you need assistance?"

Rachel silently begged Lea not to fight back, not to argue, though she knew her sister—her sister who'd seemed so mousy—had grown a determined streak, especially where Amelie's safety was concerned.

Lea stood and stepped into the aisle.

"You've made a wise decision, Frau Hartman," the officer mocked. She did not look him in the eye. "This is your luggage?" He reached for the case above her head and set it at her feet. When she bent to retrieve it, he pushed back her hat and stroked her hair. "Such lovely Bavarian braids."

Rachel's fury and fear grew inside her, but the priest stood once more. "My journey can wait. I will help you, Frau Hartman."

As Lea stepped forward, the Rottenführer placed his baton across the aisle in front of her, blocking her path. "Do not attempt to leave the village again."

She didn't speak.

But Rachel caught the priest's fearful and pitying glance and realized that he knew—knew she was hiding something.

Lea and the priest, clutching her case, stepped down from the train, Rottenführer Vondgaurdt on their heels. Lea's foot had barely touched the platform when the whistle blew again.

From the corner of her eye, Rachel saw the stationmaster swing the last of the bags to the boxcar. Two men began hefting the larger crates and trunks aboard. One of the men had just grabbed Amelie's crate when a group of SS shouted for him to stop, that they intended to inspect the luggage.

"But the schedule!" the stationmaster shouted.

An SS officer pulled a gun. The stationmaster's hands shot into the air. He stepped back without another word. The Rottenführer stepped quickly toward the commotion.

The crate beside Amelie's was pried open, its contents scattered across the platform. Across the street, SS poured from trucks. Above the whistle of the train, Rachel heard the crash of glass, the pounding of rifle butts on doorframes.

A raid! A raid! Rachel and every man and woman aboard the train gasped, crowding the windows.

The train, not waiting for the larger boxes, blew its whistle once more and lurched forward. Rachel found Lea's panicked eyes, and in that moment the priest beside her gazed straight into Rachel's. His eyes narrowed for less than a second, then widened.

He knows!

The black-clad SS at the end of the platform raised his rifle butt to smash Amelie's box. One thrust and the lid cracked in the middle. Lea screamed.

Rachel pulled her papers from her purse and thrust the open purse beneath her seat. She screamed at the top of her lungs, lunging off the slowly moving train, flying straight into the arms of the SS with the raised rifle butt. "Help! Help me! He stole my purse! A thief on the train! Stop him! Stop him! Oh, please stop him!"

The SS pushed her aside and in three long strides jumped onto the moving train. Men and women alike jumped from the train onto the platform, screaming, stumbling over one another as they landed—a cache of hand luggage topsy-turvy, flying among the fleeing passengers.

Rachel continued to scream and gesture wildly as two more SS chased and boarded the departing train. Others divided into the streets, pouring through the village, while the priest, under Lea's guidance, quietly pulled one broken crate from the platform.

36

WHEN THE CLOCK struck seven, Jason heard the train whistle in the distance. He rolled over, finally daring to breathe, trusting that Rachel, Lea, and Amelie were safely headed for Munich and points west. He'd close up the Hartmans' house in another hour, interview a couple of locals, and catch a later train, as planned.

But at 7:08 a truck rumbled up the mountain road, screeching to a halt outside his window.

Vehicle doors slammed. A German shepherd barked, setting off another. Panic pushed the remaining fog from Jason's brain. He pulled on pants, stuffed his feet in shoes. He was almost to the stairs when he remembered the roll of film, the one with Rachel and Amelie's picture. He wound and yanked it from his camera, then stuffed it into the pocket of a man's jacket hanging from a hook in the hallway, all the while praying the Hartmans had a camera, and that the jacket belonged to Herr Hartman.

There was a mad banging against the downstairs doors, front and back. Jason stumbled down the stairs, fumbling with buttons.

He'd made it to the lower hallway and was just pulling back the bolt when the door slammed open and he was shoved against the wall, a rifle butt to his jaw.

The rush of soldiers, guns, dogs, and a barrage of orders flew fast and hard. Soldiers ransacked the house, throwing open cupboards, smashing dishes, tossing books to the floor. One rushed Jason, pushing him to the center of the living room, and pointed a gun at his belly. He forced Jason to his knees, motioning for him to keep his hands clasped behind his head.

Jason flinched as beds and dressers overturned in the upstairs rooms, as jackboots stomped on floorboards in search of hollow hiding places. From outside came the shatter of glass, the crash and thudding of the woodpile, and the vicious barking of dogs.

Into the chaos strode Sturmbannführer Gerhardt Schlick, grim, in charge, triumph tipping the corners of his mouth.

Jason felt the lump of anger mixed with fear rise in his chest, constrict his throat. *Did Rachel get away? What about Amelie and Lea?*

"Herr Young, I believe," Schlick grunted. Jason could see the uncertainty collide with triumph in the man's eyes. "Quite a change since I saw you last . . . far from the ballrooms of Berlin."

"I could say the same for you."

Gerhardt's half smile faded as he looked down on Jason. "You overstep yourself. Poor behavior for a guest of the Reich."

"Overstepping seems the order of the day."

"Ah, but you see, I am the one with the gun." Schlick circled the room. "Fascinating. This—the only house in Oberammergau to receive such honor from the foreign press. Now, why would Frau Hartman invite such a guest?"

"She didn't. A village priest asked her to rent me a room—probably figured she could use the money with her husband at the front. I doubt the owners will think they've been honored by either of us."

"You seem to know a great deal about this family's affairs, Herr Young."

"It's my job—to ask questions. It's what I get paid to do. What is it you're looking for?"

Gerhardt's jaw tightened. He stepped closer.

"Asking a question's usually the easiest path to getting an answer," Jason countered, refusing to look away.

Schlick seemed to consider this. He blinked slowly, still in charge, but stepped back. SS stomped through, shaking their heads in a silent no. Schlick jerked his head toward the door, and the body of uniforms filed out as quickly as they'd come. Without turning to look at Jason, he murmured, "I will take your advice, Herr Young, and ask those questions." He ordered the guard nearest Jason, "Take him."

The soldier grabbed Jason's arm, jerking him to his feet, twisting his arm high behind his back, and shoved him at gunpoint through the door, into the early-morning light.

❦

Oma had rushed to the street when the first screams came from the village, her hand clutching her heart, prayers going up fast and furious.

She waited in the garden, gritting her teeth to keep from trembling while the SS searched, tearing apart her orderly house—again. Thankfully, she had washed the dishes and put them away, made the beds and set towels to soak after her granddaughters and Amelie had gone. She'd often heard that the extra number of dirty dishes or unmade beds or the unusual amount of laundry alerted searchers to the number of people staying in a house. But there was nothing to give them away.

Sturmbannführer Schlick marched past, frustration in every step.

She kept her eyes to the ground. *They haven't found them if they're still searching.*

The town clock chimed the hour as the soldiers jumped into the truck and it peeled from the curb. In the back she glimpsed the pale profile of Jason Young, his arms wrenched unnaturally behind him. She could not help him, dared not acknowledge him. But she prayed for him and for her granddaughters and Amelie, with every fiber of her being.

❦

The morning wore slowly on. Oma found no energy to set her house to rights.

The first to return was Lea and her broken crate. Curate Bauer accompanied her, helped her wrestle the heavy box into Oma's kitchen.

Oma wept in gratitude at the sight of Lea, unharmed, but gasped at the sight of the smashed crate top.

"Frau Hartman assures me that the carvings are well wrapped, that they'll not have broken," Curate Bauer encouraged. "I would be glad to help you unpack them, to see if we can repair any damage—"

"*Nein*, Curate! It is not necessary. I will take my time." Lea shrugged. "We both know I will not be leaving now to sell them." She turned to Oma. "I've been forbidden to leave the village."

"What? Why?"

Lea silently shook her head, and Oma saw that her hands trembled.

Curate Bauer straightened. "It was a madhouse at the station—in the village. The SS raided houses and shops, smashed luggage . . ." He scanned the raided room. "They were thorough here." He glanced from one woman to the other. "I'm so sorry, Frau Breisner, that you have suffered this. You are hurt?"

"*Nein*, Curate. I am not hurt—only grateful my Lea is not harmed."

Curate Bauer nodded, distracted. "I do not understand what they're looking for, why they keep tormenting you of all people." When they didn't answer him, he turned to Lea. "I know you counted on selling Herr Hartman's carvings. If there is something more that you or your grandmother need . . . perhaps we could ask the parents of the children's choir to provide more for the singing lessons."

"*Nein,*" Lea was quick to answer. "It is not necessary. They have no more to give."

The curate nodded. "These are strained times for everyone. Thank you for understanding that, Frau Hartman. If you are certain . . ."

"There is, perhaps, one thing, Curate," Oma ventured.

"Tell me, Frau Breisner. I will do all I can."

Oma moistened her lips. Asking was such a risk. "We could use meat . . . and vegetables. Perhaps some bread . . . that does not require our ration book."

The curate's brows rose.

"Oma, we'll manage—just as everyone does!"

The curate looked at the house, and at the women, as though he saw them in a new light.

But Oma stood her ground, gazing steadily into his eyes. She hoped she was not making a mistake.

An off-key whimper came from the crate.

Curate Bauer's eyes widened. Neither woman bent to investigate, but Lea stepped between the curate and the crate. A moment passed.

"Yes," the curate said. "Yes, I can see that you may need more provisions."

"We could trade some milk—as long as we have our cow," Oma said. "At least a little milk."

"But not too much," he responded.

"No, I think not too much," she replied.

"I understand." He smiled, a weary but hopeful smile. "I will see what I can do." He picked up his hat to go. "You must be careful. Very careful." At the door he turned and grasped Oma's hand. "God bless you. God bless you both."

Lea opened the kitchen door for him. "I'll see you at choir practice, Curate, as usual?"

"As usual." He smiled more broadly as he pulled the door behind him. "Thank the good God I will not need to beg Frau Fenstermacher! I was not looking forward to that!"

❦

Oma and Lea spent the remainder of the day cuddling a still-sleepy Amelie and worrying over Rachel and Jason. The child loved the attention and seemed no worse for wear, didn't even seem to realize the ordeal she'd endured or the peril she'd encountered, thanks to the laudanum Oma had given her. For that ignorance, both women were grateful.

Rachel finally returned at nightfall. She'd spent a cold day hiding in an alcove of the Lutheran church.

Oma could not hide her joy at having Rachel and Amelie returned to her home and care. "Thank You, Father God!" She held Rachel close, happy tears streaming down her lined face as she rubbed life into her granddaughter's chilled arms, rocking her back and forth like a little child, though Rachel was taller than she. Rachel melted into her embrace.

Lea's eyes, Oma saw, held mixed feelings, conveyed mixed messages. Oma knew Lea did not entirely welcome the return of her sister, but her glowing tale of Rachel's quick thinking to save Amelie at the risk of her own life—putting Amelie first—proved that Lea admired Rachel. *It's a beginning—a new beginning for us all.*

There was still no word of Jason Young and none likely to come. Though Oma tried to comfort Rachel, her granddaughter could not speak of him—could not say his name, so frightened was she for him. She trusted that he would not betray them, but for that loyalty he would dearly pay.

Throughout the evening, Rachel and Amelie kept close to the cupboard. Lea and Oma took turns peeking beneath the blackout curtain, holding their breath, watching to see if their tormentors might return. But no one came.

When all in the village was silent, Lea slipped out to check on her house. She returned an hour later, only shaking her head, too heartsore to share what she'd seen. Oma cradled her, too, in her arms and let her cry.

By the time the clock struck nine that evening, all four were bone weary. Rachel had forced an eiderdown behind the cupboard's false wall, not even daring to climb into the attic. She and Amelie crawled in and made the most comfortable bed they could, though neither could entirely lie down in the space.

Lea returned to her bed, and Oma to hers. But once the house was quiet and another hour had passed, Oma slipped into Lea's room and sat on the chair beside her granddaughter's bed. "Are you awake?"

Lea rolled over. "How can I sleep? I feel like I'm waiting for someone to crash through our door. She's put us at such terrible risk!"

"Then we are at risk," Oma replied softly. "When have we not been at the mercy of these Nazis?" She shook her head. "It is a miracle of God that you were all away when they came—that this was the first day we tried to get them out."

Lea opened her mouth to retort, but Oma placed a hand on her granddaughter's arm—an affectionate motion to silence her. "She and Amelie are sleeping in the cupboard. What more can we ask?"

Lea sighed. "It's safer for them there. The search party may return anytime. They often do soon after they've raided—thinking we'll let down our guard."

"*Ja, ja.* But you said that the troops talked of going to Munich, that they were already late for their assignments as security for Herr Hitler's speech. They won't be back until that's over. We could have allowed them one more night in the beds, I think."

"You weren't at the train station. You didn't see them smashing crates. Amelie could have been killed—she could have been killed!" Lea covered her face in the dark.

"But she wasn't," Oma insisted. "You must take hold."

Lea shook her head as though it was no use. "It's only a matter of time until they find her, until they find them both. And then what will become of us?"

37

JASON'S TONGUE moved over his teeth. He felt the ragged edge of his right incisor. He couldn't tell where the thickened mass that was his tongue ended and where his burning throat began. It had all melted into one miserable, parched mess in his mind.

He tried shifting his position on the dank cell floor, but the pain through his rib cage made him catch his breath—which in turn made him wince, setting off the piercing in his eye again, no matter that it was swollen shut. Jason could only imagine what he looked like—wondered if there was any part of his face still the color of skin. Certain his ribs had been broken, he only hoped his lung wasn't pierced; breathing had turned to wheezing. If he ever got out of this hole, he'd give some doctor a heyday patching him up.

He knew he could manage without food—had done it before when paychecks didn't stretch—but no water for three days, the constant bright lights in his cell, the hourly high-pitched clamor broadcast through the hallways to keep prisoners awake around the clock . . . it was almost more than his mind could take, far more than he'd ever endured.

Even so, it was the waiting that was brutal—knowing the guard would come, knowing Gerhardt Schlick in all his arrogant SS glory would circle Jason's chair, interrogate him again and again, order his underlings to slam iron fists into his face and his body like marks of punctuation with every question Jason refused to answer, then yank him off the floor and start again.

The minute he got out he'd tell the world how the Nazis treated foreign journalists under interrogation. That worried him. They'd have to know he'd report. Would they risk that? Or send him to Dachau? Or have his body dumped in the Isar River?

How easy it would be to give up, to shut down altogether, or to confess everything. But that wasn't going to happen. It couldn't. He'd never tell them what they wanted to know. He only feared that in his exhaustion and their hounding something would slip, something that could hurt or incriminate or lead them to Rachel or Amelie.

Dear God, he prayed, *don't let that happen. Save me from myself. Save them. Help Rachel find a way . . .*

Just as his head fell to his chest, a guard slammed open the cell door and jerked him to his feet. Jason squared his swollen jaw. It was a new day for Gerhardt Schlick.

❦

Early the following week, Curate Bauer returned from Munich on the late-afternoon train. He hurried up the hill to Frau Breisner's home, intent on meeting Lea after choir practice. His was not news to give her in front of the children. It was not news he wanted to give her at all.

By the time Lea reached her Oma's kitchen, the blackout curtains were drawn close and the table lamp lit. The curate held his breath, uncertain which news to share first.

"Curate Bauer? I thought you'd gone to Munich today."

Neither he nor Oma spoke.

She hung her coat and scarf on the hook by the door.

The curate stood, offering his chair. "Sit down, please, Frau Hartman," he urged. "I have news."

Oma poured tea and slid a cup across the table.

"Tell me."

"I learned today that Herr Young was to be released.

Sturmbannführer Schlick's questioning methods were . . . were such that our friend will need time to recuperate." He wanted to warn, to caution them. But he did not want to frighten them so they wouldn't continue the work they were doing—and, perhaps, something more.

They watched him with wide eyes. "I saw Herr Young to the station and aboard the train for Berlin. Do not fear. He will recover—in time." The curate swallowed. "We had opportunity to talk. He's a good man, and he hopes to help—more than he's helped already."

"I'm glad he will recover," Oma said. "It's horrible to have a guest so treated in—"

Lea interrupted, "They released him to your care?"

"I took responsibility for sending him to your home—a respectable and comfortable home with a little room available for tourists, naturally suitable for members of the foreign press." The curate paused. "A home that I hope will be open to receiving Herr Young in the future, and perhaps more guests from time to time."

Lea didn't respond.

"Herr Young expects to return soon to continue his interviews. He may occasionally bring someone with him to assist—someone who may need to remain behind."

Oma placed a hand on Lea's arm. Lea covered her grandmother's hand with her own.

"What are you saying, Curate?" Lea's eyes bore no trace of understanding.

"I am asking if you will take in refugees—Jewish refugees hunted by the Reich." He searched the women's faces. "Children, perhaps, and youths whose parents have been . . . relocated."

"We have no food to give," Oma began.

"One of our village shopkeepers will help, and two farmers from outside the village have promised meat—a little. Herr Young knows someone who will provide extra ration books." He hesitated. "And papers, if needed."

"Forged papers?" Oma's eyes widened.

He nodded.

"Oh, Curate . . . I don't think we can—"

"Yes," Lea said quietly.

"Lea!" Oma cautioned.

"How can we turn them away—children?" She turned to Oma. "Do you know what they're doing with Jews?"

"Resettlement—that's what I've heard. Some to Poland." But Oma's voice did not carry conviction, and Lea did not speak. The curate looked away. "Where, then?"

Curate Bauer wondered if Hilde Breisner could comprehend the awful truth. "There is word that they are taken to camps. Not camps awaiting transport or resettlement, but concentration camps—work camps where prisoners are considered expendable, then worked, sometimes starved, until they die. And there is talk through my sources that the Nazis are planning to establish death camps—for the express purpose of killing vast numbers of prisoners. What exactly that means or when, I don't know."

"No," Oma insisted. "The Rheibaum family left only a few weeks ago. They were going to Palestine—just going to wait for a ship to Palestine and resettlement."

Curate Bauer shook his head. "The immigration quota was full. There were no more spots, and no safety here. If they tried to go, they went illegally. But I know the port where they tried to embark, and the Nazis were there first."

Oma's face blanched and she sat back, covering her mouth.

"We would take them, Curate Bauer," Lea said quietly, "but I don't know where we can hide them—how we can hide them with the Nazis raiding our homes at their whim."

"Herr Young has thought of that too. While in your home, he saw a way."

"I had no idea you knew Herr Young when you asked me to take him in."

"I'd only just met him," Curate Bauer confessed, "but I knew there was something in the questions he asked." The creases in his forehead deepened. "And I am desperate." He opened his hands and placed them, palms up, on the table. "I have nowhere to turn and my heart is broken for those I cannot help. I risk the church, and I ask others to risk much—though I have no right."

"Then we will trust the American too," Lea said, "and you. We'll find a way. If Herr Young thinks more can be hidden in my house, we'll do that."

The curate felt the heaviness of what he must say next—what, perhaps, he should have said first, if only he'd had the courage. If he'd not been afraid they would refuse to help the others. "Before you agree, I must tell you, there is more. I have a friend in the war office. Two weeks ago I asked him to see what he could learn of Herr Hartman."

Lea straightened, her face a mixture of hope and fear.

Curate Bauer swallowed. "Your husband was wounded—critically— in the Polish campaign. He was sent to a hospital in Berlin, for treatment."

"Berlin—I must go to him!"

"No, Frau Hartman," Curate Bauer said softly. "No."

"Surely they will allow me to leave when they learn—"

But the curate shook his head. "No—they will not. I inquired. I begged on your behalf. But he will soon be returned to you."

"Returned?" Oma said.

"Herr Hartman has not . . . has not regained all the functions of his brain or his body. It is not known if he will."

Lea stared. "What does that mean?"

"It means he can lie in the bed or sit in a chair. He can be fed— simple, soft food and drink he can swallow. But his eyes remain closed. There appears no recognition, no speech of any kind."

"They will send him home like this? Is there no surgery, no treatment?"

Curate Bauer felt the heat rise within him, the same indignation he'd felt when he was first told. "Apparently they need hospital beds for those they expect to recover—to recover and return to the front."

Neither woman looked as though she comprehended.

"Friederich's leg was badly splintered. He lost an eye. The bullet was removed—very near his brain. Even so, the doctors can see no reason why he has not spoken, why he is not alert." Curate Bauer let the air hang between them, summoning courage, praying for what he must say next. "Even if he wakes, it is doubtful that he will be the same . . . as before." He hated bearing such news—to Lea Hartman, of all people.

The women sat, hands clasped, silent before him. Twin tears escaped Lea's stricken eyes, scrolling down her cheeks.

"I am sorry, Frau Hartman. With all of my heart, I am sorry."

38

BRIGADEFÜHRER SCHELLENBERG all but ignored Sturmbannführer Gerhardt Schlick's salute and "Heil Hitler," so disgusted was he with his subordinate. He'd known the man since he was a boy on his parents' knees, had served with his brave father, and had greatly admired his mother—a striking beauty with the cunning of ten women. The child of such parents held great promise. But Gerhardt had not lived up to expectations, and now his obsession with finding a woman who'd bested him—not once, but probably twice—had nearly cost the Führer his life.

"You were assigned to ensure the Reich Chancellor's protection. While you were chasing this ghost of a woman through the Alps, our enemies plotted the murder of our beloved Führer!" It was all Schellenberg could do not to rip the SS insignia from Schlick's coat. *The man deserves more than a beating. He deserves to be shot!*

Schlick remained at attention.

"You have nothing to say? Well, that is good. There is no excuse for dereliction of duty." Schellenberg sat back, staring at the failure before him, ashamed that such a man might be listed among the SS—supermen of the Reich, breeders of the master race. He was grateful Schlick's parents were both dead. The boy had held some promise as a youth, but petty grievances got the better of him even then. No matter how his mother had reprimanded, no matter how she had tried to beat manliness into him, he'd kept tally of slights and small wrongs as though a glove had been thrown before him. Petty, vindictive, shallow, weak. How ashamed they would be!

Perhaps the death of his wife and child have addled his brain, though I doubt that is his problem from the way he pursues this woman.

"For the sake of your parents' memory, I have saved your skin. This time." He leaned forward, elbows on his desk.

"Yes, Brigadeführer!" Schlick spouted obediently.

The Brigadeführer closed his eyes, turning his back on the man. He heard the pivot of his subordinate's heel, the grasp of the doorknob. "Gerhardt," he sighed wearily, "I speak to you with the wisdom of a father. Forget this woman. She is not worth your career. She may have been promised to you, but she has eluded you twice now. She is not a willing partner to the doctors' grand experiment. And we are at war. Untoward things happen during war.

"There are countless eager and suitable women—Aryan women you will find most pleasing and who will not disappoint you. Women who would welcome an SS officer as the father of their children, women ready to do their duty for the Fatherland. Do not let pettiness or pride blind you, my boy."

❦

Gerhardt bowed slightly to acknowledge the Brigadeführer's overture but did not answer, was not required to respond. Respectfully closing the door behind him, he straightened, clenching his jaw.

He pulled his leather gloves taut, punching the space between his fingers. He marched smartly across the great hall, the click of his heels echoing off the walls. Gerhardt Schlick was not a schoolboy to be reprimanded by a general who counted himself a surrogate parent. He'd taken more than enough from his mother in life; he would not listen to her chastisement and dressing-down in death.

It had been a mistake letting Jason Young go. He knew something about Rachel, Gerhardt was certain. But the journalist had not broken under pressure, and when Gerhardt's superiors had learned that he'd detained and questioned, with all persuasion, a member of the foreign press, Gerhardt had released Young. The journalist had returned to Berlin, somewhat the worse for wear.

Perhaps he must bide his time, erase this spot, this tarnish to his reputation. He was good at waiting and could keep his eye on Young from afar. His mother had taught him well—*"Wait until your enemy thinks you've forgotten, until they let down their guard; then pounce."* It had certainly served him in taking his revenge in her dotage. An overdose of medicine here, a bit of neglect there. She had not bothered him long.

In this case, waiting posed an unfortunate waste of precious time. But it could not be helped. His image as a member of the elite of Germany must, at all costs, prevail. If Rachel had not left the country by now, she would certainly not be able to leave once the German army invaded England. Border security would clamp down tighter than ever. And that could be any day now—as soon as Hitler gave the word. That, too, would require his time and attention.

But forget Rachel Kramer? Not likely.

39

FRIEDERICH HAD GROWN used to the blackness, used to the sterile smell of antiseptic and disinfectants he'd long associated with white-enamel-tiled hospital hallways. He anticipated the next skyrocketing explosions, the sickly sweet smell of blood mixed with sulfur, the rush of limbs shooting into the air. He swam between worlds of dark and darker that never reached beyond the voices—the sharp, tired voices, the barking orders—that cut the silence, then faded.

He couldn't say when the voices changed or when the prolonged rumble in his bones, followed by more jostling and finally a deep-seated comfort, pushed back his haunted dreams.

New scenes bled onto the canvas of his mind—long-ago dreams of Lea releasing coiled braids and combing her hair, long and gold and silken, before the oval mirror above her dressing table at bedtime. Sweet symphonies of Lea singing, true Alpine soprano. Homey scenes of Oma pulling stubborn weeds from her kitchen garden, rolling dough across her table, and dicing purple plums for his favorite turnovers. The scent of fresh bread baking and the prolonged silence drew him nearer the surface.

And then there were more and new voices—whispers, soft and feminine, fleeting. Friederich idly wondered if the melodious rise and fall of questions and answers, of croonings and assurances, meant that he was attended by angels. Perhaps the brush against his forehead, the warm pressure on his lips, the wisp across his cheek meant the passing of a seraph's wing. Sometimes he would dream that Lea's softly curved form slept beside him once again, that her gentle tears fell on his face, his hands, like spring rain. He knew that was heaven. But the light did not come.

—❦—

Lea could not stop the tears from flowing over Friederich's face, his chest, his arms.

The body returned to her was not her husband but a scarred, emaciated shell of the robust protector and lover who'd reluctantly gone to war.

She'd prayed and yearned for his return—but whole, as himself, not like this. He did not look at her, did not seem to hear her or even know she was near.

The first night she closed their bedroom door and lay beside him. His eyes never opened and hers never closed.

When morning came, Lea rose and washed and dressed herself. Then she washed and dressed the man who shared her bed, wrestling a fresh nightshirt over his head and pushing his fingers, his arms, his shoulders through the sleeves. She changed the sheets he had soiled. But she refused to believe this was her Friederich. She would steel her heart for this one day; there was not strength for more.

Tomorrow—perhaps tomorrow—he will open his eyes, and he will see me.

40

CONVINCING CHIEF to return him to Munich in early December was easier than Jason had imagined. The editor had been impressed with Jason's inside scoop on the failed assassination attempt at the Munich beer cellar. Just after rousing the troops with his glorified memories and much-hailed anniversary speech, Hitler had walked out, safe and sound, just minutes before the bomb went off. Despite his arrest in Oberammergau and subsequent beatings, Jason had overheard enough in the SS circle to give new inside angles to the beer hall story. The trick was in printing it, getting it beyond the censors. But his report under fire raised Jason's worth in Chief's estimation.

Getting out of the newsroom, brushing off Eldridge—convincing him that he had no ulterior motive or amazing Munich source up his sleeve—was another thing. It didn't matter that Jason's bruises were still fading, his jaw too roughed up to shave, or that three broken ribs nearly bent him double.

"So, who's the Nazi in your pocket?" Eldridge demanded.

"What—you mean the one that beat me to a pulp or the one that pulled him off? Take your pick. You can have 'em both." Jason placed his typewriter in its case.

"I mean the one that tipped you off about Hitler's little time bomb in the beer hall. The one that put you in the right place at the right time for that scoop. Maybe the one that called here looking for you shortly after you left?"

Jason's heart stopped. *Schlick called here? That's how he knew—why he came looking. He followed me. I could have led him straight to Rachel and Amelie! I might have . . .* He forced himself to clamp the typewriter into place, close the travel cover, and snap the latch. *Nonchalant— breathe—take it easy.* "So what'd you tell him—go down there and beat up the kid? He's probably digging up something scary—like, the Krauts don't like meat rationing on the home front. Let's send a letter to the Führer; that'll teach him."

"Funny."

Jason winced, gently pushing his arms through his coat. "A million laughs, that's me."

"So what's next? What's your angle?"

"Christmas markets—ornaments, Nativity carvings, bells, beer, German pastries fit to adorn your waistline—gotta challenge the system sometimes. Everybody loves German Christmas markets, and Uncle Adolf's not likely to be giving any speeches at those. Sounds safe to me." He slapped his fedora on his head, tipped it to a jaunty angle, but even that made him wince again. "The Reich Chancellor's glorious speeches are yours from now on. I've had all the 'Heil Hitler' I can stomach."

"Right." Eldridge clearly didn't believe him. "And you're retiring to the land of Bavarian fairy tales."

"The glory's yours, old boy—take it away. And Merry Christmas." Jason pushed through the newsroom door, not looking back, hoping Eldridge bought it . . . but betting the squealer wasn't through.

❦

Inspired, Curate Bauer hurried up the hill to Frau Breisner's house.

Three months ago he could not have imagined asking quiet, mousy Frau Hartman to fill such a role, but three months ago he'd not seen her muster seventeen unruly hooligans in the children's choir and transform them into neat rows of singing cherubs. He'd not known she could hide whimpering children in crates or that she was in some way connected to the older woman on the train who'd saved them both through her uproar—a woman who bore an uncanny resemblance to Lea Hartman, if only about the eyes.

As far as he was concerned, Lea Hartman could walk on water. But Lea turned him down.

"It is all I can do to care for Friederich and teach the children's choir. I'm sorry, Curate, but I know nothing of theatre, of dramatics. It's only in singing that I'm able."

"It is less a matter of significant training than of keeping the children focused, occupied. And—" he searched her eyes—"of moving Jewish children through the town among the refugees—as though they, too, are children of German soldiers fleeing the cities. It's only a little training they need—a happy afternoon twice a week."

She shook her head. "I feel I've let you down. But I simply ca—"

"I am the one to apologize, Frau Hartman. I only thought you might have more hidden talents that you've not revealed. I should have realized the impossibility of what I was asking with the burdens you already bear." He hesitated. "There is no improvement?"

Lea bit her lip. "I hope . . . every day."

Oma squeezed Lea's shoulder. "We both hope, and we pray."

The curate nodded. "The mysteries of God . . . I don't always understand them." Wearily, he sipped the herb tea Oma had placed before him.

"Curate," Oma ventured.

He looked up.

"How soon do you need someone to begin the theatre classes?"

"A week; two, perhaps. No more. It must be someone I can trust to overlook hidden guests—a challenge greater than finding someone to teach the class." He shrugged. "And truly, the children here need more structure to their time. 'Idle hands and mischief,' you know." He smiled. "Tell me, then, are you thinking of taking them on, Frau Breisner?"

She laughed. "*Nein*, Curate. These bones are too old and these nerves too brittle for a dozen sprites. But I think Lea may wish to reconsider."

"Oma, you know I can't—"

"I know you *think* you can't. But let's talk about it over supper. Let's think it through carefully. I could watch over Friederich, even feed him while you're teaching, just as I do while you're at choir practice, and—"

"No!" Lea turned to the curate. "Truly, you must look for another."

"We could certainly use the money, dear. And it would be a natural way for you to bring children home with you—as though they were refugee children, as Curate Bauer said."

The curate looked from one woman to the other, hope springing in his chest, but uncertain whose word he should take as final. At last he urged, "I know crates that whimper need food and clothing. It would be one way of raising extra funds."

"Give us two days. If Lea does not speak to you by then, consider the matter closed. But let us talk tonight."

"Oma!"

Curate Bauer was not about to stay and dodge the squabbles of two determined women. He nodded hopefully, appreciatively, and bowed his way out the door into the cold December sunshine.

He pulled his hat over his ears and tugged his winter coat tightly round him, setting a good pace down the hill into the village.

Dramatics experience or no, he'd wager that Hilde Breisner would win this round with her granddaughter. He was rather sorry for the good Frau Hartman—but not sorry enough to withdraw his plea.

❦

"It's perfect! I'll do it!" Rachel squealed, bursting from the cupboard. "That's what you have in mind, isn't it, Oma? That I'll teach the classes?"

"You can't be serious!" Lea spouted. "The moment you step outside this door we'll be shot—all of us. Tell her, Oma!"

"Not if she appears as you, my dear."

"As me?" Lea shook her head. "You can't mean it. Think, Oma! Think what you're saying!"

"I'm saying this is an opportunity to do something beyond ourselves, for the children—the Jewish children who have nowhere to go, none to take them in."

"I know; I know they need someone. I've already agreed to building the secret room in my home, but—"

"Someone the curate can trust. Did you not hear him? For these children to come here means that their parents have already been taken. And the work will bring in more food money for us—to feed them and pay for forged papers. It will get Rachel out of the house before she drives us all over the brink." She looked pointedly at Rachel. "It will give her a way to contribute."

"There must be someone else. The risk . . ." Lea looked away.

"For Friederich?" Oma asked softly.

"Yes, if we do anything more to draw the Nazis here—and Rachel parading herself in the village will—"

"I won't 'parade' myself! Give me a little credit!"

"Friederich cannot defend himself! You saw what they did here, but neither of you saw how they stabbed the mattresses in my home. They destroyed everything in their way—the walls, the furniture. The cupboards Friederich crafted and carved are ruined . . . and he can never defend himself," she repeated. "Our home is not even livable, and it was surely a warning. No." She shook her head. "No, I won't do it."

"Please." Rachel bent her knee before Lea's chair and clasped her sister's hands. "Just hear me through, think it through. This can work."

Lea closed her eyes.

Rachel moistened her lips, ready to give the most convincing performance of her life.

—❧—

Curate Bauer had not expected to hear from Lea Hartman so soon, if at all. He slit the note's seal at breakfast, assuming he'd find a firm refusal, without her grandmother's goading.

But he was more than pleased to read that she would take on the theatre classes the week following the children's public singing on the first Sunday of Advent, as long as the classes were on alternate days from choir practice and student enrollment was restricted to one class or the other. She would have her hands full preparing and executing two classes, and this would provide more children with opportunities to participate. She would also appreciate it if Maximillion Grieser could be kept busy elsewhere during her classes. He was becoming intrusive, and she didn't believe children's classes warranted Hitler Youth observation. She asked that, in return, the curate arrange for the repair of her house by trusted carpenters and for whatever other remuneration the village could afford. She formally thanked him for considering her and asked him to pray for the success of the classes.

Perfect. He would lay her letter, as it was, before the committee and encourage them to allow him to hire and oversee the carpenters—workmen he trusted. He'd assure the committee how glad they should be to agree—a relief for the village and a simple solution to occupying and incorporating the refugee children of Oberammergau into suitable—and approved—local activities.

It was also the perfect opportunity to build the secret passage, even the room, into the repairs of the Hartmans' house. Herr Young's idea was brilliant—a little thickening of the walls and a tunnel leading to the outside via the root cellar. He only hoped that the work could be completed before the end of Advent, when more children were expected, and that Frau Hartman would approve.

41

JASON AND AN attractive young blonde with dark-brown eyes booked the 10 p.m. train from Berlin. With her hair dyed, straightened, and pulled severely back, her smart American traveling suit and two-inch heels, fifteen-year-old Rivka Silverman looked every bit the Gentile and every bit the American journalist's protégé. Occupation: photographer, just as her false identity papers vouched.

Jason only hoped she wouldn't need to demonstrate expertise with a camera. It was not her strong suit.

Frau Bergstrom had assured him that Rivka's English was excellent—as long as the English of the foot soldiers at checkpoints was no better. She could certainly bluff her way through a conversation if it didn't become too probing. *What do the Jews call it? Chutzpah?* Jason grinned. She reminded him of Rachel.

By the time their train pulled into Munich, Jason's ribs ached and both were road weary, longing for a boardinghouse breakfast, even a rationed one.

"Sorry, kid. This'll have to do." Jason handed her a hard roll and a cup of tepid roasted chicory sold by a vendor. "Too many eyes and ears at my boardinghouse, and I don't think we'll find a café open at this hour."

Rivka waved a hand as if it didn't matter, maintaining her professional demeanor, sipping the bitter brew as if she'd done it every day of her adult life. She checked her wristwatch and hefted her camera bag. Jason admired how she kept up the role of a journalist on a tight schedule—no coaching required.

A sharp whistle blasted from the far end of the platform. It was all Jason could do not to jump out of his skin as they boarded the train.

"Tickets! Tickets!" the conductor called, collecting and punching as he made his way down the aisle.

A Nazi patrol trailed, checking papers, faces, papers. Even that spelled routine. Not one of the officials seemed to have their mind on spies or saboteurs so early on a Sunday morning.

Jason slumped in his seat, pulled his fedora down over his eyes, and pretended to sleep.

The first Sunday of Advent services, the Advent singing of the many choirs, and the village Christmas fair should provide great photo ops for the papers in New York, as well as more freedom than usual to get lost in the crowd. He'd find Curate Bauer first and let him escort them through the village. He expected to see Lea Hartman conducting the children's choir. But what he really wanted was to get a moment alone with her. He'd heard nothing since the raid except that Lea had been confined to Oberammergau, unable to travel to sell her husband's carvings. But what did that mean for Rachel and Amelie? If only he could know they were safe. And he needed to retrieve a particular roll of film.

How he'd maneuver a moment alone with a married German woman who directed a children's choir on this eventful village day or find his way into her home was anybody's guess. *This one's on You, Lord. I haven't got a clue. And there's Rivka, our first test case. Take care of her, Lord. Give us direction. Keep her safe.*

❦

It had been weeks since Rachel had stepped outside the house—the first time since she'd tried escaping and nearly been caught. She never thought she'd be glad to take up the garb of an older woman again, but the costume pulled from Oma's clothes was a ticket to fresh air and freedom. Rachel was glad to play the role of a distant relative of

Frau Breisner's husband from Stelle, visiting to take in the Christmas fair with her grandson.

They'd waited until Lea left for the church and the gathering of her gaggle of choir children. They'd waited even longer, until Frau Hillman, nosy neighbor in all her Sunday finery, left for mass. Finally, they'd bundled Amelie in a little boy's breeches and coat, her tousle of new short curls tucked high into her cap and a rag tied beneath her chin as if she had a toothache and couldn't speak, then strolled down the snowy hill and into town amid refugees, transient laborers, and villagers alike.

Playing a role would be good practice before taking on the impersonation of Lea next week. But if Jason Young should be there, as the curate had reported to Lea he would, Rachel was less confident of her ability to keep her heart rhythmic or the light from her eyes. She'd had long weeks to appreciate the sacrifices and risks Jason had taken for her and for Amelie, long weeks to remember his flamboyant fox-trot and the unruly hank of hair that tumbled over his forehead, sometimes hiding one eye.

"Pay attention," Oma ordered quietly, smiling in return as if she and her cousin were in deep conversation. "Keep hold of Amelie's hand. If you can't do this, you'd better tell me now, dear."

Rachel banished all thoughts of Jason from her mind. She wasn't about to be ordered back into the cupboard like a reprimanded puppy. She smiled again, but this time in character.

The outdoor Christmas fair was in full swing. Rachel glimpsed Lea ordering the children's choir into forms through the snow-shoveled square, a young man in Hitler Youth uniform close on her heels.

As the singing children wound through the village, Oma whispered the name of each one. Rachel, in turn, memorized all she saw, as if preparing for the opening night of a play.

She engraved their names in her mind, attached them as tags to some feature about them. Heidi, with flaxen tangled braids and bright ribbons. Therese, with a missing front tooth and spray of freckles across her nose. Herbert, with ears that stood like saucers against his small face. It was not difficult to recognize Heinrich Helphman from Lea's descriptions—mischief written in every feature.

Amelie stared wide-eyed at everything. Oma kept her arm about the little girl, telling everyone she was her cousin's grandson. "Such a pity the little fellow has a toothache and an ear infection! So congested he can't hear a thing. But what can you do? They'll be going home to their own dentist tomorrow. We didn't want him to miss the Christmas fair."

They'd just begun to peruse the booths when Jason rounded the corner of the table before them. He and an attractive young woman in American dress stood six feet away in stark relief against the swirl of red and black Alpine costumes. Rachel's heart did not behave. She dropped her purse and a tugging Amelie. Both ended up in the snow. Oma scooped Amelie into her arms. Stooping too quickly, too lithely for the middle-aged woman she portrayed, Rachel rummaged for the contents of her purse, fumbling her compact, handkerchief, and precious forged papers.

And then he was there, stooped in front of her, awkwardly gathering the last of her bits and pieces. So close, she felt his breath on her hair, and she couldn't speak.

"Here you go, *meine Frau*. Let me help you up." He took her by the arm, raising her to her feet. He smiled a typical chivalrous Jason smile, even as he winced, but barely looked into the older woman's eyes.

"Thank you." It came out breathless and far too clear and pure for one of her feigned age.

Jason stopped short.

"I mean, thank you. Thank you, young man," Rachel tried again.

Still Jason stood, frozen to the spot. A light leaped to his eyes and he opened his mouth to speak, but she shook her head, just a mite, and pulled away.

The younger woman with him stepped to his side. "So what do you want me to shoot first, boss?"

Rachel backed away, pulling a squirming Amelie from Oma. Amelie's eyes had lit like stars at the sight of Jason, her little arms reached for him. Hunger springing from his eyes, Jason turned away. Rachel could barely see for the joy and excitement that filled her head. *He's here and well . . . but who is that woman with him?*

Oma helped tug a fractious, struggling Amelie toward the next booth. Rachel felt Jason's eyes upon her and deliberately took up her role again. When she looked up she found Curate Bauer, the priest she'd seen at the train station with Lea, staring at her. An older priest stood beside him, and he too followed her and Oma and Amelie with his eyes. She looked away. *What a fool! What an utter fool I am!*

For the next hour Rachel stuck like a burr to Oma, as her guest, not daring to glance at Jason. The only time she managed to steal a glimpse, she found Jason holding up a gold necklace at one of the booths. The young woman at his side took it from him and coquettishly modeled it. They both laughed. Rachel turned away, breathless from the sudden knife in her chest.

When she and Oma and Amelie finally climbed the hill to home, Rachel was exhausted from carrying out her role—as much from all she refused to allow herself to experience as that which she'd performed.

But Amelie was more alive than Rachel had ever seen her. Her eyes had danced as she'd watched the dozens of children in the village, her cheeks burning bright with the cold. Up and down, up and down she hopped between her two ladies as quickly as her feet could manage. Oma laughed at the child's happiness and periodically nudged Rachel, reminding her to portray the indulgent grandmother.

By the time they'd fed Amelie and tucked her into bed for her afternoon nap, she was nearly asleep with happy exhaustion.

But Oma was wide awake and perturbed. "You were very nearly

discovered today—by Herr Young, by Curate Bauer, by Father Oberlanger, who is more aligned with the Nazi Party than not, if I'm not mistaken. I've no idea who else saw. I'm not at all sure you can manage in the village two afternoons a week."

"I'm sorry. I was just . . . flustered . . . for a moment. I was so glad to see Ja—"

"All it takes is a moment to end everything—for all of us, including your Herr Young. This is no time for you to play the lovesick schoolgirl. You hold our very lives in your hands!"

Rachel had never seen Oma so distraught, not in all the time she'd hidden in her home. "It won't happen again."

"Your promise is not good enough. I can't subject Lea and Friederich and Amelie to your whims and flirtations." She untied her apron and threw it to the table.

"Oma, I just said—"

"No more, Rachel. I'm going to check on Friederich." And she stalked from the room.

Rachel stood motionless in the center of her grandmother's kitchen. Never had Oma so severely reprimanded her. Rachel picked up her grandmother's apron from the table and hung it on the hook by the door. She leaned against the sink, digging the tips of her fingers into her temples.

When Lea walked in an hour later, Oma hadn't returned. Rachel swiped the last of her tears with the back of her hand.

"Everything all right?"

Rachel nodded.

"Did you like the choir?"

"Yes." Rachel looked at her sister with new respect. "It was wonderful. The children were wonderful . . . and so were you."

Lea flushed. Rachel realized she'd never complimented her sister. Lea was very pretty when she smiled. She'd smiled less since Friederich had come home to lie in her bed, dead but not dead.

"You've done an amazing job with them."

Lea shrugged. "The village children are raised from infancy to sing, to act, to play an instrument—one or more of those gifts run in their veins, nurtured for the Passion Play. Did you get their names? Oma told you?"

"Yes." Rachel swallowed. "Yes, she did."

"Could you pick Heinrich out of the crowd?"

Rachel laughed, despite herself. "In a heartbeat—mischief personified."

Lea laughed too, then sobered. "What's wrong? What is it?"

"I nearly gave us away today." The confession was harder than Rachel had anticipated.

"When you saw Jason Young?"

"Yes."

"You love him. I saw it in your eyes." It was said as a matter of fact. Rachel's eyes filled.

"He saved your life, and Amelie's. He's the only American you have any contact with—or had. He's the person who saved you from your father and that SS officer. Why wouldn't you love him?"

Rachel couldn't hold back the tears. "I'm sorry. I'm so sorry. I nearly gave us away."

Lea shook her head, sympathy in every turn. She walked toward Rachel with open arms, but Rachel couldn't move, couldn't step into such grace. It didn't stop Lea from folding her sister into her embrace or Rachel from sobbing quietly into Lea's shoulder.

Lea brushed Rachel's hair from her forehead and whispered, "When you love someone, it is not possible to keep it from your eyes, your face, your posture."

"But the curate saw—and that older priest."

"Curate Bauer is our friend. Whatever he knows or suspects he will keep to himself. And Father Oberlanger . . . well, I don't know. But he knows nothing for certain, and the friend who walked into town with

Oma today will not be here tomorrow. She was a slightly vain and preoccupied woman flustered by a dashing young American—much as the rest of the village women were! But she is gone—as soon as you wash the gray from your hair and take off those awful clothes."

Rachel gasped.

Lea laughed, pulling back from her sister. "I love our Oma, but her clothes don't suit us."

Rachel swiped new tears with the backs of her hands, knowing she'd probably made rivers in her makeup.

Lea pulled her handkerchief from her pocket, passing it to her sister. "When Friederich wakes I will let him know every hour of every day that I love him. I will let him know through the way I look at him, smile at him, by the way I touch his hand in passing. I can't blame you for the same."

"But Oma said—"

"What—that you shouldn't risk the theatre class in the village?"

Rachel nodded.

"Oma is afraid. She's right to be afraid—for all of us. But this is a good thing—a better and more needful thing than I first realized. The curate told me some of what is happening to Jews sent to Poland. It's worse than you can imagine."

"But I could have . . . Maybe you should teach the classes, and I can watch the children you bring."

Lea snorted. "Rachel, I can't teach acting. And you're terrible with Amelie; how will you keep three or four little ones occupied and quiet?"

"How will I teach a class if I can't do that?"

"Because it's theatre—it's what you love. You really were very good in the village today. It was only that little bit of time."

Rachel looked at her sister as if she'd not seen her before. Where had this new version, this generous new twin, come from?

"We must form a truce. We're more than sisters, more than a team now. We must behave as one person, think as one person. That's what will convince them that we are only one."

"I told you that."

"I didn't think it was possible. But today I met our first orphan. Today I know we must make this work. She's the only one of her family left—and only because she was at a friend's house when the Gestapo came for her parents."

"Where—?"

"She'll be here after dark. Forestry Chief Schrade will bring her as part of a delivery of firewood."

"Who is Forestry Chief Schrade?" Rachel felt the panic rise in her throat at the notion of more characters being suddenly thrust into trusted parts of the play.

"There are more people involved than I realized—more helping, and in different ways. We're not alone. Still, the less we know, the safer for everyone."

Rachel nodded. She knew that was true. Jason and Sheila had said the same.

"There's something else." Lea smiled mischievously. "Herr Young—I think perhaps he loves you too. The way his eyes followed you was far more dangerous than the way you responded to him."

Rachel's heart tripped. She could only remember the smart young American woman at his side—very close to his side.

42

F ROM THE CUPBOARD, Rachel heard the kitchen door close behind the man she'd heard Oma call Chief Schrade.

"Rachel," Oma called softly, "come; you'll want to meet your new roommate."

Rachel pushed open the cupboard door, prepared to look down into the brown eyes of a frightened Jewish child. She wasn't prepared for the petite but curvaceous young blonde woman who stepped from the sack in the middle of the kitchen floor.

"You!" Rachel exclaimed. "You're the photographer!"

The girl's brown eyes widened and she nodded, looking from one sister to the other.

"That was her disguise," Lea said. "Rivka, this is Rachel, my sister."

"You're . . . so alike," Rivka stammered, not sounding American at all.

"And this is our grandmother, Frau Breisner. Welcome to our home, Rivka."

"Yes, welcome." Oma reached for the girl. "Twins—my grand-daughters are twins," she said in answer to Rivka's blatant stare. "Rachel, show Rivka her sleeping quarters while I heat a bowl of soup." Oma patted the girl's shoulder—the girl whose wide-eyed expression looked anything but grown-up. "You must be starving."

Rivka nodded but looked at Rachel as if afraid she'd bite her.

"Go on," Lea encouraged. "Rachel will explain our routines. I'll look in on Friederich."

The knots in Rachel's stomach tightened, but she motioned for Rivka to follow her through the small cupboard and into the wall, up the ladder to the attic.

"This is very cleverly done," Rivka whispered once they'd reached the attic floor.

"Yes. You must be quiet here—not a word. Not a sound."

"Yes." Rivka lowered her eyes.

"That's Amelie." Rachel pointed to a small lump of covers nearest the stovepipe. "She can't hear or speak properly, but she senses things— so don't startle her. She's apt to cry out, and someone might hear her."

Rivka didn't speak. Rachel felt an unfamiliar urgency to defend Amelie. "She responds to some hand motions and facial expressions, but she doesn't know what you're saying."

"She's the little girl Jason was telling me about—he's been so worried about her," Rivka exclaimed softly. "He taught me some sign language, in case she was still here—how to call you 'Aunt Rachel,' and lots of things. Oh, I'm glad she's safe!"

Rachel bristled. She didn't know whether to be pleased that Jason had taught Rivka signs for "Aunt Rachel" or to be miffed that he'd confided so much to her. Rachel pulled her pallet nearer Amelie's, leaving Rivka's nearer the ladder.

"My sister said you came alone?" Something perverse in Rachel made her ask the question, made her emphasize that Lea was her sister, that she had a sister, had family.

"Yes." Rivka turned away.

Rachel was immediately sorry, ashamed of her intended cut, but didn't soften her tone. "You have nightclothes?"

"My chemise," Rivka whispered. "Everything I have, I'm wearing."

Rachel bit her lip. "Get ready for bed, then come downstairs. Oma will have your soup ready soon. But you must be ready to climb into the cupboard right away—stand on the rungs of the ladder anytime you hear a noise outside or a knock at the door. The trapdoor into the attic must remain closed in case we're taken by surprise. We can take no chances."

"I understand."

"I hope so—for all our sakes." But Rachel couldn't look Rivka in the eye. She climbed down the ladder and crawled through the cupboard, letting the younger girl fend for herself.

Once the house was quiet and Rachel heard the rhythmic, whiffling breath of Amelie and Rivka, she turned to her side. She'd been nothing but cruel to Rivka. Why? The girl had lost everything, everyone dear to her, and Rachel, though a captive in Oberammergau, was surrounded by people—by family—who loved her, risked their lives to hide her. Why couldn't she extend that same kindness to Rivka, who needed it so desperately?

She rolled over, knowing the answer. *Is Jason only helping the girl, or is he interested in her? He certainly looked interested as she modeled that necklace before him.*

❦

Friederich, still locked in his cone of darkness, heard the whispered prayers of Lea and the Scripture readings of Oma. Other dreams, other voices came and went—whispers of women, prayers of his longtime pastor, the urgency of men he didn't recognize. But they swirled and mixed, convoluting with nightmare orders barked by his sergeant, the roar of artillery, and the blasting of dynamite. At times he felt the heat of fires, heard insanity unleashed in bloodcurdling screams. Just as suddenly a cool Alpine breeze, just off the mountains, soothed his brow. Sometimes tiny drops of moisture traveled the length of his arm—warm rivulets of rain or tears he could feel, or imagined. Once he was certain he tasted Oma's potato soup. He tried so hard to reach out, to touch—if only his mind could make his muscles move his hands, will his mouth open to speak, his eyes to see. Still the darkness prevailed, and he could not reach beyond it.

Rachel stumbled through the children's names in her first theatre class, but the improvisational game she taught them created distraction and won them over. When the hour ended, small feet skipped and flaxen braids bounced through the classroom door.

Rachel was happily repacking small props after her second class with the children when Curate Bauer stopped in the classroom.

"We've come to a conclusion," the curate confided miserably to the woman he assumed was Lea. "There is nothing more to be done. The board met last night. Father Oberlanger notified the local newspapers this morning, and I sent word to Herr Young in Munich for his foreign press. The 1940 Passion Play has been canceled." He searched her face. "I am so sorry."

Nothing could have pleased Rachel more, given that she—pretending to be Lea, a woman and a Protestant—would not have been allowed to have anything to do with play rehearsals. Without the Passion Play, she was still needed. It was a different thing entirely—comparatively nothing—to organize after-school theatre classes in the wartime absence of their normal Passion Play directors. But Rachel dared not show her relief. Lea and Oma had explained the vital impact of the play on the villagers—the fulfillment of their vow to perform every ten years, the essential income the play brought through tourists for hotels, restaurants, and the many woodcarving industries. "I don't know what to say. The entire village will be so very disappointed."

"It's this war—the war we're told the British have forced upon us." He almost grunted. "Too many of our leading players have been conscripted. Germans can't come—no Benzin for pleasure trips. And food, meat—everything rationed. And of course the British and Americans won't come. Not that they'd be welcome." He shrugged. "When this accursed war is over, they'll want to come again, perhaps. And perhaps Germany will want them."

She'd no idea what to say to comfort him. "There's always 1941—the war will surely be done by then."

He looked at her as if she'd spoken sacrilege.

"Or 1942?" She tried to make light, to break the awkward silence.

But he simply frowned, studying her face.

They usually do it on the decade turn, but it can't matter if they need the money, the business. Whatever she'd said was not comforting him. So she turned, finished packing her bag, and bade him good night. But all the way home she wondered and worried what the curate was thinking—for oh so clearly, he was.

She'd been careful of her posture, her accent. Her clothes were Lea's. She'd even tried to think like her sister! What had he seen in her that discomfited him so?

Lea had insisted to Curate Bauer that the children and their parents choose either choir or drama—not both. He'd agreed that it seemed only fair to spread the opportunity and to develop seriously the unique talents of the children. For Rachel and Lea, it also kept the children from comparing too closely Frau Hartman, teacher of the choir, with Frau Hartman, teacher of drama classes.

The first two classes had gone far better than Rachel had dared hope, with the exception of the too-constant attentions of one of the Hitler Youth—a boy the others called Maximillion. The children were more enthusiastic, more joyfully exasperating and wonderfully alive than she'd imagined, the hour all too short. If only she hadn't drawn the attention of the curate. If only she knew what she'd done to raise his curiosity!

It took thirty minutes and a pot of tea for Lea to calm Rachel after she'd returned from the market, to reassure her that everything would be all right with the curate.

"You didn't see his face. He suspects something—wonders something."

"If he does, he'll tell me. He trusts me. We're hiding Rivka at his request!"

Rachel nodded, trying to breathe.

"Now, tell me about your class, about the children. The curate mentioned that we have a repeat student between the two classes when I saw him in town this afternoon. I could only smile as though I knew what he was talking about."

"Heinrich Helphman. It's as though he has nowhere else to go each afternoon after school and no inclination to go home. And I really think he's in love with us." Rachel smiled at last. "And that Maximillion Grieser."

"Maximillion? He can't be part of the class. He's at least fifteen!"

"He hangs around, offers to carry my books or move props—even to build anything I want. He's puffed up like a peacock, but I'm sure he's harmless—just smitten."

Lea frowned. "I asked Curate Bauer to keep him away. Please don't encourage him. He could be trouble."

Rachel bristled. "I never—" She stopped. Changing the subject was safer. "Heinrich's a creative handful but can be deathly serious." She set her cup in its saucer. "My professor always said that surviving real-life drama is the best training for the stage. I don't know what it is, but I suspect something has happened in his life, something that has given him the ability to bring depth to the characters he portrays."

"I know his mother isn't well. She lost a child last year. I assume stillborn. I only know she went into the hospital to deliver but came home with empty arms. Her husband was conscripted soon after. She seems a very sad woman."

"Heinrich is her only?"

"Yes."

"Well, he's quite enough for two or three," Rachel quipped.

Lea smiled absently. "At least she has him."

The silence stretched between them until the ticking of the clock intruded.

"I hadn't realized . . . ," Rachel began. "With Friederich—with the way things are for him . . . you won't have children." The comprehension of what this must mean to her sister—her sister who bloomed in the presence of children not even her own—struck Rachel with an unexpected force.

Lea straightened and rose to place her cup and saucer in the sink, her back to Rachel.

"I'm so sorry."

Lea stood very still.

For the second time that day, Rachel wished she'd kept her mouth closed. She didn't know what to do, had hardly ever extended herself into another's pain. But she felt this, felt it for Lea—who was part of her, and growing more so each day. "Is there anything I can do for you?"

Lea shook her head once but continued leaning over the sink. The ticking of the clock on the wall swallowed the room.

"Tell me something," Lea said without turning round.

Rachel waited.

"At the Institute in Frankfurt . . . did they ever . . . did you ever have surgery?"

"For what?"

"Anything."

"Not that I remember. No, I'm sure I didn't."

"You were never there for a prolonged visit? A few days? A week or more? They never put you under anesthesia, as far as you know?"

"No. It was always just two or three hours or so every two years—routine examinations. Sometimes too probing, but general. And maybe lunch at a fine restaurant with the doctors, or dinner and the theatre—an opera in the evening with my father and Dr. Verschuer, or that creepy Dr. Mengele. They were always very nice—very encouraging toward me. Fawning, really. I didn't care for that. And I hated being told I had to go. Why?"

Lea had gone rigid.

"What is it?"

When Lea turned toward her, her face starkly white, Rachel sat back.

The sisters stared at one another. Rachel could not grasp what had happened. Was it because Lea could never have children with her husband? Had something horrible been done to her at the Institute? "What happened to you there?"

Lea opened her mouth to speak, but no words came out.

"Lea?" Rachel reached for her sister, but a sharp rap at the kitchen door made them both jump.

Rachel grabbed her cup and saucer and made for the cupboard.

43

LEA TRIED to still the rapid beating of her heart, like the banging of bricks within her chest and brain. She flattened her palms against her cheeks, as if that would hold her face in place. The rap on the door came again.

"Frau Hartman!"

Lea took a breath, then opened the door. "Chief Schrade! I—we weren't expecting you today." She tried to think if there was something she should remember—something Oma had said or Curate Bauer had implied. *Not another refugee come to stay—not yet!*

"A surprise—a gift from your journalist friend, the renter of your house." He winked.

"A gift?"

"Stand back—just a bit of space needed!" He hefted a Norway spruce through the kitchen door.

"A tree?"

"*Ja! Ja!* A Christmas tree! Herr Young said it was little enough to send his benefactress for allowing him a place to stay. He also said to tell you that he hopes to be back again soon—another story he's working on for his American newspaper."

"It's lovely."

Oma appeared in the low doorway, hands clasped to her chest. "A tree! A Christmas tree! Oh, Chief Schrade, how good of you!"

"It's not me you must thank."

"Shall we set it in your room, Lea? When Friederich wakes up it will be the first thing he sees."

Chief Schrade laughed, eyeing Lea appreciatively, making her blush. "*Nein*, Frau Breisner; it will be the second, I think." He hefted the tree again. "Show me the way."

❦

Once Forestry Chief Schrade had left, Oma called Rachel, Rivka, and Amelie from their hiding place to see the tree, then sent Rachel back to the attic to find the box of ornaments.

When Rachel returned, Oma's arm was wrapped around Rivka's shoulders. "I don't suppose you've ever decorated a tree, my dear?"

Rivka solemnly shook her head.

"Well, you're in for a treat!" Oma declared. Amelie, taking in all she could, clapped her small hands and danced. Oma laughed.

But Rivka looked as if she'd been asked to eat pork against all her Jewish upbringing.

"It smells wonderful!" Rachel ran her fingers through the scented branches, glad in some perverse way that Rivka was not enamored of the tree. *Maybe that will help her realize she and Jason are worlds apart.*

"Best to wait until the children have gone," Lea counseled, paler than usual.

"Children?" Rachel's eyes widened. *She can't be thinking of taking in more!*

"The *Klopfelsingen*, the caroling by the village children," Lea reassured her. "I'll walk with them. You'll be able to hear, but stay hidden. We don't want a houseful of women seen peeking through curtains."

"There's something else," Oma whispered conspiratorially, crooking her finger, beckoning toward the kitchen. "Come see what else Chief Schrade brought us—another gift from your young man." She smiled at Rachel, and Rachel wondered if at last she'd been forgiven for her faux pas at the Advent market.

"Carp!" Rivka squealed at the floundering fish splashing in the metal tub.

"Oh, it's soaked my floor!" But Oma laughed.

"A carp for Christmas!" Lea wondered. "We've not had one in three years."

Oma smiled. "It can swim until Christmas Eve." She cuddled Amelie from behind. "And you, young lady, can come see it every day."

Amelie, her face the picture of light, reached up to pat Oma's dimpled wreath of smiles, as though she'd understood every word.

⚶

Jason was sick of Christmas, or sick for Christmas. He wasn't sure which. He only knew that spending the holiday in a city at war, with no presents, no family, and spartan food, was lonelier and bleaker than any other time of year.

Germans were Christmas-tree crazy—even bigger on them than folks were back home. No matter how rationed, no matter how poverty-stricken or desperate or glum the people might be, they still found a way to decorate a tree in their front window. But blackout regulations forced every shade to be drawn, every drape pinned tight. Not one glowing candle or electric bulb shone into the night. And there was something lonelier, something colder about that than if the trees had not been there at all.

So he'd taken the *"Stille Nacht"* assignment in Oberndorf, home of the Christmas carol's first performance. Nostalgia was written all over the feature—a sentiment Jason had studiously avoided in years gone by. But this year, surrounded by the darkness, the vile hatred and misery of Nazis and propaganda he could no longer stomach, and most especially because Rachel and Amelie were in a place he dared not go, he felt the need to get away.

It would be good to be part of something pure, something holy, if only for an hour. He wanted to hear and sing with locals the simple, sacred words of Joseph Mohr's poem to the tune composed by Franz Gruber.

The tiny, black-domed white chapel, known far and wide as the Stille-Nacht-Kapelle, stood on its own hillside nestled amid evergreens and festooned in pine garlands and red ribbons. Octagonal and noted for its amazing acoustics, the memorial chapel had opened a couple of years before—long after the flood-damaged original church had been torn down.

Jason circled the chapel, taking it in from every side. He'd already spent an hour with locals over a stein and thirty minutes with the clergy. The article nearly wrote itself. As glad as he was to be there, what Jason wanted most was to hear the high sweet voices of Lea's young choir sing the beautiful hymn.

Silent night! Holy night!
All is calm, all is bright.
Round yon virgin mother and child—
Holy infant, so tender and mild.
Sleep in heavenly peace!
Sleep in heavenly peace!

For the first time in Jason's life, Christ was more than the holy infant—more than a Christmas baby in a manger. He was Messiah to the Jews and humanity's Savior—the Savior that Germany and all the world so desperately needed. Jason's breath caught at the wonder and the unprecedented love of what He'd given to complete that offering. It would have been so much easier for Jesus to have turned His back on the world—the world that then, and even now, so largely rejected Him.

That's what he'd seen as he'd read through *Nachfolge* a second time. The Bible passages Bonhoeffer expounded upon had given Jason's ego—his arrogance—a beating, but he was discovering a new life, a new identity in Christ, and clear vision. He was being changed—transformed in some way he couldn't explain. And the God he'd never really known before would not let him go.

It had been easier to agree with Frau Bergstrom to move and hide children—Jewish and others the Reich wanted to destroy—than to embrace the notion of denying self, dying to self, and living only to Christ. Taking risks and walking a knife's edge was one thing—even the adrenaline rush was addictive. Loving his enemy and reaching out to him by really living in the world—not escaping from it, even through writing—was altogether new, and Jason needed time to absorb that idea, to understand what it meant, how it could play out in the midst of war.

Shadows spread across the snow-covered hill. Jason circled the chapel again and shoved cold hands deep into his coat pockets. The townspeople would soon fill the chapel and swarm the hillside. He wished Rachel could be there to share the coming service with him, to sing about heavenly peace. He wondered if she'd understand what that meant, what it meant to him.

He wondered if Rachel would like his gift—if Rivka had given it to her yet or if she was really waiting until Christmas morning.

He wished for the photograph he'd taken of Rachel and Amelie. But the risk of developing it had been too great. After his last visit with Gerhardt Schlick and friends, he dared not carry such evidence in his possession. Even if Schlick didn't recognize the profile of his own daughter dressed like a small boy, he'd never mistake Rachel Kramer for Lea Hartman, not the way she'd looked at him as he'd snapped the shutter. He'd made a risky detour to retrieve the film from Lea Hartman's house when he'd visited Oberammergau's Advent market. Now it was tucked away for safekeeping, waiting for the day it could be safely developed. In the meantime, he could dream.

❦

Wind and snow swirled round and round, rattling the windowpanes of Oma's snug house. Coals shifted, burning low in the stove. The radio crackled and sputtered until they couldn't make out the announcer's words. "This weather!" Oma sighed as she shelved the last supper dish and dried her hands on her apron. "I'm not sure we'll make it down the hill to church tomorrow."

"I'd best bring in more firewood before bedtime." Lea pulled her coat over her shoulders.

"We've enough coal for the stove, and you brought in a load of firewood earlier. We'll not use half that before morning."

"But imagine how deep this snow will be if it keeps up. I'd rather trudge through a foot than two." She pulled on mittens and pushed into the night.

Oma sighed. It was work Friederich had done—until this wretched war. Now Lea worked for them all. Rachel helped in the house, though it didn't seem to occur to her to contribute to the heavier labor. Oma knew Rachel was trying to change, to carry her weight, to lay down her inbred sense of entitlement. Family life, where each lived for the other and all lived for God, was new to her. "My fish out of water," Oma murmured. *It will be a long time—if ever—before our workforce changes.*

The man in the bed was thin—skin stretched taut over bones, his muscles atrophied. Friederich had not twitched, had not opened his eyes since the orderlies had carried him into the house. And Lea, though she bore it all with outward calm and patience, was wearing thin with worry for her husband. Oma could see it in the strain of her granddaughter's face, in the shine of unshed tears, in the slump of her shoulders when she finally, wearily sat down at night. Even her joy for the children's choir had waned.

Oma had not mentioned it to either granddaughter, but the difference between the two girls was beginning to show and certainly couldn't be hidden from the villagers much longer. What they'd do then, she didn't know.

Oma pulled her chair closer to the stove and stooped to fiddle with the radio's dial. The shouting voice of the Führer broke through. Oma pulled back instinctively, then quickly turned the dial again.

The second station reported on a Berlin Hausfrau who'd stolen ration coupons from her neighbor and been sentenced to three months in prison—just in time for Christmas.

She probably needed them to feed her family. How this war changes us at the very core!

Next came a repeated warning about listening to foreign radio stations, and the penalty: "No mercy will be shown the idiotic criminals who listen to the lies of the enemy." Oma didn't need to hear the rest. It had been broadcast and rebroadcast all week. Stiff prison sentences were meted out to those caught listening or suspected of listening to the BBC.

She heard Lea stomp her boots on the wooden mat outside the door and on the straw one inside, then the kerplunk of wood and the studied arrangement of kindling. Lea shoveled another bucket of coal into the stove. Rachel and Rivka pulled their kitchen chairs closer. Amelie was already fast asleep and tucked into her bed in the attic.

Oma changed the station once more, hoping something could be found to lighten their hearts. There would be no presents to mark the day beyond Herr Young's Christmas tree and the carp they'd filleted out of Amelie's sight for dinner tomorrow. There was no sugar to be had—no rolling and cutting *Lebkuchen* and drizzling the small cakes in sugar glaze as in years gone by.

Two more twirls of the dial and the soft, sweet notes of *"Stille Nacht"* filled the blue and white room. Oma smiled and sat back, leaning her head against the rocker's high back, glad she could count on something not to change, something to hold true. At least there would always be music in Germany—the pure, sweet carols of Christmas.

She closed her eyes as the choir ceased their humming, happy to share this first Christmas—despite the strangeness and peril of their circumstances—with both her granddaughters, with Amelie, and with Rivka, who were now as much her family as if they'd been born into it.

Silent night! Holy night!

"My favorite," she murmured to the young women. At least she could give them this.

All is calm, all is bright.

"So beautiful," Oma whispered.

But the words changed after the second line. They were not the words on the tip of Oma's tongue, not the beloved lyrics she'd sung all her life. Her eyes snapped open.

Only the Chancellor, steadfast in fight,
Watches o'er Germany by day and by night,
Always caring for us.
Always caring for us.

Silent night! Holy night!
All is calm, all is bright.
Adolf Hitler is Germany's wealth;
Brings us greatness, favor, and health.
Oh, give us Germans all power!
Oh, give us Germans all power!

The cold penetrating Oma's heart was reflected on the three pale faces in the lamp's glow.

Lea switched off the radio, and the small group of women sat in silence.

44

Lea's Christmas morning peek beneath the blackout curtain revealed snow-covered roads. After last night's storm, lanes into the village would be blocked with drifts. She'd be fortunate to shovel a path to Oma's little stable to milk their cow. No Nazis would come today, surely.

It felt good to inhale the fragrance of the tree in their room, to snuggle beneath the eiderdown and roll over, to sleep an extra hour beside her husband, to forget that she must soon rise to diaper and feed him.

It was bliss to imagine that at any moment Friederich would wake and fold her in his arms. It was her favorite dream, though getting harder to imagine. *It's more like sleeping beside a corpse.* The thought shamed her, made her wince. And then the tears trickled down her face and onto Friederich's arm, just as they did every morning.

"Please, Friederich. Oh, please wake up," she whispered. "It's Christmas morning, and there's nothing in all this world that I want but you. I love you, my dear, my darling husband. Whatever has happened, whatever you've been through or become, whatever is left to endure, let me endure it with you. Please, Friederich . . . please open your eyes."

But Friederich did not move. He barely seemed to breathe, though he never labored in his breathing.

After an hour of stroking his face, his chest, his arm, Lea rose, slipping her feet into cold slippers. Tonight she would light the candles on the tree, and she would sing to her husband—the old songs of Christmas, the ones he'd loved. That would be her gift to him, whether or not he heard.

❦

Oma did her best to make merry for her little family, though it was hard to keep her smile once she'd seen Lea's face and the solemn shaking of her head to Oma's brows raised in question. Oma had long since stopped asking Friederich's condition aloud. It was simply too wearing on Lea to admit that he was no better, that there had been no sign of improvement, that a little more of her husband had wasted away as they'd slept.

It was nearly noon when their late breakfast ended and the grown-ups finished off with a second cup of ersatz coffee—brewed from the same grounds as the day before. Amelie drained her mug of hot chocolate—chocolate Jason had smuggled through Forester Schrade—which she'd happily shared with the new handkerchief doll that Lea had made for her. Rachel had just begun to clear the table when a knock came at the back door.

Heads shot up and eyes widened. "Who? Heaven's mercy!" Oma began.

Rachel pulled Amelie toward the cupboard. Rivka followed. The knock came again, only louder. Lea scooped up the remaining cups and crumbs, tumbling everything into the wash pan. Oma straightened the chairs and disappeared to close the cupboard door behind the girls as the pounding increased.

❦

Straightening her apron and hair, Lea stepped into the cold foyer and opened the kitchen door.

"Merry Christmas, Frau Hartman!" The child held up a rectangle wrapped in brown paper, tied with string.

"Heinrich!" Lea gasped. "Merry Christmas to you! Whatever are you doing out in this weather? The snow is up to your knees!" She pulled him in the door, guiding him near the stove.

"I came with a g-g-gift, for Herr H-Hartman." The boy's teeth chattered.

"For Friederich?" Lea stopped, holding the little boy's scarf in midair. She could not imagine what gift could be given to her nearly comatose husband. "He's not . . . he's not well, Heinrich."

"He'll need this when he's b-better." The boy's teeth still chattered, and he shivered.

Lea didn't know what to say. "Pull off those boots and sit by the stove. You're soaking wet! Does your mother know you're out in such weather?"

"Sh-she doesn't. She's gone to church in our neighbor's sleigh. But I pretended to be sick, and she thought it was t-too cold for me."

"Heinrich Helphman! She was right!" Lea helped the child from his coat.

"But it's Christmas, and I must give this to Herr Hartman." The boy handed the package up to Lea. "You can open it, Frau Hartman. He'd want you to. And then you can tell him what it is."

Lea could not make herself smile into the boy's hopeful face. She sat in the rocker by the stove and took the package, pulled the knotted string bow, and folded back the brown paper. Surely it was the Christkind that Heinrich had taken weeks ago. It would be good to have it back. It was Friederich's best work, and he'd never carve another. She was prepared to kiss the forehead of Heinrich Helphman.

But when the gift was revealed, it was only a block of wood. Another cruel joke, and that stung Lea most of all. Tears sprang to her eyes.

Before she could tell him the pain he'd inflicted, Heinrich rushed ahead. "I took Herr Hartman's Christkind. It was so beautiful, and I think it's doing its work—at least I hope it is."

"Where is it, Heinrich?" Lea demanded. "Where is the Christkind?"

"I can't tell you that," Heinrich retorted, as if speaking to a child too simple to comprehend. "But Herr Hartman can carve another from this wood—it's fine wood! I worked five weeks for Herr Hochbaum at the woodcarving school—sweeping up and oiling the tools. It's a fine piece," he repeated. "A precious piece, he told me—the best that he had."

Lea shook her head, too hurt, too angry to speak. To be given a block of dead wood instead of the beautiful Christ child Friederich had carved—the babe with the face they'd hoped would look like their own—was like being given a shriveled corpse in place of her husband, a husk instead of the smiling, charming man with the strength of an ox. She was sick to death of taking whatever was left over—whatever anyone threw away once they'd taken the best at her expense.

She stood and Heinrich's gift dropped to the floor with a loud thud.

Staring up into Lea's eyes, the boy looked stricken.

Lea felt her face flame in fury and shame. But she lifted her hand to strike just as Oma stepped through the doorway.

"Lea!" Oma ordered.

Lea trembled with a violence of her own making. Withholding the slap she wanted to give the world, never mind Heinrich, wreaked havoc on her nerves. Oma stroked her granddaughter's shoulders, her arms, from behind, and pulled her hand from the air above Heinrich's head.

"Why is it you want the Christkind, Heinrich? Tell us that. Help us understand," Oma insisted.

Now the boy's eyes filled, and he shook his head. "I can't tell. It might not come true if I tell." He stooped to pick up the wood, setting the block on the rocker by the stove. "It's not beautiful yet, but I know Herr Hartman will make it so. He's the best woodcarver in Oberammergau—I tell everyone." He looked hopeful, but uncertain. "Don't be sad, Frau Hartman. It won't be long. You'll see."

But Lea turned her head into Oma's shoulder and wept.

"I think you'd best bundle up and go now, Heinrich," Oma whispered. "You'll want to get home before your mother finds you've gone."

"Yes, Frau Breisner." The little boy, worry lines creasing his forehead, pulled black boots over his shoes.

Oma continued to cradle her granddaughter against her shoulder.

Heinrich had just buttoned his coat and was pulling his cap down over his ears when he picked up the handkerchief doll from beneath the kitchen table and swiped his finger over the chocolate stain. "Is this yours, Frau Hartman?" He handed it to Lea, hope of redemption written in his features.

"No," Lea gasped, not claiming the doll. She hadn't the reserves to invent anything, had not one more cunning bone in her body.

The little boy frowned in confusion. "Do you have a little girl?"

Lea did her best to claim her senses, and shook her head.

"Mother made my sister one of these before she was born." Heinrich looked very sad. "But she wasn't able to play with it. She was too little when they took her away." He set the doll on the chair, lovingly spreading its embroidery-and-lace pinafore across its skirt. Soberly, he looked up. "Did they take your little girl away too?"

Lea moaned and tore from the room.

❦

Rachel held Amelie still in the attic, silently berating herself for not scooping up the child's new doll before they climbed into the cupboard and up through the wall. *A stupid, costly mistake! My only real job is to mind Amelie, and I failed again! Please, please don't let Oma suffer because of my stupidity!*

Rivka leaned close to the stovepipe, where it was easy to hear everything said below. As she did, Rachel saw the necklace Jason had given her dangle from beneath her blouse—a small diamond cut into the center of a gold oval locket. Rachel closed her eyes and swallowed the burning coal in her throat. Not once had Rivka spoken of any feelings for Jason, though she'd caught the girl's glazed eyes mooning over something, or someone, far away from time to time. *She's a teen! What is Jason Young thinking, leading on a girl of that age! What does he see in her that he doesn't see in me?*

When Heinrich Helphman had gone at last, Rachel released a long sigh, her neck and shoulders aching from the tension, and dropped her forehead on Amelie's crown.

***

It was the longest, most tense Christmas Day in Oma's memory. Both her granddaughters looked very close to tears, one as fractious as the other. Rivka looked as if she'd stepped into a world in which she didn't belong—and guilty to boot, poor child. Little Amelie wandered sleepily from adult to adult, peering into faces, holding her handkerchief dolly closely, as if it might tell her which of her frowning grown-ups would be willing to play.

By the time supper was finished and the dishes washed and put away, Oma was ready to lay her weary head upon her pillow. But despite the terrible ordeal of Heinrich Helphman and his twenty questions, Lea was determined that they should light the tree in Friederich's room and sing the carols.

It was almost morbid, gathering and singing round the half-dead man in the glowing light of the flickering candles. *If only he would die before he wears the very life from her. At least she could grieve and eventually get past grieving. But this living death goes on and on!* Oma felt she should regret, repent of such a thought. But she could not.

Still, she could deny her dear Lea nothing, not this year, not this day. They all dressed warmly for bed and gathered chairs in Lea and Friederich's room, round the tree. Lea lit the carefully spaced candles. Oma cuddled Amelie in her lap, let the little girl lean her ear to her chest to feel the vibrations as they sang. They all sang carols together, and then Lea sang alone—Friederich's favorite since childhood, "O Holy Night." She sang with pitch clear as handbells and the voice of an angel.

Somewhere during the second verse, Oma reached for the handkerchief in her pocket to wipe the tears of Lea's song from her weathered face. Amelie slipped from her lap. Oma let the child go.

⊷⊶

Friederich dreamed he neared heaven, the voices of angels attending his journey. The farther he walked, the nearer and brighter the lights grew. Angelic beings, heads wreathed in Bavarian braids and robed white in Christ's righteousness, sang in harmony. The weight on his chest lightened, returned, then lightened again. He recognized Oma, glad she was there to meet him, though aware his Lea must be terribly lonely without either of them.

And then the child he and Lea had daily prayed for came to meet him, to run tiny fingers across his lips and pat his face. She looked so much like the face of the Christkind he'd carved, the babe he'd prayed for as he'd worked. He wondered that prayers were answered finally, fully, in heaven.

The braided angels turned—nearly identical, so like Lea. He'd always believed angels must look like his angel wife.

The child made a happy gasp, pointing to him, welcoming him, and Friederich smiled wearily. He was so very tired. It would be good to rest from his long journey.

"Friederich! Friederich!" The angels surrounded him, chorused his name. He felt pulled in two directions—one toward rest and peace, and one toward the voices that grew more insistent.

His body began to prickle—just a little, but something new. He willed his eyes to open, not believing that they would. Faintly, out of focus, two angel faces hovered over him—two Leas. He couldn't reach with his arms, but he reached, as far and high as he could, with his eyes, his heart. "Lea," he whispered. "My Lea."

45

When Friederich had focused on Lea's face . . . Rachel could barely breathe. He was a shell of a man, his body broken, one eye lost, but what she saw in his expression was explosive and beautiful and rare. She envied Lea. She wanted what Friederich gave her sister in that moment—not from Friederich, but Rachel wanted . . . oh, how she wanted. She couldn't articulate it and couldn't deny it. She'd slipped from the room, pulling a willing but frightened Amelie with her. Rivka, stunned into silence, followed without a word.

Rachel tucked Amelie into her makeshift bed and climbed into her own pallet, pulled close alongside Amelie's. For the first time she let the little girl snuggle against her. The kitchen stovepipe, coming up through the attic floor, warmed the room just enough to sleep. Still, Rachel shivered. Amelie's breathing evened before ten minutes passed.

Rachel pulled the eiderdown over her head, willing the day to be done. She was sleeping on a pallet in a Bavarian attic with a deaf child and a Jewish teenager. She'd been raised—designed and groomed—to become the elite of society, racially and genetically superior to the masses. The philosophy had been drilled into her since childhood. And yet she felt the least of all.

Oma and Lea and Friederich got along fine without her, had lived a lifetime without her. Amelie would thrive under Lea's care. Even Rivka had grown closer to Oma in some ways than Rachel had, than she probably ever could. Oma and Lea appreciated and served those who worked with willing hearts and spirits, but they didn't seem to understand that Rachel was not raised to serve.

Changing that was less about participating in physical labor than about comprehending the levels of evolution within the human species. She could never explain that to them. She no longer understood it herself. And for the first time, Rachel wondered if it was true. Could that be one more lie from her father's lips? And if it was, how would she ever rid her mind, her very marrow, of its deception?

Rachel rolled over, drying silent tears on the sleeve of her nightdress.

"Rachel?" Rivka whispered behind her.

Rachel wanted to ignore the girl. The last thing she wanted to add to this unholy mixture was the adolescent pleas of a girl who'd stolen the one man whose nearness did raise the hairs on her arms—a man she'd finally admitted she never really had in the first place, and one her father had seen as "the lowest of the low," simply because of his dogged determination to bring the truth to light.

"Rachel?" Rivka whispered again, this time more urgently.

"What is it?" Rachel tried to sound as if she'd been asleep and wasn't happy to be woken.

"I must tell you something."

"In the morning. I'm tired. Go to sleep, Rivka."

But Rivka shook her shoulder. "No, it cannot wait. I should have told you sooner. I should have told you today—this morning."

Rachel sighed long and loudly, pulling the covers from her head. "What is it?"

Rachel felt her roommate sit up, saw her faint silhouette against the attic wall as she pulled the long and tangled ropes of her hair to the side and slipped her hands behind her neck.

"He told me to save this until Christmas Day, to give it to you first thing in the morning." She felt for Rachel's hand in the darkness and pressed the locket—Rachel could tell by the feel of the metal and the shape of the oval—with its delicate golden chain into Rachel's palm. Rivka closed Rachel's fingers. "I'm sorry that I didn't give it to you sooner. Jason said—" and now Rivka's voice trembled—"to tell you that he wants you to be well and safe and happy . . . and that he will find a way out of Germany for you and Amelie—he promises."

Rachel stopped breathing. She pressed her eyes tight, then opened them again, certain she was dreaming, angry in part that Rivka had held back Jason's gift, that she'd worn for weeks what was intended for Rachel. Still, one thought pushed beyond all the others. *He cares for me!*

Rivka lay down and turned her back to Rachel. "I'm sorry," she murmured. "I was just pretending it was mine. . . ."

Rachel didn't trust herself to answer. She closed her eyes and sank beneath the eiderdown. She couldn't see the necklace, not properly in the dark, but ran her fingers over its every intricacy, again and again. Finally she worked the clasp and fastened it round her neck. She fingered the locket's shape, imagined that Jason had fastened the clasp himself, that he admired how the locket fell into the hollow of her throat. *He cares for me. He'll come for me. He'll get me out of Germany—he promised! But how?* She could not imagine that.

❦

It was late. Christmas night and not a reporter or typist in the newsroom. Mark Eldridge had pushed and pushed for a story or a lead at the US ambassador's house—nearly begged—but it was shut up tight. The ambassador wasn't about to let reporters intrude on the final hours of Christmas Day with his family. It had been a long shot anyway, but a shot Eldridge dared in order to impress the chief.

That "Silent Night in Oberndorf" story Young had phoned in was nothing but sap, pure and simple. But the chief was delighted. It seemed that's what readers wanted this Christmas—something homespun and sappy from Germany. No Hitler atrocities for the holidays, though there was no shortage of those.

Earlier in the month Young had submitted an entire roll of Christmas market shots—all rosy-cheeked Bavarian girls and long-white-bearded men bouncing delighted toddlers on their knees as they played with carved wooden toys. Enough sap to cover the Zugspitze, tallest mountain in Germany—more than enough to make a guy sick.

Eldridge needed something fresh, something wholesome for the New Year. He wasn't likely to find that in Berlin. He pulled out the chair of Young's desk and flipped through the photos Peterson had left in the top drawer. Extras. Young had already submitted the best ones. Eldridge had seen them in print.

Frustrated, he slammed the drawer shut. It jammed. Eldridge pushed again, but it wouldn't close. He pulled the drawer out and ran his hand round the perimeter. Nothing. He tried again. It still wouldn't close.

Eldridge knelt down and peered into the space. Something dangled, like bait, near the back and from beneath the desktop. He reached in and pulled the small cylinder, sticky with tape, from its hiding place. Popping the canister's lid, he emptied the contents into his palm.

"Well, well, Ace, what have we here?"

46

"THE GERMAN PEOPLE *did not want this war. I tried up to the last minute to keep peace with England. But the Jewish and reactionary warmongers waited for this minute to carry out their plans to destroy Germany.*"

Rachel switched off the Führer's New Year speech midstream. She wished the "Jewish and reactionary warmongers"—whoever they were—truly would destroy Germany, or at least the Germany that had emerged since Hitler took power.

The New Year *Sterngang*, the walking musicians and choir of villagers led by a lantern star to welcome the New Year, had been canceled to comply with blackout regulations. Even so, Lea insisted that to lift their spirits, they hold their own singing late in the afternoon, before Friederich slept again. So once again they pulled chairs into Friederich and Lea's room.

By now, Friederich was sitting up in bed for an hour at a time, at least twice each day, to eat the thick and nourishing soup Oma made, thanks to the meat and fish Curate Bauer brought them. But physically weak and exhausted, tears streaked Friederich's face over every little thing. He couldn't sing, could barely speak, but Rachel had never seen a man's eyes communicate so much—or a woman so easily interpret them as did her sister. Lea sang her heart out in thanksgiving and hope. Friederich drank it in. Rachel slipped from the room when she could take no more.

But Friederich's nightmares and bloodcurdling screams rocked the little house and wracked the nerves of each member. Through the attic floor, Rachel could hear Lea soothing and crooning peace to her husband by night. She didn't understand the words, but she could hear the urgency in Friederich's long, sobbing explanations.

Between the holiday break and Lea's determination not to leave Friederich's side, the acting and singing classes were suspended for the week between Christmas and New Year, and the week following—all of which drove Rachel mad. She was ready to burst from being shut up inside the emotion-filled house. Jason's locket somehow kept her sane.

But Rivka had grown more distant, more despondent since Christmas, and Rachel could only imagine she missed wearing the necklace, or perhaps missed the fantasy the necklace had fostered.

She shouldn't have kept it so long. She shouldn't be fantasizing about a grown man—a man ten years older.

"Have you no pity, Rachel?" Oma asked one morning when Rivka left the breakfast table in tears after Rachel's chiding. "The child has no family left, no idea what has become of them—if they're even still alive."

"That's not my fault. My father was taken away too."

"You know that's different." She leaned across the table toward Rachel. "You have me and Lea and Friederich."

That was true, but Rachel was tired of Oma taking everyone's side but hers. "She's not like us; she's Jewish," Rachel whispered. "What do you expect? Even Friederich can barely look at her."

Oma stood abruptly, knocking her teacup over, so horrified that Rachel thought she might slap her. "Friederich remembers the horrific things his unit did to Polish Jews. He's ashamed."

Rachel felt the warmth spread across her face. "I see that, but Germany's at war, Oma. That's what war is," she defended. "You can't stop it. Friederich couldn't stop it. I can't stop it—it's everywhere! So please don't blame me."

Oma straightened, her mouth trembling in fury, and left the room.

Rachel rolled her eyes. Oma would not stay and fight with her, and Rachel itched for a good fight.

She knew she should treat Rivka better, that she was being nothing short of a brat to her and sometimes to everyone in the house. But everything she'd said was true—none of them could stop Hitler's madness.

Still, Rachel knew that fueling her desire to squash Rivka's fantasies of Jason were memories of her father's tirades about Poles, Jews, Slavs, Negroes, and Asians—how they cursed the world by being and breeding, how they must be contained before they further weakened society, dragging it down to their level. This cleaving—sterilization at the very least, he'd declared—was truly a mercy, and for the good of mankind.

Rachel bit her lip. She knew the idea was madness—as mad as anything Hitler had conceived. She could never admit such dogma to Oma, or that she'd once bought into it. Even now, knowing eugenics was a crock, it was too easy to think of herself as better than the others. So much craziness, so many lies to sort out, and all of them woven, like plaits, into her mind.

47

CURATE BAUER knelt for morning prayers beside his bed. He prayed that God would blind the eyes of the Gestapo and—God forgive him—Father Oberlanger to his Munich activities with Jews and political dissidents, and to his trading for food on the black market to feed them.

He prayed God's protection on Mayor Schulz and the couple the mayor had recently illegally wed, Jewish Zebulon Goldmann and Aryan Gretel Schweibe.

He prayed for Administrator Raab and the two junior monks who'd recently begun a weekly religious discussion group for boys in Raab's home, under the guise of a Hitler Youth program, ostensibly learning and developing signal skills.

He begged God to help Friederich Hartman accept the forgiveness offered him. Such atrocities as he'd known in the Polish campaign could break any man. The heart of the gentle woodcarver was not made for such evil.

He prayed that Jason Young would find a way to tell the world Friederich's story. He thanked the Holy Father for the spirited young American, for his steadfast heart and crusader nature. He could not ask for a more determined partner in resistance or a more passionate brother in Christ. His ability to move freely within the country, to collect forged papers and passports, was indispensable in helping Jews to safety.

And Lea Hartman and her sister . . . The curate laughed in the midst of his prayer. He'd not known whether to believe Frau Breisner when she'd finally confessed to him there were two. All three of them were good enough for the stage! But it had explained so much—why Frau Hartman had suggested performing the Passion in an odd year, how she'd bloomed with newfound confidence and boundless energy and talents, why she could be shy and demure one day and nearly flirtatious another.

He shook his head. Herr Hartman must grow dizzy with two such beautiful women beneath his roof. If he didn't miss his guess, Herr Young would happily relieve him of one of the twins. *Please, Lord, let them go on fooling us all.*

He'd passed Jason's copy of *Nachfolge* to Rachel. Herr Young had such hopes for the Fräulein's heart. But Curate Bauer wondered. She'd been reared in the haughty spirit of eugenics. Faith in the One who so loved all the world that He'd offered Himself as a ransom for sin was a humbling journey. *Heal and mold her heart, Holy Father.*

Such a vast network to keep straight and so many lives at stake—Curate Bauer spent more time than ever on his knees.

And he spent so much time trying to avoid Father Oberlanger that he was greatly surprised when later that morning the priest stopped him in the square and quietly affirmed the Marian instructional sessions and Bible studies for older girls, as long as they could safely be slipped beneath the noses of the Gestapo.

"Even those parents who are members of the Nazi Party are not eager to give up our Catholic traditions or the training of their children, Curate. That's not the way of the people of the Passion." Father Oberlanger leaned close and tapped the curate on the shoulder, as if confiding something more.

Curate Bauer wished that the village parents' staunch spirit led to helping those who truly had no voice in this Nazi regime. But he dared not say that aloud. He wasn't certain where the old priest stood; he met so frequently with the Nazi officials lording over the village.

It wasn't that Jews were eager to hide in Oberammergau. Dramatized and distorted scenes of the Passion Play and the vicious responses of some theatregoers made the village a potential hotbed for anti-Semitism, easily compatible with Nazi propaganda. It had become a place for Hebrews, whether Christian or not, to avoid. But a few Jews could be safely slipped among the refugees flocking to the village, especially if the map of their heritage was not written on their faces.

Curate Bauer sighed later as he polished the crucifix in the church. More resisters could be such a help—especially if they were willing to supply food or hiding places within their homes or shops.

Father Oberlanger stopped in the church, clearly preoccupied. "I'm meeting later today with our Nazi official, seeing if I might convince him to keep his hands off our festival and Corpus Christi procession." He was halfway down the aisle when he appeared to just think of something. "If you happen to be away today, Curate, it won't matter. I'll be meeting with the Hauptsturmführer."

Curate Bauer felt again that the priest was urging him forward, though he couldn't be certain.

⋘⋙

Jason loosened his tie and raked his hair into place, pulling his typewriter closer. He had stories to get out—Friederich's stories, related through Curate Bauer, of Nazi atrocities in Poland that should rock the world.

He prayed they would incite governments sitting on the sidelines to band together and crush Hitler before he obliterated the Jews and Poles and everyone else in his mad path to world domination.

It was not a story the chief would print or sell, but Jason had other avenues. As soon as he phoned New York through his private source—he'd never get typewritten copy past the censors—he'd contact Dietrich Bonhoeffer with the number Frau Bergstrom had given him. Dietrich would want to know all that Friederich had told the curate, if he didn't know already.

The fact that the Nazis were driving Poles from their homes so Germans could resettle there, taking over their houses and possessions, was new information. More "living space." Meanwhile, Poles were sent to concentration camps or simply massacred.

Learning that a friend had participated in herding Polish Jews into a synagogue and watching as they burned alive had been the last straw for Friederich. He'd placed himself in the line of fire, knowing he could not carry out another sadistic order and face his God.

Jason knew that by the time distorted Polish war propaganda reached the German people, it would in no way resemble the truth. The Volk, no doubt, would go along, apathetic, or nod their heads, turning a blind eye. "After all," he'd heard a thousand times, "Herr Hitler is rebuilding Germany. As he told us from the beginning, there will be sacrifices required."

Jason grunted. *As long as the sacrifices required belong to others.*

Despite the Party line, no one could pretend they'd not seen the inhumane treatment of Jews on the streets of Germany each day—the complete stripping of Jewish rights and citizenship, the expulsion of Hebrew Christians from churches, expulsion from civil service, schools, universities, symphonies, and newspaper ownership. Marriage to Gentiles was forbidden. Confiscation of goods and property was the norm, as was denial of medical and dental treatment, stricter and more severe rationing of food and clothing—of everything—than for Gentiles. And then there was the "relocation" and constant intimidation, the threat of concentration camps, rape, and torture by the Gestapo and SS.

He could only hope that America and Britain would listen and respond with greater force. What worried him most was something Dietrich had mentioned observing during his visit to America—the way Americans treated Negroes. Not so different in some ways than

German citizens treated Jews at the beginning. *If Americans treat our citizens in such a way, will they step up to the plate to protect their own or the world's Jews?* He wasn't sure.

❦

"No, no," Rivka admonished. "Not that way. Try again. Open your palm, hold it against your chest . . . There, that's it. Now circle." She stopped. "You're circling the wrong way, Friederich. Please pay attention."

Friederich humbly nodded and shifted in his chair, stretching his game leg out the best he could. Amelie tugged on his sleeve and he opened his arms. She climbed onto his lap and looked at him expectantly. He would try the sign again—for her. It was a good thing Rivka and Amelie were patient and encouraging teachers. He didn't mind that they found his fumbling efforts amusing. His large fingers didn't seem to bend and curve so flexibly as those of the women—even Oma's, no matter that his were stronger from years of wood-carving. And he was still regaining the ability to focus for lengthy periods of time.

Amelie laughed as he made the wrong sign once more, grabbed his hands between her small ones, and did her best to maneuver his fingers into position. Friederich wondered if pretzels felt this way.

"You'll get it in time, my love." He felt a soft kiss nuzzled into the back of his neck and smiled. Practicing the signs had added benefits. Lea loved to watch him with Amelie and he knew his efforts pleased her. There was nothing he wouldn't do to please his precious wife.

"What would we do without Amelie to lighten our days?" he sighed.

"I hope we never need learn," Lea whispered in his ear, sitting beside him, trying the new sign Rivka continued to demonstrate.

Friederich hadn't realized that he'd spoken aloud. He did that a great deal lately—spoke his thoughts without meaning to. He looked around the room. His comment had sobered each of the women and caused little creases in their brows, as well as Amelie, who'd responded quickly, pulling away, so sensitive to the reactions and nuances of her grown-ups.

Friederich deliberately smiled again, hugging Amelie to his chest, tickling her cheek until she, too, smiled again, laughed again, and pulled his fingers into the shape of the sign. Friederich, much relieved, determined to be more careful in the future. They all needed as much joy, as much hope as their lives could afford. He must do his part in providing that.

Lent had barely begun when the Nazi order came that all crucifixes and Catholic imagery were to be removed from classrooms. Even normal school prayers were banned. Father Oberlanger turned grayer. At first, parents were too stunned to react. But before the week ended, the outraged village parents—mostly mothers left at home, thanks to the war—protested, demanding that the symbols and freedom to pray be returned. How could a village whose entire identity was defined by the Passion Play be expected to give up their hand-carved imagery?

In neighboring Ettal, Curate Bauer saw protesters who threatened to desert Nazi Party organizations and withhold donations to the winter funds designated to assist the poor and needy. Men in the beer hall claimed those funds went straight to Nazi coffers and that threatening their wallet was a sure way to garner attention. Irate wives vowed to write their husbands at the front and tell them of the Nazis' latest ploy, creating dissension in the military ranks—the Reich's greatest fear.

In the throes of the battle, Curate Bauer lamented to Rachel one afternoon after the children's theatre class. "That such a thing could happen in Germany!"

"Nothing in Germany surprises me now, Curate."

"You are too cynical."

She shook her head, packing her small prop bag. "Just a realist. I've looked at the world through the glasses I was given. Now I've taken them off. It's surprising how distorting the wrong pair of glasses can be."

He sighed. "I suppose nothing like this could happen in America."

"Banning prayer from schools? Stripping crucifixes from walls? That would be like taking down the Ten Commandments in the United States. I've never been a churchgoer, but I can't imagine such a thing happening. The churches, even the people who aren't church-goers, would never stand for having their rights stripped away like that."

⸙

By the end of the week, Berlin resounded with the tremendous clamor and crucifixes were restored. Curate Bauer watched as Father Oberlanger, proud of his parish for their pro-Catholic stance, applauded the fortitude of the parents at every opportunity.

But Curate Bauer knelt alone in the darkened church before the altar and wept. What if these same parents had risen up and so vig-orously protested the Nuremberg Laws stripping Jews of citizenship and rights? What if they had demanded that the elderly, the handi-capped, the mentally challenged, homosexuals, Jehovah's Witnesses, Gypsies, Poles, the Jews themselves—so many targeted by Hitler—be spared? What if the church, Catholic and Protestant, had refused allegiance to Hitler and maintained Christ as its true head?

Have mercy, and forgive us, Father. We've saved our sacred images, but sacrificed Your image within our souls.

48

THE BITTER winter cold gave way. The city's snowbanks all but disappeared. Jason was recalled to Berlin to cover for a correspondent sent back to the States.

"So, why was Keifer sent home? I thought he was here for the duration."

Eldridge dumped a sheaf of papers on Jason's desk. "Shot off his mouth to a New York paper about the Gestapo throwing dissident priests into concentration camps and torturing them. They figured he'd leaked the stories about Poland. Chief was lucky to get him out of the country before the Gestapo took him. Nazis don't think much of having their handiwork exposed, or didn't you know?"

Jason ignored Eldridge's sarcasm. He was sorry Keifer had taken the blame for the Poland stories, but at least he hadn't been sent to one of the prison camps—a foreign journalist's unspoken threat. If Keifer's early trip home meant there was still a chance Jason could expose more Nazi dirt, that was a plus. "So what's my assignment?"

"Church news, old boy. You did such a fine job on that Bonhoeffer story that the chief thought you could take on something new—with more discretion than Keifer, of course." Eldridge grinned. "It's not my cup of tea, if ya catch my drift."

Jason did, and he was glad for the assignment, though he wasn't about to let Eldridge know. He nonchalantly leafed through the pages.

The church news—Catholic and evangelical alike—wasn't good.

From reports in the field, the number of priests and pastors arrested for speaking against Nazi aggression had grown. Even those who weren't speaking out—if they weren't heiling Hitler—were being watched, their letters intercepted, their phones tapped. Gestapo routinely sat in to observe and report on sermons.

Jason's immediate concern was for Curate Bauer. He knew of at least two dozen refugees hiding in Oberammergau and the surrounding countryside, all under the curate's protection. How many more there were, or who could help them if Bauer were arrested, was anybody's guess. At least the curate was quiet about his business and had no private phone to be tapped. It was his constant busyness, his running to and fro, that drew attention.

And busyness was what worried Jason about Dietrich. Bonhoeffer did not deliberately draw attention to himself, but he refused to hide behind the Nazified skirts of the National Reich Church. He was allowed in Berlin only to visit his high-profile parents—surely because of them he'd not yet been arrested. Either that or the Nazis hoped he'd lead them to others equally deserving of their attention.

But Jason knew his new friend would find a way to stand and serve, no matter where, no matter what they did to him—even if it meant cloistering himself for a time to write another book, a book that would no doubt incite and turn the church on its ear.

Nachfolge had certainly done that for Jason. He prayed it would do the same for Rachel.

Jason spent the next week pounding out story after story. He saturated the chief with Berlin church news, which made it easier to wrangle an assignment for the story that took him just where he wanted to go—Holy Week in the Passion Village without a Passion Play.

He tried to convince himself that his motives were selfless, that he could use the opportunity to deliver more passports and forged papers to Curate Bauer. That he needed to touch base with Friederich

Hartman and see for himself that little Amelie was safe. But he couldn't wait to see a certain young woman, couldn't wait to see what she thought of Bonhoeffer's book.

That reminded him of the film.

Jason waited until evening, when the newsroom was empty. Just before leaving for Munich, he reached into the back of his desk drawer for the small cylinder he'd taped to the inside top. The first time his hand swept the empty space he wasn't concerned, certain he'd just missed it. But the second swipe and a third left him empty-handed. He pulled out the drawer, checked the back, checked each of the drawers and the floor. Finally he switched off his desk lamp and sat, every imaginable scenario racing through his brain. None of them good.

49

"The children were magnificent!" Curate Bauer whispered in Rachel's ear as the roomful of parents rose to their feet in applause. The Easter skit had come off beautifully, down to the tiniest performer. Rachel, nearly bursting with pride, crowed over her charges. She was thrilled to play Lea for the day, and grateful to her sister for exchanging places and watching Amelie.

It wasn't the Passion Play by any stretch of the imagination, but a story about a child who came to know Jesus, a skit she and Lea had secretly written together—an Easter miracle all its own.

In the process, Lea had insisted Rachel read the Gospels, focusing on Jesus' last week. Initially, Rachel had balked at the notion, remembering her father's claims that Christianity and its book were crutches for the weak, a soft religion for those unable to navigate life under their own steam. The Nazis said the same, ridiculing the idea of a sacrificial, suffering Savior rather than one strong in military might like their Führer.

But once she realized her prior programming, Rachel was willing—determined—to investigate for herself. She was surprised to find that Jesus was not the weakling her father had insisted, but a strong and radical man who stood against the hypocrisy of His time. That unsettled her, shifted her moorings. But she kept at it.

When she'd finished reading, she and Lea wrote the skit in a sitting, then edited and edited for days, until every line sang. Rachel had imagined the story from Amelie's viewpoint, a little girl who came to Jesus in need of help—Lea added that she came in need of forgiveness.

But Rachel knew she was that little girl, that parentless child who recognized her need at last. She wanted her ending to be as happy as the child's in the skit, but that required belief in Jesus as the Son of God. Rachel winced. Belief—in anyone or anything—was more than she could swallow.

Rachel saw the light of that belief and accepted forgiveness in Lea's eyes and life, in Oma's and Friederich's. She wanted that feeling of being clean and whole too, but yielding, humbling herself, raked against the grain of her self-sufficiency.

"An unusual rendition, Frau Hartman," Father Oberlanger suggested, making her jump, bringing her back to earth. "May I ask what script you used?"

"I wrote it myself." Rachel could not keep the pride from her voice.

"I see." But Father Oberlanger looked none too pleased. "You understand, do you not, that all scripts must be presented to the council and are subject to their approval?"

"No, I didn't—I mean, yes, I understand that about the Passion Play," she stammered, "but I didn't think it applied to simple skits for the children."

He raised his chin. "You've lived here your entire life, and yet you don't know this? You are mistaken. Because we are at war does not excuse us from conforming to established guidelines."

"It was just a little skit," she defended. "I thought the children did very well, didn't you?"

Curate Bauer stepped into the breach. "The children were wonderful, Frau Hartman. We very much appreciate your fine endeavors with them." He glanced at grim Father Oberlanger. "Please forgive me, Father. I should have spoken with you about the script. I did not think."

"Not thinking," Father Oberlanger replied, "can be very dangerous, especially in these times. You may have noticed our Gestapo guest?"

"Yes, Father." Curate Bauer spoke humbly, much to Rachel's chagrin. "It won't happen again."

"I hold you responsible, Curate."

"Yes, Father."

Rachel waited until the older priest had walked away. "Why did you kowtow to him? You know the play was well done. The parents were pleased as punch! What is his problem?"

"His problem," Curate Bauer whispered, "is the Gestapo agent scribbling away in the last row. And Maximillion is not on duty outside the door because he loves the church. He's a snitch in Hitler Youth uniform—not one of your American Boy Scouts."

Rachel waved the notion away. "Maximillion is moonstruck and harmless. And what can the Gestapo possibly complain about? This is the Passion Village. Plays about Jesus are the norm, not the—"

"Anything that declares our need for anything beyond the perfect Aryan man or woman or recognizes any savior but Hitler is frowned upon." Curate Bauer and Rachel glanced at the door and the agent leaving, writing in his notepad. "We must be careful, very careful."

The gild was off the lily. Rachel smiled mechanically at the parents who thanked her, the children who reached their arms to hug her on their way out the classroom door.

She'd written the play from the best that was in her. She'd believed that the Passion Village powers that be would love it—love her for it. Now, to be reprimanded for doing the first truly good thing she could remember doing—for sharing, in her way, what she'd been given—was a slap in the face.

And where was Jason? Rachel had heard he was in Oberammergau, conducting interviews. She was sure he'd hear of and come to the play, that he'd find a way to visit her at Oma's one evening after curfew. She'd wanted him to see what she could do, had hoped it would relieve his unspoken anxiety as to the state of her eugenics-drilled soul. But he hadn't come.

When the room was empty, she packed her bag of scripts and collected the small hand props to store, tossing them into the box with more energy than necessary. She swiped at tears that sprang unbidden.

"Frau Hartman?" Maximillion stood at the classroom door, his hands behind his back. "You are crying." He was across the room and at her side in a moment.

"No." Rachel blinked her eyes and dried her face. "Just something in my eye. I'm quite all right."

Maximillion pulled a handkerchief from his pocket. "Allow me, please."

Rachel smiled, self-consciously, trying to decide how Lea might behave in this situation. Would she be meek? Appreciative? Standoffish? Rachel couldn't decide, and allowed the teen to brush the last of her tears away.

"There. Is that better?"

"Yes," she sniffed. "Thank you." She turned away, but the boy took the liberty of pressing her arm.

"Perhaps these will cheer you." He handed her a lovely, mildly fragrant bouquet of hothouse flowers. "I grew them myself."

"They're lovely, Max!" Rachel meant it. It had been ages since she'd seen flowers, even longer since she'd been given a bouquet.

Maximillion smiled. "Max—I like that. Always call me Max."

Rachel blushed, realizing she'd betrayed her American penchant for nicknames. "It suits you."

He stepped closer. "I heard of the priest's reprimand. That was not warranted."

"You saw the play?"

"No, I am sorry; I did not. I was on duty in the hallway. But I'm certain that whatever you did was in the best taste. You've given so much—music, singing, and acting classes for the *Kinder*. The priest should be grateful. He should not question you." He pocketed his handkerchief. "I'll be sure to check my duty roster the next time your class performs. I will not miss it again."

Rachel's heart was warmed by his righteous indignation, though she knew he was just a boy adoring a teacher. "That's very sweet of you, Max." She touched his face, just as she'd seen Lea do to Amelie when the child had especially tried to please her. "I look forward to that."

But Maximillion did not respond gratefully in the cherub-like manner of Amelie or her students. His eyes lit with a lust Rachel had seen only in grown men. He covered her hand, clasping it to his cheek. Too late Rachel realized her mistake and tried to pull her hand away, stepping back. But Maximillion was not put off. He grabbed her hand and stepped forward, too near, inches from her face, his eyes riveted on her lips. Rachel's heart gripped. She realized for the first time that the boy was at least three inches taller than she and a good thirty pounds heavier. She had nowhere to go.

A loud knock at the open door intruded. Jason Young stepped into the center of the room. If disgust were a lance, the Hitler Youth would have been impaled. "Frau Hartman, I was wondering if I could ask you a few questions about the children's skit for the newspaper."

Maximillion turned, his cheeks a furious shade of red, frustration shooting from his eyes.

Rachel nearly sank to her knees in relief. "Yes, yes, Herr Young. Gladly." She straightened, pulling her hand away and regaining her composure. She placed the flowers on the table beside her. "You must go along now, Maximillion."

Maximillion, still shooting daggers at Jason, didn't move.

"I believe you heard the lady." Jason stepped closer, pulling a notepad and pen from his coat pocket, never taking his eyes from the Hitler Youth.

Maximillion grabbed the cap he'd tossed to the table, defiantly placed it on his head, and marched past Jason, his shoulder brushing hard against the journalist.

When he was out the door, Rachel slumped against the table, heaving a sigh of relief. "Thank you."

"Looks like you have a problem on your hands."

Rachel shook her head. "Lea cautioned me, but I thought he was harmless. He's just a boy."

"A big boy," Jason warned.

"Yes." Rachel swallowed. "A big boy."

Jason looked about to say more but stopped. "It's good to see you." A smile lit his eyes.

"And you, Herr Young." She grinned.

He reached for her hand, froze, and glanced quickly back at the door.

"I guess you'd better stay on that side of the table, and I'll stay on mine," she whispered.

He pouted. "What fun is that?"

"None," she said, meaning it. "I've missed you."

"You have no idea," he lamented. After a moment he straightened. "There's something I have to tell you."

Her brows rose expectantly.

Jason pulled a magazine from his coat pocket and plunked it on the table between them. The cover—graced by a stunning Rachel, smiling into the camera with a winsome Amelie clasping her face—took Rachel's breath away. "You took this." She picked up the maga-zine. "I remember when you took this. But you published it?" She felt the room sway and the floor drop beneath her.

"No." Jason frowned. "It was on a separate roll of film—just those couple of pictures I took of you and Amelie." He tossed his fedora to the table. "It was stupid, foolish, I know. And selfish. I just wanted your picture, and Amelie's—I never thought anybody'd see them. I didn't even develop them—didn't dare."

"Then how—?"

"Check the attribution—the name at the bottom of the photograph."

She squinted to bring the fine print into view. "M. Eldridge. Who's M. Eldridge?"

"My archrival, a guy in the Berlin newsroom who's made work a living nightmare. It's a race for every story, the Indy 500 for photo sales. He must have been snooping in my desk."

"You left my photograph in your Berlin desk?" She couldn't believe such stupidity.

"I left the cylinder of film there, taped to the inside, sure nobody would find it. And they wouldn't—couldn't—if they weren't looking for something."

"And you didn't think after being interrogated and beaten by the SS looking for me that someone might go snooping through your desk?"

"I said it was stupid on my part. Taking the picture in the first place was stupid, and I'm sorry. I'm sorry, Rachel."

"Is this on the newsstands in Berlin?"

"No. He sold it to this rag in New York. Berlin's not likely to see it."

"Not likely? This could get us killed!"

"I don't think anyone would recognize Amelie. She looks like a boy—is dressed like a boy."

Rachel wondered if he'd lost his mind. "How did you find it?"

"I searched the newsroom—Eldridge's desk. He was evidently proud enough of it that he kept it in his own desk drawer—stupid move number two." He leaned forward. "The thing is, if anybody in the Party sees this—"

"Gerhardt."

He nodded. "If Schlick sees this, he'll think it's Lea."

"Does this look like Lea to you?" she demanded.

"No, it doesn't," he confessed. "But she's dressed like Lea, and a case can be made. You'd better warn Lea to own it, to make up some story about the kid she's holding."

Rachel felt like tearing her hair out. After having been so careful so long . . .

"The German censors keep tabs on all the foreign newspapers and periodicals. They're bound to see it, and eventually somebody's gonna realize this is the spitting image of the missing Kramer woman." Jason sat on the table's edge. "We might get lucky where Schlick's concerned. We might not."

"If he realizes this is me . . ."

"He'll be back. Maybe not soon." He almost smiled. "I think that nearly letting the Führer get blown up—all for chasing the ghost of you through this remote Alpine village—has convinced him to toe the line in Berlin for a while."

"How do you know?"

"Sources." He sobered. "If there were a safe way to get you out of Germany right now, I would. But the borders are locked down. Trains, roads, waterways, ports, checkpoints—drum tight. Getting out through Switzerland is our best bet, but even that . . ."

"This makes leaving less safe." Rachel wasn't sure how she felt about that. She'd wanted desperately to leave before, but now she didn't know.

"It raises awareness again." He closed his eyes. "Things are closing in everywhere. Remember me telling you about my friend Dietrich?"

"Bonhoeffer!" Rachel remembered the book the curate had passed on to her, the book she'd barely skimmed, then set aside to work on the skit.

"The Gestapo closed down his school in Sigurdshof. He's no longer allowed to teach ordinands."

"But why? He's not militant, is he?"

"Because he's teaching allegiance to Christ, and because by challenging people to live as Jesus lived, he's challenging them to think beyond blindly following the dictates of the Reich."

"Is that what you're doing in helping the curate, by helping Jews and forging papers?"

He nodded. "Giving targets lower on the Nazi radar a way out of Germany wherever we can. But it's getting harder."

"That's about the most dangerous thing you could be doing, short of raising a coup to assassinate Hitler. I'd have thought reporting real news was risk enough—even for you, Mr. Scoop."

"Guess I don't feel much like 'Mr. Scoop' these days." He studied her long enough to make her squirm. "I've met someone."

She sat back, sure she'd been punched in the stomach.

"I mean, I've met someone who's shown me things about myself that I didn't know before—things about life, the world."

"Blonde? Blue-eyed? Aryan, long legs?" Rachel couldn't keep the blister from her voice.

A grin crept up one side of his face. "You sound jealous. It's not like that." He leaned forward and took her hands in his. "What do you know about Jesus Christ?"

Rachel pulled away. "So now you've decided to become a priest. Where's the real Jason Young and what have you done with him?"

"I've changed—in ways I never imagined."

"You weren't so bad the way you were," she joked self-consciously. "I'm not sure I want you to change."

"Too late." Jason's eyes probed hers. "Did you read the book I sent?"

"*Nachfolge*? I started it, but—"

"Dietrich wrote it. Read it—in light of what you know about the eugenics movement here and at home, what you know about experimenting on and euthanizing people, all you know about Hitler and his Nazis and this war."

Rachel sighed. "It's not exactly a gripping English novel."

"Better than. It will change the way you think."

"My father will turn over in his grave. I'm sitting in the middle of the Passion Village teaching church plays." She shook her head, knowing she'd read the book anyway. "He always said that Christianity is a crutch—"

"For the weak," Jason finished. "That's pretty much what the Nazis say. Only now they're trying to replace Jesus with Hitler as the savior of the people. Hitler's got it all bound up with pagan rites and blood and soil and nationalism. Sick stuff."

"I hear parents of the children in my class, when they stop in to pick up their kids. Calling themselves the 'people of the Passion' and saying how the Passion rules their lives. And then I hear through Lea how this one or that one turned informer on their neighbor or even their relatives—for privileges, money, rations, or just brownnosing the Nazis. I see kids who've copied the adults they hear—yelling that Jews are Christ killers and that the Jews deserve what they get. Their brand of Christianity certainly doesn't seem to make any difference in how they treat each other or how they talk about Jews."

"I see it too. They don't realize how Hitler's changed the culture, changed their thinking, that he's doing just what he said he'd do in *Mein Kampf*." Jason kneaded the back of his neck. "He's eliminating the weak and poor, people Christ died for. He's determined to wipe out the Jews, the very people God chose to reach the world through. The ones He entrusted with His Word. They're cutting off the arm of Christ and they don't see it."

"No, they don't," Rachel confessed, uncertain what she thought.

"Most don't know or care what will happen to those they relocate outside Germany."

"It's not their problem—they don't see it as their problem."

"It's only beginning," Jason warned. "I have a feeling we've seen nothing yet."

50

Jason sat in the newsroom, reading the latest—Germany's invasion of Norway and Denmark, proclaiming it their duty to protect the "freedom and independence" of those countries from the Allies. Hitler warned that "all resistance would be broken by every available means by the German armed forces and would therefore only lead to utterly useless bloodshed."

Jason shoved his fedora onto his head and pushed into the cold spring morning. He doubted very much that the flabbergasted Norwegians or Danes saw Hitler's invasion in such a magnanimous light, let alone the correspondents who were driven from their beds at dawn only to be locked up in the Kaiserhof while their countries were "protected."

The Swedes were too scared to aid their Scandinavian kinsmen—a decision Jason felt certain they'd rue. But later, over the BBC, Jason heard Winston Churchill vow from the House of Commons that Hitler had "committed a grave strategical error" and that the British navy would now take the Norwegian coast and sink all ships in the Skagerrak and the Kattegat. Jason prayed the British would make good their threat. If they didn't, what—or who—would stop Hitler from systematically taking over the world?

But just before Passover, British and Norwegian troops were driven from Lillehammer, and Hitler celebrated once more.

⊶⊷

Nearly a month had passed since Easter. Rachel knew that Curate Bauer had scrounged and bartered to provide all he could for the

Passover feast for Jews in hiding—those who embraced Jesus as their Messiah as well as those who did not.

Once the blackout curtains were drawn, Rachel, Oma, and Rivka carried to the attic napkins and plates, bowls and candles, food and wine needed for the seder. Lea helped Friederich hobble up the attic stairs. The girls spread their pallets and pillows across the floor in a circle, wide-eyed Amelie delighted with the impromptu picnic and eager to help. Rivka placed two candles in the center.

"There's no lamb and no egg, but we have horseradish root and unleavened bread. Thanks to Curate Bauer, we have wine." Oma held up the decanter.

"Is it enough?" Rachel asked Rivka, seeing the girl's sad face.

"It's wonderful." Rivka choked back tears. "It's just . . ."

"The first Passover without your parents?" Oma asked.

Rivka nodded, unable to hold her tears at bay. Oma's hands were full, and Rivka desperately needed a shoulder. Rachel pulled the girl into an awkward embrace, letting her cry. Amelie patted Rivka's leg, and Rachel stroked the little girl's hair in return.

Rachel didn't understand how people, especially those who claimed to be Christian and to follow the Jesus Bonhoeffer wrote about, could stand by and watch as their neighbors were stolen away in the night.

Curate Bauer had shaken his head when Rachel had asked him to explain. "Is there an explanation for blindness, for hatred? For sin? I don't know the answer. I only know the remedy is Christ's great love as we've been shown in His Passion."

Rachel thought about that as she held Rivka—Rivka, who'd lost her family at the hands of a madman and a world gone mad.

Rivka pulled from Rachel and wiped her eyes. Rachel drew Amelie to her side as the entire makeshift family settled onto the pillows and pallets, gathering round the small seder plate Rivka had placed on the floor. She set three matzohs on the plate, covering them with the large white linen napkin Oma had provided. Then she looked up at the family, her eyes still glistening. "There was no time for the bread to rise before we fled Egypt, so we baked it unleavened."

She arranged the horseradish from Oma's garden and a bunch of watercress Friederich had found in a mountain spring. "Our slavery was bitter—as bitter as these herbs. We're missing the shank bone, showing the lamb's blood that marked our houses—our lintels and doorposts."

"Jesus is our Passover Lamb," Friederich whispered. "He knows our hearts, and He covers us with His blood."

Rivka blanched at the notion but continued. "My mother used to let me mix the nuts and cinnamon, the apples chopped with a little wine." She swallowed. "We're missing that tonight too, but it represents the mortar used when my people labored so hard to make bricks in Egypt."

She picked up a little bowl of salt water. "And these are our tears, for we were slaves."

She touched the four small wine goblets Friederich had filled. "These are for the promises Adonai made to us, of all He would do and be to us."

Rivka sat back, breathed deeply, then lit the two candles, drawing their flames toward her. Rachel thought she might be praying or remembering seders past, but she looked up and reverently began, "*Barukh atah Adonai Eloheynu Melekh ha'olam asher kidshanu bidevaro uvishmo anakhnu madlikim haneyrot shel yom tov. . . .* Blessed are You, O Lord our God, Ruler of the universe, who has set us apart by His Word, and in whose Name we light the festival lights."

Each of the foods caught in Rachel's throat as she listened, transfixed, to Rivka. *I've lived my whole life and not known such things existed.* She looked at the faces of her family in the circle: Oma, Lea, Friederich, and little Amelie, whose trusting eyes danced in the candlelight. They weren't Jewish, but the little service held something sacred for them—she saw it in their faces, in their unshed tears. *What did Friederich mean about Jesus being our Passover Lamb? And Rivka—she's Jewish. How can she share this ceremony with Christians after Gentiles arrested and may have murdered her family? What is this connection she holds with my family that I don't have?*

When the seder ended and the candles burned low, Rachel heard Rivka whisper beneath her breath, "Next year . . ."

"Next year?" Rachel asked, reaching for Rivka's hand.

Rivka, tears streaming, gripped Rachel's in return. "Next year in Jerusalem!"

⬥⬥

That night, as the others prepared for bed, Rachel tucked Amelie beneath her covers. The little girl fell fast asleep with her thumb tucked into her mouth. Only then did Rachel turn to Rivka. "I don't understand about this Passover. How is it connected to Jesus?"

"There is no connection to the Christian Jesus—it's about our flight from Egypt and Adonai's protection over us. The night the firstborn—"

"I get that; I do. But what did Friederich mean about Jesus being our Passover Lamb? About His blood covering us?"

Rivka sighed. "My brother believed that too."

"Your brother? You mean—"

"My brother believed that Jesus was Messiah, and not only that, but that He was the Son of God, that He was the atonement for our sins—for the sins of all the world."

"A Hebrew Christian?"

Rivka nodded. "A fat lot of good that did him with the Nazis. 'Once a Jew, always a Jew,' they said." She snorted. "The 'chosen people.' Chosen for persecution! I say, choose somebody else!"

"But your parents—"

"Orthodox."

"Did they know your brother—?"

"The night he told us of his conversion . . . it was Shabbat, two months after my bat mitzvah. We lit the candles—the silver candlesticks my mother said would one day be mine. The ones those pigs stole." Rivka stopped. Rachel looked away as Rivka swiped her tears. Minutes passed. "My brother said the prayers. We were eating." Rivka looked in some far-off place, remembering. "My brother told us he was helping our people get out of Germany, that he could get us all passports. He'd learned to forge them—he showed me how it was done. He urged my parents to go, but they would not hear of it. They thought it could not be so bad, that the persecutions would stop.

"When he saw he wasn't getting anywhere, he told us something more astounding. At first, we didn't understand. He talked about his Gentile friends and their *Kirche*—how he'd gone with them once, on a dare. My father looked like thunder, and my mother kept trying to change the subject.

"But Jacob said he'd learned things he never knew before, and that he'd come to see that this Jesus, this Yeshua, was truly Messiah. He tried to convince my parents to go to the *Kirche* with him, to listen to the pastor's words. Before he could say more, my father howled and tore his shirt. He ordered Jacob from the house, from the family, then turned his back until the door latched behind him. My mother wailed, like the mourners. The rabbi came the next day, after Shabbat, and we sat shivah for Jacob. After that, my parents would not allow his name to be spoken."

"Never?"

Rivka blushed in the candlelight and shook her head. A moment passed before she whispered hoarsely, "I disobeyed them. It was the only thing I remember doing that rebelled so against their wishes."

Rachel waited.

"The last night I went to bed early, pretended to sleep. When all was quiet, when I heard *mein Vater* snoring, I slipped through my bedroom window and climbed down the tree outside. I ran to my friend Anna's. Jacob was waiting there for me." Tears trickled down Rivka's face.

"So your brother's safe? Do you know where he is now?" Rachel couldn't believe Rivka had never spoken of him.

But Rivka shook her head, sniffing. "*Nein, nein.* Anna lived just down the street from my family. She is Gentile, but a good friend. It was not the first time she'd arranged for Jacob and me to meet. We were talking—so precious the minutes, they flew—when we heard the truck squeal to a stop at the top of the street. No one should be out that time of night—the curfew. We heard the dogs, snarling, barking. We knew right away. They ran from house to house, pounding on doors, barking orders, searching for Jews, dragging them from their beds."

Rachel swallowed.

"Anna would have hidden us both, tried to hide us beneath their stairwell. But Jacob pushed me into the hiding place, insisted I stay there until morning. He raced to our home to warn our parents." Rivka began to cry uncontrollably.

"They took him, too?"

Rivka nodded and repeated, "It never mattered that he'd converted to Christianity."

"No, it wouldn't," Rachel whispered, hearing in her mind the hate-filled rants of Hitler, remembering the dogma of her father denigrating every race, every skin color other than those whose papers could "legitimately" be stamped *Aryan*.

"But I think," Rivka ventured, "that it mattered to Jacob. Saving himself was not why he converted. He believed—with everything in him. I think, in the end, he was glad to be taken with our parents. He'd said that night that he expected to be taken soon, that he wanted to talk with our parents one last time, to share with them what he'd learned about Messiah Yeshua. To urge them to believe."

"He was very brave to warn them. He could have stayed hidden."

"For a long time I was angry with him for going, for leaving me, when he was sure to be caught. But now I, too, think he was brave." She hesitated again. "And I think, though I don't understand it, that it was his love for this Yeshua, and for our parents, that made him go. I only hope . . . I hope my father forgave him . . . loved him again."

"Don't give up on them. Maybe, when this is all over . . ." But Rachel couldn't finish, didn't believe her own encouragement.

Rivka didn't answer, but lay down, turning over. Amelie stirred in her sleep. The candle had burned low.

Rachel lay down too, stroking Amelie's hair, soothing her brow and staring up at the darkening ceiling, the last of the candle flame's shadows fading. What it all meant, exactly how everything fit together, she wasn't sure—only that there was a connection. What Rivka had said about her brother sounded like the same love, the same relationship with this Jesus, that compelled Oma, Friederich, Lea, surely Curate Bauer, and perhaps Jason to help so many—to help her. It was something shut up inside them that filled them until it forced its way out, compelling them to share what they'd experienced, insisting that they help others, even when it meant that they must risk their lives to do it. It was that thing Bonhoeffer wrote about—"costly grace."

Rachel sighed and closed her eyes. It was beyond her. She didn't understand why she couldn't feel what they felt, see what they saw. She certainly didn't want to buy into any hocus-pocus. That would be as futile as her father's pseudoscience. But the more she thought about it, the more she read and lived with them and witnessed their lives, their faith, the more she knew there was something real and empowering in it. Whatever it was, it would not let her go.

51

April gave way to May. Jason worried over the photograph of Rachel and Amelie. Every day he wondered if Schlick or one of his cohorts would come across the magazine cover, wondered if he'd return to Oberammergau.

He didn't have long to stew. Jason was recalled to Berlin, where rumors spun out of control. Tension in Wilhelmstrasse was palpable, every correspondent on edge and packed to be sent out at a moment's notice. Where would Hitler attack next—Holland, Belgium, the Maginot Line, Switzerland?

After a long and frustrating day pounding pavement, trying to get quotes from the Gestapo for a story nobody wanted to acknowledge, Jason plunked his reporter's pad and pencil onto his desk and slumped in his chair, only to be ordered to cover a black-tie embassy dinner in an hour's time. He groaned.

Peterson, the staff photographer, shrugged in sympathy. "Sorry, pal. Chief's orders."

"Why me? Covering the dandies is Eldridge's beat now."

"You didn't hear? Eldridge has vamoosed—gone stateside."

"When?" Jason couldn't believe it. Eldridge would never leave when the news was this hot.

"Last week. He got an offer from the *Chicago Trib*."

Jason whistled. "Lucky break. That's near his hometown."

Peterson nodded. "Took him all of two minutes to accept."

"So why'd they come after him?" Jason knew Eldridge was a decent reporter, but he'd not have thought he was sought-after material.

"Some great picture he took, near as I can tell."

"Something you developed, no doubt." Jason underlined the irony.

"Nope. He took that one all the way, though I have to say it looked more your style than his—a Bavarian Madonna and child, they called it, along with a sappy feature. Sure got somebody's attention."

Jason straightened. It was the first time he'd heard that spin for the photograph, but he could see how it fit. The sleaze. He prayed it was all American attention and that it kept Eldridge over the pond, far from any connection to Oberammergau, Rachel, or him for the duration. He had no desire to share a cell or find themselves dangling on identical ropes when the thief squealed. And squeal he surely would, if interrogated. It was better this way. If caught, Rachel, Amelie, even Curate Bauer and the entire network would line up like dominoes, waiting to fall.

Jason covered the black-tie dinner without complaint.

Two days later he was sent on assignment to Britain, where Neville Chamberlain resigned as British prime minister and Winston Churchill took up the post. Hitler launched an invasion of the Low Countries.

Unkempt, with three days' stubble and no shower, Jason shouted his makeshift article through poor telephone lines to New York. "Germany marched at dawn into Holland, Belgium, and Luxembourg, where Hitler proclaims he is 'safeguarding the neutrality of the Belgians and the Dutch.'"

A German communiqué delivered to the pressroom read, *From now on, every enemy bombing of German civilians will be answered by five times as many German planes bombing English and French cities.*

❦

Lea heard the news, but her problems with the Reich pressed closer to home. Mother's Day in Germany had long been hard for her, but never as demeaning as now. The Cross of Honor was publicly awarded to women who had borne four or more healthy children for the Reich. But to have borne none was shameful, an ignominy that could not be ignored, one that members of the Nazi Women's Party noted. Lea did her best to smile, to hold her head up as women of Oberammergau paraded from church, proudly displaying their medals of honor.

Just outside the church door, Lea looked up to find the eyes of Maximillion Grieser boring into her, uncharacteristically full of compassion. The unexpected sympathy made her misstep. Friederich caught her hand. When they straightened and regained their pacing, Lea glimpsed Maximillion staring at her husband with nothing short of contempt—a thing which unnerved her more.

Friederich kept his hand at the small of her back, as if willing strength into his wife's spine. But at Oma's home, alone in their room, Lea gave way and wept.

Lea knew that Oma tried to keep the others in the kitchen, to divert their attention from her granddaughter's room, and she was grateful.

But later, when a soft knock came at their door and Amelie was gently pushed inside, Lea was even more grateful. No arms around her neck so filled her heart as did Amelie's. They needed one another, and that made the little girl's hugs all the sweeter. Lea had no words, and Amelie didn't need them. Even the few signs they shared seemed extravagant. After a time, the two drew Friederich into their precious circle. And Lea prayed they would have one another always.

52

IN MID-MAY when the First Mountain Division entered French territory, Friederich thanked God for his limitations, that he was considered unfit for service. He could only imagine the cruelty his old unit would be ordered to wreak on the Jews of France. Gratefully, he returned to his woodcarving, thankful that he'd lost only one eye, that he still had the use of both hands.

Lea stopped by the shop from time to time, but she was not Friederich's most frequent visitor.

Though Heinrich Helphman did not return the Christkind, the little boy haunted Friederich's shop each afternoon—as regular as the clock over Friederich's workbench.

Heinrich leaned over the carving table, watching Friederich's push and pull of the knife. "Did Frau Hartman give you the Christmas wood I brought?"

"*Ja, ja*, she did. That was very kind of you, Heinrich. I appreciate it. Though I must admit, I would like it best if you'd return the image I carved."

The little boy ignored the hint. "Will you carve another Christkind with it, Herr Hartman? I know you will! You're the best woodcarver in all of Oberammergau."

Friederich laughed. "I think you're prejudiced. There are many more accomplished than I."

"But you carve the most beautiful faces, the best smiles."

"Do I?" Friederich smiled at the praise.

"*Ja*, they are the smiles of angels. I think even Herr Hitler could find no fault in them—nor his doctors or nurses either."

Friederich looked up at the child, turning his head to better see him, and frowned at his strange remark. But Heinrich flushed and stepped back from the woodcarving table, as though he'd said something he ought not.

"Heinrich? What is it?"

The boy shook his head, worry filling his eyes. "I must go, Herr Hartman. I'll see you tomorrow!" Heinrich grabbed his schoolbooks and tore from the shop.

Friederich followed the boy to the door and watched him race over the streets and out of sight. "Heinrich!" he called. But the child never turned.

Friederich scratched his chin. He was tempted to go after him, to see what was behind this glimpse into the boy's odd behaviors. But he was late in filling Nativity orders, and a game knee was no match for Heinrich's young and pumping legs. Friederich closed the shop door, allowing the bell overhead to jingle, and limped to his workbench.

53

By the time yellow daisies and monkshood, large blue harebells, sweet butterfly orchids, and meadowsweet with long white tassels spread across the Alpine meadows, Rachel's fears of Gerhardt discovering her photograph on the magazine cover began to fade. *Maybe the magazine never reached Berlin. Maybe Gerhardt's found a new obsession. Maybe we're safe.* It sounded too good to be true.

It seemed less important when, in May, the BBC reported that old women in Belgium trudged the roads, carrying crying babies in their arms as they followed young mothers burdened down by their families' belongings—and pursued by relentless German tanks.

When reports followed that German forces were halfway from the French border to Reims, on their way to devour Paris, Rachel left the room. She could listen to no more of the plundering of small French villages, of farmland trampled and livestock shot, of unmilked cows left bellowing beside the roadway, of the raping of women and girls at will. *This in the name of creating a master race, a thousand-year Reich of horror!* She retched in the kitchen sink, then washed the filth away.

In the name of advancing racial purification, the German army relocated elderly Tyrolians to Oberammergau and surrounding villages. The irony of taking those considered inferior and moving them among the "German elite" was not lost on Rachel.

The first week the Tyrolians appeared in the village streets, Rachel, on her way to theatre class, saw the backs of a crowd of children gathered, jumping up and down, calling and jeering. Such scenes were rare in Oberammergau, and her heart tightened in her chest.

She edged the crowd, keeping her head down. A group of five Hitler Youth had surrounded an old man. They were teasing him, calling him names Rachel couldn't quite capture—some sort of slang, she supposed—and knocked the hat from the old man's head. The poor man, doing his best to maintain his dignity, bent down to retrieve his treasure, but the youths kicked his hat farther down the street, swiping the swollen knuckles of his arthritic hand with their boots.

Women bordering the group turned away, and Rachel heard one whisper loudly to another, "Well, we didn't want them anyway. There's no more rooms, and they eat what little we have. Why couldn't the Führer send them somewhere else?"

Two younger children from Rachel's class had wormed their way through the crowd and, following suit, clapped and jeered from the curb. Rachel feared trying to stop the bullying, feared the attention it might draw to herself, but she pushed through the crowd and grabbed the two children's hands. "You're going to be late for class, and you know I won't abide that. Come with me now."

"But we want to—"

"Now—come!" And she herded the young children into the building.

Why grown people tolerated such cruelty escaped her. But the Hitler Youth were strong, robust boys, and their bullying was nearly encouraged, nearly out of control.

It hurt her heart to see that poor man or any of the senior folks mistreated and demeaned only because their customs were different, their language obscure, their values so simple. It was seeing her father's theories in action—her father's theories and Hitler's realities—and that frightened her most of all.

Jason was right from the beginning. It's as though we didn't believe

Hitler would do what he said he would. Or was the world simply waiting for someone to step up and do it? She groaned inwardly. She'd once considered her father's rhetoric as innocuous as the morning newspaper. *Is my fear, my apathy—indifference—any better than perpetrating evil?*

❦

Rachel begged, but Curate Bauer refused to let her help, loath to draw her onto a more dangerous path than the one she already walked.

"Keeping Rivka and Amelie safe, and even yourself and your family, must be your first priority. None of us can save everyone, but we can each do something."

"But everyone else is doing that for me. Who am I helping?"

"Your grandmother—she needs you. And little Amelie. Prepare her to live in her silent world through sign and self-sufficiency. And Rivka—she has no home, no family, no country."

Those were not the answers Rachel wanted.

"The point is to live—faithful each day." Curate Bauer looked as if he were speaking to a child. "And we must prepare and be prepared to go on living. Most of life is not high drama or danger. It is our responsibility to help those around us to live."

"Be our brother's keeper—that's what Friederich says."

"Or our sister's." He smiled. "Sometimes taking up our cross is doing the thing in front of us, not the glamorous, high-risk thing afar off."

Rachel felt her face warm. She didn't like being so transparent. It was true that she wanted to do something exciting, something dangerous, something truly rich in self-denial. She wanted . . . and that, she knew, was the problem: it was still about what *she* wanted.

She nodded at last. "That's what they say Jesus did, isn't it?"

Curate Bauer's brows rose. "You understand, then."

"He probably didn't think that giving Himself up to be beaten and spit upon and crucified was very glamorous."

"For our sins. He did it for us because it was what we needed."

"What we needed," Rachel repeated. She'd not thought she needed anything or anyone. But now . . . now she wasn't sure.

❖❖

In June, as the Germans marched toward Paris, the last evacuation ship loaded with British and French forces left Dunkirk for England's shores.

Prime Minister Winston Churchill vowed that even if an invasion of England came, the British empire would "carry on the struggle until, in God's good time, the New World, with all its power and might, steps forth to the rescue and the liberation of the old."

Rachel could not understand why the United States—her part of the New World—did not enter the fray, why they didn't step "forth to the rescue."

Rachel and Rivka lay awake at night in the attic, listening to their forbidden, hidden radio. The BBC reported heavy British bombing in faraway Frankfurt. Rachel hoped the Institute was leveled to the ground. They wondered how long until British bombers would reach Bavaria. Proximity to Munich made them feel like sitting ducks.

Friederich argued that bombing in the Alps was unlikely, that the mountains made finding and hitting targets difficult. "That's why the Germans are building factories in the mountain valleys and caves—they believe it's safer."

But nothing felt safe, and morale in the village waned, especially when letters from soldier husbands and sons did not come, and no casualty lists were posted.

"Hitler's forbidden the posting or printing of casualty lists, no matter the victories in the field," Friederich explained. "He doesn't want us on the home front comparing our losses with the Great War."

Oma agreed. "The outcry against the war effort could be his undoing."

But Rachel knew the uncertainty and fear for their sweethearts, husbands, sons, and brothers were nearly overwhelming to those waiting at home, and she pitied them.

❦

By mid-June Rachel had finished reading Bonhoeffer's book and portions from Oma's Bible. The characters and their stories, their strengths and many failings, their desperate needs, were not so different from people she'd known—not so different from herself.

To Rachel, the most startling part was Jesus—not only who He was but how He lived until the very end, and how His life was not meant to throw out the Jewish law He was born under—the law that seemed so harsh and severe at first—but to fulfill it. To live within its protection and within its privileges, and to meet its demands for atonement by offering Himself as a sacrifice for all humankind. All of that ran counter to her upbringing—the very idea that the Bible was anything but destructive to human ambition. Sometimes Rachel was thrilled by what she read; sometimes she felt almost as if she was doing something wrong. It was hard to leave behind the voices of her past.

Rachel and Rivka whispered long into the nights, plowing through questions about the law, about the Passion Play, about the quandary of Bonhoeffer's radical Jesus, as well as his insistence that the church commit to saving the Jews hunted by Hitler.

Rivka claimed she could make no sense of the disparity between Bonhoeffer's view and the Aryan clause in the German National Reich Church. "Even some Nazis call themselves Christians, but they expel all the Jews, even the ones who believe in their Jesus—the ones who claim Him as Messiah and Savior. It makes no difference that they have become Christians. They arrest them anyway—just like my brother. You can't believe what those cross wearers say."

It made no sense to Rachel, either, but she understood the Nazis' perverted eugenics reasoning. If one was Jewish, it was a matter of blood—inferior blood—not religion. She'd been fed those "facts" from infancy, and it made her sick.

Some nights they fell asleep talking, disagreeing, exhausted by their questions. What did the apostle Paul mean about Gentiles who believed being grafted as wild branches into the olive tree, and what was that about Jesus being the living vine? Did that mean the vine united all—Jews and Gentiles alike? That would fit with the greater picture, but Rivka wasn't sure. Rachel wasn't sure.

While Rivka and Amelie slept, Rachel wept over her parents and their too-small world—a world as sad and narrow-minded as the Third Reich's philosophies. *Father's arrogance kept him from even imagining that there could be things he didn't know—possibilities he could not foresee.* She pitied him and was surprised at the stirrings of forgiveness within her heart.

But sometimes, especially in dark moments of weariness or anxiety, the old bitterness wriggled through. Memories of his manipulation and betrayal tore at her stomach, her heart. The process of forgiving had to be repeated.

She wondered, if God really existed, how He did it, day by day, year after year, century upon century—why He never gave up, why He bothered with humankind.

She was on her way home late one afternoon in June, pondering just that question, when Maximillion Grieser and his band of Hitler Youth marched past her toward the beer hall. Since Jason had interrupted his inappropriate behavior in the spring, Maximillion had not patrolled the halls of the school.

The boy beside Maximillion jabbed him in the side as their eyes boldly followed Rachel. Maximillion looked away, but his neck, several shades brighter, betrayed his blush. Rachel pitied him. He'd probably spouted off about being smitten with a teacher, and his friends wouldn't let him forget. Jason had been hard on him, though the youth had certainly deserved it. Neither she nor Lea needed that kind of harassment.

She didn't realize she'd been staring after them, or that Maximillion had turned to watch her. She couldn't read his facial expression, but smiled self-consciously at the boy, embarrassed to be caught staring. His face lit, and he waved. She waved in return, smiling, glad to put to rest any animosity or shame he might feel. She turned away, idly hoping he'd not misinterpreted her greeting. It was nothing.

❦

It had been quite a day for Maximillion. He'd participated in his first vandalism at the direction of the Gestapo when a local shopkeeper was accused of handing out provisions without the proper ration stamps.

The shopkeeper, beaten and arrested, had begged for mercy along with her daughter. But pity was not the Gestapo's concern, and it should not be Maximillion's, according to his Youth leader, who'd helped the boys drown any qualms by taking them on a drinking binge.

The first tankard of beer had helped Maximillion remember that consequences suffered by lawbreakers were their own responsibility and had nothing to do with him. The second tankard helped him forget the woman's split lip, her bruises, her daughter's tears and pleas. The third had reminded him why he so enjoyed looking at the beautiful Frau Hartman—and that lifted his spirits and ambitions immensely.

He wondered why he'd ever stopped pursuing her, why he'd paid any attention to the overbearing American correspondent. After all, who was he? Frau Hartman clearly thought well of him, and he of her. But the newspaperman was a nobody, and gone.

The difference between Maximillion's age and Frau Hartman's was not so very great. Her husband, though a war veteran, was little more than a cripple. If anything, Maximillion decided he'd wasted valuable time where the beautiful young Frau was concerned.

54

PARIS WAS DECLARED an open city, and within days the Nazis marched in unchallenged. Less than an hour later, Hitler's ebony spider fluttered from the Eiffel Tower. French prime minister Reynaud, refusing to agree to an armistice with Germany, had barely resigned when General Pétain stepped into the gap. Pétain, desperate to avoid the division of France between Axis powers, humbly requested the armistice. The Vichy Government, puppet to Hitler, was born.

Part of the victorious entourage to Paris, Sturmbannführer Gerhardt Schlick raised plundered champagne flutes to repeated renditions of "Deutschland über Alles" and the "Horst Wessel Song" while the masses in Germany rejoiced, heiling their Führer. Gerhardt applauded Hitler's order that the armistice be signed in the very railcar in the very forest in which Germany had been made to surrender in 1918.

Delighted to assist in the ripping of the railcar from a French museum, Gerhardt saw it placed once more in the Forest of Compiègne. Returning to the scene of Germany's defeat increased Hitler's sweet revenge and the total humiliation of France—a life philosophy Sturmbannführer Gerhardt Schlick embraced with an eye to the future.

***

Despite the war, Lea was content. Friederich was home and getting stronger each day. He returned to his woodcarving more and more often, as his strength allowed, and she her painting of his carvings. The children's choir made them both happy, and Amelie completed their joy. If only the war would end, if only the SS would forget them, and it would be safe to bring her into the light of day.

Lea knew these were fantasies, yet she lived them in her heart. Friederich cautioned her against setting her hopes on things unattainable, but Lea only smiled, grateful for the strange fortunes of war.

Even Oma's nosy neighbors loomed as less of a threat. Despite the Nazis' determination to create racial purity, numerous prisoners of war from occupied Europe were spread among local homes and camps to live and labor on public works projects. Frau Hillman was preoccupied with Oberammergau's sudden influx of French visitors—their lilting tongue and rhythmic ways. She could no longer be bothered with the peculiarities of her neighbor, though she frequently commented on Lea's extraordinary energy.

"You teach children's choir and acting classes, you help your grandmother, you paint your husband's carvings, and you work yourself to death in that garden—it's like you were born with the energy of three women! Though some days you seem all thumbs. Why is that?"

It was *two* women, to be precise, and two very different sets of thumbs, but Lea simply smiled whenever Gerda Hillman leaned over the fence to gawk. Rachel or Lea—whoever was gardening that day—frequently offered the busybody a bunch of greens or pulled a luscious plum or fig from Oma's orchard trees to appease her.

Oma was not so easily appeased and still worried over her neighbor, still feared that Sturmbannführer Schlick would see Rachel and Amelie's photograph, still spent much time on her knees at night.

But Lea sang more than she ever had, and between Friederich's love and Amelie's adoration, she glowed. It was impossible not to notice.

55

Summer came.

Maximillion had grown much taller over the past year. His hair was bleached and his body bronzed from the Alpine sun. His arms had grown thick and his waist trim from climbing ropes and mountains, rowing back and forth across the mountain lake, and chopping wood with his troop of Hitler Youth.

He decided he would wait no longer to pursue his dreams. He combed his hair and buttoned the shirt of his uniform across his broad chest. He fitted his cap to his head, tipping it to a jaunty angle. He'd not take Frau Hartman flowers this time, just himself. He would wait until she was alone, then surprise her, but quickly assure her of his intentions.

Perhaps they would begin with a walk in the woods and a picnic, perhaps a blanket.

Maximillion wasn't certain what lay ahead. There was the husband to contend with, of course, but Maximillion was not especially worried. The woodcarver was no match for him, and he'd not given his wife children. Frau Hartman was good with the village children—doted on them. She deserved her own.

He'd even talked the question over with a couple of his friends, drinking around a campfire late one night. They'd agreed that the crippled woodcarver was an inconvenience, not one Germany would miss. Survival of the fittest, after all. An accident could be arranged—not so very difficult. They might even be willing to help him. Now that they were all experienced in dealing with "situations" for the Gestapo, they had become creative problem solvers in their own right.

Maximillion waited until the last child left choir practice, until he was certain the Hitler Youth on duty had gone for the day. He grinned in anticipation, straightened his tie, and walked into the darkening school.

※—❦—※

Lea had just turned off the overhead light after collecting her students' worn song sheets. Little fingers, despite their best intentions, had a way of dog-earing corners and smudging print. Or was it dirt ground across the bars and treble clefs? She smiled. It didn't matter. The children were still precious. She thumped the worn sheets into a straight stack. The last afternoon rays through the small window gave just enough light to find the cupboard.

She heard a slight shuffle at the door but didn't turn. "So you're back! Your lunch pail is on the piano, Heinrich. You'll need that for tomorrow."

She'd just finished shelving the song sheets in the cupboard when she sensed that someone stood close behind her, someone bigger than Heinrich. Before she could turn he'd covered her eyes from behind and pressed his body against hers. He didn't speak, but nibbled her neck, just in the curve between its nape and her shoulder—Friederich's favorite kissing spot, one he hadn't made good use of since coming back from the war.

Lea giggled, surprised by her husband's boldness in the school. Her suppleness spurred him on and he nestled deeper, into her hair, his hands seeming to forget her eyes, but traveling down her cheeks, her neck, her arms, encircling her waist.

"Not here!" Laughing, breathless, she tried to turn, only to find herself held tight, smothered with kisses, the hungry kind of kisses Friederich had given her before her last visit to the Institute had crippled her and the war crippled him. She squirmed, turning just a little, not wanting to discourage her husband but wanting him to take her home and finish what he'd begun.

She grasped his arms, but they were not Friederich's still-too-thin arms. Even in the dim light she could see and feel that the sleeves were not Friederich's flannel shirtsleeves. Her heart raced; fear gripped her brain. She pushed away, turned, and found herself staring into the hungry eyes of Maximillion Grieser.

He pulled her to him, but she beat against his chest with her fists and screamed. "Get away! Take your hands from me!"

He laughed. "What are you doing? You invite me in, then push me away? You know you want me, Lea—as much as I want you."

"No!"

"Stop pretending. There's no need. We're alone." And he pulled her to his mouth with such force that she could not push him off.

She squirmed and pummeled, but he laughed and kissed her harder, aroused by the hunt and her resistance. His hands groped above her waist. She bit him, and when he grabbed his lip she pushed against his chest and slapped him, hard, across the face.

The lights of the classroom snapped on. Curate Bauer stood in the doorway. The sudden blinding light, the absolute stillness that followed, stole Lea's breath until she thought she would faint. "He attacked me. He attacked me!"

The horror, the sorrow and misery of understanding, dawned in Curate Bauer's face. "Get out. Get out, and don't come back."

Maximillion checked the blood on his hand, the blood from Lea's bite, and swiped it away. He looked from the priest to a frightened Lea. "We love each other."

"We do not!"

"But you teased me—everyone saw. You teased me, and then you get what you ask for but pretend you don't want it? What is this?"

"You're crazy, Maximillion! I have a husband—I love my husband!

I will tell your mother!" It was the worst thing Lea could think to threaten, the only thing she could imagine that would humiliate Maximillion or make him afraid.

"Tell my mother?" Maximillion looked incredulous, as if scales had been ripped from his eyes, as if he saw Lea for the first time. "You think I am a schoolboy that you will run and tell my mother?"

"You *are* a schoolboy!"

But Maximillion did not look at her as a child would look. He swore and his eyes ran over Lea's body, as though he owned her, as though he'd finish what he'd dreamed of doing, no matter what she said. He stepped forward, threat in his eyes. "So, you're like your mother. I've heard the stories."

"I said get out," the curate repeated, pushing between them and shoving Maximillion into a small desk so he fell backward. "Get out, or I'll throw you out."

Maximillion scrambled up from the floor. Before he could regain his footing, he stumbled again.

Flashes of anger and humiliation sprang to the boy's eyes. He brushed back the greased hank of hair that had fallen across his forehead, looking like an overgrown pouting and dismayed child who'd been deprived of his toy and his will. He pushed himself up from the floor. "You'll pay." Spitting blood from his mouth, he glared at the priest and at Lea. "Do you hear me? You'll both pay!" Then he tore from the room.

Curate Bauer exhaled mightily and looked at Lea, who'd collapsed against a desk, her hand to her heart. "Are you all right?"

She nodded, breathless and shaking. "Yes, he didn't hurt me. He just . . ." She began to cry, despite her desperate wish not to. "I never led him on. I never did what he said!"

"I saw what he tried to do. I'm so sorry, Frau Hartman, so very sorry. Thank the good God I was here."

"Yes," she quavered. "Thank you!"

The curate helped her to her feet. "You must be very careful, Frau Hartman. We have made an enemy. You must tell Friederich, and you must warn your sister."

❧❧

Lea shuddered, frantically whispering in Rachel's ear so Rivka could not hear the sordid tale of Maximillion.

"Okay, I believe you, but don't you think you're overreacting? Really, what can he do? He knows nothing. He's just a hormonal teenage boy. He has no power over us."

But Lea, terrified, argued, "You didn't see his face. He vowed that we'd pay."

"I just smiled at him and waved." Rachel shrugged. "It was nothing—really nothing."

"It was something to him. Rachel, I'm frightened! What if—?"

But Rachel shook her head, cavalier, as though such flirtations and infatuations with teachers were everyday affairs. She almost convinced Lea that she was too provincial in her thinking, that despite the ugliness of Maximillion's tantrum, there was truly nothing to fear.

56

By the time Gerhardt returned to his Berlin office, he was in high spirits. Weeks of life in Paris had proven invigorating. He'd not lacked for female companionship and had come to the conclusion that regardless of the disappointed expectations of youth, life goes on. Perhaps Rachel Kramer truly had perished aboard the ship on which her passport was found. Perhaps it was time to end that frustrating and ignominious chapter in his life.

He closed his office door and removed his uniform coat and hat, his gun from its holster. He loosened his tie and took the chair behind his desk. His office seemed smaller than he remembered, and dim.

Gerhardt leaned back, lit a cigarette, and inhaled.

Perhaps he should think about requesting long-term reassignment. Nothing held him to depressing Berlin, and life in Paris had its rewards. It wouldn't be a bad place to wait out the war.

The more he thought, the more he liked the idea, and there was no time like the present. In fact, with recent victories, his superiors might be in an excellent frame of mind to grant his request. He checked his watch. There was still time to complete the paperwork before calling it a day.

An hour later he picked up the phone to call for a courier. He'd rather have his request hand-delivered than leave it to the delay and uncertainty of regular channels.

As he dialed, a junior officer entered with a stack of mail and waited at attention.

"Twenty minutes? Very good." Gerhardt spoke into the receiver, pleased. He nodded an indication for the junior officer to leave the mail on his desk, gave a perfunctory salute, and watched as the young man turned on his heel, closing Schlick's office door behind him. "I will expect him. Heil Hitler." He replaced the phone, feeling quite in charge of his destiny.

Gerhardt lit another cigarette, flipping through the mail, tossing to the trash everything nonessential; most of it he deemed nonessential. There was a letter dated June 15 from a Hitler Youth in Oberammergau, claiming he'd found the woman the Sturmbannführer was looking for, that he could help him and could expose those in league with her. It wasn't the first letter Gerhardt had received from youngsters who idolized and wanted to ingratiate themselves to an officer of the SS by claiming they could accomplish what the SS could not. What red-blooded German boy would not aspire to the ranks of the Führer's supermen? He tossed it aside. He'd have his aide send a form letter and a signed photograph of the Führer.

At the bottom was the latest batch of propaganda newspapers—"Goebbels's fairy tales worth reading," as Gerhardt privately dubbed them. He'd take them home. True or not, they provided a good evening by the fire when he lacked companionship.

Between two of the papers was an envelope—large enough to hold an important communiqué. It was from Dr. Verschuer, who'd moved to the Institute in Berlin. Curious, Gerhardt ripped the seal and pulled out a handwritten sheet clipped to a magazine cover.

Sturmbannführer Schlick:

I find it difficult to believe this comely Madonna is the demure Lea Hartman, despite her Bavarian garb. Are you quite certain our mutual friend is no longer in Germany? Please advise.

Dr. Otmar von Verschuer

Gerhardt pulled the cover sheet from the periodical, blood rushing to his brain.

Provocative and arresting, the woman smiling from the cover was undoubtedly Rachel. Lea Hartman, even in her wildest fantasies, could not exude such confidence or that unique combination of refreshing innocence and come-hither look.

The child she held in profile looked vaguely familiar too. Something uncomfortable stirred in Gerhardt's memory. The child bore an uncanny resemblance to his dead daughter, but this child appeared older, much happier, more fit—and apparently male, if somewhat effeminate. He pushed the thought away. He was becoming morbid. What Aryan child was not blond and bouncing?

A knock came at his office door, making him start. "Enter!"

The courier stood sharply before him, saluting. Gerhardt returned the salute. "What do you want?"

"Your communiqué, sir?"

"What?" Gerhardt couldn't think, but he needed to think clearly, to plan.

A flash of uncertainty crossed the courier's face. "You called for a courier, sir?"

Gerhardt stood. "Yes, yes, of course." He plucked his prepared envelope from his desk but stopped, just out of the young man's reach. He pulled back, reconsidering.

"No." Gerhardt sat down. "No, I won't be sending anything at the moment. I've changed my mind." He saluted the air and turned his chair to look out the window, to get his bearings. "That will be all."

When the door closed, Gerhardt pulled the Hitler Youth letter from his slush pile and a magnifying glass from his desk drawer. He peered at the small print in the bottom corner of the magazine cover. He could barely make out the photographer's name—M. Eldridge. Gerhardt smiled, tapping the photograph, remembering his phone conversation with the newspaperman who'd guided him to that cocky

Jason Young—the one who either knew nothing or was extremely clever.

Gerhardt sat back in his chair, considering. He'd been naive, barking up the wrong tree—or led to the wrong tree by a smooth-talking American. He certainly wouldn't make that mistake again.

❖ Part III ❖

July 1940

57

ONE WARM July afternoon, the curate stopped Rachel in the school hallway, just as she was about to leave the building. He pulled a small parcel from the sleeve of his robe and passed it into Rachel's market basket. "Chocolate, from a friend."

"Jason's been here?"

The curate shook his head. "*Nein*, but I've seen him in Munich." He smiled. "A good fellow, your young man."

Rachel felt warmth surge through her. "Is he well?"

The curate nodded. "Though he says he's sick of sitting in cellars with Berliners night after night, waiting for British bombers, and he hates the censorship. He says there is no truth in the news and no good news worth telling."

Rachel smiled. It sounded just like him.

The curate sobered. "His friend Bonhoeffer is suffering some difficulty with the Gestapo. I believe the Confessing Church has given him an official leave of absence for 'theological study.' However, Herr Young made it clear that Pastor Bonhoeffer will be stationed between Munich and Ettal."

"Ettal? That's the Benedictine monastery—just over the way."

"*Ja*. I think his friend Joseph Müller initiated an invitation from the monastery. It's a good place to work, to write. I pray Pastor Bonhoeffer will find peace there, though there is little peace anywhere now, I'm afraid. And there is danger. More of the foreign correspondents are returning to England and America."

"Jason—will he—?"

"He stays as a courier for those in need. I don't know how long before he's . . . These are uncertain times, Fräulein, especially for the disciples of Jesus. You must prepare your heart and mind. Do you understand what I am saying?"

Rachel's heart sank, but she nodded, as bravely as she could.

"There is something more." He pulled her into the shadows. "If I am taken—"

"Please don't say that!"

The curate smiled sadly but continued. "If I am taken, you must get word to Herr Young not to bring the papers. It will mean our network has been infiltrated. It would mean death for him and discovery for those we are trying to save."

"We couldn't manage without you—the rations, the passports. How would—?"

"God will provide all that is needed. He will show you the way. None of us are unexpendable."

Rachel was not at all sure she believed that. She wanted to ask him more, but the heel clicks at the far end of the hallway told her that the Hitler Youth on patrol was making his rounds. Curate Bauer pressed her hand and was gone.

❦

Rachel pulled Lea to the attic as soon as she got home and sent little Amelie and Rivka scurrying. She told Lea everything Curate Bauer had said.

"I was afraid of this. I knew last night something was wrong. Just as Friederich and I were leaving the church, a black car pulled up. I'm sure Maximillion was in the backseat. It was the first time I've seen him in weeks. He's been avoiding me like the plague ever since that day—"

"But what could he possibly know?"

"He patrolled the church and the school for nearly a year. Perhaps he saw things, heard things."

Rachel shook her head. "Curate Bauer is no fool. I'm sure he was careful."

"Of course he was—he is. But there are many he's helping. It would be so easy—just one slip of the tongue, a paper, a passport, a door left ajar." Lea rubbed her temples.

"Stop it! We can't think like that. We must make a plan. What we will do if—?"

A loud banging came at the back door. Lea clutched Rachel's arm.

"I'll go—I'll be you," Rachel insisted. "Stay here and get hold of yourself."

"No!" Lea pushed her away. "Get in the crawl space. Oma will send in Rivka and Amelie. I'll get the door."

There was no time to argue. Rachel did as she was bid. She crawled through the trapdoor and onto the ladder just as she heard Lea open the back door. She met Rivka coming in through the false wall of the cupboard. But where was Amelie?

❦

Lea opened Oma's kitchen door and caught the little boy pounding so frantically. "Heinrich! What is it? What's the matter?"

"I went back to the church. I went back for my lunch pail!"

"Yes, it's all right. I'm sure it's still there. Did you look on the piano?"

He pushed away, shaking her arms. "Listen to me! They took him! They came and took Curate Bauer away—in handcuffs! I saw them!"

Lea felt her face drain and her knees go weak. "Who took him?"

"The Gestapo. I think it was the Gestapo—a black car!"

Oma appeared beside Lea, kneeling before the little boy. "Was there anyone you recognized?"

The frightened child nodded, the threat of tears brightening his eyes. "Maximillion. Maximillion Grieser was there. He wasn't nice to Curate. I thought he might help him. I begged him to help, to explain to the men that Curate Bauer is a good man, that there must be a mistake, but he just stood and watched. He laughed and pushed me away." Great tears scrolled down the child's face. "I couldn't stop them. I tried, but I couldn't stop them!"

Lea folded the boy into her arms. "No, you couldn't. Of course you couldn't. But you did right to come here and tell me. We must pray for Curate Bauer. You're so very right. He's a good man—a very good man. He helps many people. . . ."

But Heinrich seemed to have frozen, to have suddenly lost interest, fascinated by something over Lea's shoulder. "Who's she?"

Lea and Oma turned quickly.

Amelie stood with one arm wrapped around her handkerchief doll, the other hand a fist with a thumb in her mouth.

Oma gasped.

"She's your little girl?" Heinrich was fascinated. "She's beautiful."

"No, no," Lea stuttered. "A boy—he's visiting—a friend's child." She stood, turning Heinrich toward the door. "You must go home now, Heinrich. You must go along."

"She's not a boy, Frau Hartman." He looked at her as though she'd lost her mind, then back at Amelie. "I've never seen you, but I saw your doll. What's your name?" He waved to Amelie, who didn't answer but laughed her inharmonious laugh, waving back.

Oma swept toward Amelie, pushing the little girl out of the kitchen and pulling the door behind them.

"Are you hiding her?" Heinrich's eyes grew wide. "From the Gestapo?"

"No, no, of course not." Lea could see that he didn't believe her. "It's just that . . . that the child has a fever and must be kept quiet. He's visiting. I wouldn't want you to catch it. Now you really must go home." She pushed him gently but firmly toward the door. "Perhaps it's best that you don't mention . . . that you've been here."

Heinrich stopped in his tracks and, standing firm, fixed her eyes with his. "I won't tell—not that I've been here, and not about the girl. I know secrets are not meant to be told. You can count on me, Frau Hartman."

Lea stared at the little boy—the menace of her class who suddenly showed eyes as old as time. He was smart, and he offered her . . . what? What was he offering? Could Amelie's secret be safe with him? Lea didn't know, couldn't guess, was terrified to imagine. She wrapped her arms around Heinrich, squeezing him tight—a sign of trust. He returned her hug and touched her face before running through the door and down the path.

Lea closed the door behind him and wept.

58

RACHEL AND RIVKA crept from the hiding place, joining Oma and Lea in the kitchen.

Rivka trembled. "I'm so sorry. I thought she was in the attic. I wouldn't have gone in without her. I—"

"I know, my dear; I know." Oma held Rivka close. "What's done is done. It can't be undone."

"I think we can trust Heinrich," Rachel said, pulling a worried-looking Amelie from the kitchen doorway and into her arms. "I believe him."

"He's a child!" Oma insisted. "He'll tell, just to have something sensational to share."

"No," Lea said. "It's a great risk, but I think Rachel's right. There's something he's hidden for the longest time—something about his taking the Christkind. He knows how to keep a secret."

"The important thing is what to do about Curate Bauer." Rachel bit her lip.

"What can we possibly do?" Oma lifted her hands.

Rachel shook her head. "He thought this might happen. He told me, if he was taken, to get word to Jason not to bring any more papers. He said it would mean death for him and the discovery of the entire network."

"How can you get word to him? You can't pick up the telephone and call!" Oma insisted, her voice rising. "It's too dangerous."

"Dietrich—his friend Dietrich is in Ettal. I can find him, tell him. He'll reach Jason."

"Oh no!" Oma begged.

"What about the people hiding in your cellar?" Rivka asked Lea. "The curate supplied them food."

"Did he? Or did someone else do it for him? What about Forester Schrade? He knows something. He helped us." Lea pushed her hair back. "I must tell Friederich. We'll have to go by the house, see what's needed."

"Not with the Gestapo crawling through the streets!" Oma nearly cried again.

"No, of course not. We'll check on Friederich's way home from work. I'll walk with him. It won't seem at all strange that we stop by our house for something. We may even need to stay the night." Lea guided her distraught grandmother to the kitchen rocker. "There's nothing to worry about, Oma. It will all be so easy to take care of." She motioned to Rachel from behind Oma's back. "It's time for a cup of tea. Rivka, will you bring the kettle?"

Rachel saw that the danger had grown beyond Oma's ability to cope. The risk to her heart was too great to draw her into their plans more than necessary. She shifted Amelie to her other hip, tickling the little girl under the chin to make her smile. "I'll go in disguise," Rachel whispered as Lea poured. "That way I have papers, even if I'm stopped."

Rivka offered, "And I'll keep Amelie with me in the cupboard. We won't move until you return."

"I heard that," Oma insisted, motioning for Amelie to come to her.

"It's perfectly safe, Oma," Rachel chided, releasing the little girl to her grandmother's arms. "Who will notice a middle-aged woman walking to the monastery?"

❧

Rachel set out before the summer sun broke over the mountains, hoping to make the journey before the heat of the day, before the Gestapo rose for rounds, before other eyes roamed abroad. By the third kilometer, a dozen scenarios had raced through her mind. *What if Pastor Bonhoeffer isn't there? What if he has no safe way to reach Jason? What if he's somehow connected to Curate Bauer's work and has been taken by the Gestapo too? Jason said they were watching him closely.*

When she finally reached the monastery, a local cock crowed and a milk wagon stood in the lane. She skirted the wagon, keeping her head low, and made for the great door. Locked tight, no matter that she jiggled the handle in desperation.

There must be another way. She stepped back to get her bearings and spotted the rectory.

So anxious was she that she forgot to maintain her aged character and nearly ran to the small side door. *Stop it!* She scolded herself into breathing, smoothed her skirt, and knocked softly on the door.

No one answered. No one came. Rachel tried twice more, then gave way to frustration. It took five minutes of incessant pounding, but the door finally opened to a large, rotund man, who introduced himself as assistant to the abbot.

"Father, help me. Please, Dietrich—Pastor Bon-Bonhoeffer." She couldn't get the words out for her fear of the passing time. "Is he here?"

The priest stepped back, admitting her without a word. He closed the door behind her. "You are Brother Dietrich's family, *meine Frau?* Come in, come in."

She hadn't anticipated needing a story. "A friend of his family. Please, I must speak with him—it's urgent."

"He is leading a psalm reading for our brothers now. He'll be through soon. I'll send him in then." He stopped at the door. "You've walked far?"

"Not so far. I'm just out of breath." She tried to add years to her voice. "The sun rose hotter than I expected."

"You're not from Ettal."

"No, no. I'm visiting friends. But I must see Dietrich." She knew an older woman, a family friend, might use his Christian name.

"Would a cool drink help?"

Rachel nearly shook her head just to be rid of the man, but thought again of her return walk to Oberammergau. "That would be excellent—*danke schön*."

The monk nodded, his forehead creased, and left the room, only to return momentarily.

She drained the glass, grateful to the priest for the pitcher he left.

Half an hour passed before the door opened again and a man, much younger than she'd imagined, stepped through. A sturdy and muscular build, blond, with wire-rimmed glasses. He bent to take her hand. "You've come to see me, *meine Frau*? Brother Peter said you know my family?"

"Pastor Bonhoeffer?"

He nodded.

"Are we—?" Now that the moment had come, Rachel could barely catch her voice. "Are we quite alone?"

The man opened his hands, looking about him, and smiled. "Quite, I think."

Rachel swallowed and whispered, "Curate Bauer has been taken— by the Gestapo."

Bonhoeffer's smile vanished. He pulled a chair closer to Rachel. "When?"

"Last night. They came in the early evening."

"Do you know where they've taken him?"

She shook her head, a willful tear escaping her eye. "He knew it was coming—he must have known. He told me, if he was taken, that I must get word to—"

"To me?" Bonhoeffer looked puzzled.

Rachel bit her lip, knowing she was putting everyone at risk. *Dear God, let my instincts be right about this. Let him be the friend, the man, that Jason believes he is!* "A friend—a journalist."

Now Bonhoeffer's eyes registered caution. "Do you know his name?"

"Jason," Rachel whispered. "Jason Young."

Bonhoeffer stared at her, narrowed his eyes as if trying to discern the truth. "You're Rachel."

"Yes," she admitted, relieved. He could only know that because Jason had told him.

Bonhoeffer's lips turned up in a half grin. "You're not precisely as he described."

"Begging your pardon, but I'm probably exactly as he described."

Bonhoeffer laughed. "Yes, I think perhaps you are." He sobered. "The curate was expecting a delivery from our friend?"

Rachel nodded, feeling the weight of her world fall away. "He said that Jason must not come, that if he was taken, they'd be waiting and watching, ready to break the network. If Jason is caught—"

"Yes, yes, I understand. We can't let that happen." Bonhoeffer sat back. "When is he expected?"

"This week—he's stationed in Munich. Please, can you get word to him?"

"I can do better than that. I'll go to Munich and intercept him myself. I need to go anyway. I have my own difficult appointment there."

Rachel did not like the sound of that.

"Not to worry; it's not as it sounds." Bonhoeffer searched her face. "I'm not at liberty to discuss my activities, but you must trust me when I say that things are not always as they seem."

Rachel knew that to be true. She spread her hands, smoothed her skirt. "Apparently." She smiled.

"Yes." He smiled in return, a clear and genuine smile. "Apparently. And you must call me Dietrich—but perhaps not in public, if we should meet again, Frau—what is your new name?"

Rachel lifted her chin. "Frau Elsa Breisner, age fifty-seven, from Stelle."

"Well then, Frau Breisner, leave this to me."

"Thank you. Thank you, Dietrich."

"Jason has told me much about you, and about your Amelie, how you are helping Rivka. You are a brave woman, Fräulein Kramer. It is no wonder our mutual friend is taken with you."

Rachel's heart beat faster. Jason had confided his feelings for her to Dietrich. "And I with him." But she could take no credit for the good that had come of their friendship, what she hoped would become more than friendship. "Jason gave me your book."

"Ah, so he said. And did you read it?"

"Yes. I'm not certain I understand it all, but I'm learning."

"An honest answer. We are all always learning."

"Jason told me of the trouble the Gestapo's given you. I hope I don't bring you more trouble, more scrutiny, through what I'm asking."

"*Nein.* Jason is my brother. I love him and will do all I can for him." She frowned, trying to understand the man before her. "You barely know him."

"Grace." He shrugged, smiling.

"Your book talks about that," Rachel whispered, still trying to grasp the concept.

Dietrich tipped his head to the side, as if considering her. "'Love I much?'" he quoted. "'I'm much forgiven. I'm a miracle of grace.'"

She recognized the words from Oma's hymnbook. "Costly grace," she said, feeling the warmth of understanding kindle inside her chest.

Dietrich's eyes shone. "We are all miracles of costly grace."

59

Lea did not go to the church to teach her choir lesson that afternoon. Father Oberlanger had telephoned that morning, just after Rachel left, saying that classes were canceled for the day. He made no mention that Curate Bauer had been taken by the Gestapo.

To maintain a semblance of normalcy, Lea accompanied Friederich to his woodcarving shop in the village after lunch. She would paint and gild carvings. He had nearly an entire new Nativity set ready. Rivka and Amelie would be safe with Oma, and Lea desperately needed to keep busy.

Worry for Rachel filled her head, and fear for Curate Bauer. If the Gestapo beat him, if they tortured him, what might he say? And if they locked him up—sent him to one of Germany's many concentration camps—what would become of all those refugees he'd hidden and placed throughout the countryside? He was the one connection to the black market for food, and Jason's contact to provide forged passports and ration books. He was the key to moving the Jewish children out of the Alpine valley. Even she and Oma depended on Curate Bauer for extra food for Rachel, Rivka, and Amelie in exchange for milk their cow produced.

"You're painting the sheep red, Lea," Friederich quietly observed. "Pay attention, please."

Lea dropped her brush. "I'm sorry—I'm so sorry!" Never had she done such a thing. She covered her face with her hands.

Friederich left his carving table and wrapped his arms around her. "It's all right. A little sanding, a few wisps from the wool, and it will be new again." He pulled her to her feet and held her close. "You've borne so much for so long, *meine liebe Frau*. This is too heavy."

"No." She shook her head. "It's no more than others bear. I'm just so frightened. I'm frightened for the curate—and for Rachel, for Amelie, for us."

He kissed the top of her head. "I'm frightened too."

Friederich was still holding his wife when the shop door opened and Gerhardt Schlick strode in.

❦

It was dark in the attic when Amelie woke from her afternoon nap. She didn't like afternoon naps and she didn't like the dark made by the blackout curtains over the little attic window. It reminded her of hours squished into the cupboard with Rivka and Aunt Rachel. She was tempted to put her head beneath the covers and stay there.

But she needed to use the chamber pot. She couldn't wait much longer. Aunt Rachel got angry if she waited too long and wet the pallet. And that was worse than getting up in the dark and padding across the splintered floor and down the attic ladder.

Amelie didn't know why she couldn't have a pot in the attic. But the grown-ups were very strict about that. And about rolling her bedding tight each morning and keeping her clothes and shoes and even her picture book and dolly in the cupboard. There must be no sign of Amelie—or even of Aunt Rachel or Rivka—anywhere. Anytime, day or night, they might rush into the cupboard and close the door. She supposed it was a game. But she didn't like the game, and she hated the cupboard.

When the door finally opened and she came out, the older lady, Oma, always hugged and petted her. She gave her a little Kuchen or porridge and milk and let her sit close beside her at the table. Amelie loved to finger the creases in the old woman's face and make her smile. Then the creases lit up, like birthday candles.

The younger women smiled sometimes. But mostly they looked worried, and when they worried, they frowned. Amelie didn't know if it was because of something she'd done. Her father used to frown at her, and that frightened her. But the pretty aunts weren't like him. They often even cuddled her, like her mother used to do. And the man—oh, Amelie smiled to think of the man. Uncle Friederich smiled great big whenever he saw her, as if she brightened his day. It made Amelie feel glad to be alive.

Still, there was a great deal of time when the two pretty aunts who looked alike were gone, and Uncle Friederich, too. Aunt Rachel, who shared her attic room, was often reading, and the dark-haired lady—Rivka—seemed sad.

Sometimes, when Amelie felt lonely, she fingered the locket at her throat—the one with the picture of her mother inside—even though it was getting harder and harder to remember her.

When Amelie finished with the chamber pot she slid it back into its little cupboard in Oma's room. She padded to the window and lifted the curtain, just a little. She could see the road, the front garden gate, and the walkway round to the back door from there. That was the path the pretty aunts walked whenever they came home.

The sun was shining brightly over the path leading from the road to the front door. There was no sign of either aunt. She'd almost dropped the curtain when she saw a truck pull to a sudden stop on the road, just outside the front gate.

Amelie knew she was not supposed to pull back the curtain, so she held it close to the window and peered through the very edge. Why were men in uniform jumping out of the truck? And big dogs? Amelie had never seen such big dogs! She stepped back.

Amelie didn't like the men in black uniforms. Black uniforms reminded her of her father—her father who'd grown dark and angry whenever she'd approached him.

The men looked very much like her father—tall and broad-shouldered, the same severe posture. She peered closely, but the limbs of the ash tree shadowed their faces.

Soldiers ran toward the house in different directions—to the front and around the sides. And they carried guns.

Amelie dropped the curtain. She was afraid to confess that she'd been peering out, but she was more frightened by the uniformed men with guns. She ran to the kitchen for Oma. But she'd barely crossed the threshold when Rivka jumped from the table and dragged Amelie with her into the dark cupboard below the stairs.

At the same time she saw Oma pale and walk slowly toward the kitchen door. She made the "be still" motion to Rivka and Amelie, just before the cupboard door closed. Through her bare feet Amelie felt the rumble of more banging. She thought of the soldiers and the big dogs and Oma, all alone. Amelie began to cry.

Rivka covered her mouth, but Amelie bit her and cried harder. And then Rivka shook her, which didn't help.

Amelie felt the thunder of boots through the floor, and that, more than anything, made her catch her breath in fear. The boots rumbled angrily, and everywhere all at once. She could feel Rivka tremble beside her. Amelie reached for her in the darkness and Rivka pulled Amelie into her lap—not gently. Amelie could feel Rivka's heart beat wildly through her dress, felt her fear in the way the older girl gripped her around the middle.

The pounding through the floor went on a long while, sometimes coming very near the cupboard. When Amelie reached her hand to the wall or the little door, she felt them shudder.

The smell of urine seeped through the cupboard wall. Amelie knew it wasn't her own. Rivka clapped a hand over Amelie's mouth. Amelie was so frightened that she didn't struggle to free herself this time.

At long last Rivka relaxed her grip on Amelie's mouth, and on her middle. She didn't push her away, but laid her head on Amelie's back. She felt Rivka's tears through the back of her shirt, and felt the jerking of her body. There was not room for Amelie to turn around to comfort Rivka. So she remained very still.

When the older girl stopped sobbing, Amelie leaned her head against Rivka's shoulder. No one came to the cupboard door, and they didn't move for what seemed a very long time. At last Amelie fell asleep. She dreamed of her mother and how she used to lay her head against her mother's chest. She dreamed of her soft skin, of her smell, of the times she cried and the way she'd let Amelie kiss the salt away.

When Amelie woke, she was still in Rivka's lap. But Rivka's heart was beating rhythmically now, slowly. Amelie thought she might be sleeping. She sighed and fingered her heart-shaped locket. She needed to use the chamber pot again, so she tried to move, to push open the cupboard door.

Instantly Rivka was awake, pulling Amelie's hand away. And so they waited, and waited some more.

❦

Dietrich had gone immediately to Munich but urged Rachel to wait a few hours, so their departures would not be linked. He'd arranged for the groundskeeper to give Rachel a ride into Oberammergau.

She could walk from the grocer's shop near the town square to wherever she wished. She might pass Friederich's shop, but of course she wouldn't go in the front door. She must show no connection to them unless absolutely necessary.

She was thinking of this, and if she should take a back road home to Oma's, when the driver slowed. "What is it?"

"Trucks ahead."

"What kind of trucks?" Rachel tried to keep her voice natural.

"Gestapo, if I had to guess. Or—no, maybe not."

But Rachel recognized the vans of the SS, and her heart sank. Did

Curate Bauer break down? Oma . . . and Amelie? What about Rivka and Lea and Friederich? She thought she might be sick.

The driver turned down a side street, avoiding the town square. "I won't be shopping for the abbey today."

"No, of course not," Rachel said. "You can let me out here. I'll be all right."

"Are you certain? It's not far to the shops, if that is where you're headed."

"Not far at all." She tried to smile. "*Danke schön.* You've been most kind."

The driver tipped his cap, not making eye contact. She didn't blame him for being afraid. One didn't have to do anything wrong to fear running afoul of the SS.

Rachel adjusted her kerchief to cover as much of her face as possible and climbed from the truck cab. Keeping her pace slow, she circled the village, coming up behind Friederich's shop, thinking she might slip unnoticed through the back and wait there until dark. She dared not draw attention to Oma's home by returning in daylight. But just as she reached the walkway, two SS guards stepped through the shop's back door, and Father Oberlanger came round the building.

Rachel's knees went weak and she stumbled, nearly losing her footing.

"Careful, *meine Frau!*" one of the guards shouted.

"Ja, ja—danke." She waved, breathless. The old priest's eyes shot up, but Rachel stared at her feet, as if trying to command them to hold her up.

"Papers," the other guard ordered.

Rachel stopped and opened her purse to comply. Women were stopped and searched every day. She must remain calm, give them no reason to search beyond a cursory glance at her papers.

"Elsa Breisner? From Stelle?" One guard looked at the other. "Isn't that the name of the woman Sturmbannführer Schlick sent troops to question earlier?"

Rachel nearly fainted.

"*Nein*, that's Hilde Breisner. She lives just up the road. It's a common enough name."

"Stelle. I'm from Stelle." Rachel made her voice crack.

"Frau Breisner!" Father Oberlanger interrupted. "I've been waiting for you. I thought you weren't coming for our talk. Did you have trouble with the train?"

Rachel searched the old priest's face, unbelieving. She clasped a hand to her heart.

"You are here to see the priest?" the soldier asked. "You just arrived in the village?"

"*Ja, ja.*" She nodded, bending over. "My heart."

The priest pushed between them, taking her arm. "Allow me. You've checked her papers; now let me take her to sit down. You can see she's not well."

The guards stepped back, and the priest wrapped a protective arm around Rachel as they limped toward the church. "Say nothing," he whispered. "I remember you from the Advent market. You were with Frau Breisner. I don't know your game, Fräulein, but you're a better actress than you are a teacher."

Rachel couldn't have agreed more. They returned to the main square and headed for the church. From the corner of her eye, Rachel saw a furious Gerhardt Schlick slam open the door of Friederich's shop and drop into the backseat of an official black car, swastika flags flying. The car whipped into its turn and sped up the hill, just past Rachel and the priest, close enough for her to feel the spit of gravel from its tires on her face.

60

"Oma!" Lea, badly shaken from Gerhardt's interrogation in her husband's shop, reached her grandmother through the open door first. Friederich, grim, limped right behind her.

Oma groaned as her eyes opened, fluttered, and closed again.

"I'll lift her. Support her leg," Friederich ordered. *"Eins, zwei, drei . . ."*

Together they lifted their precious Oma from the cold tile floor.

"It's broken—her leg is broken!" Lea's teeth chattered in shock. She'd never seen her grandmother so ill-used—bruises across her cheek, her lip split, a cut just above her temple, her leg unnaturally twisted, surely broken. And the slight stench of urine. Lea's heart broke. That, above the rest, would humiliate her proud Oma.

Lea pulled back the eiderdown and Friederich laid the old woman on her bed almost reverently, as though she were the crowning star from his Nativity scene. He adjusted the pillow beneath her head, and he and Lea arranged another pillow beneath her twisted leg.

"What monster would do such a thing to an old woman? To this dear, dear woman?" Lea cried.

"I'll go for the doctor." Friederich's voice grated as he turned. Lea knew he was heartbroken and angry—angry enough to strangle the life from the men who'd dared to lay hands on their Oma.

"Amelie . . . Rivka," Oma moaned.

Friederich's eyes grew round. "They took them?"

"The cupboard," Oma moaned again.

Lea's heart caught. "No more talking, Oma," she ordered. "Friederich, check the cupboard. See if they're there."

Lea could hear Friederich opening the cupboard, could hear Amelie's guttural expression of delight upon seeing him. Lea closed her eyes, thanking God the little girl was safe. She heard Rivka's soft whispers as she climbed from the hiding place, saw Amelie tear through the room to the chamber pot.

Rivka could tend to Amelie. But where was Rachel? Was she not back from Ettal?

Lea didn't wish either woman harm. But after seeing her dear Oma beaten, she wished them both safely away.

She'd not finished the thought when Rachel appeared in the doorway, her face streaked and dirty from pulling off her disguise, her eyes nearly wild. "What did they do to Oma? What did they do?"

"Her leg is broken, I think. Friederich is going for the doctor." Lea turned back to her grandmother and began removing her soiled dress. "Take care of Amelie and Rivka. You must hide before the doctor comes. They might return."

"Let me help you with Oma." Rachel pulled a fresh nightgown from the drawer.

"There is no need. I can manage."

"I need!" Rachel countered. "I need to help her!"

"This is not about what you need, Rachel. It's about what Oma needs. And she needs for you to be safe and out of sight." Lea pulled the dress gently over Oma's shoulder, but it took everything she had not to jerk the fabric in anger and frustration. If only her sister would do as she was told!

"I heard them." Rivka appeared in the doorway. "I heard them scream at her and beat her! I heard her slump against the cupboard door. She was trying to shield us, to hide us."

"Please let me help," Rachel cried.

Lea wanted to shout at her sister, *They beat Oma because of you!*

Because they didn't believe her when she said she was not hiding you, that she didn't know where you are! I know this because I know Oma and how she loves you! And we all know why the soldiers came! But she didn't shout it, didn't say it. She swallowed and repeated, "The doctor may be here any moment. Please, Rachel—for Oma's sake, do as I ask. Oma knows that you love her. Now show her by doing what is needed. Take care of Amelie and Rivka—and yourself. Get into the cupboard."

Rachel looked as though she was struggling—what she wanted and what was wanted of her warring at the top of their lungs within. She kissed Oma's free hand but stepped back and disappeared through the bedroom doorway.

Lea heard the quiet rattle of crockery in the kitchen, the kettle being filled and placed on the stove. A few moments later Rachel reappeared in the doorway. "Everything's ready. We'll take Amelie into the cupboard, and we'll wait there until you come for us."

Lea nodded without turning. "I hope it won't be long. But I think he'll set her leg. I don't know how long that will take."

"Please," Rachel whispered, "when she wakes . . . tell her I'm sorry. Please tell her I'm so very sorry."

Lea gritted her teeth, conscious of the tension in her arms, her shoulders, her neck and face. She forced herself to breathe, to turn, to say, "You can tell her yourself tonight. Now into the cupboard, and please—please keep Amelie still."

❧

Jason handed over the forged passports to Dietrich's contact. Despite their best sources, neither had been able to track down Curate Bauer—where he'd been taken or what he'd been charged with.

It was another week before Jason got wind of Schlick's transfer to Oberammergau. But a call from a phone box to the chief told him why the SS officer had requested transfer to the Bavarian village.

"What do you know about that photograph Eldridge took—the Bavarian Madonna, they're calling it?" Jason could hear the chief chewing on his cigar through the telephone lines—no typewriters clattering in the background. *He must not be in the newsroom. So what's up?*

"Not sure I can tell you anything," Jason answered. "Seeing it in that US rag was the first time I laid eyes on it." *That's the truth—best stick to the truth.*

"That's what I told that Sturmbannführer Schlick who keeps pestering. Apparently he's out looking for the broad—says she's the American, Rachel Kramer. The guy's on some kind of crusade, if you ask me." The chief yawned. "I'm just as glad Eldridge went back to the States. I've a feeling this thing with Schlick could get ugly."

"Ugly is an SS signature," Jason agreed.

"Censorship, my boy. Watch yourself," the chief warned.

"Roger. Over and—"

"Wait. I've a lead for you. Word on the street is that mercy killings are up."

"What do you mean, 'up'?" Jason could barely breathe.

"The Gestapo's 'relieving society of the mentally deficient of the Reich.' No idea what that means in numbers. Probably only Himmler and a handful of his cronies know. There's an asylum in Bethel. Nazis are pressuring the pastor to give the kids up. Word is neither will give and something's gonna blow. Ever since Hitler got France, things have gotten even nastier, more out in the open. See what you can dig up—but be careful."

"Roger." Jason dropped the receiver into its cradle, sick in his stomach, wishing Rachel and Amelie were stateside, knowing that with Schlick stationed in Oberammergau, they'd run out of time.

He picked up the phone again and dialed. Three rings and a woman answered. *"Ja?"*

"I'm looking for a stenographer. Know any good ones?" It was his regular code question.

"One or two?" Her standard response.

"Three." *Rachel, Amelie, Rivka.*

"Not three. I'll be in touch." The phone went dead.

Jason replaced his receiver. *Not three. Whose life do I save? Whose do I lose?*

61

FRIEDERICH MADE the train trip to Munich himself. He was the least likely of his household to be followed, and he could legitimately take care of a little business in the city. He also took the opportunity to speak with Jason, albeit not face to face. Back to back on benches in the train station would have to do.

"The train is impossible. There's no way to get them out in cars or trunks. Schlick has checkpoints at every entrance to the city. The entire village is on tenterhooks and treating Lea like a pariah, waiting for her twin to show up. Schlick has shown Rachel's picture all over the village. There is a reward for the one who finds her."

"Rachel's lying low?"

"She's not teaching the theatre classes anymore. It's too risky, and Lea's stalling—saying Oma needs more care since her 'visit' from the SS. Lea's not an acting teacher. She's frightened out of her wits. Schlick comes to watch her teach choir—anytime he wishes. Lea will have to start the theatre class up again soon, but we've no doubt he'll show up there, too."

"Intimidation. Schlick's trademark." Jason sighed. "Okay, so no trains, cars, buses—nothing on the road. We need a diversion to get her out."

"Something to keep every guard from his duties?" Friederich nearly grunted. "Impossible." He sat for a moment, hating to confess one more need. "We're low on food. Oma's garden is not enough, and there are those hungrier—pilferers we cannot turn away."

But Jason didn't seem to hear. "Smoke and mirrors."

"What?"

"Smoke and mirrors. Making something look like something it's not."

"I've no idea what you're talking about."

"Rachel will understand. Ask her for an idea—a diversion that will keep them all busy long enough to get her out." Jason stretched, checking his watch against the clock. "I'll be waiting."

❦

Rachel had put Amelie to bed in the attic. The five adults sat in the kitchen, blackout curtains pulled tight and pinned.

"Smoke and mirrors?" Lea asked.

Friederich shrugged. "That's what he said, and that Rachel would know what he meant."

All eyes turned toward Rachel.

"I know what he means; I'm just not sure how to make that work."

Oma shrugged helplessly, then peeked beneath the blackout curtain, keeping watch from her rocking chair.

"It's just what Lea and I have been doing with our classes—or were doing. By me pretending to be Lea, we could pull the wool over the eyes of everyone who saw us."

"And those who didn't," Rivka added thoughtfully, tapping the table.

"Yes?" Lea asked.

Rivka turned to Lea. "You were in two places at once. You were at the church, and you were here. You were able to accomplish twice as much because there were two of you, pretending to be one. The same would be true if you both pretended to be Rachel."

"I still don't see—" Lea began.

"I do," Rachel said, grasping Lea's hand. "What if, instead of everyone thinking I was you, Gerhardt really thought you were me?

379

What if he thought you were me, and was diverted—kept busy just long enough for Amelie and Rivka and me to get away? And then he would realize that you're not me after all—that he was mistaken."

"No." Friederich stood up now. "It's been risky enough having you pretend to be Lea. I won't have Lea pretending to be you, to be put in such danger. That man, thinking my Lea is you, that he could do with her as he wishes, even for a minute, is out of the question! No, that is the end of such talk."

Rachel looked at Lea, pleading. But Lea shook her head, pulling away. "I agree with Friederich." She shuddered. "Maximillion trails the Sturmbannführer like a shadow. No telling what he's told him, what lies or half truths, what distortions. Any moment I expect them to tear me away as they did the curate! I'm afraid. . . . And how would we ever get you out of the village? There's no way—there's simply no way!" Lea's voice had risen; her panic spread round the table.

Rachel reached again for her sister. "You're right. I'm sorry. I'm so sorry."

But the days of July passed, and inspiration did not come.

Rations in the little house thinned without Curate Bauer's intervention. Friederich worried over the Jewish family hidden in the cellar of his and Lea's home. Others were helping to feed them, but lines of communication had broken down, and not enough black-market food was getting past the Nazi patrols into the village. Amelie cried herself to sleep in Rachel's arms at night from hunger, no matter that Rachel saved her little bits from her own food to provide a bedtime snack. After that, Rachel and Rivka halved their shares, insisting that those who were working eat. Oma continued to recover physically from her beating, but slowly, and everyone's nerves frayed.

62

THE FIRST WEEK in August, Forestry Chief Schrade stopped by Friederich's shop to place a Nativity order and to slip him wedges of cheese and one of beef. "I'm sorry it is not more."

"Thank you, Chief Schrade. You're a godsend to us." Friederich meant it.

Chief Schrade glanced over his shoulder, waiting until the guard outside the shop door passed the window, then quickly pulled a slim, zippered pouch from inside his vest. "Herr Young sent these. He said to say that he's sorry he could not do three—there are so many needed. He wants to know how you will get them out."

Friederich glanced at the papers but had no idea how he could transport high-profile refugees under the nose of Schlick. He momentarily closed his eyes against the hopelessness, the enormity of the question.

"I've been thinking that with all the roads blocked and those Nazi bloodhounds on the prowl, there is only one way," Chief Schrade whispered.

Friederich was ready to listen—ready for anything.

❖❖❖

Now that Sturmbannführer Schlick was stationed in Oberammergau—an apparently long-term fixture—it was entirely too risky for Rachel to leave the house.

But Lea had never taught dramatics, did not understand

improvisational games or the high drama of children's skits, had no concept of the American humor Rachel naturally interjected into her classes under Lea's name. Lea's first class fell flat and the children left disappointed and bewildered. Lea excused her odd behavior with a stomach disorder. The mothers who came to retrieve their children sympathized but went away as puzzled as their children by Frau Hartman's abrupt change in teaching methods.

That night Lea grilled Rachel, begging her to better prepare her for class, to help her devise a skit and assign roles that would take the attention off of her and place it on the children once more. They didn't get far that night. Lea taught choir the next day.

Sturmbannführer Schlick strode, arrogant and commanding, into Lea's second dramatics class, an alternately fawning and gloating Maximillion Grieser glued to his side. Between the two, all of Lea's training under Rachel flew from her head.

"Sturmbannführer Schlick," Lea began, her throat drier than the cardboard clock prop she held in her hand. She hated that the man had this same effect on her each time she encountered him, hated that her own body betrayed her, that her heart raced and fingers trembled. All she could remember was his raid on Oma's house—his intimate humiliation and cruelty to them both. What could stop him from doing as he pleased again? The children—perhaps the presence of the children!

"Frau Hartman—" he circled her once—"we meet again." His eyes roved, calculating, over her face, her hair, her body, then turned suddenly cold. "You will not mind if I observe your class today."

She swallowed, knowing her fear was palpable and noting he'd not asked a question. Jason had warned her that to act afraid served only as enticement to cruelty. She fumbled with the prop in her hand, closing her eyes, willing herself to breathe. *What would Rachel say? How would she respond? What has Maximillion told him?* "You are welcome to observe, Sturmbannführer. We are working on facial muscle skills and voice projection today. Heinrich, set chairs for the Sturmbannführer and his guest."

But Heinrich stood his ground, glaring at Maximillion until Schlick, distracted by the boy's sullenness, focused on him. Maximillion did not have the decency to be embarrassed by the youngster's challenge.

"Heinrich, please. Do as I've asked," Lea gently admonished. The last thing she wanted was for Heinrich to come under Schlick's scrutiny.

Lea did her best to muster the confidence she felt when conducting singing lessons, but the facial and body movements Rachel had taught her were not natural to her. So she fell back on what she taught her young choir about breathing from their diaphragms, about projecting their voices to the mountains, about lifting their chests and chins and singing from the depths of their being, not from their throats. This must be true for acting, surely. But Heinrich looked worried, the other children looked uncertain, and Maximillion whispered incessantly in Sturmbannführer Schlick's ear. Schlick narrowed his eyes, drilling an imagined interrogation into Lea's mind. He reminded her of Dr. Mengele at the Institute. She could barely hold her head up from the cringing in her soul.

Never had the clock on the classroom wall ticked so slowly. Never had she stumbled so incompetently through a class.

Once the children had gone, Gerhardt Schlick accompanied her to the town square, where she tried valiantly not to crumble. "An enlightening afternoon, Frau Hartman. Not what I expected based on your choir classes or the laudations of parents and children alike."

"That's because—" Maximillion began, but Schlick cut him off.

"As I said, enlightening," Schlick finished.

Lea did not trust herself to respond, but nodded and measured her steps toward home. Knees trembling, she stumbled into Oma's kitchen, letting her prop bag fall by the door.

"What is it?" Oma asked, drying her hands on her apron. "What has happened?"

"Sturmbannführer Schlick—he dogs my every step. He haunts Friederich's shop and now my drama practices—classes that even the children know are horrible! I'm not Rachel—I can't act or teach as she does. Maximillion knows I am a fraud. They both sat today and watched me. Sturmbannführer Schlick looked one moment as if he wanted to eat me and the next as if he'll grind me into the dirt with his boot."

Oma propped her cane beside the table and gingerly sat down across from her. "It was bad enough the two of them sat behind us in church on Sunday. Will he never stop?"

"Not until he finds me." Rachel appeared in the doorway. "We can't possibly keep this up. The only way to make him stop is to turn myself in."

"And have him know we've hidden you all this time?" Lea shook her head. "We'd all be arrested."

Oma knotted her fingers. "Can you imagine what that fiend of a man would do to his daughter if he found her alive?"

Lea buried her head in her hands.

"What, then?" Rachel pleaded. "I can't put you through this any longer."

Rivka stood in the doorway behind Rachel. "Amelie's sleeping—she'll never know I'm not there. There's something I want to say. I've been thinking. What Friederich said about Jason—'smoke and mirrors' . . ."

"And?" Lea looked up, desperate. "Friederich said it was too dangerous."

"Yes, I know. But I can't stop thinking about it. Just think of this: What if you and Rachel created a special musical or a play—a play you invited the officers to, and as many guards as possible? What if, the night of the performance, Rachel actually directed the children, and Sturmbannführer Schlick saw her there—knew, somehow, that it was her and not you? Then sometime during the play, the two of you switched places, and the woman he'd seen—Rachel—sneaked away, and the woman on stage became Lea?"

"Whatever are you talking about?" Oma demanded.

"Smoke and mirrors," Rachel said, the light dawning in her eyes. She pulled out a chair and sat before Lea. "We could do it during scene changes—switch clothes. If the lights were dim, he couldn't tell the difference between us."

"But you and Rivka and Amelie would have time to escape the village." Lea was beginning to see it.

"Escape? With all those guards at the checkpoints?" Oma looked as if they'd both gone crazy.

"They'd have to be kept busy," Rivka said. "They'd have to believe Rachel was really there, in front of them, with no worries of losing her. And it would have to be safe afterward—for Lea. As though Lea were the only one there all along."

"Could it be done?" Lea asked.

"Impossible! The whole town would have to believe—and be there! That horrid man has put a price on your head!" Oma stood firm. "There's nothing—"

"King Ludwig's Fire—the birthday celebration!" Lea sat up.

"*Nein, nein*, the Nazis will never allow it—not with the blackouts and curfew," Oma protested. "Not with them in power and wanting to distance themselves from the very notion of the old monarchy."

"The King Ludwig's what?" Rachel asked.

"It's a tradition—to honor his memory. Weeks before his birthday our fire-makers carry wood up secret paths to the top of Mount Kofel. They construct a gigantic crown—eight meters high with a cross beneath it! And six more fires on surrounding mountains—some in the shape of a cross, sometimes the letter *L* for his name, sometimes a great bonfire. Then, the night before his birthday, the fire-makers and the brass band steal up Mount Kofel. Just as darkness falls, a chorale begins the celebration. Then the band plays as all the fires are lit."

Oma nodded. "The hills are ablaze."

"They burn for hours, and finally, when they burn very low, the fire-makers and musicians descend the mountain by torchlight—a parade of light and music, down the mountain and through the village streets."

"We sing and celebrate at the inns all night and into the new day—the king's birthday."

"Fires on the mountain to honor a long-dead king?" Rachel's brows peaked. "I don't think they'll—"

"But if they did allow it, it would provide the perfect opportunity to get away—to walk out of town during the parade, and to some other place to be picked up. And even if they won't allow it, we could create some alternative form of entertainment—one that honors the blackout and provides cultural entertainment for the troops. They're always wanting that," Lea insisted.

"Maybe the fire lighting in story form, performed by the children?" Rivka wondered. "Invite them all—the church, the town, the guards, Schlick—everyone!"

"You'd have to make it in honor of the Reich or Hitler or Gerhardt to get him to come. He wouldn't come for some folkish festival or to honor a dead monarch," Rachel objected.

"Then we'll do it. If the villagers know the play honors King Ludwig, they will come. If the Nazis believe it honors them on the day we would normally honor King Ludwig, *they* will come," Lea insisted.

"It might work, but it's a huge risk," Rachel challenged her sister. "You would do this for me? Risk your life for me?"

"For you and Amelie and Rivka . . ." Lea swallowed hard. "Yes. Yes, I would."

"We could make the switch while they're all in the hall, but how will we escape? How will we leave the village?" Rivka asked.

Lea turned to Rachel. "Does your friend Pastor Bonhoeffer have a car—a way?"

"No, but perhaps he knows someone who does—someone he can trust."

"Even if we can find a car, those Nazis would never leave the checkpoints unguarded." Oma placed her cup in the sink. "Even if you invited them all to the production—even if they believed Rachel was there. And Friederich is certainly not going to like this."

Lea held up her hand for silence when they heard the scrape of boots outside the kitchen door, but too late. Friederich had pushed open the wooden door even as Oma spoke.

"And what is it your Friederich isn't going to like, Oma?" Friederich leaned his cane against the doorframe and pecked the old woman's cheek. He pulled off his hat and vest, his smile fading when he saw the women watching him, holding their breath. "What is it?"

"We've thought of a way to draw the Nazis from their posts—or at least some of them—to get Rachel and Amelie and Rivka out. We just don't have the means of transportation."

"Or the papers," Friederich said.

"Or the papers—yet," Lea agreed.

"But Jason's working on those." Rachel's voice sounded more hopeful than certain.

Friederich drew a deep breath. He looked sadly at Rivka.

"Friederich?" Lea reached for her husband's hand.

"Jason sent new documents, but he could only get two sets. I'm sorry, Rivka. Perhaps later."

Rivka's eyes fell, but she straightened, attempting a smile.

"What good will papers do if there is no way out of the village?" Oma worried.

"Herr Schrade said there is a way—one way left to us." Friederich hung his vest by the door. "Through the forests and over the Alps on foot, through Switzerland and unoccupied France, then eventually to Lisbon. It's still possible to get out through Lisbon."

"The Alps—on foot?" Lea cried. "Even if they left tomorrow, by the time they'd reached halfway, snow might set in. And if they are delayed along the way . . ."

Friederich shrugged and looked at Rachel. "Can you ski? If Herr Schrade guides you through the mountain passes and connects you with others?"

"Yes, yes, I'm strong on skis. But I'm certain Amelie's never skied; she's too little. I'm not sure I could carry her."

"That's what I said."

"Would Herr Schrade—?"

Friederich shook his head. "*Nein*, it's too dangerous for a child—the uncertain weather high up, the cold. Besides, he can only take you so far; then others will assist, and there's no way to know if they could carry her. She might have to be left along the way."

"I would never leave her," Rachel vowed, but amended, "not now."

"I told him that, too."

Silence stretched across the moments.

"Then we're no better off," Oma said.

"Can I see the passports?" Rivka asked.

Friederich pulled them from a small pouch. "They're perfect. I don't know how they do them."

Rivka took the papers to the light and held them close. "Yes, they're very well done. But they can be altered. My brother told me that it's possible."

"What do you mean?" Rachel peered over her shoulder.

Rivka turned to face her. "I mean that I ski. I ski very well."

63

THAT NIGHT Rachel slept with Amelie in her arms. She'd come to love Amelie as her own, or as near to her own as she could imagine. Supposing Amelie's passport could be doctored and forged again for Rivka, could she leave Amelie with Lea and Friederich and Oma? Could she leave her to save Rivka? Could she leave her at all?

She'd taken Kristine's daughter to raise—unwillingly, at first. But in the last few months she'd come to imagine their future, forming a makeshift family with Jason—Uncle Jason—the three of them. It was a fantasy, Rachel knew, but with or without Jason she would raise Kristine's child as her own. From duty? From honor? Partly.

But Amelie's deafness was no longer an issue in Rachel's estimation of her worth. Being able to sign, to communicate together at least some, broke down barriers. Rachel had realized that the barriers were of her own making, not Amelie's. When they got back to the US, Rachel would make certain they both received all the training they needed. *Amelie will have everything I can provide. That's what I want—at last. I love her. But is that best for Amelie?*

She can't possibly make this trip on foot—not so close to cold weather in the mountains. But if I don't leave now, when can I? When will the two of us ever be able to leave together with Gerhardt posting the "Bavarian Madonna and Child" photo across the Alps and offering a reward for me? Amelie's at greater risk with me than without me. If I don't leave soon, no one will be safe.

And what about Rivka? What hope is there for an orphaned Jewish girl in Germany? Perhaps even less than for the golden-haired deaf child of an SS officer.

Rachel closed her eyes against defiant tears. Why was the world so stupid, so cruel? Both Rivka and Amelie were innocent—treasures, rubies, diamonds beyond worth—and yet the likes of Gerhardt Schlick and Adolf Hitler bent perverted energies to destroy them. She bit her lip. Until recently, she'd been just as blind through belief in her own superiority, and through apathy.

Amelie squirmed in her arms. Rachel released the little girl, realizing she'd been holding her too tightly. She smoothed Amelie's curls, kissed the crown of her head, and rolled over, swiping away her tears. There was no sound from Rivka, no even breathing to indicate a peaceful sleep. Rachel knew her friend lay wide awake, pondering her fate.

❦

Lea listened, two nights later, as Friederich confided to her across their pillows, "It wasn't pleasure but Brigadeführer Schellenberg that recalled Schlick to Berlin. Herr Schrade heard it at the post today—the Brigadeführer got word of Schlick's oppressive ways among our locals. I expect he wants to have a little talk with the man."

"Should we thank Herr Young for that 'word'?"

"I suspect so. Jason's a good man to have in a pinch." Friederich reached for his wife in the dark.

But Lea held him at bay. "Did you think more of the plan we ladies contrived?"

"I did." She heard the frustration in his voice. He pulled away and lay on his back, his arm behind his head. "You know the risks if you impersonate her. Schlick is no fool. He—"

"You know the risks if we don't get Rachel out."

"And what about Amelie?" he challenged softly. "If we find a way, are you ready to let her go?"

Her voice broke in return. "I would give my life to save her, and I would do anything to keep her with us. If only the two could be one." Lea's breathing grew ragged. "I don't understand myself. I've come to love Rachel—she's my sister, and I know that none of this craziness is her fault. But it seems . . . it's always seemed that everything is for her—the good life, the approval, the affirmations, the education, the success . . . and now Amelie. She doesn't even have to give birth—another thing taken from me forever—and yet she gets the child of our dreams!" She felt Friederich reach for her again, this time overcoming her protests and pulling her close.

"I don't always understand the ways of God, *meine liebe Frau*." He nestled a kiss in the curve of her neck. "Sometimes I understand better the ways of evil men. But I know this: you were both an experiment—specimens to them. Identical in every biological way, but one twin was given every advantage they could devise, and one twin deprived of those advantages. In their distorted minds they wanted to see what your environments—her nurturing according to their standards or your lack of nurturing according to their standards—would do to each of you. And now they want their specimens back, to tear apart and peer at beneath their microscopes. Thankfully you are useless to them without her to compare, or without Rachel to bear out their plans for a new generation."

"It's so unfair."

"They presumed you would fail, that the life they dictated and their undermining, their intimidation, would destroy you. They never counted on love in their experiments—not Oma's love, or my love, or Amelie's love, not even the love of village children. They know nothing of God's love or the women He made you both." He wiped tears from his wife's face, replacing them with kisses.

Still she shuddered and sobbed aloud, unable to hold in the pain.

"Lea, Lea . . . do you not know that you are my heart, my soul?" She trembled against him. Friederich pulled her closer still and continued to kiss her eyes, her brows, her cheeks, her nose, her lips. He rubbed her back and cradled her in his arms, whispering her name, repeating the steadfastness of his love.

Slowly, slowly but surely, envy for all that Rachel possessed, and for all that her sister was, unwound its tentacles from Lea's heart. More slowly, fear of losing Amelie unwound from her body, then from her mind. Gradually, and at last willingly, she yielded to her husband's love. Minutes passed, and all the voices stilled.

—❖—

Two nights later, the clock in the dark kitchen cuckooed ten. Oma, Amelie, and Rivka had gone to bed when Rachel knocked softly on Lea and Friederich's door.

"Come," Friederich said.

Rachel tightened her robe about her and tiptoed in, pulling the door behind her. The message she gave her sister and brother-in-law, the parting gift she gave them that night, cost Rachel more than she'd expected. But when she saw her sister's tears of joy and Friederich's great relief, she knew she'd done the right thing—for them and for Amelie.

Friederich promised to see Chief Schrade first thing in the morning. He'd already confirmed Rivka's suspicion that changes could be made to the passport. He knew a local man, a discreet man able to do the work.

When Rachel closed their bedroom door, she knew there would be no sleep for them that night. Happiness would not contain itself. She waited in the silent kitchen until she could compose her heart and emotions. She didn't walk up the stairs, but crawled humbly through the cupboard and climbed to the attic, where Amelie slept and Rivka read from a tiny pool of light made by her candle.

"I spoke with Lea and Friederich tonight," Rachel whispered across the room.

"They've found a way to get you and Amelie out." Rivka nodded, her eyes unnaturally bright. "I'm glad—for you both. I'll miss you, but I will pray for your safety, each step of the way."

"Pray for us, Rivka—for you and me."

"What?"

"Will you go with me? Will you be my sister?"

Rivka sat up. "But Amelie—"

"Amelie's too little for a trip on foot across the Alps. She's safer here, hidden with Lea and Friederich. As long as Gerhardt can be convinced that I'm not here, he'll stop pestering Oma and Lea. I'll make sure he knows I'm in America when we get there."

"Do you mean this?" Hope, fear, wonder rose in Rivka's eyes.

Rachel laughed, though she could barely see her friend through her own tears. "Yes—" and she finger-spelled *R-i-v-k-a*—"we're bound together in hope."

"Binding—that's what my name means!"

"Yes, little sister, we're bound together."

Rivka sat up on her knees, her hands pressed together. She whispered hoarsely, recounting Ruth's vow. "'Where you go, I will go. Where you lodge, I will lodge. Your people will be my people!'"

"I have no people but here," Rachel whispered, unable to stop the tears, "and we must leave them—for all our sakes. You and I—we'll go to America. We'll find a way."

"Then I will be your people," Rivka paraphrased. "And you will be mine."

"And my God, your God," Rachel returned, remembering Oma's Bible, holding her breath, wondering if she believed that, if it could be true.

"Yes," Rivka whispered, "oh yes!"

64

OMA WANTED PHOTOGRAPHS, and Rachel agreed, as long as the film was hidden beneath floorboards and not developed until it was safe to bring them into the light of day—whenever that might be. Photos of the twin sisters alone and of both with Oma, of Oma with Lea and her husband and new daughter, of Rachel and Rivka—of every possible combination.

Once Rachel dyed Rivka's hair a ripened-wheat shade of blonde and applied a little makeup, Rivka sat for her passport photo.

Doctoring Amelie's passport to fit Rivka was cleaner, easier than Rachel had imagined. Changing the numerals in the year of birth was not so difficult for a local printer turned expert forger, nor was aligning Rivka's new photograph.

Explaining the coming changes to Amelie had been more difficult. Preparing her to sit quietly alone in the attic or cupboard, sometimes for a few hours in case of a raid, was harder still. Rachel could only imagine how frightened the little girl would be without her or Rivka.

But when Rachel saw Lea's freedom and joy with her new daughter, she knew she'd done the right thing for both of them. For all of them.

Rivka's dark eyes lit like warm amber, her smile so radiant the entire family marveled at the change. Rachel decided it was a good thing Rivka was stuck in Oma's house. It was hard enough for the older women to keep their secret from their faces. Only Oma seemed distressed.

The Nazis forbade fires on the mountain, citing blackout restrictions, even as Rachel had suspected. But dissension among the villagers over the cancellation of their beloved holiday increased tension, which prompted Sturmbannführer Schlick to condescendingly grant their petition to present an alternative indoor form of entertainment—as long as it was dedicated to the Führer and observed blackout restrictions.

Friederich reported that Forester Schrade, Father Oberlanger, and even the mayor, each with his own agenda, played their roles well in organizing the theatre hall and inviting troops stationed in and around Oberammergau.

Word raced through the village that the Ministry of Propaganda had gotten wind of the event through foreign news sources in Berlin. Goebbels was sending Brigadeführer Schellenberg to join Sturmbannführer Schlick for the grand affair, hoping to mend Nazi relationships with the Passion Village willing to honor the Führer and their Sturmbannführer. Word came that Goebbels was delighted to take advantage of photo ops for worldwide papers, all surely hungry for "German news."

Rachel dared believe the ruse might work, that it might be the answer. While Gerhardt was in Berlin, she taught the acting classes, assigning roles and prompting lines. No matter that it was only two classes—it helped Lea get started with the production and enabled Rachel to better visualize potential pitfalls.

Exciting as it was, it spelled the end of her time with Oma, Lea, Friederich, and Amelie. Rachel told herself that it was best, that it was what she wanted . . . if only her heart would believe.

❦

Gerhardt was not pleased and not taken in. Not for a moment did he believe the people of the Passion wished to present the gift of this event because they held him in high esteem. Villagers fearfully fawned to his face . . . or spit behind his back.

Still, he could not determine where the plan had originated, who was behind the push or why. Father Oberlanger didn't seem the type—too frightened of Nazi intervention in the Catholic Church rituals he held so dear to try railroading an officer able to send him to a concentration camp. Lea Hartman was too mousy, reduced to a bundle of nerves at his very presence. And what could the community pull together that he'd not seen in her rehearsals, pitiful as they were? Still, it wouldn't do to snub the officious Brigadeführer Schellenberg or let word of his lack of cooperation get to Goebbels.

Gerhardt had just returned from a grim recall to Berlin and a stern warning. He was "encouraged" to play the gracious recipient of this goodwill gift from the German people. It was the perfect opportunity to put to rest rumors among villagers and suspicions growing within the SS that he'd become obsessed with a dead woman to the point of madness.

Gerhardt had played the dutiful surrogate son to the overbearing Brigadeführer who'd been ordered to warn him. But he knew with every fiber of his being that Rachel Kramer was alive, that she was hiding somewhere—if not in Oberammergau, then nearby, somewhere in Bavaria. He knew not only from the photograph, but because the thing that Rachel Kramer had run to as a young woman, at least before her university experience increased her attitude of independence, was family—even when that family was no one but her scientist father.

The thought of family reminded him of the photographed child's uncanny likeness to Amelie. The more he looked at the photograph, the stronger the resemblance, though he didn't see how that could be.

While in Berlin, he'd visited the scene of the clinic explosion where Amelie had died. He tracked down and interrogated the matron. She'd blubbered that it had all happened so quickly, moments after his wife had left the clinic. The fire was intense and the fire trucks misdirected. There was simply not time to get everyone out. She was so very sorry for his loss.

He was not satisfied.

Left to his own devices, Gerhardt would have arrested the old woman, Frau Breisner, and interrogated her personally. Persuasion during raids had proven unsuccessful, but now he wondered if seeing her granddaughter tortured might lead to greater success, or if torturing the old woman might loosen the young Frau Hartman's tongue. Seeing his wife upon the rack might influence the stoic woodcarver. The possibilities pleased him, though he did not see how he could conduct such interviews under the Brigadeführer's watchful eye.

On the way through the village, Gerhardt had his driver stop outside the woodcarver's shop while he took a short stroll round the square. Just to let the provincials know he had returned. Gerhardt enjoyed the trepidation he brought to the eyes of the villagers. There were those who scurried by, averting their eyes, and those who all but genuflected.

He ordered his driver to pick up a pound of cheese, one of the few foods he did not import from Berlin. By the time he returned to the car, the driver stood at attention, an envelope in his hand.

The man saluted. "This was in the car when I returned, Sturmbannführer."

Gerhardt took the ivory envelope—good-quality linen stationery—with only his name penned across the front. He recognized Rachel's handwriting immediately.

Gerhardt ripped it open. Her perfume, rising from the page, made his blood race.

I regret that these months have been so devastating for both of us—all of us. But a new beginning is at hand—one in which we may each forgive and, I pray, be forgiven.

Be patient just a little longer. Consider this production my gift to you—the start of happier days, and the best these quaint people know to offer. I look forward to seeing you there.

After the show, when all have gone for the night, come behind the stage curtain. You won't be disappointed.

Gerhardt read the missive twice, smiling the second time. He returned the note to its envelope, tucking it securely within his coat's breast pocket. *Yes, Rachel, I'll indulge you this for the sake of showing the world and my superiors that I have been right all along. A promotion is more to my liking than a trip to the front. For Schellenberg to see you come humbly, willingly, to me will be worth a few days' wait. I'll be patient for you, but do not try my patience longer.*

❦

When Gerhardt walked into his office, he found Maximillion Grieser nervously awaiting an audience.

The boy had been useful at first, ferreting out rumors, playing Gerhardt's eyes and ears among the villagers. But he'd grown tiresome, and his infatuation with Lea Hartman, a married woman, put Gerhardt's pursuit of Rachel in a squalid light. Word had even reached Berlin of their mutual pursuit, though how, he didn't know.

Now that Rachel had contacted him, he had no need of the boy. His nearly drooling devotion was, in fact, a liability. He'd have to see about having Grieser shipped to the front after the celebration. He was nearly old enough to be conscripted.

"What do you want?" Gerhardt threw his gloves to his desk.

"I have new information, Sturmbannführer—information about Frau Hartman."

Gerhardt considered the teen. He wondered for a moment if he'd disgusted the Brigadeführer as Grieser disgusted him. The thought tightened his jaw.

Grieser stepped forward. "While you were away, a woman impersonating Frau Hartman taught the acting classes. She was bold and decisive—a different person from the woman we observed last week. They are two different women, surely, though identical twins, as you said."

"This is your astounding news? That you confirm my suspicions?"

"Yes, sir." Grieser now seemed less certain. "They tried to fool me as they have fooled you."

Gerhardt took a seat behind his desk, making a pyramid with his fingers.

Grieser licked his lips, a crease of worry lining his forehead. "To deceive you, sir." He rushed on. "There is some trickery planned for the King Ludwig celebration—the performance being prepared. Something strange. I overheard Frau Hartman tell Father Oberlanger that a big surprise is planned for you. I don't know what it is yet, but I do not trust Frau Hartman. You will need to take precautions."

Gerhardt would have liked to slap the boy for his presumption. Instead he leaned back in his chair. "That will be all."

Grieser frowned, confused. He leaned in. "Did they call you in for the raids? I don't think they should have done that. You were only doing your duty."

Such overstepping was the last straw. Gerhardt could feel his collar tightening around his neck. "Get out!"

Grieser's face fell. His eyes flashed confusion. But he shot out his arm. "Heil Hitler!"

Gerhardt raised his hand in a perfunctory salute as the youth spun on his heel.

65

When Uncle Friederich had slipped through the back door and untied the brown paper package, all the women had gathered round him, their mouths shaped like *O*'s. Amelie squirmed between them just in time to be covered by floating, cool waves of blue silk—a little bit of sky fallen from the heavens. Where he'd found it, she couldn't imagine. That it was a secret, she knew right away. That Oma and Aunt Lea could fashion such a thing into a magnificent gown in three days was like watching fairy godmothers at work.

The night of the play, Amelie watched Aunt Rachel apply her makeup carefully, unwind her braids and curl her long and golden hair, then step into the long, dusky-blue silk gown and pull it up to her shoulders.

Aunt Rachel looked, to Amelie, like a princess dressed for the ball—the Cinderella of her storybook. The vision stirred some deep memory of her mother—a memory sustained through daily peeks into the tiny silver locket she wore beneath her little boy's shirt.

Amelie laughed to see Aunt Lea dress as Oma's friend, the woman who'd accompanied them to the Christmas market last year, where she'd seen Uncle Jason. She watched, fascinated, as Aunt Rachel painted Aunt Lea's face to look almost as old as Oma's. She wondered if Aunt Lea still felt the same age beneath her old face.

She watched Oma dress in her best frock as Rivka packed two small knapsacks. When the ladies finished, Aunt Rachel motioned for Amelie to crawl into her lap. Amelie knew she musn't crush her pretty dress, but Aunt Rachel didn't seem to mind.

Aunt Rachel had explained days ago that she must go away without her, but she must have forgotten that she'd told Amelie, because she did it again, using the simple signs that Amelie understood.

She signed that Amelie would be Aunt Lea and Uncle Friederich's little girl now—always. They would be her Mama and Papa. Amelie loved that idea. She'd wanted her mother for a long time, but even with her picture in the silver locket, it had been hard to remember her mother's arms about her, the feel of her mother's voice as it rumbled in her chest. Aunt Lea—no, Amelie must call her Mama now—sang all the time, especially when Amelie sat in her lap. Amelie loved to press her ear against Mama's chest and feel the vibrations. It made Mama smile, and Amelie saw that she and the singing brought Mama joy. Papa Friederich had signed that God in heaven is like that—that He rejoices over us with singing.

Aunt Rachel promised again to love Amelie always. She pointed to the picture in Amelie's locket, promising that she would always love Amelie's first mother. She promised to someday return to Oberammergau to hold Amelie close once more. She didn't know when that would be—someday, when all the bad men went away.

Amelie understood those conditions. She wasn't afraid. There had been so many more things to fear in life. Knowing she was loved by many people, even if they couldn't always be with her, was not one of them. She knew that Aunt Rachel would come back to her when she could. And maybe she'd bring Uncle Jason. Amelie loved Uncle Jason. She had dreamed of him becoming her papa, but she loved Uncle Friederich, too. Amelie sighed. It was happiness to be loved and wanted.

Aunt Rachel and Mama Lea explained that Amelie must go to sleep early and remain in the cupboard until someone came for her, that in the morning Oma would be there to give her breakfast.

Amelie saw the two women—identical on the outside—exchange anxious glances. That was the only thing that frightened Amelie: the uncertainty that flashed between her grown-ups.

She was not sleepy, but she allowed Aunt Rachel to tuck her into her little pallet bed in the cupboard and kiss her good night. Amelie watched as her princess aunt swiped away tears that fell and streaked her makeup, and then the door was shut.

66

JASON ENTERED the theatre with Peterson an hour before showtime. Jason didn't want to miss a moment of either production—the one onstage or the one behind the scenes. He should be able to capture everything needed to complete his story of the evening's production for the newspapers—even make it pass muster for Goebbels. Peterson could keep the propaganda press ball rolling with his flash photography.

They'd missed call time by ten minutes. The directors and cast were backstage, getting the kids ready to perform.

Half an hour before the opening number, troops filed in, boisterous and glad to be freed from duty for any reason. Villagers began to arrive, straggling in through the next twenty minutes. He recognized Frau Breisner and her relative from Stelle—the one he'd bumped into at the Christmas market. But was she Rachel or Lea? He dared not look too long or appear too interested, only prayed that all would go well this night.

He wished he could have said good-bye to Amelie. Chances of seeing her again weren't high. He couldn't think of many more good reasons to visit the Passion Village without a Passion Play. He couldn't have stood for Amelie to go to anyone less loving and motherly than Lea, and there was no better man than Friederich. Of that, Jason was certain. He'd have to be content with that.

Just before the lights dimmed, Schlick and Brigadeführer Schellenberg marched in, surrounded by lower-ranking officers and security, as though they were the show. Jason felt his stomach grip, the sickening grip that had never quite disappeared in his years of covering the Reich.

Peterson stepped quickly in front of the stage and snapped a picture of the Nazi entourage. The Brigadeführer gave his best profile. Jason smirked to see the nod Schellenberg gave Schlick, the "smile for the camera" order. Things were going according to plan.

House lights went down and the orchestra began to play. Gradually, a soft spectrum of lights filtered across the stage, looking almost like fireflies. Into the center-stage spotlight walked Rachel Kramer, golden curls flowing past her shoulders, voluptuous and magnificent in a floor-length blue silk gown that draped low on her ivory neck. It was a dress eerily similar to the gown she'd worn to the Berlin gala. A collective gasp ran through the audience. Rachel blushed, smiling appreciatively.

From the corner of his eye, Jason saw Schlick rise in his seat, then suddenly plop down, as if the brass next to him had jerked him into place.

Rachel swept the audience with her arm. "Welcome, Brigadeführer Schellenberg and Sturmbannführer Schlick. Welcome, officers of the SS and soldiers of our illustrious Fatherland. Welcome, *meine Damen und Herren* of Oberammergau—old friends, dear friends, and all who are new in our midst." She rested her eyes on Schlick, whose posture straightened even more. "We are delighted that you came. We trust that this evening, this new twist on our longtime celebration of King Ludwig's birthday—prepared for your pleasure by the children of Oberammergau—will lighten your hearts and make you smile. May our good memories of former traditions be honored and preserved—though we will be lighting no fires on our mountain or in this hall tonight."

The chuckles through the audience fed the performer onstage, and she laughed with them—beautiful, intoxicating. Jason swallowed hard.

"May this special evening mark a new beginning in forging stronger relationships between us all for the good of our Passion Village and our nation."

"Heil Hitler!" Schellenberg shouted, saluting.

Hands shot forward throughout the room in response. "Heil Hitler!"

Rachel's eyes fell again on Schlick. She smiled warmly before taking her seat in the front row, nearest the stage entrance.

Jason could not still the erratic beating inside his chest. If Schlick, seated on the opposite side of the auditorium, was affected anything like he was, it would take the Brigadeführer and every officer in the room to keep him from rushing the stage and sweeping Rachel off her feet, show or no show. He knew that playing up to Schlick was part of Rachel's staged scheme, but he didn't like it. She was playing with fire.

Peterson waved his hand in front of Jason's face. "Earth to Young," he whispered. "You're here to do a story, sport, remember? Can't say as I blame you. She's a looker. A year or so in hiding hasn't done her any harm."

"Who?" He tried to sound innocent.

"Kramer, genius—the elusive woman of the hour."

Jason scribbled notes in the darkened room, notes he'd never be able to decipher. "Read the program. That's Lea Hartman. But they sure do look alike." He couldn't take his eyes off Rachel's back.

In the stage lights he could see that Schlick had the same problem, only he eyed her like a ravenous wolf.

Halfway through the play, the curtains closed for a short intermission and the lights went up. Schlick stood, excusing himself from the Brigadeführer. Rachel slipped from her seat and hurried backstage before Schlick could reach her. From Jason's point of view, her sleight of hand only appeared to frustrate Schlick. He tried to push his way backstage, but Friederich stood in the gap, apparently urging the officer to take his seat.

Jason saw Schlick's neck redden, heard his voice rise, though he couldn't tell what he said. Schellenberg leaned over, whispering to an aide, who quickly made his way toward Schlick. There were strained words between them before both men returned to their seats, Schlick not smiling.

"What I wouldn't give to have been privy to that exchange," Peterson whispered.

Jason nodded, glad his colleague was there.

Overhead lights flickered and theatregoers filed down the rows to their seats. Rachel appeared once more by way of the stage steps and slipped into her chair just as the lights went down. *Or is that Lea? She walks confidently like Rachel, looks like her.* Jason checked his watch. *When will they make the switch? The intermission would have been the perfect time.*

The play continued, lost momentum, picked up, and finally climaxed. The ending came victoriously with all the cast onstage, rounding out the story. Thunderous parental applause, echoed by a pounding of feet from the troops, brought the entire auditorium to their feet, calling for an encore bow. The young players had barely exited before they trooped back to the stage, bowing once again.

Proud parents pointed out their children. Peterson snapped pictures and Jason edged closer to the front, pretending to scribble names and quotes, nearly crazy in his worry for Rachel. *Why didn't she go? How will she get out now?*

And then she glided once more to the stage, holding up her hands for silence, thanking everyone for coming, encouraging them to join the special celebrations to follow, to be sure and thank Sturmbannführer Schlick for lifting the curfew this night. "Remember our Führer, our troops, and the goodwill of this night. Let us all pray to God for peace on earth."

Is she crazy? Jason saw the Brigadeführer frown. Germans weren't supposed to pray for peace; they were told to pray for the Führer's victories, if they prayed at all. And then she smiled at Schlick, that seemingly innocent but alluring smile that only Rachel could give. Schlick's eyes lit. Jason gritted his teeth. She walked offstage but turned just inside the curtain, in view of anyone who cared to watch, though everyone else seemed oblivious. She held up ten fingers, smiling at Schlick again.

Schlick lifted his chin. He'd received his signal.

The audience filed out, subdued now that troops and Nazi officers were revealed by electric light.

"What now?" Peterson threaded a new roll of film through his camera.

"Glad-hand the entourage—shoot a few pictures to make Schellenberg happy and get Schlick on film with the mayor, as promised. I think they're planning something backstage in a few; then it's off to the beer halls and inns to watch them drink like fish. Maybe we can get in on that."

"Do we want to?" Peterson grunted.

"Yeah, well, the backstage part, anyway." Jason made his way in a wide arc around the Brigadeführer and Schlick as the theatre emptied. "You shoot the artwork. I'll see what I can learn."

Jason pushed through the stage door, no matter that Friederich tried to stop him. "Where is she? Why hasn't she gone?" he hissed.

Friederich's eyes told him plainly enough to shut up, but Jason was terrified.

"You are the journalist," a voice behind him accused.

Jason whirled. The boy had grown half a head taller and muscled a hefty thirty pounds since Jason had seen him last. "You're the Hitler Youth kid."

The youth stepped through the stage curtains. "Maximillion Grieser." He squared his shoulders. "Just who are you looking for, Herr Young?"

Jason looked past Grieser's shoulder, into the eyes of Hilde

Breisner. "Frau Breisner—" he pushed past Grieser—"I thought you'd gone. I have a car and wanted to offer you a ride. I understand the Hartmans must stay and break down the set."

"How kind of you, Herr Young, to think of me. Walking is still quite difficult." She tapped her cane against her cast. "I'll gladly take you up on that good offer, if you're able to wait just a few more minutes." She stage-whispered, loud enough for Grieser to hear, "We have a surprise for Sturmbannführer Schlick—one I very much think he'll enjoy. Why don't you come and see?" She glanced at Grieser. "You, too, young man. It will do you good to see how kind people treat others."

Maximillion's neck flared red, but Jason cut him off. "Your lord and master's getting a gift, I understand, for human relations. Best stop and take note."

Friederich shushed them all. "Come in, but be quiet! You'll ruin the surprise!"

Jason offered his arm to Frau Breisner and squeezed onto the darkened stage, hugging the side curtain behind Friederich, Grieser close on their heels.

On the opposite end of the stage, a crevice of light gleamed as the curtains parted. A deep voice from the far end called uncertainly, "Rachel?"

A collective shout of "Huzzah!" rose from the darkness as lights flooded the stage. Actors, singers, musicians, and noted town officials took up a rousing rendition of "Deutschland über Alles."

Jason had never seen Gerhardt Schlick register shock, confusion, or betrayal, but his eyes flashed all three in quick succession. The Brigadeführer was suddenly at his back, beaming like a proud father as two of the loveliest Fräuleins Oberammergau boasted wheeled a beautifully decorated tiered cake before the officers.

Peterson stepped to the side, shooting photographs, switching flashbulbs as fast as he could, tossing the hot bulbs to a flabbergasted

Grieser. Schlick's dismay shot toward the camera's flash and stopped on the Hitler Youth, who looked like Peterson's assistant—the picture of betrayal, his hand in the cookie jar.

Jason searched the crowd for Rachel, didn't see her, and dared to breathe.

But as the song finished, she stepped through the curtains, the same vision in silk, confident and smiling, that all-too-familiar glint to her eye, and held out both hands in welcome. "Your surprise, Sturmbannführer Schlick—do you like it?"

"Rachel!" Schlick seemed to find his moorings. The boastful gleam in his eyes returned. He stepped forward to claim her. Brigadeführer Schellenberg's eyes widened. Jason thought he'd be sick.

But she stopped, frozen, just before reaching Schlick. "Rachel?" She looked genuinely confused and stepped back. "Oh no, Sturmbannführer. You've confused me again. I'm not the Rachel you seek. I'm Frau Hartman—do you not remember?" She looked to her husband, perplexed, then saddened. The blue orbs of her beautiful eyes appealed to Schlick, who seemed to be engaged in a cardiac explosion, and then to the Brigadeführer standing behind him. "We'd all hoped you were feeling better after your time away in Berlin. We wanted to begin anew, all the unfortunate past forgotten."

"Don't take me for a fool." Schlick smirked. "The little Bavarian Frau has no such swivel to her hips, no such gleam in her eye." He took another step forward and boldly fingered the neckline of her dress. "I remember this gown from Berlin last year, the night we danced." He leaned toward her ear as she cowered.

Friederich, who'd been at the back of the crowd, pushed between the astonished onlookers, his limp pronounced, and pulled her back with a jerk. "I'll thank you to take your hands off my wife."

Schlick rose in height. "This woman is no more your wife than—"

"Sturmbannführer Schlick," Schellenberg ordered, "join me for another picture."

The vision in blue melted into Friederich's arms. Schlick did not move, but his face raged. "You lying vixen!"

"We invited you here to honor you, and you disgrace us?" Friederich challenged.

Mayor Schulz intervened. "Sturmbannführer, surely you don't mean to insult us? We'd hoped this would be a happy occasion, a—"

"And it is." Schellenberg stepped forward, his arm firmly around Schlick's shoulders. "Sturmbannführer Schlick was mistaken."

But Schlick shrugged from the general's grip. "A mistake?" He pulled a folded magazine cover from his breast pocket and slapped it with the back of his hand. "Is this not the same woman? Do you not see they are making fools of us?"

Schellenberg frowned. He glanced at the photograph and looked carefully at the woman before him. "The likeness is certainly remarkable," he admitted.

"Let me see," ordered Friederich.

Schlick looked ready to backhand the impertinence, but Friederich stood his ground, his hand extended. "You speak of my wife."

"Show him," Schellenberg commanded.

Friederich took the picture, held it as though it were not the first time he'd seen it. "*Ja*, this is my Lea." He held the picture before the crowd. "We all know this is my Lea." He handed it back to Schlick. "It was the American press that made such a thing of the photo— calling her the Bavarian Madonna. We never did. You persecute us because you lost someone who looks like my wife?"

Whispers and side glances stole through the partygoers, while the Brigadeführer's eyes registered the tide turning against the SS.

"So, Brigadeführer, how do we report this evening of anticipated Reich endorsement to the international press?" Jason added to the fire.

"You!" Schlick turned on Jason. "You are behind this! You came between Rachel and me in Berlin, and now—"

Jason raised his hands in surrender. "I just report the news—to the world."

An aide whispered into the Brigadeführer's ear. Schellenberg straightened. His eyes narrowed, searching the face and figure of the woman beside Friederich. "If this is you, Frau Hartman, where is your child?"

The woman's face fell. Friederich took her in his arms again, but recovering her features, she stepped away from him and spoke, her voice broken but strong. "It is easy for those in authority to know that I have no children, that after my enforced visit to the Institute in Frankfurt, I never will . . . and why. Of course the child is not mine."

Schlick stepped forward, revelation dawning in his eyes. "No, the child is mine. Isn't she?" he demanded. "This is my daughter—made to look like a boy, so as to hide her from me." He shook his head in wonder, incredulity. "Kristine, Kristine—you were more clever than I thought," he whispered. Then his eyes focused on Lea. "And you, Miss Kramer, were brilliant—too brilliant for your own good."

Tension rose across the stage. The Brigadeführer asked, "Who is this child, Frau Hartman?"

At this her confidence wavered. Her eyes swept the crowd, as if needing help, but found none. "Just a child—a child in the village. Why would I hide your daughter, Sturmbannführer Schlick? *How* could I hide your daughter?"

"Whose child?" Schellenberg demanded.

"A refugee—passing through, if I remember correctly." Father Oberlanger spoke from the back of the group. "The child and his mother did not stay."

"Priest? You dare to lie?" Schlick's scathing glance parted the crowd. "You will join your curate—"

"Sturmbannführer," Jason intervened, "I understood that your daughter died in a clinic explosion—after you or your wife had her committed. There was something wrong with the little girl, wasn't there? Something not quite up to SS standards?"

Schlick reddened. The Brigadeführer looked ready to explode.

"Was it because of her mouth?" Heinrich Helphman called, peering between grown-ups' skirts and pant legs. He pushed his way through to the center of the stage and looked up into the face of Schlick. "Men came and took my little sister when she was born with a crooked mouth. They said she was a monster and they killed her, and then they did something to *meine Mutter*—I don't know what. They took my sister's body away so we couldn't even bury her. Did the bad men kill your little girl too?"

The eyes of women circling the men in uniforms widened, horrified. Murmuring villagers stepped back.

"Because if they did," Heinrich insisted, "you can ask Herr Hartman to carve you a perfect Christkind with a beautiful mouth, and you can keep him at home until your Frau has a new baby. It will help, I'm certain." Heinrich turned to Friederich. "That's why I stole the Christkind from your Nativity. But I'll give it back just as soon as *meine Mutter* has a new baby."

A gasp spread through the crowd, and a sob from one end.

"Baby killing? Is that what the New Germany specializes in?" Jason pushed, his pen poised to write. Peterson's camera flashed and Schellenberg came to life.

"*Nein, nein!* The Reich is in no such business. Clearly there has been an unfortunate misunderstanding." Schellenberg turned to the Hartmans. "You will forgive Sturmbannführer Schlick. He—"

"Forgive me?" Schlick shouted. "These *Dummköpfe* have—"

Schellenberg glared at Schlick, raising his voice. "These villagers have extended their folkish gifts in gratitude and goodwill, and we—the Reich—thank them for this splendid evening."

"But—"

"Enough!" Schellenberg nodded to two men in uniform behind

him, who stepped up to escort a struggling Schlick, nostrils flaring, from the stage. The Brigadeführer bowed to the group. "It is a long drive back to Berlin, so I must ask you to excuse us. Forgive me for taking your guest of honor, but Berlin is in need of Sturmbannführer Schlick at this time. Continue your party, and accept our gift of a lenient curfew this night."

The sweep of questions not answered was drowned in tentative applause. Jason couldn't tell if the half cheers were for a night to drink without curfew or for Schlick's enforced departure.

Either way, Jason bit down on his grin. *Whose idea was it to stage the kid? He was brilliant.*

Schellenberg paused on his way off the stage. "I look forward to reading your rendition of this evening, Herr Young."

Jason nodded. "If I hurry, maybe I can get it in tomorrow's paper."

"Allow me to make myself clear. I am most anxious to read this particular story—before it goes to press."

Jason searched the Brigadeführer's eyes. "Of course."

"*Schön gut.* You may write in my hotel. I will leave a car and driver at your disposal—for when you are finished."

Jason hadn't counted on hanging around to have his story censored. He'd already written the party line—the only one that would fly. The last thing he wanted was to be held up. He had another appointment to keep this night.

67

FORTY MINUTES before Brigadeführer Schellenberg and his aides escorted Schlick from the theatre, Father Oberlanger had stepped from the shadows of the darkened church. He'd searched the street before and beside. Seeing no one, he'd furtively beckoned Rivka from the darkness and helped her into Forestry Chief Schrade's wagon. He and Chief Schrade had helped her step in a burlap sack, surrounded her with wooden boxes—eight bottles to a box—and pulled another sack over her head, covering it with straw. Together, they'd driven to the theatre. Father Oberlanger had jumped as nimbly as his old bones could muster from the wagon and deftly handed up the middle-aged woman who'd just stepped out the back door.

❧

Rachel trembled when she realized their cohort this night was Father Oberlanger. If he recognized her or called out, if he reported them, all would be lost. But as she climbed into the wagon beside Forester Schrade, Father Oberlanger whispered, "Godspeed, Fräulein Rachel. Godspeed!"

She peered into the old priest's face—the priest who'd helped save her a second time—and found mercy and hope in the eyes she'd never quite been able to read, in the creased forehead she'd always thought evoked disapproval. She squeezed his shoulder and touched his face, her heart too full and too frightened to speak. There were so many mysteries in life—Father Oberlanger was one more.

Chief Schrade cracked his whip above the horse's head. Together they clopped steadily through wide, familiar village roads. Passing the village's edge, the road opened quickly into a winding ribbon of late-summer moonlight.

Rachel reached her hand beneath the straw and burlap behind and caught Rivka's hand raised in return.

"The first checkpoint is just ahead," Chief Schrade said. "Get a bottle ready, or two."

The words were barely out of his mouth before a light flashed across the roadway, and soldiers, guns raised, stepped into its beam. "Halt!"

Chief Schrade reined in his horse, gliding to a stop. "Heil Hitler! We bear gifts from the village and good wishes from Sturmbannführer Schlick! It's a shame you're stationed out here in the dark—that you're missing the celebration. So we bring you a little party, eh? Something to warm you through! No cake, but something better, eh? Helga, hand me a bottle for our strong soldiers!"

"Schnapps? The Sturmbannführer sent you?" The soldier in charge didn't believe it.

"*Ja! Ja!* For the celebration—Brigadeführer Schellenberg is there too! No curfew tonight!"

Rachel handed bottles to men on each side of the wagon.

"Don't be stingy!" Chief Schrade laughed. "The Sturmbannführer ordered a bottle for every man! Drink up! He may rue his generosity when he's sober!"

The men could not raise a bottle and a gun at the same time. Bottles won.

"Where are you going?"

"Just beyond Ettal. We're not to miss a soldier—deliver every bottle. Only the best for you men serving our Fatherland!"

"Serving the Führer!"

"*Ja! Ja!* Heil Hitler!"

The soldiers stood back, raising their bottles in good humor. "Heil Hitler!"

Chief Schrade waved a merry good-bye to the troops and was gone.

Two more checkpoints brought them to the base of the mountain. Chief Schrade pulled his horse off the road and through the field.

"We're leaving the road?" Rachel felt her panic rising.

"*Ja*, it's better this way—just to reach the road beyond the wood. We want them to think we drove on, beyond Ettal. I don't want them to think we took to the mountains."

"What about our tracks?"

"Can't you smell? Rain is coming. By the time they've figured out we're gone—if they realize you existed at all—our tracks will be washed clean."

Rachel prayed it would be so.

The moon swept between clouds. The horse emerged at last onto a mountain road. Up, up, and around they went, the horse going slower the higher they climbed.

"Will he be able to make it to the top?" Rivka peeked from beneath the sack.

"*Nein,*" Chief Schrade replied. "It's much too steep . . . but you will."

"What?" Rachel could not imagine walking the mountain in the dark.

The man nodded. "Sit back. Enjoy the ride, for we'll all be walking soon."

Less than twenty minutes later, true to his word, Forestry Chief Schrade pulled the wagon off the road and through a grove of trees. A faint light broke the darkness. By the time they'd come within close view, Rachel realized there was a cabin. The door opened. A woman, silhouetted against a softly burning lamp, beckoned them inside.

But Chief Schrade refused, calling instead for the woman's

husband. "*Danke*, but we must be on our way. I'll be back tomorrow for the horse and wagon."

"I'll take good care of him," the farmer replied, stepping around his wife. "He'll be ready for you."

Rachel had hoped they could stop for a cup of something resembling coffee, or anything at all to steady her nerves. But Chief Schrade helped her down, uncovered Rivka from the straw, and urged them to follow him quickly into the dark forest. He handed each a length of rope to keep connected. But neither woman was used to strenuous hiking these last months, and they stumbled in tandem.

"Can we slow down a little?" Rachel called.

"You must keep up," Chief Schrade hissed. "You must keep up or you risk being shot!" Rachel didn't waste her shortened breath on another word, but bent her head into the climb.

Up, up, and up—forever they climbed, until Rivka slowed and Rachel felt her legs would break.

At last the terrain leveled and they stepped onto a crooked path, descending into a small glen. Rachel prayed they would not have to climb back out.

The trees thickened so they could barely see one another through the darkness and branches. One moment Rachel was holding the rope and following Rivka, and the next minute she stood alone, empty-handed. "Rivka! Rivka!" she called.

"Silence!" Chief Schrade whispered fiercely. "We're nearly there. Stay close to one another."

Rachel groped silently in the dark until Rivka grabbed her hand. Rachel breathed deeply, relieved but tense, and followed her friend.

A small clearing opened and something tall and dark loomed before them. At first Rachel thought it was another copse of trees. But Forestry Chief Schrade reached the darkness first, and she heard the thumping of shoes against a door.

"Thank you!" she whispered.

"Come in, come in," Chief Schrade urged. "We rest for one hour, and then go. We must meet our contact before midnight." He struck a match, and the lamp's sudden flare hurt Rachel's eyes. But she was grateful for the shattered darkness, even for the crazy shadows that danced upon the walls, across the broad tables and chairs.

"What is this place?" whispered Rivka.

"A lodge—used by hunters in times gone by. Since the war, the Nazis use it as training barracks for the mountaineers."

"Do you think—?"

"*Nein, nein.* No one will come up here tonight—they'll all be celebrating till dawn. The Sturmbannführer doesn't even know of this place."

"What about Maximillion?" Shivers ran the length of Rachel's spine.

"*Ja*, he knows, and he knows whom to tell. Let's hope he's not that smart." He handed them a lamp. "Do not worry. Before it crosses their minds you'll both be safely on your way to Lisbon."

"I pray you're right." Rachel had done more praying, more almost believing, that night than she'd done in her life.

Chief Schrade nodded. "We'll all pray, Fräulein Kramer."

It was so strange to hear her own name; to think she would soon hear it every day seemed a miracle. If only she could hear Jason say it—aloud—once more. All the way up the mountain she'd wished she could have spoken with him, said good-bye. To see him in the audience, unable to smile at or acknowledge him, seeing the hurt and betrayal in his eyes when she'd brazenly flirted with Schlick from across the room—it seemed too cruel an ending, and one Jason didn't deserve after all he'd done to help. Surely Lea would explain that it was safer he not know their exact plans ahead of time, so he could better act as surprised as everyone else.

By the time they'd bedded down, Rachel could barely keep her eyes open. She and Rivka shared a sofa, and Chief Schrade kept watch by the window. Rachel was nearly asleep when Rivka whispered, "Oma and Amelie and Lea and Friederich will be safe now—won't they? And we'll be all right?"

Rachel forced her voice to smile in the darkness. She pressed her new younger sister's hand. "More than all right. Everything will be wonderful—for all of us. You'll see."

Rivka squeezed her hand in return.

Rachel closed her eyes. *Let it be true.*

68

RACHEL DIDN'T WANT to wake when Forestry Chief Schrade touched her shoulder; she wanted to finish her dream. And all her bones ached from the evening climb.

But he shook her, insisting that she waken. He shook Rivka. "We must be on our way. I have rolls for you. But hurry! We must make it look as if no one has been here."

"Coffee?" Rivka yawned.

"No fire—no smoke," he ordered. "Hurry!"

Rachel pulled herself together. There was no way to change her clothes or do more than wipe the worst of the homemade stage makeup from her face. But at least the face that peered back at her from the cracked mirror over the washbowl was her own—a little bleary, a little older and more careworn than the young woman who'd come to Germany the year before, but her own.

Soon she would be free to be herself, would not need to pretend to be Lea Hartman or her grandmother's relative visiting from Stelle. She wondered for a moment what that would be like, who she would be now that she'd lived this other life, now that she'd learned all her life before had been a lie.

Rachel and Rivka took the rolls Chief Schrade handed them and stuffed them into their pockets to eat along the way. They wrapped their jackets tight against the cold mountain air and followed him into the night.

They climbed and climbed, for an hour or more.

"It's not far now—not far at all," Chief Schrade whispered, hoarse.

Suddenly the trees stopped, the mountain dropped, and the moonlit path swerved almost back upon itself through a sharp cleft.

"A pass!" Rivka called behind her. "A pass! The going will be easier."

"Thank you!" Rachel whispered to the night. Her calf and thigh muscles strained to the breaking point.

Hidden at the base of the pass was what looked like the outline of a building. Chief Schrade motioned for the girls to stop, to wait. Rachel caught up to Rivka, and they stood close in the shadows of the trees. Chief Schrade continued down the path, disappearing inside what looked like nothing but a makeshift hut, a shack. Sounds of two men, maybe three, talking, possibly arguing, floated toward them.

Three minutes must have passed before a man started up the shadowed path toward them. But it wasn't the shape of Chief Schrade. They couldn't see his face as it bent toward the climb, but he scrambled up and up. Rachel was ready to turn, to pull Rivka back through the trees the way they'd come, to stumble down the mountain. Perhaps they could make it back to the lodge, lose the man, make it to Ettal or even Oma's attic.

"Rachel! Rachel!" the man called.

The swimming, swirling fears in Rachel's head stopped short. "Jason?" She gasped, trying to escape hallucination. "What are you doing here? How did you—?"

"I couldn't let you go . . . without seeing you." He reached them, panting. "Rivka . . . good to see you again."

"And you, boss."

"How did you get here ahead of us? It took us all night to get this far—we only rested an hour."

"Schellenberg was grateful for good press and offered me a ride with his motorcade. I picked the nearest ski lodge—told him I'd been assigned to do a story on Bavaria's ski resorts, reasons the world might still like to visit Germany this autumn. The last hour I took on foot."

"What about Gerhardt?"

"I believe our good Brigadeführer's going to keep Schlick very busy coordinating concentration camps deep in Poland for some time." He stepped closer. "Lea told me where to find you. We don't have much time."

Rivka squeezed Rachel's hand, said, "See you later," and continued down the path toward the shack.

"How long do we have?" Rachel didn't want to think of Gerhardt Schlick again, didn't want to miss this moment.

"Five minutes. Just enough time for the two of you to drink something hot and change clothes. You can wear a set of mine—with suspenders." He grinned. "Your contact's ready to go—got to get you through the pass and to the other side before daylight." He wrapped an arm around her back. "Chicory's on. I want you warmed through. You've got a long road ahead."

But she needed to stop time. It had all been such a rush, such high risk, and now there was no more time. "Jason. When will I see you?" She knew she should thank him for all he'd done—for saving Amelie, for saving her from a father who would have sold her to the Nazis, for helping her find her real family, for saving Rivka, for introducing her to Bonhoeffer and, more importantly, to Jesus—his Jesus and perhaps, one day, her Jesus—someone she needed to know better. She should say a thousand different things. But just now, this was all that mattered. "Tell me."

He cupped her face in his hands and turned it to the night sky. "Do you see that half moon?"

She sniffed, unable to keep the twisted knot from rising in her throat.

"Each night I want you to look at that moon, and know that

I'm looking at it, thinking of you, counting its cycles until I see you again—in New York."

"And what will happen when you reach New York?" She could barely breathe.

He turned her face back to his. "I'll be looking up Miss Rachel Kramer. I'll be asking her to meet me for coffee that very day, then lunch, and dinner."

"Dinner? Isn't that pretty serious?" she whispered.

He pulled her closer. "Very serious. For the rest of my life."

"And mine," she promised.

"Mrs. Jason Young—has a nice ring."

"Rachel Young," she countered.

"Rachel Young," he agreed, then kissed her boldly, fully, warmly on the mouth.

The heat that rose from the tips of her toes traveled up her legs and into her torso, filling her heart, rushing to her head. She couldn't think, couldn't reason, didn't care to, but pushed her fingers through his hair, letting his hat fall to the ground, and returned his promise tenfold.

Epilogue

IN 1950, the people of Oberammergau pooled their resources and committed to their first Passion Play season since 1934, hoping to show the world a more Christian and temperate side of Germany. General Eisenhower planned to attend with his wife, Mamie. Jason figured that was a sure sign that it was time—it was safe, at last—for his Rachel to return home to her family.

The Youngs flew first by way of Israel and spent five days with a radiant Rivka, RN, and her new husband, Dr. David Schechem, recently settled in a fledgling kibbutz. The Schechems had opened the kibbutz's first medical clinic, joining other Hebrew believers in building a community, and hoping to welcome many more.

For years from the time that they'd learned of the murder of Rivka's parents and brother, Jason, Rachel, and Rivka had donated money to help build the new state of Israel, to plant trees and vine-yards, praying with Rivka that their efforts would help to save the Jewish remnant surviving the Holocaust.

"And here we are!" Rivka exulted. "It is a beginning."

"A wondrous beginning." Rachel embraced her little sister, who'd grown beyond her now, anticipating a life, a family, a community of her own.

Walking onto the plane, waving good-bye to the sister she'd come to love just as much as her birth sister, was harder than Rachel had imagined. Rivka had hidden in Oma's attic with her and witnessed the biggest transformations in Rachel's life. She'd trekked over the Alps and skied into Switzerland with her. She'd begged and bargained by her side for two seats on a weekly, rickety, packed bus through unoccupied France to Barcelona, hopped a moving train with her from Barcelona into Madrid and finally Lisbon. Together, they'd miraculously sailed from Lisbon to New York and battled immigration.

In a story stranger than fiction, Rivka was the sister who'd wrestled and journeyed beside her for five years to the heart of Jesus—Yeshua, the Messiah. A journey neither had imagined in their younger lives, and a journey that had changed them both forever.

When their feet finally stood on German soil in Munich, Rachel trembled, but Jason stood close, his hand on her spine.

The train ride to Oberammergau brought a rush of memories and no small amount of trepidation. *What will it be like, seeing Amelie again? Will she remember me?*

They'd received no word from Oma, Lea, or Friederich until six months after the war ended in Europe. Jason and Rachel, reunited and finally able to marry, had immediately sent relief packages. Each month's package contained a tin of coffee, a tin of tea, and four bars of chocolate, wrapped in clothing or shoes for one family member or another. Sometimes the packages made it through.

Oma wrote most recently that Amelie had grown into a beautiful and capable young woman, one of Oberammergau's finest up-and-coming dressmakers. So changed was she from the picture of the little boy in the "Bavarian Madonna and Child" that she was certain Rachel would not recognize her. No one in the village questioned her origins—no one except Heinrich Helphman, Friederich's wood-carving apprentice, who was smitten from the moment he'd seen Amelie as a child in need of a protector.

Years of fierce bombing had made deafness and hearing difficulties common—a casualty of war. Oma's story to all who asked was that the little girl had been orphaned. The child's grandmother was a relative of Oma's from Stelle, who had disappeared during the bombing. How natural for Lea and Friederich Hartman to adopt her.

Rachel knew that, in walking German soil again, the unsettling ghosts of the past were not hers alone. She'd sensed the tension in Jason's posture, in the grim set of his mouth, in the grip of his hand.

Jason had left Berlin in 1941, having been reassigned to London until the end of the war. He never saw or heard from Dietrich Bonhoeffer again, but learned from colleagues that his friend was arrested in 1943 and charged with conspiracy when his part in the failed plot to assassinate Hitler was discovered. After months of inter-rogation, and shortly before the end of the war, Dietrich was moved from Buchenwald to Schönberg. The Sunday after Easter, just after leading a service for inmates in his prison cell, Bonhoeffer was taken by Gestapo agents to Flossenbürg. He was hanged at dawn two days later. Among his last known words were, "This is the end—for me the beginning of life."

Nearly a year after the war, Jason learned through the Red Cross that Curate Bauer had been sentenced to hard labor in Sachsenhausen, a concentration camp on the outskirts of Oranienburg. On Christmas Day, 1942, he'd insisted on taking the place of a young Jew con-demned to death for stealing a ration of bread. The curate stood before the firing squad, without blindfold, praying aloud for the soldiers who raised their guns to kill him. The Jewish boy was shot anyway.

So many losses, so much pain. Rachel didn't know if she was strong enough to face a Germany with such sadness. At least she'd put the ghost of her father to rest, and she no longer feared the Institute or Gerhardt Schlick.

Six months after the war, a new secretary at the Cold Spring Harbor Institute had mistakenly forwarded a letter to Dr. Kramer's former address. The letter, to the Institute, from the office of Dr. Verschuer of Berlin, made its way to Rachel. Dr. Verschuer regretted to inform the Institute that Sturmbannführer Gerhardt Schlick had fallen ill during the last month of the war and died in Poland. Miss

Rachel Kramer's participation in their mutual experiment was no longer of interest.

Incriminating files disappeared near the end of the war; Dr. Verschuer was not tried for war crimes, but continued to conduct research in the related field of genetics. His assistant, Dr. Josef Mengele, better known as the "Angel of Death" for his horrific human experiments at Auschwitz, had escaped to South America in 1949 with the help of his family.

How can we make peace with such a past as this? How can we move into a future, build a home, a family born of so much pain?

But when Jason traced her arm and fingered her wedding ring, Rachel knew. *I am not alone. We are not alone.*

Rachel breathed deeply as the train neared the station. *What will Lea think when she sees me? What does she look like now? Do we still look the same?* Rachel sighed, rubbing her stomach, which seemed to grow larger by the day. She knew they no longer looked anything alike, and that might be the greatest hurt of all for her sister.

She turned to Jason and whispered, "Maybe we should have told her before we came. Maybe this is a bad idea."

Jason pushed his fedora back on his head and whispered in Rachel's ear, "Did I ever tell you that you don't look much like that old woman I kissed on her way out of Germany all those years ago?"

"By the time you got around to kissing me, I'd washed that gunk off my face, so you never kissed that old woman," Rachel countered.

He grinned and sat back.

"This woman's a lot fatter," she mumbled, casting what she hoped was an appealing glance his way.

"This woman—this fabulous woman—is carrying our perfect baby."

"You forget whom you're talking to—there are no perfect babies."

He smiled. "Lea will tell you that every baby is perfect, no matter the packaging."

"She would, wouldn't she? And Friederich will say each child is rejoiced over with singing," Rachel remembered.

"And Oma will say, 'Knit by God in its mother's womb.'"

Rachel sat back, thankful as their little one kicked, almost on cue. *Yes, she will. I just hope they'll truly be glad to see us.*

But there was no need to wait, to wonder, until they reached the station.

"Look!" Jason pointed out the window of the train. "On the hillside!"

Wildly jumping up and down with a bouquet of Alpine flowers crushed in one hand and waving fiercely with the other arm was a beautiful young woman, flaxen hair splayed round her face in the late-afternoon breeze.

"Kristine! She's the image of Kristine!" Rachel wept, waving wildly in return.

Beside her was a boy—a young man—who could only be Heinrich Helphman grown up, running, suddenly tugging Amelie along with him toward the station.

As the train slowed and finally lurched to a stop, the whistle blew one long and final blast. Rachel spied Lea and Friederich eagerly searching the windows of the train. Holding hands. They looked a little more mature about the face, perhaps a tad thicker about the waist, but two parts of a lovely whole. Oma leaned forward in a wheeled chair beside them, hands clasped beneath her chin, her face a rapture of joy, of hope and expectation.

Lea's eyes found Rachel's and she whooped for joy, pulling Friederich, still limping, with her, closer to the tracks.

Rachel clasped Jason's hand in both her own and pressed them to her heart. *We're home. We're truly home!*

Note to Readers

ON THE NIGHT of May 10, 1933, less than four months after Adolf Hitler was appointed Reich Chancellor, members of the SS and the SA (brownshirts), Nazi students, and Hitler Youth trooped into Bebelplatz, a square near Humboldt University in Berlin, where they lit a raging bonfire and sent approximately twenty thousand books up in flames.

In 2009, my daughter and I joined an emotional anniversary ceremony on the very spot. Nearby, a plaque, engraved with a line from Heinrich Heine's play *Almansor* (1821) reads, *Das war ein Vorspiel nur, dort wo man Bücher verbrennt, verbrennt man am Ende auch Menschen*—"That was only a prelude; where they burn books, they will in the end also burn people."

I doubt that in 1933 any of those students, so intent on burning books and championing their new Führer, imagined that within a few short years they would be ordered to force Jewish men, women, and children from their homes and ultimately into cattle cars en route to concentration camps, or that they would eventually help load their bodies into crematoriums.

I've never understood how one of the most enlightened nations of the world was seduced and reduced to stripping portions of its populace of rights to citizenship and human dignity, to living complicit in the murder of entire groups of people. What made Nazis believe that their wants and needs were most important, that they constituted a superior race, and that anyone their leadership deemed inferior should be eliminated? Why did the people—and the church, in particular—fail to rise up in protest? And if such a drastic change in culture and behavior happened then, could it happen today? Could it happen in America?

In my quest for answers, I traced the evolution of the pseudo-science of eugenics in the United States and Germany, with its determination to eradicate disease and its design to eliminate certain bloodlines while promoting others, along with Hitler's fascination with eugenics and his writing of *Mein Kampf,* outlining his intentions. I also explored Hitler's rise to power, the evolution of the Third Reich, and the events of World War II. I needed to understand how it all began—why any of this madness made sense to those living at that time.

The answers I've gleaned are varied and complex, and saddest of all, not altogether a thing of the past. At the most basic level, I believe that fear, greed, arrogance, and the desire to be above others—the cause of so much of the world's strife—encompassed a nation grasping at straws for a savior, a nation desperate to climb from the pit in which they found themselves after the devastation of World War I and the long-term consequences of the Treaty of Versailles. I also believe much truth can be captured in this familiar saying: "The only thing necessary for the triumph of evil is for good men to do nothing."

Dietrich Bonhoeffer, a dissident German pastor, was one of the few who early recognized the danger of Hitler's absolute power and his insistence on total allegiance to him rather than to any other, including Jesus Christ. Bonhoeffer wrote, "The Church has only one altar, the altar of the Almighty . . . before which all creatures must kneel. . . . He who seeks anything other than this must keep away; he cannot join us in the house of God. . . . The Church has only one pulpit, and from that pulpit faith in God will be preached, and no other faith, and no other will than the will of God, however well-intentioned."

Bonhoeffer also realized, after reading *Mein Kampf,* that Hitler was systematically setting about doing exactly what he'd written he would do. He saw the horrific ramifications for Jews in the Nuremberg Laws and the Aryan Clause, which stripped German Jews of their citizenship and rights and eliminated Hebrew Christians from all public and church roles. Historically there were tens of thousands of Hebrew Christians in Germany. Under Hitler's regime, nearly all were killed in the camps beside their Jewish brethren and many other groups the Reich sought to eliminate.

Bonhoeffer saw the burning of synagogues for the hate crimes they were, saw sterilizations and "mercy killings" of the physically and mentally handicapped as murder; he saw that the church, by not protecting Jews or anyone else outside Hitler's concept of an Aryan ideal, was not living out Jesus' commandments. And he realized that with the passing of each of Hitler's edicts, the German people lost their liberty to protest the madness.

History is one thing. The current, urgent questions are ours: What have we learned? How do we make sure we are not taken unawares, that we are not seduced into giving up our rights and taking away the rights of others? Where do we find the courage to rise from our apathy, our indifference, from political correctness and fear of offending to stand for God's truth? How do we make certain we keep God on the throne of our hearts and minds, that we do not place political or charismatic leaders or our own comfort and wealth before Him? How do we make certain that we have not deemed ourselves more worthy or important than others whom Jesus died to save?

I found many of the answers to these questions in Bonhoeffer's book *The Cost of Discipleship.* It's not a simple read. But it's a book I wish I'd read earlier in life, one that challenges and convicts and draws me into a deeper relationship with Christ. It reminds me that

I'm not called to some ethereal monasticism outside this world, but to live, fully equipped by Christ, in this world as His disciple.

In 2010, my daughter's new in-laws told my husband and me about a tour they would soon join to Oberammergau to see the Passion Play. They invited us to accompany them, as a couple of spots had opened up on the tour. At the time, I had no plans to set my story in Oberammergau. But after that tour, I began to see the contrast between a people who'd vowed to perform the Passion Play every ten years (and—to the best of their ability—to live that culture) and a regime set on claiming primacy in the hearts and minds of its citizens. It sounded so like the contrasting struggles of the Christian's journey that I could not resist.

Some of the events explored in *Saving Amelie* are real and follow the historical timeline. For example:

There was a strong eugenics movement in the United States as well as in Germany and other countries that practiced sterilization. International conferences (including the conference Dr. Kramer and others attend in Scotland) and the sharing of research between countries were common. At the time this story opens, years before Dr. Josef Mengele's infamous human experiments in Auschwitz, Dr. Verschuer was assisted by Mengele at the Institute for Hereditary Biology and Racial Hygiene in Frankfurt, where they did extensive research on tuberculosis and on twins. Notes in the epilogue regarding both men are true. Eugenics research was conducted at the Institute in Long Island, though Dr. Kramer is a fictitious character.

Much of Jason Young's timeline came from William L. Shirer's *Berlin Diary: The Journal of a Foreign Correspondent, 1934–1941*. It is a profoundly different experience to read a diary written as events unfold rather than a history written after the fact.

Dietrich Bonhoeffer and the books he wrote are real, including *Nachfolge*, later translated as *The Cost of Discipleship*. I've tried to follow the timeline of Bonhoeffer's life during these years. However, he did not arrive at the Benedictine monastery in Ettal until later in the fall of 1940. My scene at Ettal with Rachel is fictitious.

For the sake of story, the villagers of Oberammergau replaced their August 24 King Ludwig's Fire celebration (an annual event) with the production directed by Rachel and Lea. Though the Munich State Library was not able to conclude whether or not the fires on the mountain were forbidden in 1940, it seemed a fair supposition since the country was under blackout.

Adolf Hitler attended the Passion Play in 1934. General Dwight D. Eisenhower and his wife, Mamie, attended in 1950.

Some characters and their activities—like Frau Bergstrom, Father Oberlanger, Curate Bauer, Forestry Chief Schrade, Administrator Raab, the mayor, and the shopkeeper who was arrested for giving extra food to refugees—were, in part, modeled after real people who lived in Berlin or Oberammergau at the time. While they were not connected to the resistance network I have portrayed, each of these characters serves as a reminder that in desperate situations there are those who quietly go about resisting oppressors and helping others in ways they are able. I pray for courage to do the same.

God's blessings,
Cathy Gohlke

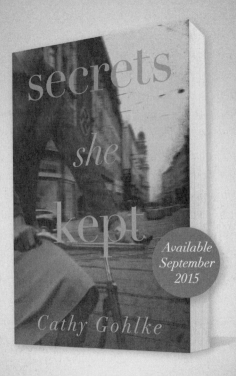

Don't miss these other great novels by

CATHY GOHLKE!

Turn the page
for a preview of
*PROMISE
ME THIS*

"A gripping tale."
Publishers Weekly

"Riveting . . . mesmerizing . . . compelling."
Fictionadditict.com

"Dramatic . . . heart-wrenching."
Library Journal

"A sweet, compelling story."
Shelf-awareness.com

"Grabs the reader from the first sentence."
Romantic Times

"Excellent storytelling."
Radiant Lit

"Captivating."
Christian Book Previews

"Keeps the reader riveted."
Titletrakk.com

"Impressively emotional storytelling."
Freshfiction.com

"Wonderful."
Romantic Times

❋ CHAPTER ONE ❋

THE GREAT SHIP returned late from her sea trials beyond the shores of Carrickfergus, needing only her sea papers, a last-minute load of supplies, and the Belfast mail before racing to Southampton.

But in that rush to ferry supplies, a dockworker's hand was crushed beneath two heavy crates carelessly dropped. The fury and swearing that followed reddened the neck of the toughest man aboard the sturdy supply boat.

Michael Dunnagan's eyes and ears spread wide with all the fascination of his fifteen years.

"You there! Lad! Do you want to make a shilling?"

Michael, who'd stolen the last two hours of the day from his sweep's work to run home and scrub before seeing *Titanic* off, turned at the gruff offer, certain he'd not heard with both ears.

"Are you deaf, lad? Do you want to make a shilling, I say!" the mate aboard the supply craft called again.

"I do, sir! I do!" Michael vowed, propelled by wonder and a fear the man might change his mind.

"Give us a hand, then. My man's smashed his paw, and we've got to get these supplies aboard *Titanic*. She's late from her trials and wants to be under way!"

Michael could not move his feet from the splintered dock. For months he'd slipped from work to steal glimpses of the lady's growing. He'd spied three years ago as her magnificent keel was laid and had checked week by week as ribs grew into skeleton, as metal plates formed sinew and muscle to strengthen her frame, as decks and funnels fleshed her out. He'd speculated on her finishing, the sure beauty and mystery of her insides. He had cheered, with most of Belfast, as she'd been gently pulled from her berth that morning by tugboats so small with names so mighty that the contrast was laughable.

To stand on the dock and see her sitting low in the water, her sleek lines lit by electric lights against the cold spring twilight, was a wonder of its own. The idea of stepping onto her polished deck—and being paid to do it—was joyous beyond anything in Michael's ken.

But his uncle Tom was aboard *Titanic* in the stoker hole, shoveling coal for her mighty engines. Michael had snuck to the docks to celebrate the parting from his uncle's angry fists and lashing belt as much as he'd come to see *Titanic* herself. He'd never dared to defend himself against the hateful man twice his size, but Michael surely meant to spit a final good-bye.

"Are you coming or not?" the dockhand barked.

"Aye!" Michael dared the risk and jumped aboard the supply boat, trying for the nimble footing of a sailor rather than the clunky feet of a sweep. Orders were shouted from every direction. Fancy chairs, crates of food, and kitchen supplies were stowed in every conceivable space. Mailbags flew from hands on dock to hands on deck. As soon as the lines were tossed aboard, the supply craft fairly flew through the harbor.

Staff of Harland and Wolff—the ship's designers and builders—firemen, and yard workers not sailing to Southampton stood on *Titanic's* deck, ready to be lightered ashore. The supply boat pulled alongside her.

Michael bent his head, just in case Uncle Tom was among those sent ashore, though he figured it unlikely. He hefted the low end of a kitchen crate and followed it aboard *Titanic*, repeating in his mind the two words of the only prayer he remembered: *Sweet Jesus. Sweet Jesus. Sweet Jesus.*

"Don't be leaving them there!" An authoritarian sort in blue uniform bellowed at the load of chairs set squarely on the deck. "Bring those along to the first-class reception room!"

Michael dropped the kitchen crate where he stood. Sweeping a wicker chair clumsily beneath each arm, he followed the corridor-winding trail blazed by the man ahead of him.

He clamped his mouth to keep it from trailing his toes. Golden oak, carved and scrolled, waxed to a high sheen, swept past him. Fancy patterned carpeting in colors he would have wagered grew only in flowers along the River Shannon made him whistle low. Mahogany steps, grand beyond words, swept up, up to he didn't know where.

He caught his breath at the domed skylight above it all.

Lights, so high he had to crane his neck to see, and spread wider than a man could stretch, looked for all the world to Michael like layers of icicles and stars, twinkling, dangling one set upon the other.

But Michael gasped as his eyes traveled downward again. He turned away from the center railing, feeling heat creep up his neck. Why the masters of *Titanic* wanted a statue of a winged and naked child to hold a lamp was more than he could imagine.

"Oy! Mind what you're about, lad!" A deckhand wheeled a skid of crates, barely missing Michael's back. "If we scrape these bulkheads, we're done for. I'll not be wanting my pay docked because a gutter rat can't keep his head."

"I'll mind, sir. I will, sir." Michael took no offense. He considered himself a class of vermin somewhat lower than a gutter rat. He swallowed and thought, *But the luckiest vermin that ever lived!*

"Set them round here," the fussy man ordered. Immediately the first-class reception room was filled with men and chairs and confounding directions. A disagreement over the placement of chairs broke out between two argumentative types in crisp uniforms.

The man who'd followed close on Michael's heels stepped back, muttering beneath his breath, "Young bucks busting their britches."

A minute passed before he shook his head and spoke from the side of his mouth. "Come, me boyo. We'll fetch another load. Blathering still, they'll be."

But as they turned, the men in uniform forged an agreement and called for Michael to rearrange the chairs. Michael stepped lively, moved each one willingly, deliberately, and moved a couple again, only to stay longer in the wondrous room.

But as quickly as the cavernous room had filled, it emptied. The last of the uniformed men was summoned to the dining room next door, and Michael stood alone in the vast hall.

He started for the passageway, then stopped. He knew he should return to the deck with the other hands and finish loading supplies. But what if he didn't? What if he just sat down and took his ease? What if he dared stay in the fine room until *Titanic* reached Southampton? What if he then walked off the ship—simply walked into England?

Michael's brow creased in consternation. He sucked in his breath, nearly giddy at the notion: to leave Belfast and Ireland for good and all, never again to feel Uncle Tom's belt or buckle lashed across his face or shoulders.

And there was Jack Deegan to consider. When Deegan had injured his back aboard his last ship, he'd struck a bargain with Uncle Tom. Deegan had eagerly traded his discharge book—a stoker's ticket aboard one of the big liners—for Uncle Tom's flat and Michael's sweep wages for twelve months. As cruel as his uncle had always been, experience made Michael fear being left alone with Jack Deegan even more.

To walk away from Uncle Tom, from Jack Deegan, from the memory of these miserable six years past, and even from the guilt and shame of failing Megan Marie—it was a dream, complex and startling. And it flashed through Michael's mind in a moment.

He swallowed. Uncle Tom would be in the stoker hole or firemen's quarters while aboard ship. Once in Southampton he would surely spend his shore leave at the pubs. Michael could avoid him for this short voyage.

"Sweet Jesus," Michael whispered again, his heart drumming a beat until it pounded the walls of his chest. He had begged for years, never believing his prayers had been heard or would be answered.

Michael waited half a minute. When no one came, he crept cautiously across the room, far from the main entry, and slid, the back side of a whisper, beneath the table nearest the wall.

What's the worst they could do to me? he wondered. *Send me back? Throw me to the sharks?* He winced. It was a fair trade.

Minutes passed and still no one came. Shrill whistle blasts signaled *Titanic's* departure from the harbor. Michael wondered if the mate who'd hired him had missed him, or if he'd counted himself lucky to be saved the bargained shilling. He wondered if Uncle Tom or Jack Deegan would figure out what he'd done, hunt him down, and drag him back. He wondered if it was possible the Sweet Jesus listened to the prayers of creatures lower than gutter rats after all.

"I simply cannot keep the child alone with me any longer," Eleanor Hargrave insisted, stabbing her silver-handled cane into the pile of the Persian carpet spread across her drawing room floor. "While I am yet able to travel, I am determined to tour the Continent. My dear cousins in Berlin have been so very patient, awaiting my visit while I served my father, then raised your father's orphaned child."

It was the story of martyrdom Owen had heard from his spinster aunt month after month, year after year, designed and never failing to induce guilt. It was the story of her life of sacrifice and grueling servitude, first to her widowed and demanding father, whom her younger sister had selfishly deserted, and then to the orphaned children of that sister and her husband. His aunt constantly referred to that sacrifice as her gift to his poor departed father, though no mention was ever made of her own sister, Owen and Annie's mother. Owen tried to listen patiently.

"It is unfair of either of you to presume upon me any longer. You simply must take the girl and provide for her or return here to help me look after her. If you do not, I shall be forced to send her away to school—Scotland, I should think."

"I agree, Aunt. I'll see to it immediately."

"You cannot know the worry and vexation caused me by—" His aunt stopped her litany midsentence. "What did you say?"

"I said that I agree. You've been most patient and generous with Annie and with me—a saint." What Owen did not say was that he, too, was aware that his sister grew each day to look more like their beautiful mother—the sister Aunt Eleanor despised. It was little wonder she wanted Annie out of her sight.

"You will return here, then?"

He heard the hope in his aunt's voice.

"I've made arrangements for Annie to begin boarding school in Southampton."

"Southampton? You mean you will not . . ." She stopped, folded her hands, and lifted her chin. "No one of consequence attends school in Southampton."

"We are not people of financial consequence, Aunt. We are hard-working people of substantial character, as were our parents." Owen had yearned to say that to his aunt for years.

Her eyes flashed. "Your pride is up, young man. My father would say, 'Your Allen Irish is showing.'"

Owen felt his jaw tighten.

And then his aunt smiled—a thing so rare that Owen's eyebrows rose in return.

She leaned forward to stroke his cheek. "Impetuous. So like

Mackenzie. You grow more like him—in looks and demeanor—each time I see you."

Owen pulled back. He'd never liked the possessiveness of his aunt's touch, nor the way she constantly likened him to his father. And now that he'd set his sights on the beautiful, widowed Lucy Snape, whose toddler needed a financially stable father, it was essential that he establish his independence.

Eleanor sniffed and sat back. "It is impossible. Elisabeth Anne must remain in London. It is the only suitable society for a young lady. You will return to Hargrave House." She took a sip of tea, then replaced her teacup firmly in its saucer. "Your room stands ready."

"Not this time, Aunt." Owen spoke quietly, leaning forward to replace his own cup, willing it not to rattle. "I will support Annie from now on."

"On gardener's wages. And send her to a boarding school—in a shipping town!" She laughed.

"A convenient location for those going to sea." Owen paused, debating how to proceed. "Or those crossing the sea."

"The sea?" His aunt's voice took on the suspicion, even the menace, that Owen feared. But he would do this, afraid or not.

Owen leaned forward again, breathing the prayer that never failed him. "Do you remember Uncle Sean Allen, in America?"

She stiffened.

"He and Aunt Maggie offered Father half of their landscaping business in New Jersey after Mother died."

"A foolish proposition—a child's dream! The idea of whisking two motherless children to a godforsaken—"

"It was a proposition that might have saved him from the grief that took his life—if you hadn't interfered!" Owen stopped, horrified that he'd spoken aloud the words harbored in his heart these four years but delighted that at last he'd mustered the courage.

She drew herself up. "If it was not an accident that sent him to his grave, it was his own ridiculous pining for a woman too silly to help him manage his business! I offered your father everything—this home, my inheritance, introduction to the finest families. He needn't have worked at all, and if he had insisted, I could have procured any business connections he dreamed of in England. I can do all of that for you, Owen. I offer all of that to you."

And it would be the death of all my hopes for Lucy—or even someone like her—just as you were the death of Father's hopes and dreams. "I'm grateful for the roof you've given Annie and me these four years, Aunt. But it's time for us to go. Uncle Sean has made to me the same offer he made to Father, and I've accepted. I sail Easter week."

"Easter!" she gasped.

"As soon as we turn a profit, I'll send for Annie."

"He has been in that business these many years and not succeeded?" She snorted scornfully, but the fear that he meant to go did not leave her eyes.

He leaned forward. "Do you not see, Aunt? Do you not see this is a chance of a lifetime—for Annie and for me?"

"What I see is that you are foolish and ungrateful, with no more common sense than your father! I see that you are willing to throw away your life on a silly scheme that will come to nothing and that you intend to drag the child down beside you!" Her voice rose with each word, piercing the air.

Owen drew back. He'd not hurt Annie for the world. At fourteen, she was not a child in his eyes; that she remained so in Aunt Eleanor's estimation was reason enough to get her away from Hargrave House.

Eleanor's face fell to pleading, her demands to wheedling. "Owen, stay here. I can set you up in your own gardening business, if that is what you want. You can experiment with whatever you like in our own greenhouses. They will be entirely at your disposal."

Owen folded his serviette and placed it on the tea tray. The action gave him peace, finality. "I'm sorry you cannot be happy for us, Aunt. But it is the solution to our mutual dilemmas."

A minute of silence passed between them, but Owen's heart did not slow.

"Leave me, Owen, and I will strike you from my will." The words came softly, a Judas kiss.

Owen stood and bowed.

"My estate means nothing to you?"

"It comes at too high a price, Aunt." Owen breathed, relieved that the deed was done. "I'll stay the night and then must get back to Southampton. I'll return to collect Annie and her things early next week." He bowed again and walked away.

"There is something more. I had not intended to tell you—not yet."

Owen turned.

His aunt folded her hands in her lap. "It was your grandfather's doing."

※ ※

Annie knelt beside the stair rail, her nerves taut, her eyes stretched wide in worry. When at last Owen stepped through the parlor door, she let out the breath she hadn't realized she was holding.

But Owen didn't move. Annie leaned over the railing for a better look at her brother. His hands covered his head, pressed against the doorframe, and she was certain he moaned. She stood back, biting her lower lip. She'd never heard such a sound from her older brother. "Owen? Owen!" she whispered loudly into the hallway below.

At last he climbed, two stairs at a time, but she'd never seen him look so weary.

"I could hear her shouting all the way up here. What has happened?" Annie met him at the landing and rushed into his arms.

"Come, close the door, Annie." Owen spoke low, pulling her into her room. "Pack your things, everything you want to keep. We'll not be back."

"Pack my things? Why? Where are we going?"

But her brother would not meet her eyes. He pulled her carpetbag from the top of the cupboard and spread it open. He picked up their parents' wedding photograph from her bedside table. "You'll want this."

"Whatever are you doing?"

Owen wrapped the frame in the linen it sat upon and placed it in the bottom of her bag. "I'll tell you when we've settled for the night. Now you must pack, and quickly."

"Am I going to live with you?"

He shook his head. "Pack, Annie."

"Is Aunt Eleanor sending me away?"

"She knows we're going. She—"

They both started when Annie's door swung wide.

"Jamison!" Annie gasped.

The old butler's bent frame filled the low doorway. He looked over his shoulder, put a finger to his lips, and motioned Owen closer. "Do you have a place for Miss Annie, sir?"

Owen ran his fingers through his hair. "In Southampton, as soon as I can arrange it. I don't know what we shall do tonight."

Jamison nodded and pushed a crumpled paper into Owen's hand.

"Jamison!" Eleanor Hargrave bellowed from the first floor.

"What's going on?" Annie begged.

"Take this round to my old sister, Nellie Woodward. Her address is on the bottom. She will do right by you for the night," the butler whispered.

"Jamison! Come—at once!" Annie heard their aunt rap her cane against the parlor doorframe.

"Good-bye, Miss Annie." Jamison's ever-formal voice caught in his throat.

"No." Annie shook her head, confused, disbelieving, and reached for Jamison. "I can't say good-bye like this!" Her eyes filled. "Someone tell me what's happening!"

The butler took her hands in his for the briefest moment, coughed, and stepped back. "God take care of you both, Mr. Owen. Write to us when you get to America. Let us know you are well, and Miss Annie, too." He nodded. "You can send a letter to my Nellie. She'll see that I get it."

"America?" Annie gasped. "We're going to America?"

Jamison caught Owen's eye, clearly sorry he'd said so much, and looked away. But Owen wrung the butler's withered hand. "Thank you, old friend."

Jamison turned quickly and crept down the polished stairs.

"Owen," Annie began, hope rising in her chest.

"Don't stop to talk now, Annie! Hurry, before Aunt Eleanor sends you off with nothing!"

Annie whirled. "America! Where to begin?" She plucked her Sunday frock from the cupboard; Owen grabbed her most serviceable. She tucked in stationery and coloring pencils; Owen packed her Bible, *The Pilgrim's Progress*, and the few books of poetry their mother had loved.

"You must wear your spring and winter cloaks. Layer everything you can."

"It isn't that cold!" Annie sputtered.

"Do it," Owen insisted.

They stuffed all they could into her carpetbag and a pillow slip. Ten minutes later they turned down the lamp, slipped down the servants' stairs, and closed the back kitchen door softly behind them.

About the Author

CATHY GOHLKE is the two-time Christy Award–winning author of the critically acclaimed novels *Band of Sisters*, *Promise Me This* (listed by *Library Journal* as one of the best books of 2012), *William Henry Is a Fine Name*, and *I Have Seen Him in the Watchfires* (listed by *Library Journal* as one of the best books of 2008), which also won the American Christian Fiction Writers' Book of the Year Award.

Cathy has worked as a school librarian, drama director, and director of children's and education ministries. When not traipsing the hills and dales of historic sites, she, her husband, and their dog, Reilly, divide their time between Northern Virginia and their home on the banks of the Laurel Run in Elkton, Maryland. Visit her website at www.cathygohlke.com.

Discussion Questions

1. Though Dr. Kramer may have started his work with pure intentions, it seems somewhere he crossed the line in his quest to eradicate disease. Do you think he recognized his step onto a slippery moral slope? Is this line easily crossed without realizing it, or must this step be a conscious choice? Can you cite similar examples in today's world?

2. Eugenicists ranked people according to bloodlines. Today, society commonly ranks people according to physical beauty, skill, and intelligence. How do you think God measures us? Read Exodus 4:10-12 and 1 Samuel 16:7. What do those verses say about God's criteria?

3. Kristine, having learned of Nazi plans to eliminate children with disabilities, begs Rachel to save her daughter, Amelie. What do you think of Kristine's choice? How would you act if placed in her position? How would you have responded in Rachel's position?

4. Rachel struggles with feelings of entitlement and superiority, an indoctrinated belief that her life is of more importance and inherent value than the lives of others. Before she can change, she needs to acknowledge that this is not true. What are a few defining moments in Rachel's transformation?

5. It is human nature to compare our worth to others'. Rachel was taught to believe that she is superior to others, while

Lea wrestles with feelings of insecurity and inferiority. Did you identify with either woman's struggle? How can we change our thinking and actions to see our own worth—and others'—clearly?

6. In chapter 29, when Amelie first arrives, Oma demands that Rachel, rather than Lea, care for Amelie, even though she knows how much Lea longs to help the little girl. Have you ever had to be severe with someone, knowing that in the long run it would be better for them? Or have you been in Lea's situation? In either case, how did you handle it?

7. Friederich places himself in harm's way because he can no longer participate in shedding innocent blood. Have you ever found yourself forced to compromise your beliefs, but knew of no way to withdraw without suffering hurt or persecution of some kind, either for yourself or those you love? What did you do?

8. In chapter 19, Lea says to Oma, "I'm almost afraid to be happy, especially in the midst of such madness and uncertainty— as though it might be wrong. As though *I'm* wrong." Have you ever felt guilty about being joyful amid a time of great suffering? How did you overcome this feeling of guilt?

9. Rachel is gifted and trained in theatre. Lea is gifted and trained in music. Each uses her gifts and training for higher purposes than herself. Do you recognize the natural internal and external gifts God has blessed you with and the way in which He has called you to use them at this time? If so, please describe. If not, how might you unearth these gifts?

10. During the church service Jason attends, Dietrich Bonhoeffer says, "Grace is costly—it took the death of our Lord Jesus Christ, our Savior, to achieve that grace. It requires just as

much from each of us. But we've come to practice cheap grace—grace that appears as a godly form but costs us nothing." How does this fit or conflict with your view of grace? What effect does the concept of "costly grace" have on Jason?

11. What obstacles did Rachel have to overcome before she could accept the truth of Jesus Christ? What were the obstacles for Rivka? Why do you think it took them years before making such a decision?

12. Which character did you most identify with? In what ways are you similar? In what ways do you differ?

13. Despite the stringent Nazi laws confining him, Curate Bauer helps Jews and Gentiles, Catholics and Protestants at risk. He does not differentiate between those in need—an unpopular stance for the German people, including those in the Passion Village. Do you ever struggle to put aside differences with others to reach a common goal?

14. In chapter 53, Curate Bauer tells Rachel, "Sometimes taking up our cross is doing the thing in front of us, not the glamorous, high-risk thing afar off." How might this be applicable in your own life?

15. How does saving Amelie act as a catalyst for changes in Kristine? In Rachel? In Jason? In Lea?